BLOOD

PALMETTO
PUBLISHING
Charleston, SC
www.PalmettoPublishing.com

Copyright © 2024 by Steve Steed

All rights reserved

No portion of this book may be reproduced, stored in a retrieval system, or transmitted in any form by any means—electronic, mechanical, photocopy, recording, or other—except for brief quotations in printed reviews, without prior permission of the author.

Hardcover ISBN: 979-8-8229-4070-3
Paperback ISBN: 979-8-8229-4071-0
eBook ISBN: 979-8-8229-4072-7

BLOOD
THE SANGUINE PRINCE

Steve Steed

CHAPTER ONE

I love hot water. Considering how much time I spend in it up to my neck, it's undoubtedly a way of life, not a hobby. While I'm soaking, time stands still. It washes away the future as well as the past. I remember an old television commercial where this magnificently beautiful woman is luxuriating in a Roman suds-filled tub. There's a sweeping mountain scene out the window with vineyards cascading down the hillside. The catch phrase is "Calgon, take me away." In my case though, the water takes everything else away. Only I remain. I never really appreciated the therapeutic effects of a bubble bath while I was human.

Coincidentally, some years ago I actually met the Calgon lady's daughter, Kimberly, a beautiful prima ballerina in Dallas. Her boyfriend was pretty damned primo, too. He looked like a Greek god and smelled like musky ambrosia. Naturally, I wanted a taste from the moment I first laid eyes on him. Undoubtedly, I've never swallowed a more beautiful or arrogant prick. He should have known I was trouble when Caroline and I crushed the two of them playing doubles at the club that day. Even from across the net I could taste the frustration on his face as anger and futility mingled with sweat. Forty–love? You bet. Game? Come on. Match? Hardly.

After smashing the last ball unapologetically into his feet, I imagined how sweet it would be to have both my balls crashing into his teeth. That would come later, when he thought he'd regained the home court advantage. Boy, was he wrong. Dead wrong, in fact.

We left the tennis complex in Caroline's Corvette. Pretty Boy and the ballerina were in a zippy little Porsche. At the light, he started racing his engine. Caroline was more than willing to serve up one more round of humiliation, and I try never disagreeing with a woman who knows what she wants. It occurs so rarely.

The light turned green, much the same as I would've if lunch hadn't been canceled. Together we burned half the tread off four perfectly good tires, as Caroline tore from the inside lane with the Porsche right beside us, neck and neck. Sixty, then eighty, and it was only two-thirty when we blew through the school zone. I could hear her heart racing against Pretty Boy's rpms, While I was watching the artery pulsing along the length of her neck as we crested the hill, suddenly her hand slammed against the steering wheel. "Well, fuck!" she yelled at the garbage truck blocking our lane. Hot Rod and the ballerina zoomed past us in their self-satisfied little prophylactic cruise missile, Kimberly's finely French-manicured middle finger stabbing the air like some sort of a raving, maniacal conductor launching into a withering rendition of the *Nutcracker Suite*.

Slowing to pull in behind them, the Porsche's brake lights came on without warning. Caroline swerved to avoid buying the back bumper of their car as the motorcycle cop came into view, waving and smiling from behind mirrored Foster Grants. Pretty Boy pulled over first. Caroline had no choice but to park in front of officer Studly Do-Me-Right. Watching him swing his beefy leg over the Harley's leather seat, I was in a haze of homoerotic heaven hoping he'd brought his handcuffs and would find probable cause to violate at least a few of my less than civil liberties. Setting down the radar gun, he walked deliberately, slowly, over to the Porsche, each shoulder rising squarely up and back, then down and forward. His *True Grit* swagger had obviously been perfected to such an extent, John Wayne would have been jealous. If the Barbizon School of Modeling had taught that particular runway walk, I might have stayed long enough to graduate.

Officer Studly Do Me Right in his black stretch pants was bent over Pretty Boy's window, further fueling my lustful fantasies, when Caroline gunned it. After nearly biting off the tongue that seconds before had been dangling out of my mouth, I screamed, "You crazy bitch! What are you doing?"

"My Dad will kill me if I get another ticket!" Downshifting hard around the corner, she nearly turned the car over skidding into an alley. I was considering jumping and rolling when we hit the curb hard, barely missed the yelping, startled Doberman behind the chain link fence, then took a brief tour through the otherwise deserted dog park. Suspension systems be damned—I had to hand it to her—the girl knew how to drive a stick shift. Several torturous turns and squeals later, we ended up behind her house. I was still listening for sirens and helicopters as the garage door clamored noisily down behind us. The prospect of being a shut-in had never seemed so sweet as when we fell on her bed laughing that afternoon.

"Oh my God!" she cried. "I think I pissed myself. I can't believe we ran from the cops!"

"It was only one cop, but he was hot as hell. Admit it, you know you wanted him," I teased. "I saw you licking your lips."

She asked, "Do you think we should go back and confess? I know a shortcut. If we hurry, they may still be there!"

"Jane, you ignorant slut, don't you know you're never supposed to return to the scene of the crime?" *If that were actually true, I probably wouldn't get out much,* I thought while she dialed up the castle to see if Kimberly had made it home yet. After listening to several minutes of screaming and laughing, I couldn't take the "girl thing" anymore. I wrestled the phone away, offering humblest apologies and dinner to the princess and Pretty Boy.

We agreed to meet at TGI Fridays around seven. I told my partner-in-crime I was going home to take a shower and I'd meet her at the restaurant later. She offered to pick me up, but I politely declined, suggesting instead that she should go fuck herself. I'd had more than enough of her driving for one day. We'd need two cars anyway if I was going to lift and separate Pretty Boy from the party later. I didn't think it would take much effort. His deflated ego might need a little stroking and fluffing, but I was willing to wager that before morning we'd both feel completely different about things.

I'd met Caroline the year before at the March of Dimes headquarters and had grown to love her like the sister I never had. She was sweet, smart, a damned fine tennis player, and supremely, beautifully confident in her own skin. She also had me wrapped around her finger or else I would have never volunteered to do makeup for their annual Haunted House fundraiser with a group of her friends from SMU.

I called her my "Pretty Ghoul," and she was fabulous, even playing dead. We went through gallons of white greasepaint, creating ghosts and goblins. It was the first time in years I'd looked tanned, at least comparatively speaking. During a break one Friday night Caroline and company asked me to paint their faces for the midnight showing of *The Rocky Horror Picture Show* at the Village Theatre afterward. I had no interest in, or intention of, tagging along until the school's hottest lacrosse player begged me one too many times to join them. Something about the way he crooked his head when asking told me the invitation was anything but casual, and naturally dirty blonde had always one of my most persuasive colors.

Waiting in line we teased transvestites and did the time warp until the doors opened. My Pretty Ghoul was lost in the crush of the crowd, but I didn't have to turn around to know whose hand had the back of my shirt knotted in his fist. Once we were seated in the darkened theatre, he kept touching my arm and laughing. I was whispering some joke in his ear about the next scene when I felt his fingers come to rest on my thigh. Even in the dim light, the eye contact that followed was almost as superfluous as the length of his long, breezy lashes. He'd have been perfect in any light, but his slightly nervous smile made him the penultimate poster boy for "don't ask, don't tell." I had no intention of doing either. Permission, much less forgiveness, is best left to Catholics.

We grabbed a bite on the way back to pick up Caroline's car. He'd already accepted my offer of a lift to his frat house near campus. Luckily, my Pretty Ghoul was going in the opposite direction and I had keys to the haunted house. After she'd left, I suggested we go in and smoke a joint before calling it a night.

The sexual tension hanging in the air was thicker than the pot smoke swirling around our sleepy heads reclined against a pair of mock tombstones in the graveyard. Lying there laughing, I wondered whether the scene was really all that funny, or tragic, or were we were just extremely high. Clenching the joint between my aching teeth, I offered him a shotgun and nearly lost it when he licked my lips after drawing the hit deeply into his lungs. His head fell back against the grave marker as he exhaled the bittersweet smoke and reached between my legs. I'd closed my eyes by the time I felt his silky blonde hair draping my face and the snap of jeans coming undone. Were it not for the eager, expert tenderness of his lips and tongue, the blood dripping from the walls would have been much more plentiful and realistic during the next night's "Tour of Haunted Terror."

Spent and laden with guilt for wanting more, I moved down his torso—safely away from his neck—and watched as he came in small, thrusting spasms. Every jerk of his hips was accompanied by the peculiar sound of his head drumming the hollow plywood tombstone. I wondered whether it was the same sound as a headboard banging against the proverbial wall? I couldn't honestly say—none of my dates had ever lasted long enough for me to find out.

We'd finished the joint in silence by the time I dropped him off near campus. As he was getting out of the car, I asked if he was planning on coming back to the haunted house again that week. He said he thought he could work something out and would see me later. I wasn't sure whether it was his slightly crooked smile or sparkling blue eyes, but I must admit working the graveyard shift had paid handsomely, even if neither of us was eager to report the overtime.

Two nights later I saw him again. Man, was it worth the wait. I was in the makeup room working on a group of ghoul friends when he sauntered in with his teammates. I'd never seen corpses reanimate so quickly. Tight jeans, tighter torsos, and enough testosterone to put prizes in a lot of Happy Meals, the guys were all perfectly packaged beefcake worth coming back to for seconds. Everyone was choking on pheromones by the time I banished the tits and clits to howls of protest, but the show had to go on, and the boys' pants had to come off. Behemoth boners clad in tighty-whities seemed like a rapidly spreading contagion as I helped them monster up and find the pre-game predator lurking within us all.

Four or five stiff cadavers later, I was beginning to get a bit feverish when the idea hit me to give my star-studded lacrosse lover a second shift in the cemetery. We'd elevated the vignette so one of the zombies could pop up from a waist-high opening disguised as a grave mound. It was perfect for scaring the Jesus juice out of any unsuspecting passersby, and, if things went according to plan, I might get lucky enough to end the evening with a little goblin gravy on my own chin.

When we got into full swing, I walked through the maze of corridors making sure there was enough blood and sufficient screaming to satisfy the price of admission. I checked the floor for pee puddles: I could always tell we were full-up on the fright factor if someone had wet themselves.

One of the darkest rooms was so unexpectedly startling we kept a couple dry mops handy for the horror of sudden incontinence. I followed a group in and watched. No one was slip-sliding away, so I moved on down the hall to the graveyard scene and found my sweet Caroline resplendent in her white lace, blood-splattered, wedding gown. Next to her flailing corpse was the equally dashing groom, replete with severed arm and gashes galore. Perhaps a bit peaked for newlyweds, death had never made a more attractive pairing. The way the jagged glass protruded from their anguished faces, shimmering in the light, was absolutely inspirational. It made me wish I'd gone through a windshield instead of being run over by a train.

Ushering a group through the grisly scene while stressing the need to always wear one's seatbelt—"…especially on your wedding day"—I managed to slip behind the Tour of Terror guide unnoticed, then through the trap door in search of the lacrosse player's basket. He was popping in and out of his grave, grabbing wildly at the crowd, when I located his stick and commandeered his balls. People were screaming wildly, so no one noticed as I pulled him shrieking back through the hole. One fistful of college cock later, his face had to be the most startled of anyone's in the building.

"Oh my God, Dude! You scared the fuck out of me! What are you doing down here?"

"Nothing yet. You won't stop wiggling."

"You're a twisted little motherfucker! You know that don't you?" he scolded nervously.

"Compliment me later, but right now we both have a job to do. Get back up there and frighten some people. I'll stay down here and tend the salt mines." Laughing, I pushed up on his knees and ass. "Now, where did I put that scary canary?"

Crawling under his robe, I gnawed through the cotton briefs until signs of life began to emerge. While he kicked, screamed, and moaned bloody murder from above, I tried throwing myself into the thankless tasks below. After falling on his ungrateful sword one too many times, I sputtered in protest, giving him the opportunity and excuse to swoop down from his lofty perch and fire me in the hole when I was just about to strike the payload.

"That feels so hot man, but you gotta stop cause this is really blowing my mind."

"It's not your mind I'm trying to blow," I wheezed and hacked, trying to explain how much I was enjoying my work in spite of the dark, dank, sweaty conditions.

"Can't we hook up after the show, like we did the other night?" he pleaded. Those were exactly the words my aching fangs were longing to hear.

"You got it, Daddy-O."

Smiling in relief he shot back up through the hole, leaving me face to cheek with two mounds of temptation. I only bit one. He screamed in protest as I felt my head slamming into one of the contributing members supporting the stage. I was still laughing as I crawled out from underneath the platform. "It's all just part of the show, folks. Keep moving. Keep moving."

My cheek was still red and stinging when it came time for the actors' rotations. I suspected his was too. Never having been bitch-slapped by a lacrosse player before, I wanted to play nice and suggested we get some air during the break. Outside, leaning against a brick wall, I offered him my cigarette and watched the cool night breeze drying his sweat-knotted hair while he took one long draw after another. Though he never attempted to sit down, I could smell the forgiveness in his perspiration. There was even a smile on his face when I told him I'd leave a little before closing, go get some beer, and be back by the time the coast was clear.

Back inside, Caroline seemed to be hitting it off well with her newly deceased husband. It was sort of bizarrely surreal watching the two of them aimlessly chatting away, laughing as light refracted off the glass shards stuck to their faces, casting prismatic colors on the surrounding walls. Disco of the dead—David Bowie meets Hellraiser. Hey, it's a look…

She introduced me to her dearly departed, one of my own cute and creepy creations. His name was Randall and I noticed again how his ears seemed oddly large fitted to such an average-sized head. I was still contemplating Randall's handles when he and Caroline asked if I'd like to join them after closing to go downtown. I apologized and asked for a rain check since I'd already made plans with a friend. *Note to self: Ask Caroline if she got to use the handles.*

I'd forgotten all about Bob's knobs or Randall's handles, whatever the fuck his name had been, by the time I saw Caroline again a few days later. We were running behind getting the actors ready. I asked her to help me paint faces. She wanted to know if there was any news about the lacrosse player from SMU. "No," I told her, "but the police were here last night talking to some of his friends."

She said there hadn't been anything else in the newspaper, either. "I can't believe it. We were all at the movies last week and now this. It's just so weird. I hope they find him." The concern on her face was genuine, and I hated hearing the worry in her voice.

It wasn't much, but I offered what comfort I could. "I know, honey. I do, too. Maybe they'll find him soon," although I strongly suspected they never would.

CHAPTER TWO

For months after the Haunted House, I did everything possible to avoid Caroline. Without fail, when I saw her it dredged up memories of the lacrosse player. It was like knowing, remembering, you ate all the lasagna, but every time you opened the refrigerator door, there was another serving. It had caused me to form an unnatural attachment to him and I found myself unable to let go, even though by that point he was very much a ghost of his former self.

Guys don't fall for guys, even dead ones. This is a way to fill a physical need, period. It's a bodily function, you dumb fuck. You have a need. Someone fills it. Move on. Move quickly. Don't look back. You know there's no going back. Lamentations are for pussies. That's called religion. This is nutrition. Blood sport. Winner takes all. No prisoners, no feelings, no spectators. Seriously, just suck it up and get a fucking life, dude!

Taking my own advice that morning was without a doubt one of the worst mistakes I've ever made. Caroline had been badgering me for days on end to play doubles with her at the club. "Come on, you've got to get out of the house. I want you to meet Kimberly's boyfriend. I'm sure you'll like him, and, besides, I miss you. Who knows, it might even help take your mind off that stick you've had up your ass lately. Be at my house in an hour or I'm coming to get you." The line went dead before I could protest.

After an eventful day I realized she'd been right in one respect. I hadn't thought about my shriveled all-star the entire time. We'd had a resounding victory on the tennis court and outrun the police, and, although dinner at TGI Fridays wasn't exactly my idea of the perfect place to spend an evening, it did have a full bar.

Running a bubble bath, mixing a stiff drink, and cranking some tunes sounded like the perfect pre-party formula until after I'd settled into the tub. During Donna Summers' "Last Dance" she was indecent enough to remind me why I was having to move. 'Cause when I'd been bad, I was so, so bad. "Thanks, bitch. That's really what I need right now," I growled under my breath as I reached for a towel and trudged out of the bathroom dripping bubbles in my wake.

"Get the fuck out of here!" I screamed, flailing my arms. They scattered, but I knew they'd be back. The ugly goddamned things had taken up residence on the ledge outside the bedroom windows, and I had two walls of glass for their beady, hungry eyes to peer into night and day. It was only a matter of time before the maintenance people came knocking at my door and I couldn't afford to be living there when they did. The smell didn't bother me, but it sure as fuck was driving the vultures crazy. It was well past time to de-clutter and call the Realtor.

God, I loved that apartment. The guy had been smoking hot, but his top floor crib was on fire. Twelve stories up with no doorman, a great pool, and endless eye candy, it was a dream; but I figured if he could part with it, so could I. The carpet was ruined, and I nearly had to break the hinges off to get the closet doors open. My lacrosse player may have been cuter than a midget, but he took up a hell of a lot more room, even shrink-wrapped.

I know. I know. I'd violated my own rule. *Never in the nest.* One time, the only time, I'd ever invited a guy over to my place, and things had gotten out of hand because I wanted to know what the sound of a banging headboard was really like....How was I supposed to know it was upholstered on both sides?

It was also after six. I needed to get my head out of my ass, into some clothes, and across town by seven. *What to wear? What to wear? Oh, I know. Yeah, those black paso doble pants I bought last summer. Bolo tie: check. White peasant shirt: check. Bullfighting never goes out of style. Grab Pretty Boy by his horns...*

I'd done it again. *Goddamn it, stop looking in that fucking mirror!* I'd been trying to quit for years, but old habits die hard and I just couldn't seem to kick that particular one. Sometimes I'd try telling myself that immortality means there's no such thing as a waste of time, but it was still irritating as hell. I knew perfectly well I always looked the same, dashingly....*Maybe if you could get your dashingly handsome ass in the car, you'd get there on time.*

Restaurant, good; gin and tonic, better; friends and fun, the best. The rest, well I'd had mine and I could only hope Pretty Boy had managed to squeeze in a nap as well. His next one was bound to be longer than expected. When I spotted him across the room, our eyes locked for the briefest second. On the way to the table I felt like an alligator with his eyes rolled back in his head saying, "Dive! Dive! Dive!"

"Caroline, you look stunning! I can see now why you're so desperately wanted in the southern states. I know my offspring must be lurking somewhere in your bosom, but promise me when the time comes, there'll be no stretch marks. We haven't even been to Aruba yet." I kissed both her cheeks and glided immediately to the ballerina's eyes. "Mea culpa, Bella," I said in my sexiest, most apologetic foreign accent. I kissed her hand, stuck out my bottom lip in the slightest pout, and cooed softly, "I'm sorry we had to run this afternoon. We had another, more pressing engagement, but do tell, how well did you get on with the Italian Stallion? I saw him trying to get your number in his little black book."

"Yes, he took my number, thank you. Two hundred and sixty-five of them. Fuck you and my sister here very much, but thanks for asking." We all laughed and I glanced briefly at Pretty Boy as I took my seat across from him.

"I don't know about you, but that match was pretty intense for me today. I'm a little sore. It may take a couple of days for me to get over it." I smiled in his general direction.

"Yeah, I've got a few kinks myself," he responded dryly, to no one in particular. *Good. No eye contact yet. He's nervous and pissed and gorgeous. This should be a piece of cake and I'm so ready for dessert.*

The girls were ravenous and, as usual, I was unquenchably thirsty. I insisted that Pretty Boy do a shot with me. I knew he wouldn't puss out in front of the girls. I was counting on it. He didn't disappoint, even after the third round, and began to relax a bit. The evening was going swimmingly until Caroline stuck a mushroom cap in my face and said, "Eat. You're not eating anything. You have to keep up your strength for the sake of the baby!"

I smiled and complied, but food sucks when you're perpetually bulimic. Excusing myself twenty minutes later on the dot, I went to the john and parted company with my fungal foe. A line of coke, a little water on the face, and I was a new man. The price of perfection. Another gin and I'd be good to go. Back at the table, everyone was offering after-dinner suggestions. The Stark Club? No, too many pretenders. Lizard Lounge? No, too much duct tape and eyeliner (and that was just the guys). I offered the Just Off Greenville Bar. "They have this killer drum circle on Friday nights. The best of the best drummers come for this one. Tribal thunder, no preening, wenches serving ale. Last time I was there, they had foreign chickens that shat Scottish eggs." Everyone seemed game and I was gratified by their enthusiasm. Getting up from the table, I hoped the delight in my paso doble pants wasn't too obvious.

We could hear the percussion thundering, buoyed by the cool wind, from blocks away. It was crowded as shit. People were everywhere. I could smell the patchouli and nag champa mingling, inviting, intoxicating, drawing us in. The girls' nipples were hard in the night air. They took small, quick, nervous steps while Pretty Boy was strident and alert, with shoulders erect, head level, chin protruding commandingly. Completely aloof, he was above it all. I loved that quality in men. It could be such a precarious posture.

Once inside, drinks in hand, I offered the grand tour. There was one drum circle in, one out. Sometimes they competed fiercely, at others, complemented, but always by drawing each other higher and higher. Their sound was semi-controlled, frenzied passion at its finest and they just happened to be playing my song.

On the patio I spotted Seth, a handsome little Sumerian drummer boy. His was a magical voice like none other. He was the consummate teller of tales. More than once, I'd sat around a revel fire peering under his loincloth, listening to him regale us all with his bawdy tales of inglorious lies and improbable conquests. I knelt beside him and whispered in his ear, asking to borrow his drum. Seth put the strap around my neck, then said hello to all.

Clenching the drum between my legs, I found the rhythm and spun toward Caroline. She tried to find the beat, but it kept changing. When she gave up, I turned to Pretty Boy, thrusting the drum at him like a giant cock. The point didn't escape his notice, even slightly. He took the challenge, crooked his knees, bent down, and started wailing away.

I have to admit, he was actually pretty good. The girls were appropriately impressed and took on swirling-goddess roles. No longer paying attention to us boys, they laughed, twirled, and mindlessly found their own circular bliss.

Pretty Boy and I were quickly finding our own rhythm, pounding furiously on the drum's head together. His tongue was lapping at the left corner of his mouth and his eyes were locked directly on mine. I wanted to sink my teeth into his neck with a ferocity I'd seldom felt before that night. Sensing that the audience-approval factor for such a spectacle would be close to zilch, I took the strap from my neck and placed it around his. My thumb traced the length of the throbbing vein running up from his collar. Feeling the heat of his blood under my touch set my mind on fire as he took the drum between his legs. Even when my face came dangerously close to his own, he wouldn't back away. I wondered if he could hear the deafeningly loud thumping of my heart. I could sure as hell hear his.

Fuck you. No, fuck you. Smack it harder. Beat it faster. Beat it together. Louder, louder. I couldn't look down, but I'd bet anything his dick was as hard as mine. It was sublime thunder. Transcendental masturbation. Then Seth came back and we reluctantly surrendered our phallic hammer. I put my arm around Pretty Boy's sweating shoulder, smiled broadly, and said, "You give good drum."

He laughed loudly, threw his arm around my shoulder, and we set off in search of our misplaced wenches. They were inside talking to two, tall, very excited, pagan, wannabe hippie guys. Sadly, the guys were clearly out of their league, though it was fun watching them froth. Pretty Boy and I kept glancing and smiling at each other, feigning pity for them as they tried plying their wares. The darker one did have a beautifully long, strong neck and a shock of raven hair. He was wearing a souvenir puka shell necklace with a little gold-plated peace sign dangling in front of his throat. Under my breath I said, "Any other time I'd be glad to give your piece a chance, but not tonight."

That was about the time the Oracle, aka Donna Summer, spoke to me. "Let's dance!" I yelled as I grabbed my crew and pulled them into the circle. It was thick with bodies, heat, sweat, and energy. The magical thumps thronged, pounded, and pulsed. It wasn't disco or techno, but something more akin to the crazed flailings of an old-fashioned tent revival. I was a preacher, healer, and snake handler—all in one. Granted, with my black hair I probably looked more like a Spanish bullfighter in the paso doble pants and cockroach-killer cowboy boots.

Along with everyone else in the circle, I was mesmerized watching the ballerina transform the room into an otherworldly realm. She was an exquisite blend of grace, control, and poise, infused with wild abandon—the pinnacle of bacchanalian hedonism. I lost all hope or caring in the moment. Time and matter held no import as I danced away, out of my body, looking down at the Dionysian madness. Possessed by some spirit who actually knew how to dance the paso doble, I could only obey and follow the lightning rhythm of my own pounding heels.

One of the drummers, sensing what was happening, took the beat to my feet. The other players followed. My entire body was completely owned by the dance. It was rapturous. I was not dancing with the stars; I was a star exploding in dance. The ballerina. The thunder. Collapsing in. Returning to earth's heavy orbit. Slowing, gasping, attempting to cohere that which cannot be bound by mind, it was Pretty Boy who kept me from falling.

"I'm not sure I can stand up." He'd grasped me under the arm and was helping me outside for some air as I managed to wheeze at Kimberly, "You were so beautiful."

"Thank you. You were pretty amazing yourself. Have you ever thought about dancing, seriously?" she asked.

"No, I only dance thoughtlessly. Can't you tell?" I was still shaking and in imminent need of an enormous cocktail as my handsome helpmate squired me to the bar while the girls went to pee.

They were gone seemingly forever. When they finally did return, Caroline was standing like some kind of bodyguard in front of the ballerina. "Hey guys, Kimberley started her period." Scowling at me, she said, "You must have jiggled something loose on the dance floor. I'm gonna take her home. Can you two manage on your own?"

We said we'd muddle through somehow. After we walked the girls to Kimberley's car and kissed them goodnight, Pretty Boy didn't even ask, we just turned around and went back inside.

Later, full of myself, him, and more than a few drinks, I said I thought it was time to call it a night. He said, "Fine, be that way. Will you call me a cab?"

I looked at him sternly and said, "Yes, of course. You are a Hansom cab, but I'm still taking your ass home. No taxis tonight for you, buddy."

We took my car back to his house. He played the drunken straight boy very well on our way home to a nice neighborhood and even nicer house. Huge, red brick Georgian, two stories, massive columns. *Can't possibly be his.* We got inside with the requisite minimum of key fumbling and drunken stumbling—a requirement if a straight boy wants to be properly seduced. The interior was surprisingly modern. *Maybe it is his.* Pool table and pinball machines in the formal dining room. *Must be his.*

The family room sported a very large, obviously custom, crescent-shaped, white leather sofa. What was unique was the contoured, burled walnut, coffee table that exactly matched the sofa's curvature. In the middle was something I'd never seen before, something resembling the largest hookah pipe imaginable. The bowl was hand-hammered bronze, with a beautifully curved swiveling stem at least six feet long. I pointed and asked, "Life support for rich hippies?"

When we managed to stop laughing, he asked if I wanted him to turn it on. "If it needs batteries, I'm already turned on."

"Watch this." He punched a few buttons on a remote and my evening was complete. The lighting softened, soothing music started to play, and the strangest little whirring sound came from within the coffee table.

"What's that noise? Is your coffee table getting itself off?"

"No, that's how I get the swans high." He wasn't laughing.

"You have swans? They get high? Show me, dude!"

We went out onto the terrace. It was dark, but I could tell it was beautiful. The lawn cascaded down in steps to a creek. The water was calm, with just the slightest ripples, and had the appearance of night oil—black, glistening, and thick. He picked up a little brass pipe that looked like a one-hitter and blew in it. There was no noise, but the water began stirring. Suddenly, two beautiful white swans appeared out of nowhere, gliding effortlessly, silently, toward the bank. They made ground and waddled toward the terrace, announcing their arrival more noisily with each and every step.

"Oh my God, you weren't joking! You really do have swans."

"No big deal. They haven't had their nightly bong hit yet. Hang loose a minute. I'll be right back." The swans looked at me, with impatience, impertinence, or some such sense. Pretty Boy came back out with a plastic grocery bag inflated like a balloon. The swans didn't wait. They waddled right up to him, seeming as if to say, "Me first! No, me first!" He stuck the gathered end of the bag around first one beak, then the other, and squeezed.

Fuck a goddamned duck! They were actually getting high. *Six stoned swans a' smoking. Five golden cock rings.* I was hoping we could skip the lactating maids. "Dude, this is seriously wrong on so many levels...." I was almost choking on my own laughter.

"For the birds, they do not toil without toking," he said as solemnly as possible. "St. Francis, I think. And wasn't it Jesus who said if you want to get really high, follow me?" Turning toward the door he walked inside.

I plopped unceremoniously on the couch next to him. He lit the frankincense and passed it over. I could not stop laughing. I had suddenly, unwittingly found a friend. That wasn't supposed to happen.

Sitting there, I was wondering what I should do next. In my wildest imaginings, it was going nothing like I'd planned.

He passed the peace pipe and suggested we go swimming. I said, "Capital idea, old boy, yet I have no trunks, not to mention it's cold as fuck outside."

"Oh ye of little faith and lesser trunks, the fucking pool is heated."

He was naked before he hit the water. I took the path less traveled. Shedding garments as silly and seductively as possible while sauntering toward the diving board, I had on nothing but my Joe Boxers as I walked the plank. I stood on the board's edge, pulled them down to my knees and somersaulted. They came off as I plunged into the water. I swam up to him surfacing naked, barely grazing against his body. I proceeded to crown his head with my Joes.

"Crabs, you're it." I laughed. Apparently, he didn't think it was all that funny. His expression changed entirely as he grabbed my face and kissed me. There was no mistaking it for a drunken frat-boy dare. My fangs were retracting as his tongue forced its way past my lips and eagerly inserted itself into my mouth while one of his hands moved down my back and strong fingers lifted me by a single cheek tightly against his body. He was on top of me in the water, pressing flesh and grinding organs in a hungry frenzy I understood all too well. One quick, hotly drawn breath later he kissed me again, swallowing my lips inside his own. He wasn't supposed to do that either.

Delirious, confused, I kissed him back, hesitantly, not knowing what else to do. He'd now managed to stun me twice in fifteen minutes. The situation was clearly out of control, at least mine was, anyway. I wasn't at all sure why it felt so awkward. Gauging from his fevered response, we weren't about to explore my feelings. When he finally did come up for air, I smiled awkwardly and asked, "Are you always this cute when you're drunk?" I knew I was buying time, which suddenly seemed to defeat the entire purpose of immortality itself, but I guess even gods have moments of uncertainty.

Pretty Boy shrugged, replying dryly, "Of course, why do you ask?" He was mocking me. He wasn't supposed to do that, either. One part of me wanted to drain him right there in the pool for being an exquisite asshole. Another part of me was falling in love with him for exactly the same reason.

We were in the shallow end, but I was clearly out of my depth emotionally. I confessed, "My dick is hard, the swans are stoned, and you have crabs. Did I mention that my dick is hard? I think maybe it's time for me to split."

"Why don't you stop thinking so much and try splitting this?" Before my frazzled mind could wrap itself around the tangle of emotions, his legs snaked themselves around my waist, urging, taunting, daring me to be who I was. "Take me to bed," he whispered as his tongue explored the hidden curves of my ear. Chills streaked up and down my body as I lifted our mingled torso out of the water and took the first tentative steps toward the point of no return.

Do it! Do it here! Do it now! Drain him where you stand! My mind was screaming at itself, against itself. My body was incapable of listening to anything other than the ecstatic moans coming from his mouth as my hand fumbled for the door.

I know this was as stupid as it sounds, but I was so completely overwhelmed by the awesome truth standing before me, I actually said, "Invite me in."

Taking my hand, he quietly said, "I want you to come in. Come inside me."

When I awoke the next day with my face nuzzled in his neck, amazingly he still had a pulse. I pulled away gently and looked at his body. Except for a few scuffs and scratches, he seemed to be no worse for the wear. Slowly I sifted through the tattered fragments of the second most memorable night of my life. This time no one had died, and at least part of me had consented to whatever had consumed us both. I was searching for my Crabby Joes when he began to stir. With first one arm, then the other, he grasped, reached, and stretched toward some invisible bar with which to pull himself up and awaken out of the fog of love and war.

Hands scruffed at tousled blonde hair and a long lazy yawn preceded the broken silence. "Morning. Man, I hate to say it, but I think I could use a little hair of the dog that bit me. I can tell I took one hell of a drumming last night. Dude, you should come with a warning label."

I smiled. "My parvo and rabies are up to date, but I'm afraid it won't do much for your crabs. Do you have a pair of pants I can put on? These are so yesterday."

Throwing off the covers, he bounded out of bed with surprising agility. It almost hurt to watch as his naked body took a few overly long strides toward the bathroom. From the doorway he tossed me a robe, went to the toilet, and stood there pissing a torrent for what seemed like half an hour. He came back tying his robe, saying, "The bar's probably open downstairs by now. Let's go see what's on special."

Two Bloody Marys and strong black coffee accompanied us to the terrace. He rubbed one of his butt cheeks before gingerly taking a seat. "Man that was some serious fucking. You tore my ass up last night. Guess I must've needed it. I bet you make all the girls scream."

Not really, only the boys. Just the thought of it was enough to send what little blood I had left racing back to my swelling pride. I stood up and shrugged, looking down at the spontaneous tent that had hastily erected itself inside the borrowed bathrobe.

Pretty Boy's eyes grew pained and large at the sight of the interloper who'd ravaged his back forty during the night. "Damn! Keep that thing away from me. I'm already going to be walking funny for at least a week." He reached out and whacked it hard before squeezing it in the vice grip of his fist.

"Sorry, you can't kill it. It's immortal," I laughed. "Let's go for a swim."

Several rounds of drinks, laps back and forth, and one silly swordfight later we were sitting on the edge of the pool using the last of our energies kicking water at each other.

Cupping his hand over his eyes for shade, he asked, "Dude, are you like Casper-certified or something? Your ass is, like, seriously white."

"Yeah, something like that. I never got called anything but a white boy in school. I suspect I'm adopted and my real parents were Yeti, but so far my folks haven't admitted it."

"Let me ask you a question, Frosty." His voice was completely nonchalant, even monotone. "Do you think I should marry Kimberley?"

After the several moments it took to locate and reinstall my wayward tongue, all I could muster was a lie. "Yes, of course you should," I stammered. The absolutely casual disconnect between the question, its implications, and our immediate history hit me like a bag of bricks in the gut. Fortunately, my face couldn't have lost any more of its color. Nausea washed over me as I excused myself, attributing it to the sun and alcohol. In the blink of an eye, life had suddenly become very complicated.

On the way upstairs, the internal chatter chewing away at my brain grew louder with each step. *Why does it have to get so messy? I'm such a tidy person. Everything fits in its place. I need order. There's a place for everything, including people. Compartments, drawers, ditches, stereotypes. If it has a name, it has a place. Everything and everyone fits somewhere, except this crazy shit. I am not a fag. I am not a fag. I am not…*

I needed to soak my new friend away. Bubbles, water, music. Neil Diamond seemed to fit my mood for some strange reason. I ran a steaming tub of suds, put on the music, and immersed myself in forgetfulness. Every inch of hot water I could stand brought another raft of words from "I Am I Said." L.A. and New York had little meaning. I'd never been to either of them, but I did have an emptiness deep inside. Neil crooned as I immersed myself further into the murky waters of denial. Like the song said, I tried, but the truth wouldn't let me go.

Talking to a chair? Seriously, the guy must be mental. Pretending not to think about the previous twenty-four hours wasn't helping. My mind was unraveling, instead of the knots in my back. "Should I marry Kimberley?" The words kept repeating like a skipping record. *You've got to be kidding, dude. Do you have any concept of how hard I plowed your ass last night? Not to mention how much you enjoyed it…*

Then it happened, of course. I don't take nearly enough long, luxurious bubble baths to begin with, but it seems to be a fucking immutable law of the universe: Get in the tub. The goddamned phone rings. It was *him*, of course — not Neil Diamond, but Pretty Boy.

"I just wanted to say thanks. I had a blast last night. We should hang out again soon." *Gee, you think?* But I could hardly hate the guy. He seemed to effortlessly glide between two worlds. No wonder swans were his fucking spirit animal, and stoned swans at that.

We talked awhile and he hinted about how we might want to keep it on the down low. Original thought always excites me.…It was just as well, I told myself. Handsome as he was, he still needed help getting his shit packed, and I wasn't much of a homemaker.

Man, it seems like yesterday went on forever, the voices yawned in my head. *How the fuck do people do it? Honestly, sometimes it's all I can do to get into bed.* I knew I was starving as I pulled the covers over my head. It was my own fault since I'd so brilliantly chosen to pass up dinner and dessert the night before.

One mind a' swimming. Two swans a' toking. Three guys a' choking, on my big…Getting sleepy. Sleepy is good. Sleepy is very good. Very, very good. No dreams. No dreaming. Pretty boys a' screaming in my…No singing either. Shut the fuck up and get some sleep.

The Dream was the bane of my existence and it always started out the same. The raccoons are trying to steal the balls while we're playing the back eighteen at Peter Pan Mini Golf. It's Tony's birthday and the guys are all drinking Little Kings and getting tanked. Everyone's laughing as I tee off my ball into the brontosaurus's alternately gaping and closing mouth. If you're lucky and the timing is right, his swishing tail shoots your ball out for a perfect hole in one. I'm not quite that lucky this particular night.

I end up in the weeds near the creek. There's a rustling sound in the darkness. I assume a raccoon is looking for a handout in exchange for ball-washing services. Then He steps out of the shadows onto the trail, staring straight at me. I stare back, helplessly. It's disconcerting and exciting. Too weird for words, too many Little Kings I tell myself as I line up the shot and swing. I miss. I turn back around and he's still there silhouetted by the shadows—tall, good looking, blonde, and vaguely European. Even in the dim light I can see his eyes quietly sparkling, almost speaking. He smiles slightly, as if to say, "Sorry, you suck at Goofy Golf." I'm embarrassed and rejoin my friends with the hair still standing on the back of my neck. I feel the slightest nausea, wanting to turn around again, but I'm afraid. By the time I can summon my courage, he's gone.

Remmy, the "golf pro" on duty comes over asking us to finish the round. It's eleven and he's ready to close. He's also a sniveling little asshole who attends church with my mom. Looking us over suspiciously from his tiny little upturned piggish nose he whines, "You know the rules. There's no drinking on the course." My buddies start razzing him. Rather than having to eat a plate of shit for Sunday dinner because of the little twat I tell the guys to take the brews and split so I can distract the little pecker head. I walk back up to the "pro shop" talking to church boy while the guys escape with what's left of my beer. I hardly hear a word he's saying as the register slams shut and the mechanical animals bed down for the night.

I'm in another place, listening to someone or something else. It's not so much listening as hearing, though not with my ears. My body hears. My chest feels the thoughts my mind is afraid to form. My shoulders, my legs…My God, I haven't drunk that many beers. Remmy whines goodnight and drives away as I stumble toward the truck. I'm feeling sick. No, wonderful. Sick and wonderful. It's coming in waves. *I must be having a stroke.* Reaching for the door handle, all the hair on my neck and arms lurches to attention. I turn, knowing why. He's there again. He must be.

We stand there, both of us, for what seems an eternity, his tall, muscular body perfectly framed by the graffiti-stained railroad trestle he's leaned against. Cars pass almost unnoticed as time crawls to a standstill. His thumb is hooked in a front pants pocket with long fingers cascading impatiently down toward his inner thigh. He motionlessly beckons, commanding. I won't listen. I can't. Stop. My legs. The sound of tiny pebbles being crushed beneath my feet is almost inaudible, impossible as I trail behind, following him down the path into darkness.

Wake up asshole. Wake up! Crawling out of the raccoon-infested fog surrounded by the familiar dark belonging only to me, I thought for the thousandth time, *I hate that fucking dream. I should really get some help, but right now I'm starving.* Ft. Worth sounded good. All I could think of while getting dressed was devouring some prime beef and a long, tall drink to wash it down. Always worth the drive, Ft. Worth men tasted better for some inexplicable reason. Considering most of them were locally grown, instead of from God knows where like the guys in Dallas, my best guess was that it must be something in the water.

CHAPTER THREE

No hair fussing or teeth checking in the mirror. I could tell it was going to be a killer good night. The interstate was only sparsely dotted with traffic and nothing behind me in the rear view. I ask myself out loud, "How long's it been since you had a big, steaming hunk o' beef at the Stockyards? Well, that's too long, neighbor." On cue the radio took over from my impromptu commercial interruption and Willie Nelson began singing, "Mamas, don't let your babies grow up to be cowboys...."

I pulled into the parking lot at Changes. Their motto was "A great place to get away from best friends." I couldn't have agreed more—not a goddamned mirror in the place, always plenty to choose from on the long-legged menu, and no reservations required or tolerated. I started toward the front door imitating Pretty Boy's walk. Head up, chin out, eyes forward, shoulders back, I felt completely silly. *Honestly, how does he do this and keep a straight face?*

The bartender was a hottie, though, with nice tats, a sleeveless muscle shirt—actual muscles included—and a completely disarming smile. Rockabilly guys had always been one of my favorite food groups. "What's yer poison tonight?" He asked, as if really wanting to know.

"Hemlock and tonic, with a twist of lime, thanks." I smiled.

"Sorry, bud. We've got plenty of him, but we're fresh out of locks. And before you ask, we don't sell bagels neither. What else can I getcha?"

"Gin, please. And could you strangle the lime?"

"One gin and a couple of dead limey bastards, coming right up," he exclaimed prophetically while energetically scooping the ice into my glass.

I like to play pool, sometimes very well. When men are overly chatty, running the table tends to shut them up for the most part. I could tell when I surveyed the rack of Wranglers and beefy Levis it would be a night of few words.

Sizing up the competition, I felt eyes on my back and turned around. That's when I spotted them: silver, shining, sparkling. *Spurs? You gotta be kidding me. Not a chance in hell.* I could just picture big long legs flailing and thrashing in the air. Honestly, those damned things could've put somebody's eye out! He must've read my mind because he kept walking. I could still hear him jingling and jangling all the way across the bar as I slapped a couple of quarters on the edge of the table and staked out a spot to wait. It wouldn't be long as the room was beginning to heat up nicely. After a while I'd learned that body temperature and pheromones begin to act like a meat thermometer. A good cook can always smell when the meat's done. Stick it in, pull it out, and voila! It's chow time! Actually, it was time for another drink. Waiting can be such thirsty work…

I detoured into the pisser to kill a little time before clocking back in. It was one of my favorite latrines. Big, long, and metal—I think they sell them at feed stores. This one was always filled with crushed ice. I sidled up to the trough next to a tall cowboy, acting as if I were going to paint smiley faces in the snow. I don't think he even noticed my lack of artistic ability, but I could tell he was keenly interested in my brush and strokes.

"How you doin' tonight?" he asked, in a deeper than expected, rich baritone voice.

"Better and better all the time," I replied softly. They love that. I looked up at him coyly, batting my eyelashes as boyishly as possible, wishing I could still blush.

He asked my name. I felt a "Cody" moment coming on, not that it made much difference. It would in all likelihood be the last name he ever heard. Back at the bar I sucked down my drink and he bought us another. While we chatted, I confessed that only recently had I come out as a rustler of steers. He was understandably, sympathetically aroused by my lack of experience on the open range. Being the consummate gentleman, he graciously allowed me to head out the door first.

BLOOD: THE SANGUINE PRINCE

Leaning against the car I explained that, since my first trail ride not so long ago, I'd developed a love for the great outdoors. He agreed to follow me to Lake Benbrook. Not the most romantic Corps of Engineers' lake ever dammed, it was remote and I was hungry. The darkness and desolation on the drive in lifted my spirits and piqued my appetite.

Without a soul in sight, we parked the cars and made our way to the water where I spotted a fallen log. Lying back on the hard wood, I propped my head on a gnarled branch, inviting him to take a load off. Locking my fingers behind my head, I gazed up at the moon while he walked up and down the shore checking for company. I could have told him we were very much alone, but I let him nervously savor the moment of his triumphant conquest anyway.

When he'd satisfied himself and returned, I ran my hand up his leg, asking, "Will you show it to me? Take it out, I want to see it." He unzipped his pants obligingly, stepped over me, and straddled the dead stump, flopping out his stiffening tool for my approval. The wind coming in off the lake was chilling me to the bone. He seemed not to notice anything other than his own overheated lust. The desire on each of our faces was palpable, yet worlds apart. Soon enough, in the last brief instant of his life, our beings would merge in understanding. We'd shudder together, quake at the mighty awe of it, clench at each other madly, desperately, in a fearsomely terrible ecstasy which no human can comprehend until salvation is beyond reach.

He stood there, swelling in anticipation as I reached up, tugging at each subsequent button of his shirt to reveal his stomach and chest, snapping away one fake pearl after another. With my tongue I began slowly wetting the path between his opened zipper licking my way up and swirling back down as he tried pressing his hips into my face. Making my final ascent, I began tugging and working his jeans down his thighs. I was in no mood to chase him even a few feet. He moaned softly in protest as my tongue moved from his crotch, kissing my way up his belly, up his chest, farther and farther. I nibbled, nicked, and teased at his nipple until he grabbed a fistful of my hair and began begging, attempting to push my head back down.

Pulling his fingers out of my hair, he'd unwittingly just shortened his life by a good sixty seconds. Maybe Pretty Boy was right and I should've come with a warning label, but it was still no excuse for fucking up my hair. Rock hard, he ground his furry body against my own as I stood and stepped up on the log looking him in the eye.

"You like that, don't you?" I whispered, licking and scraping my way under his chin and throat, along the side of his neck. *Just a little more. It's coming, Daddy. It's coming and it's going to be so good, so good.* It hadn't been a question and I wasn't waiting for a reply as I reached between his legs wrapping my fist tightly around his manhood. It was the moment we'd both been waiting for as he threw his head back in ecstasy. My hand was pumping furiously as my fangs plunged deeply into his neck. I could feel him exploding between my fingers, bucking his hips as I swallowed, sucking hungrily in rhythm with his wildly beating heart until he collapsed into my arms, spent beyond care or repair.

I held him until his color turned ashen and his temperature matched my own. Once he'd cooled off, I gently laid him on the ground and retraced his steps back to the shore. Kneeling, I cupped the lake's cold water in my hands and splashed it over my face. It wasn't absolution. That train had left the station years ago. It was sure as hell refreshing though and I was more than satisfied, even if the other guy was the only one who'd gotten off.

"What can wash away my sins? Nothing but the blood of cowboys..." I sang as I opened the trunk and prepared a place for him next to the lacrosse player who'd once weighed so heavenly upon my body and mind. It had been a real bitch though coaxing him out of the closet earlier in the evening, but everyone seemed happy now and there was no jockeying for position. Shutting the trunk, I thought back to the time someone had asked me why I drove a Cadillac instead of something sportier. I'd wanted to answer honestly. "Dumb ass, how many bodies can you fit in the trunk of a Ferrari?"

I started out of the park with my midnight cowboy and his withering companion in tow. We had a long trail ride in front of us, so I stopped at the bathroom to check myself in better lighting. It was one of those lovely cinder-block affairs. Big, new, and clean, it still smelled as if someone had only recently expelled a denizen of dead, decaying armadillos in one of the toilets. I was holding my nose when I heard the motorcycle pull up out front.

Feeling full of myself, and not just a little cowboy, I lingered, pretending to piddle, at the trough. There were five urinals in the row and Evil Knievel, still wearing his helmet, decided to stand at the one next to me. Really, some guys do have all the luck. He whipped it out, although neither of us was peeing. I stood there a moment waiting to see whether or not it was just another silly love song, when suddenly his leg swung up behind me with incredible speed and ferocity. The leather boot slammed my face into the cinder-block wall, and I was kissing mortar before I could even think about what was happening. He was definitely intending to hurt me and we hadn't even been properly introduced or had any sort of discussion about a safe word.

I bounced off the wall, falling to the ground with my pants undone. I tried staggering to my knees since he obviously had no intention of helping me up. Instead the bastard kicked me again. Really, it was more than I'd hoped for. *He really likes me,* I joked to myself, crawling toward the door like a dying man in the desert pulling on an imaginary rope of hope. My pants had trailed almost to my knees when the fucker kicked me for the third and final time with a little too much sadistic glee. Hearing one of my ribs crack would've seriously pissed me off if I hadn't been in such a jovial, jocular mood.

Using both hands I firmly grasped his steel-toed boot and launched him backward into the air. He must have been on better drugs than anything I'd ever taken. Nothing else could adequately explain what he did after slamming into the wall so violently I could see the concrete dust forming a cloud around him. In the unlikely event I'd only stunned him instead of rendering him unconscious, I was intending to crawl away just for dramatic effect. After shaking his head like a cartoon character, against all odds, he actually managed to stand back up. I have to admit, curiosity got the best of me and I simply lay there in the doorway oozing perfectly good bronco blood from my busted lip as he walked over, dropped his trousers, and knelt down in front of me. Obviously he was confusing me for one of his regular Thursday night date rapes because he grabbed my hair and said, "Suck it!"

Until that point, I'd only been looking at his eyes. When I came face to face with…whatever it was, I realized the boy had some seriously troubling diseases of the dick to keep his other issues company. *No wonder most of his dates are unconscious.* Very carefully, I shoved him and his mangled monster as far away as I could, pulled up my pants, and ran out the door.

Unfortunately, he was too crazed to take the hint and pursued me outside. Since the trunk was rather full, I passed up the car and ran across the road, jumping over a low-slung chain surrounding the athletic fields. I was running toward the shore when I heard him start the engine of his motorcycle. When I stopped and turned to look, he was zooming down the road trying to cut me off at the pass. I stood and stared at pustule boy in complete amazement. When he came to a stop, I started walking calmly toward him. I'd had more than enough, regardless of how cramped the quarters and whether he had reservations or not.

Maybe a hundred paces would have closed the distance between us when he killed the engine, got off the bike, and opened the seat. The moon was behind him and I barely noticed the glint of metal until the flash exploded from the barrel of the pistol. Startled birds took flight as the shot rang out, piercing the silent night and a good-sized chunk of my abdomen. I was really beginning to take it personally as my knees buckled and I slumped to the ground. I'm out there in the middle of fucking nowhere with half my goddamned dinner running down my leg and his diseased dick was all I had to show for it. I was sorely pissed as I regained my composure and stood back up. "Hey Buddy," I yelled. "I think we need to talk."

Naturally, he was somewhat taken aback as I walked toward him trying to contain myself and what was left of my stomach. Sensing that there was no possibility of patching things up between us, he jumped on his bike and sped away. Under other circumstances, I would have called him a gutless bastard…

The added weight of the still-fresh cowboy in the trunk gave surprisingly good traction as I tried catching up on the winding blacktop road.

BLOOD: THE SANGUINE PRINCE

We were rounding a curve doing at least 110 mph when I spotted the infected little fucker. He knew I was there, too. Inching up slowly and softly, I tapped at his back tire. He fell for me immediately. Although I'd never been on a speed date, I felt certain we'd set some kind of new record, at least on land.

It took me two or three minutes to find him running through the woods. I was somewhat surprised. He hadn't struck me as a sprinter or the shy type on our first date. Regardless, he was so overcome once I had him in my arms, he wept openly. In retrospect, I probably overdid it a tad on that first hickey. Looking at what was left of his body as I dragged him through the woods, it was hard to imagine him ever leaving me again, even for a hot date with a horny, one-eyed, turkey vulture.

The closure I was feeling gave me enough energy to drop off Cowtown and the College Boy on my way home. It was a nice spot next to a shuttered lead smelter in south Dallas. That particular sludge pond had been abandoned for years after being declared a toxic Superfund site by the Feds. I had grave doubts it would ever be drained if their other clean-up projects were any sort of indication. Several of my short-lived loves were already in residence there. I hoped they wouldn't mind making room for a couple of new pond mates.

Too tired for even a quickie bubble bath, I was completely exhausted by the time I got home. Toxic fumes aside, my half life was killing me. It was no way to live, or die. Between the spurs and syphilitic gunmen, I'd been licked, kicked, shot, physically and emotionally drained, and exposed to the noxious fumes of my past and present, and none—not one bit of it—came even remotely close to addressing any of my real issues. All I'd done was run out to get a bite after spending the night with another man, the first who hadn't died in service to my secrets.

Not that I had a contract, nor even a how-to manual, but I'd thought I was going to live forever with the world as *my* oyster. That was supposed to be the payoff, the exchange, the currency for which I'd unwittingly traded my soul. *Blood in. Bleed out.* Whether me or someone else, it hardly seemed to matter anymore. I felt trapped either way, pressured from every side. I didn't need a mirror to see that none of it was transforming me into a pearl.

STEVE STEED

    Pulling the pillow over my head, I wanted only to hide and sleep. Not counting sheep, lying there with my stomach shredded, I wondered how many raccoons it would take to laugh me out of bed before morning. I'd long ago stopped believing in the innocence of lambs.

CHAPTER FOUR

Dreams? Even the word itself had become a misnomer. I only called it dreaming for lack of a better word because I didn't have them anymore, at least not the dreams I had when I was human. Since turning, they've always been literal, precise, and seemingly true. Whether of the past or the future, I have exact recall of nearly every detail when I wake up. It can be great when I envision something wonderful that hasn't yet happened. At the same time, it sucks when you know a plate of shit is coming straight your way and there's not a damned thing you can do except grab the salt shaker and wait. The ability to see the future is not a "gift" anyone should ever want.

Honestly, I don't know where Hollywood gets these horseshit attributes they assign to people like me. For instance, one of my favorites: You always see somebody rip the board off the window of the abandoned building and the beam of sunlight comes streaming valiantly in and Count Chocula bursts into flames. Bull fucking shit! I remember the first few days after, well, you know, when I wore dark sunglasses and kept the drapes closed. I only ventured out at night. Looking back, it's actually pretty funny how I started figuring things out.

My mom's a Realtor and goes to church a lot. She wears a little gold cross necklace my dad and I gave her for Christmas one year. In the beginning, every time I'd see her, I worried about having to throw my hands up in front of my face and back out of the room drooling, snarling, and clawing the air. It never happened, but other stuff did. Anyway, I realized after a few non-events of the cross, I should probably start testing out some of the other crazy misconceptions. It's not exactly like you can order *Vamping for Dummies* on Amazon.

It was kind of scary at first. Sometimes, actually, it still is. But, I decided to open the drapes in my room and stand there to see what would happen. If it went poorly, mom would probably be pissed about the scorched carpet, but, oh well. If you're exploding in flames, can you really hear your mother screaming at you? Nothing happened, so I just stood there until I realized I was buck ass naked, waving my willie in the window like some kind of demented flasher. It was kind of an upscale, buttoned-down neighborhood, so I grabbed some shorts and scratched that one off my list.

Slowly, I began to venture outside during the day. No shriveling or burned bacon smell. Believe it or not, sunscreen actually did help. When you know you're going to live that long, it's probably really important to moisturize anyway. The only thing that did happen is I would begin to get noticeably weaker and thirstier if I stayed out too long. It was kind of like being at the beach all day and drinking too many margaritas.

The first day after it happened, surprisingly, I didn't eat anything at all. Hey, at nineteen, you're always hungry, horny, or both. It was Saturday and I stayed in bed all day. My folks were gone so I slept, freaked, slept, and stared in the mirror at my recently ravaged neck, which was healing nicely. By five o'clock that evening, I began to wonder if I was losing my eyesight. I got up for the umpteenth time and looked in the mirror again. My reflection had been getting fuzzier and more translucent every time I checked.

That's about the same time my stomach started hurting. No, I don't mean hurting in any conventional sense. I was really, really starving with a hunger like nothing I'd ever experienced. It felt like I was being eaten alive from the inside out. After one particularly violent spasm, I lurched over so hard I slammed my head against the dresser. It hurt like a motherfucker, so I kept banging it again and again, but the awful gnawing just wouldn't go away.

I stumbled concussively down the stairs and opened the fridge. I grabbed a slice of Danish ham and stuffed it in my mouth. I could barely taste it as I swallowed the whole thing in one big gulp. That's exactly the same way it came back up. The gut-wrenching pain was getting worse by the minute. I was about to lose my mind when I flashed on some movie I'd seen where the guy grabs a raw, bloody steak and starts sucking away. I looked again and obviously Mom hadn't been to the store in, like, half a century, so I did what any newly minted teenage American vampire would do. I took a frozen rump roast out of the freezer, threw it in the microwave, and hit the defrost button.

Waiting, waiting, waiting...*Oh fuck this shit!* I grabbed the half-frozen roast and started gnawing and slurping with everything I had. Sitting there at the breakfast table with my face buried, I must've looked like an insane Eskimo chowing down on his first all-beef snowcone. It was cold, damned cold, but after a few minutes of "roast diving" the pain actually lessened, even if my table manners were completely disgusting.

Before long I felt like I was going to blow chunks again. Flipping on the light in the powder room, I looked in the mirror. Big mistake. I was almost completely transparent! I'd seen ghosts with more meat on their bones. I would have cried but my face was so frostbitten my lips were frozen in place. I couldn't even blink. I don't know if you've ever tried throwing up with your eyes completely open, but it's more difficult than you might think. I was still splashing warm water on my face when the hunger came roaring back with an unimaginable vengeance.

Nearly blinded, even in my bare bones condition, I could still see the mess I'd made on the kitchen table. I knew my mother would kill me if the pain didn't get me first. I couldn't put the roast back and had serious doubts the four-pound dog could put away five pounds of Tastee Freeze Tenderloin Treats before she came home.

Once I'd scooped the remnants into the trashcan, I grabbed the bag and lurched toward the back door. Weakening by the second, I stumbled haltingly toward the alley and hit the gate latch before falling. Two houses away, I collapsed again. I was dying. I'm still not completely sure how I knew, but I knew.

With the last ounce of strength remaining in my body, I reached for the lid of the neighbor's trashcan and pushed the bag up over the edge. Lying there between the recycling and the regular trash, I was freezing and afraid. I didn't want to die. *Not like this. Not in the alley. Not at nineteen years old with half-frozen roast on my breath instead of booze.*

Swimming in and out of consciousness, I'd grown too weak to shiver and my eyes would no longer focus. Either the sun was setting or my own lights were fading. I supposed it didn't much matter. Even the death rattle of my failing lungs had begun to take on an oddly comforting gurgling sound as my heart slowed. No matter, someone would find my body by morning.

While lying there waiting for the end, I thought I could feel the last bit of warm blood lazily pulsing up through my right leg. Then either the flow of blood changed direction or I was pissing myself. I didn't have enough energy left to care at that point. The purring in my lungs was growing louder when the warm blood stopped, reversed itself again and started running back up my leg. I had to be losing my mind.

Weakly, I pulled my hand to my crotch to check for wetness. That's when I felt the sandpaper licking my hand. *Sandpaper? You've got to be kidding me.* Instinctively I grabbed the cat by the scruff of its neck with such a swift, blinding ferocity, fur was flying before either of us knew what was happening. Trust me, it really was as revolting and disgusting as it sounds, but I felt so much better afterwards, even if Fluffy didn't.

The next day I helped Scott put out the fliers offering a reward. I liked him. His yard was the nicest on our block and his house looked like something out of a design magazine. He was also a very snappy dresser. My parents called him "bohemian." I just thought he was probably gay. I cut the articles out of the newspaper that week about the coyote supposedly "disappearing" the area's pets. No one suspected they were being given proper burials along the creek behind our house.

Brushing their fur out of my teeth was the most unpleasant aspect of it all, I suppose. In very little time, I grew quite grateful I could no longer see myself in the mirror. Had I been religious, that could have easily renewed my faith in an intelligent and merciful God. As it was, his four-legged creatures were dwindling in size and number by the day while my own appetites grew in scope and scale each night.

BLOOD: THE SANGUINE PRINCE

I knew it was only a matter of time. I tried holding myself back as long as possible, but when petrified possum is the last thing on the menu, it's time to move on. The only other animals remaining were just as pathetically geriatric. It couldn't be called justifiable homicide or even mercy killing any more. It was beef jerky with a tail—and I needed to get mine out of there before my parents started to seem attractive...

Craig, one of my buddies, was absolutely the most half-baked, lazy stoner I'd ever known. With slouched shoulders and perpetually glazed-over soggy doughnut eyes, he made the perfect roommate. His powers of observation hovered at nearly zero-to-the-nothing degree, making his oblivion my bliss. If I were to guess, his sense of awareness was about as large as the length of his underappreciated, apparently undetectable penis. He'd never had a second date; the joke at school was that he needed tweezers to jerk off. At least that's what the girls said. I made it a point not to look or comment. He was depressed and depressing enough on his own. When my parents found out whom I was living with, they thought I'd lost my mind.

Even if mom couldn't understand, at least my dad unwittingly ran interference by showing more concern about his golf game than my address. Mom pleaded unrelentingly. College would be starting in the fall. Why did I need to move out right then, with Ohio State just around the corner? She was worried about me getting involved with drugs and falling into the wrong crowd. I tried, very consciously, to give her the vivid impression that her worst fears were, in fact, being realized. She was clueless that Goofy Golf was where the real monsters lurked.

I began by perfecting the fine art of avoidance. My friends, feelings, roommates, parents, all of them were shut out as I began withdrawing. I had no choice. Sometimes, the quiet loneliness was deafeningly loud. Obviously, I couldn't talk to anyone about it. I couldn't even look at my own face in the mirror. More than once I wanted to scream, but I had to hate Him in silence, except in my dreams.

For months afterward I walked through the trails at night, searching, hoping, and fearing that I might confront that from which I had been wrought. It was not to happen. Slowly I began coming to the frightening realization that no one could unmake me. I was who and what I'd become. Whoever I might have been or become was gone. That person had died at the hands of a nameless stranger, one more terrible than any fictional monster. The uncertainty and shame that followed were the only familiar feelings that hadn't faded along with my reflection.

I'd always been afraid since childhood that someone, anyone, maybe everyone might one day discover who and what I really was. Those same shadows in which I'd hidden for years became my salvation, my comfort, and my constant companions. Nothing and no one else mattered. I'd been born a monster and was to remain one, even in death.

I'd tried dating girls in high school. It just never seemed to work out. Their skirts, pants, blouses, and minds were impenetrable. I was a failure at every miserable attempt. No one could help me, not even the consummate ladies' man, Daniel. In what I mistook as pity, he tried one Friday night after the football game. We took two girls parking at the lake, Cindy and Dietra. The former had braces; the latter had Double D's.

It would be impossible to describe how desperately I wanted that hastily deranged coupling to work. The only way I could describe the big moment is to say that it was like kissing a fish with a mouth full of bobby pins. She made the most metallic moaning and groaning noises, bumping, scratching, and scraping against my teeth and nerves with the steely abandon of a sword-wielding piranha. By the time I gave up, my ego was eviscerated and my lips were lacerated. For weeks afterward I had nightmares about Freddy Krueger trying to jerk me off.

Daniel knew I was deflated, to say the least, after dropping off the girls. He suggested we go for a drive, get high, and forget the whole thing. We ended up on a lonely country road next to a nonexistent lake that seemed incredibly real at the time. In retrospect, it's amazing what a wheatfield can become when you're young, high, and horny. Facing each other on the front seat, we passed the joint back and forth, our knees barely touching. Just that small, nebulous contact of denim to denim was enough to send stars shooting through my boyhood body. It was perfect and terrible at the same time. Sometimes it still is.

BLOOD: THE SANGUINE PRINCE

Rockets and space exploration happened that night on the front seat of Daniel's car. We went where I thought no two men had ever gone before. The next day, it was like it had never happened, at least for him. I knew instinctively to never bring the subject up again. It made me feel loathsome and dirty. I'd been cursed by a cruel and carelessly bestowed destiny that would always find me lurking, lusting, in the secretively shameful shadows of deception.

My mind, my spirit, my very essence—who and what I am were completely, utterly bound to that insatiable hunger, the need to belong to someone so completely for one moment of perfect communion and completion. Therein began the Great Lie, one I thought could only be cured by death because, once satisfied, it always began again. The thirst eventually replaced the remorse. The hunger slowly usurped the guilt. The guttural need would mount and ride the limp pony of conscious derision and denial of self. I feared I would need to feed always—again and again.

Needless to say, it made high school kind of rough. I had friends everywhere, but belonged nowhere. I was well liked, learning was almost effortless, and I lived a nice, upper-middle-class existence. My parents didn't dote, fuss, or harangue me unnecessarily. They gave me money, cars, love, and support. I lacked for nothing except ownership, pride of ownership in myself, which seemed impossible to purchase, even the smallest stake, at any price.

I wasn't stupid. I knew I was good looking and had a great body. Everyone said so. Each and every time I looked in the mirror, I tried really hard to see what others saw. I wanted to be a believer too, but I could never see beyond the ugly truth. What would they think if they knew who and what I really was? I couldn't allow that to happen. It was my burden, and mine alone. The truth simply wasn't an option.

Secretly, I harbored some hope that college might help clear up my complex condition. I was looking forward to being in a new place where I could reconstitute myself and become something other than a handsome piece of fiction. My dreams died on the railroad tracks that summer night alongside my life and virginity when all three came screaming to an end. Mine were not the only casualties. My mother's heart shattered and my dad's once-proud golf game suffered while I fumbled around, trying to continue half-in, half-out of a shadow-filled charade of existence until such a time came when I felt my final exit was credible.

I stayed stoned, making sure the requisite amount of alcohol could be smelled on my breath often enough. I became dismissive, combative, and recalcitrant enough to satisfy any parent's underlying fear of his or her own inadequacies of tutelage or genetics. After the appropriate passage of time and handwringing had occurred, I left The Note.

"Mom and Dad, Don't blame yourselves. It's not your fault. It never was. If there's any fault to be had, it's mine. I know this will be impossible for you to understand, but I can't go on this way anymore. I never was and I'm not now the son you thought you had. I know you both love me, and I love you immensely. But sometimes even that isn't enough to cure what ails us. I need this time to find my own way, and I need to do it alone.

"Please don't try to find me. Some things a man has to work out for himself. Maybe in a better world, after I've faced my demons, things can be different. Until then all I can do is apologize and ask your forgiveness. Take care of yourselves, and if you can, each other."

It was difficult to write and even harder to leave that day. In the years that have passed, I feel certain too many tears may have dulled the words, but not their sting.

I moved slowly, deliberately west and changed my name along the way. In Denver I changed it again. A casual conversation at a bar in Boulder left me sidetracked and snowed in. I'd intended to land in San Diego, but what can I say? I was hungry, horny, and stuck. The University of Colorado basketball player I met that night would probably have said the same thing. Nude snowboarding in the dark can make you do some crazy shit.

After cramming together for his final, I decided to enroll. Not the best decision I've ever made—I blamed it on my penchant for frozen rump roast. The whole affair ended up a terrible, expensive mess. I had to hire a computer hacker to create high-school transcripts and a community-service history. It was a pain in the ass considering how well my real ones would have worked, but I couldn't afford to take the chance.

BLOOD: THE SANGUINE PRINCE

Don't get me wrong, Boulder was beautiful, and I loved going to college there. It was like something out of a storybook fantasy, a snowy postcard from heaven. Making friends proved easier than I'd thought. Not eating them proved to be considerably more difficult. Impulse control was not my forte in my freshman year and I was flunking badly, at least according to several local police departments. By the end of my first semester, the nightlife really sucked and everyone had become way too frigid for my taste, or because of it.

One of the things I did learn during the winter of Denver's discontent was about getting off. In that final moment when I'd look into a guy's face and the absolute realization occurred, his eyes would always get unbelievably large. The guy never seemed to know whether to cum, piss himself, or try to run. I've never actually seen anyone choose all three at once, but I imagine it could happen under the right circumstances.

Anyway, he always shuddered when he felt the piercing pressure biting into his neck and the blood started flowing in reverse. I imagine it must have been akin to being a rapturously orgasmic Quaker. *Your life is flashing before your eyes. Check. Hottest and last sex you'll ever have. Check. Meeting your maker. Check.* Ironically, I'd found out the hard way how well that last one works, regardless of your beliefs. If I drained a guy completely, Heaven was only a heartbeat away. If I didn't, he'd already met his maker—me. That's why I always made a point of introducing myself. Accidents can and do happen.

My point here is how much I like feeling that orgasmic quivering against my body. It's so fucking hot when it's happening and Denver is always so damned cold, everybody's always shaking and shivering, sex or not. How can you tell whether it's really Olympic gold or if they're just extremely cold?

Moving to Texas solved that problem. At least there, when they're shaking and flailing all over, you know they're either seriously getting off or else they're Pentecostal.

I found an apartment and got something to eat, in that order, because I don't really need to feed that often. That's one of those myths I was talking about. People always assume the stereotypical bullshit about corpses stacking up in the corner night after night. It's wholly untrue, a completely gross misrepresentation of reality, not to mention very bad housekeeping.

The first apartment was kind of a bummer. It was almost like living in the drive-thru window of Burger Queen. I'd never been to Dallas, except with my folks once when I was twelve. I really didn't know much about the place. I picked the apartment because it was centrally located near downtown, in a neighborhood called Oak Lawn. The place had these beautiful skylights, nine of them in fact, over the dining area and stairwell. There was also this secluded, tranquil little patio. I bought a pagoda, some bamboo, and a nice teak bench for an instant Zen garden. It was serene for the first few days while I was busy moving in.

Then I noticed the smell. It was everywhere. Daytime, nighttime, Saturday afternoon, I could hardly go outside at all. The leasing agent had conveniently omitted one small fact about this "desirable" location. It wasn't just called Oak Lawn. It had another name, "Homo Heights." I was living smack dab in the middle of the biggest, queerest area of any city in the southern United States. It also had what was affectionately referred to by the locals as a "cruise route." My driveway happened to be on the entrance ramp to the Fairy Freeway.

One of the selling points of my little piece of heaven, according to the agent, was the lovely, historic Lee Park right across the street. Truly, one man's paradise is another's hell. Remember about the pheromones and the body temperatures acting like a meat thermometer? Well, forget all that. My life was a nine-alarm fire and I was a hardwired, smoke detector. I couldn't stop going off. It wasn't the least bit funny, either. I couldn't sleep, go out, stay in, read a book, or watch TV. Paradise was infested with crotchroaches, and they were swarming everywhere! Sweaty, horny men were prowling constantly. Truly relentless, they teased, taunted, tortured, and titillated me down to my last nerve. I didn't even know I could be titillated, but I looked it up. I'd thought that could only happen to girls.

Fuck it. It cost me my deposit, but I moved before completely turning into a fat, half-human, blood-gorged tick. Living in that place had been like being a big, fat, chocolate whore, perpetually trying to lose weight, all the while living in Hershey, Pennsylvania, next door to the factory. I was glad to be out of there and back on a sensible diet.

The new place was so much better, even if it did have its moments. One of them was walking in the front door for the first time. You really couldn't tell from the outside that there was anything unusual going on inside. I'm kind of naturally drawn to that sort of place…The exterior was nothing but plain brick and a nondescript cedar wall with a cutout for a door in the middle. There were no windows whatsoever and no door handle of any kind, just a discreet keyhole, which almost became my undoing.

The Realtor unlocked the door and we stepped into this amazing, light-filled atrium with a soaring glass ceiling. Lushly landscaped with palms, banana trees, a huge ficus, and blooming bougainvillea vines dripping down the walls, it screamed tranquility. There was a small natural-looking rock waterfall in the corner that saved the day. While my rental agent babbled away about her koi pond at home, I walked through the French doors into the living room.

The space itself was stunning. I nearly fainted when I saw it. If I'd had a reflection to begin with, the look on my face would have been one of stunned horror. The back wall of the entire fucking room was covered in mirrors, floor to ceiling and end to glorious end! Had she turned around any sooner, her own end would have undoubtedly been far from glorious.

After nearly revealing less of myself than intended, I hauled ass back to the atrium, asking her to check upstairs while I figured out how many howler monkeys to order for my new jungle paradise. It could have been such a complete fucking disaster, and I was so relieved, that once I moved in a few days later, I sent her the most expensive goldfish I could find along with a gushing note of thanks.

It's kind of funny and more than a little off-putting how Hollywood never deals with the mirror problem. Vamps in the movies have busy social lives. They get invited over and go clubbing, to restaurants, everywhere. They hang in all kinds of fashionable places and it never seems to be an issue. You have no idea how many times I've had to quickly bend over to tie a shoelace or pretend to search for a contact lens on the floor. I've learned to be quite the contortionist at a moment's notice. Believe me, it's an image problem you wouldn't want to have.

Holy water, rabid priests, crosses, garlic, snarling dogs, and sunlight, for the most part anyway, are just not issues for me. Mirrors are an entirely different matter. As for the wooden stake thing, I have no earthly idea. You try it first and let me know how it works out. Mind control, thought reading, and other Svengaliesque parlor tricks do seem to work, at least some of the time. I began noticing my skills were always more pronounced after I'd fed. It's a shame they don't work so well when I'm really hungry. It may just be me, but I find it difficult to concentrate when I'm starving. Either way, most people are just so easy to read in the first place, they'll pretty much believe any bullshit I shovel in their direction. Superpowers aren't skills usually required for herding sheep. That's why I have a tendency to solve my problems pretty much like everyone else.

For instance, my Caddie died late one afternoon about a month after I moved into the mirrored jungle. I'm talking about my car; I don't play golf anymore. I figured it was an electrical problem since it just stalled at a red light. There was a garage a couple of blocks away. I walked over to see if anyone could help me out. It was about four thirty and there was only one guy there. He rolled out from under a car, got up wiping his hands with one of those red shop rags, smiled, and ambled over toward me. He was dark, just beefy enough, about twenty-five or six, and had the bow-legged gait of death. If he'd had a Stetson, cowboy boots, and a bronco slapped between his thighs, I'd have bought anything he was selling at twice the price, and been damned glad to pay it. He was even wearing those drab gray Dickies coveralls. It was enough to nearly make me forget why I was there in the first place.

"What can I do ya for?" he asked in a low keyed chuckle. Pretending not to understand the nature of the inquiry, I told him about the car instead. He responded, "Gimme just a sec and I'll take the wrecker over there and see whatcha got." By five o'clock, he'd hooked me up, towed me over, and backed me in.

"I was just about to close up shop, but I can get to you first thing in the morning. You gotta ride?"

"No, but if you're offering, I'll buy you a beer on the way home for helping me out."

He said, "Sounds like a deal. I could use a cold one." I thought it sounded like the best proposal I'd had in weeks. It was about time for dinner anyway.

He wrote up my ticket, closed the shop, and we got in his smelly old Jeep International. We drove a few blocks and pulled into a joint called The Crow's Nest. It was dark and crowded, but we found a couple of stools at the corner of the bar. I bought us a round of beers and shots, more beers and more shots…repeating as needed. There was still that damned smell, though.

He got up and went to the pisser. The scent was still present, so I crossed axle grease off my list of suspect odors and looked around. I noticed that the clientele was completely male. He came back a couple of minutes later and I broke the news, "Dude, I think this is a gay bar."

He smiled at me with a slightly drunken, feigned look of shock, saying, "I think it's okay, they probably won't bite unless you ask 'em real nice." We laughed and he continued telling me his story. He loved cars and horses and lived alone. He was from a small town and didn't have many friends in the big city. I liked what I'd heard so far. I was a bit distracted by the smell and the fact that it was my first gay bar, but I tried paying attention. I hadn't fed for days and he was a tall, long drink of A-Positive if I'd ever seen one.

My soon-to-be dinner companion was getting adorably shitfaced. Easy, unassuming, he was very down to earth; there was not much to dislike about him. I suggested we get out of there and go back to my place nearby. He said he was dirty and needed a bath. I told him there were these marvelous new inventions called indoor plumbing and soap, and luckily I had both.

When I unlocked and opened the front door he said, "Holy fucking shit! This is like a rain forest or something."

"Thanks, I picked it up in Brazil on vacation last summer. I'm expecting the monkeys any day now. Let's get you a beer and I'll show you that new indoor plumbing. I might even be able to find you something to eat."

We went upstairs to the bedroom and I offered him some sweat pants. He found the Jacuzzi another source of revelatory amazement. I began thinking maybe he really didn't have indoor plumbing, but, fuck it, I'd eaten worse than monkey grease.

"Damn, I've never seen a bathtub this big. You think I could take a bath instead of a shower?"

"Sure. Knock yourself out. Live a little," I said. *Fuck, I'll never get the ring out of the tub after he's done.* Begrudgingly, I ran the water and tossed in a handful of Pearls from Heaven. Replacing the box on the shelf, I thought of the biblical admonition about casting pearls before swine. Hopefully, in the celestial scheme of things, cleanliness next to godliness would trump his porcine pedigree. Either way, he was headed for hog heaven because I was hungry and I wasn't about to waste my Calgon on some bumpkin.

I closed the door, went back downstairs, and put on some music after pouring myself a gin. *Easy pickings; I think I'm going to like Texas after all.* I went in the kitchen and opened the freezer door. Needless to say, the food choices were pretty pathetic. Permafrosted chicken fingers were about it. I popped them in the oven and stretched out on the sofa, not intending to fall asleep. I'm not sure how long I was out, but when I did wake up the whole place was deathly quiet. Upstairs it was the same way, no noise whatsoever.

Damn, he's been in there a long time. I rapped lightly on the door. "Are you okay?" Nothing. I knocked louder as I opened the bathroom door. No response. He wasn't there. He just simply was not there.

I panicked and began looking around. *He couldn't have gotten out of here. There's only one way out.* His Dickies were piled on the floor. The towel was still neatly folded. The tub was full. *The tub. Oh no.* Lurching over, I reached under the bubbles. Yep, there he was.

"Oh my fucking God! There's a dead hillbilly in my bathtub! Jesus fucking Christ!" I yelled while pacing back and forth frantically. It didn't seem to help for some reason, so I calmed myself down, turned off the jets, found his shoulders, and pulled him up through the suds. He may have looked very relaxed, but, I can assure you, the motherfucker was extremely dead.

Before I could dry-dock him, the smoke alarm started going off. The chicken fingers were downstairs burning and my dinner had drowned. "Well fuck me dead!" I shouted. When I realized how redundant that would be, I couldn't help but laugh. *Okay, get a grip. It's not that bad, even if there is a dead guy in the Jacuzzi. Breathe, just breathe, and be calm.*

Even though the ring-o-grime did eventually scrub off, I could never take a bath in that tub again without thinking about my cowbuoyant friend. Consequently, I didn't live there much longer. Waterlogged hillbilly corpses can really put a damper on your Calgon moments, and besides, they weigh a ton. Wrestling him down the stairs and into his Jeep was no small feat. He could have stayed the night, I suppose, but I doubted that even if I had waited until morning he would've dried out much.

Since he was already wet, I dropped him off in the pool at the Roadway Inn across the freeway. I left the keys in his Jeep's ignition and parked it where someone would surely take notice as well as advantage of the situation. It probably wouldn't be much of a joyride when the unlucky car thief had to come up with an explanation for the bubble bath in the dead guy's lungs the next day. I walked home and went to bed on an empty stomach. By then, I'd lost my appetite anyway.

CHAPTER FIVE

The decorator, Gabrielle, came over early the next afternoon. She brought her son Jay along to help hang the rest of the art. I hadn't been relishing the thought of company until he walked in. Large, lazy blonde curls wound their way effortlessly off his head, spilling down around his neck and shoulders. Under other circumstances his too-large, powdery blue eyes would have seemed out of place on such a normal, pleasant face. Instead, those baby blues lent him a cherubim-like serenity without all the fuss of baby fat and alabaster overspray. Admittedly, I was intrigued by the angelic effortlessness with which he ascended the ladder while I tried remaining steady from below. It almost made me wish I'd been home when he'd installed the tapestry drapes over the god-awful mirrors in the living room.

While Jay chatted amicably away, I was left to admire how well-hung he and the art were. It didn't seem to bother him in the least how ardently I admired either of his talents. He was definitely a piece of work. Handing him the tape measure while he held a painting, I thought I might faint when he asked if I could pull it out for him. I was still reeling as I found myself accepting an invitation to join him at the March of Dimes the following evening. I'd been suckered by an angel and since he was off limits as a food group, I decided I might as well tag along for the hell of it. Volunteering was in my blood anyway; my mother had said so more times than I cared to remember.

Fortunately the repair shop guy called, towing my mind back from Heaven's gutters, saying my car was ready. It wasn't necessarily the call I was expecting, considering he was probably short on help that day. Gabrielle and the Holy Most graciously offered to drop me off. The owner was there by himself, wringing his hands, writing my ticket, and telling me his woes. Five memorable minutes later, he surrendered my keys while inadvertently unlocking a mystery.

His employee hadn't shown for work that morning. Somehow I managed to keep my feelings of relief pent up inside while he told me how he'd given the guy a chance to prove himself, knowing he had that "HIV thing. He was always havin' to stop and eat somethin' 'cause of all them damned pills. I didn't pay no mind to that when I hired him. I reckon some folks are gonna disappoint you, no matter what you try an' do to help 'em."

I couldn't have agreed more, or much less, given the circumstances. Smiling, I pulled slowly out of the drive, waving goodbye, when it hit me. *HIV! That's what I was smelling?* It had been in his car. It was in the bar. *I couldn't smell it on him, but I could smell it in the upholstery. Jeezus H. Christ, I'm turning into my own fucking mother!* The few times I'd ever come home after smoking a cigarette, my mom would invariably hold her nose and make snarky comments. It had never occurred to me that she might end up on the list of scariest things I could become.

Vampiric senses aside, if I'd gotten even a scintilla of a hint, the smallest clue, I'd have skipped the March of Dimes altogether and just bought some fucking cookies and a bag of weed. Girl Scouts and worthy causes have brought better men to their knees. "Sucker" must have been emblazoned across my forehead. And before you ask, yes, it's true: Never listen to your better-endowed angels, especially one who flaunts his crotch in your face from dizzying heights.

Mine even came pre-packaged with accessories. Her name was Caroline and, as it turned out, she and Jay were very close friends. In retrospect, my life would be simpler today if I'd drained her the night we met, but I'd never thought of girls in that way. It just didn't seem natural. *Don't kill what you're not willing to eat.* I know that must be written somewhere.

Of all the extraordinary things a guy can experience, "My best friend's a girlfriend," is not one of them. Closer scrutiny would have revealed many things. Luckily for both of us, I was a great liar and gifted self-delusionist. Neither of us ever gave the other a second glance, which should have been the first order of business. Who cares if the emperor has no clothes as long as he's handsome, has a hot body, and lots of money? She was pretty, privileged, and personality plus. I managed to ignore the rest of her psychotic quirks just as easily.

The March of Dimes loved my flawlessly G-rated string of lies and deceptions. Coupled with Caroline's death-defying smile, we became a fixture of the fun-raising set and a damned fine toothpaste commercial in the making. We were the models of wholesomeness: wealthy, white, and, in my case, fictional. I'm still the youngest person, dead or alive, ever elected to the national board of any major charity in these United States. Thus was the beginning of my long-suffering, oft-knotted Criminal Conspiracy with Caroline. Rarely does someone come along so seemingly innocuous, so devoid of agendas, so completely full of shit that she unwittingly, unfathomably, somehow becomes the sister you often wish you'd never had.

Luckily, neither of us was the type to spend a lot of time looking back. Wreckage of the past can be such a downer. Forward, sideways, or at each other were equally suspect in our contagion of boundless lack of direction and posthumous possibility. In those days, I still believed the world was indeed our oyster, even if my own mother-of-all-pearlized personas had to be refashioned out of shifting sands each and every day. Lying can take a lot out of a person, but at the same time it can also add a lot back in. Besides, I kept telling myself it was all for a good cause.

Clueless to the end, I had little to no idea how much the line between truth and fiction had already begun to fray into a hopelessly tangled web of contradictions. I'd sprung up on the off-chance as a close relative of Big Oil. I never made my exact relation to the greatest, richest oilman in Texas history precisely clear, and no one bothered to ask. There was already a seemingly inexhaustible supply of them from which to choose. Why force the issue? My family tree was large and gnarled, laden with nuts and cash—a veritable gift horse for protein-deprived, conspiratorial vegetarians and charitable causes alike. It allowed me discreet wealth, no need for work or income, unassailable secrecy, and the means to power. Not quite Republican, it was almost perfect. Mythical, in fact.

BLOOD: THE SANGUINE PRINCE

The problem with myths is that they're like great beauty or brand names. They last awhile and then begin to fade from age and over-exposure. The patina wears thin and people eventually begin to kill and destroy in the name of preserving that which always becomes the holy-fattened, sacred cow. Fortunately, I wasn't a fan of the papacy or prenuptial agreements. Neither can really protect you from the effects of aging or poorly planned press events.

Being a neophyte on both accounts, I thought nothing of it when one of the most famous faded faces on the planet, pleasantly, persistently opposed birth defects of any sort on our behalf. After he made two public service announcements for the March of Dimes, it became clear to some that he wasn't seeking higher public office or financial compensation. His aspirations were of an entirely different nature. One of the keen-eyed board members took note of his oft-affectionate gaze in the direction of my derrière and generously offered me up, along with the organization's thanks, over Beef Wellington and a bottle of Merlot. Lunch between the fictional princes was lovely for about twenty minutes. Much to his own credit and my surprise, he never once tried to use the force on me, in spite of the media's assertions to the contrary.

Shortly after rejecting the advances of the galaxy-hopping, butt-loving, Death Star destroyer, I discovered they'd elected me, by secret ballot, to the charity's national board of directors. Everything suddenly went straight to hell. My phone wouldn't stop ringing. One minute I'm painting goblins and munching on lacrosse players, the next, they're trying to book me on *Good Morning America*. As I was soon to learn, you can never put the Jedi back in the bottle.

Several torturous months passed. I wrote painful, heartfelt letters of resignation, offering apologies and sprinkling them with explanations as needed. Staying mostly out of sight, I tried as best as I could to smooth things over with Caroline. Of necessity, I moved again with no inkling as to whatever became of the howler monkeys or my flirtation with fame. Distracting myself by playing mostly with Pretty Boy and his polo ponies while he readied himself for his wedding with Kimberley, I became a decadent shut-in of sorts. I know what it must sound like when you don't own a single cat or have a trust fund, but, to this day, I still love playing croquet, especially from horseback. Simply because one has an aversion to publicity in no way means one doesn't want to be pampered and adored.

And adored I was, but it began to bother me more and more in the end. Pretty Boy and I became very close. We were perfectly paired, in fact. At first, I'd thought of him as a friend, a playmate of sorts. The whole affair seemed to unravel itself quite naturally. Privacy and privilege cloaked us from the outside world for a while. Over time, his mood subtly began to change and my eyes started to open. The wedding was drawing nearer and alliances of the heart were becoming clearer. Late one afternoon, sitting by the pool, he proposed an idea about some petty detail regarding the wedding reception, and, without thinking, I suggested otherwise.

He exploded. Once the screaming tirade ended, I felt like I was the one getting married, and to a complete asshole of a man, no less. It was sickening. How could I have let it happen? I stared at him in horrified disbelief. He'd dismissed me completely without regard to word, deed, or circumstance. I was nothing more than an interloper in his world and he let me know how comfortable he intended to remain inside it. For him there was no disconnect. Flashing back to that first morning we'd spent together, when he'd asked me if I thought he should marry Kimberley, I realized what I'd had no idea of at the time. He'd been proposing to me, too. She was supposed to become the face of his life. I would be his heart.

Fuck that. I'm not your heart. I'm not your mistress. I'm not really even your friend. You're just a faggot poorly pretending to be something else. Fuck a swan, fuck a pony, I'd rather you were dead and I was lonely. Something like that, exactly like that, shot through my mind at the moment. If he could play lord of the manor, I could damned well play God.

I decided to call off the grand wedding in favor of a smaller private service without consulting the bride or groom. I'd convinced myself it was for the public's good, after all. Me, Kimberley, nor anyone else ought to suffer that kind of humiliating, denigrating fate. I was no silly faggot's plaything, he would soon discover. I felt completely, righteously justified at the time, but God was not a role I would ever play with such childish relish or indignant abandon ever again.

BLOOD: THE SANGUINE PRINCE

Sandy Shores Play Land, an amusement park with pony rides, seemed only fitting as his final resting place since we were both acting like children at the time. The place was dark, deserted, and deathly quiet as we climbed the fence. Creeping halfway down the trail, we'd finished smoking the first joint when we happened upon the corral. The sign at the entrance warned, "You must be this high to ride." It seemed funny enough that we woke the horses. It was the last time we'd ever laugh together.

"Dude, we're gonna get arrested," he whispered nervously as the ponies delighted in our unexpected arrival. Leading him past their late-night whinnying, down the beautifully adorned path toward artificially sandy shores, we found the perfect place to spread our blanket. I must confess it felt awkward taking the glass from his hand after he'd prepared the drinks. It was my first real funeral. I'd never buried anyone so close to me before. Our knees were still touching when he laid his craning neck on my shoulder. The magnificence that had been his chin thrust itself up toward a starry moonlit sky while I drank my fill at the fount of adolescent folly.

The police questioned me. Naturally, I made myself available as well as concerned. Understandably, Pretty Boy was from a family. Having several of them myself, I reached out expectantly to his. Answering questions, looking torn up inside, if not quite out, came easily enough at first, ahead of the police and the yearning curves I would soon suffer as I began the slow process of devouring myself from within. Attempting to bury that much self-loathing alongside his body, beneath heaping shovels full of denial and indignation—the agony on my face became real, acutely real. I'd never known such futility as trying to bury something that wouldn't, that couldn't die.

In the beginning, I was unwilling to acknowledge the rumors circulating that he and I had been more than just friends. After all, reality is what we make it, right? I should know, considering I'm about as improbable a statistic as you'll ever encounter. Ignoring the rude whispers, raised brows, and ridiculous questions was easier than admitting something I didn't fully understand, much less believe. *Everyone lies.* I tried convincing myself, *just to get through the day.* How could I possibly be any different than anyone else in that regard? Now if I'd stopped lying, even for an hour, that would've been something truly remarkable to talk about. I may be half dead, but I'm not completely stupid.

Telling the truth was inadvisable, if not impossible, except possibly when jerking off. My right hand was both forgiving and forgetful. My other relationships hadn't proved nearly as successful or long-lived. I'd been fucked exactly once, and someone had died, namely me. I'd fucked exactly one guy's ass and he'd died also. The occasional blow job, ditto. Sex was deceptively lethal. For me anyway, the "down low" usually meant "six feet under." How could I be gay if someone always died? *That's not sex*, I reasoned. *It's homicide.*

The only time no one died was when I stroked my own cock. Death didn't invade my fantasies, only my reality and dreams. No rocks and thorns. No screaming or trains. I never had to stand naked and trembling before an awesome, beautiful God when I jerked off.

But in my dreams, He would always see me for exactly what I am, who I am. I hear the distant rumbling as He lays me down. I know what's coming. I've always known. It grows, louder, faster, raging, bearing down on top of me with the earth pressing into my screaming back. Pain, fear, ecstasy, and blood all mingle in a mindless rampage, swirling, searing, soaring through my veins, fusing us together. Forever inside me, two worlds collide in a fateful, fitful explosion. Stars spin at dizzying, terrifying speeds as the train thunders by, roaring into the night above my head. Shouting, scraping, the piercing and gnashing of teeth tearing at flesh—these are the last, terrible, exquisite sounds I hear as the God of my making forsakes me in the darkest hour. For the terrible thing I have become, even the raccoons must wash their hands and turn away.

Ravaged and torn apart, I lie there dripping, drenched in my own blood and cum. The taste of clotted copper and semen coat my mouth and fill my throat. Breathing is a labor—not of love, nor from the mouth, but through the gaping wounds in my neck. Thorns and rocks prick, dig at my ripped flesh, each a painful remembrance of the life I can feel slipping away with every whistling wheeze, as the air rushes in and out through the blood-crusted remnants of my shredded throat. *I'm not dead. I'm not dead*. I keep repeating the same mantra over and over again until I pass out, beyond life, beyond redemption.

The fur-matted mongrel dog licking at my face nudges me toward consciousness. We're both startled as I stir to the impossibility of life. For the briefest second I think I've entered Heaven until I see the fatted ticks clustered around his frayed, yellowed collar. He backs away warily as my eyes flutter into the glaring light and confusing certainty of a being shattered, a body broken. Rent asunder, the detachment I feel from the torn flesh of my limbs tells me I must have died, yet I can feel the wounds closing, healing around my ass and throat. The heated metal of the steel rail warms the back of my neck while the morning sun tries in vain to dry the salty, burning tears pooling in the open pockets of flesh on what once had been my face.

The trees look familiar, all burned and scorched. I want to believe it's still August because I'm dying of thirst like every other half-living thing.

Tattered rags and fragmented memories are the only belongings within my reach. Trying to get a grip, some sort of grasp, on reality, I see a half-spent Little King lying in the broken rocks and suck the bottle dry, swilling my tongue into the neck like a drunken sailor in the desert. Knowing *I can't go home* I scavenge for any remaining body parts and some sort of clothes to cover them. Malt liquor seeps from the largest of the holes in my neck, running down my chest until it pools on my stomach. *I must be alive. I'm leaking. I can feel it.*

No matter how many times it happens, it's always the same. I wake up swimming in a bath of imaginary slaughter and very real semen. My heart is racing wildly. Blood is slamming through my veins with rage, lust, fear, and awe pre-mixed in a powerful cocktail of emotions.

Trust me, rattlesnake venom and coffee is not the way to start your morning, or end your evening, for that matter. I knew I needed help. Dreams don't tell lies. The notion of talking to someone, though, was about as absurd as the rest of my life—completely out of the question.

I could only imagine the conversation. "Well, Doc, you see, it all starts with these recurring wet dreams. Only they're not dreams per se. It's more of a vivid, excruciatingly detailed recalling of events. I can't stop reliving the past unless I'm seeing the future, and right now that's not looking too bright either."

He was always smug, bearded, and Freudianly self-assured. I never drained him, especially at a hundred-and-seventy-five dollars an hour. Hookers with a massage license would've been more practical, if not plentiful. He always started by saying, "So let me see if I understand you correctly. You have no dreams, yet you have visions of the past and the future. And you're having orgasms during these visions? In my professional opinion, I'd say you're a lucky man. But just to be on the safe side, take two Handi Wipes and call me in the morning if the condition doesn't persist."

"Thanks, Doc. You're a funny man. It's always funny isn't it, until somebody gets bit?"

"I'm not sure I'm following you," he says with an expensive-looking crook of his head.

"Oh, I'm sorry, did I forget to mention that I'm a vampire? But, no, let's not dwell on that. It's not really why I'm here." Then I blurt out, "I think I might be gay." There, I'd finally said it aloud. Well, maybe not literally, but I think you get my point.

"I am, I said. To no one there. And no one heard at all, not even the chair…" Maybe Neil Diamond knew something I didn't. Either way, I needed a new dream and maybe a hobby. I needed something, anything, to get me out of the quagmire I'd slogged myself into. I had to face it: I was depressed. Immortality is great for clearing up zits or healing a fractured femur, but it can't do shit in terms of lifting one's spirits.

Under the circumstances, I thought maybe I should try to write. I had all the prerequisites: anguish, tormented dreams, loneliness, isolation, and a broken heart. Poetry seemed like a natural fit, and it was. The Dream slowly began subsiding, and, before long, I felt ready to venture out into the world again. Whether more for company or dinner, I couldn't be certain, but my taste for humanity had returned.

After a few pints with a new friend, I slept like a dead baby for two days. The next morning I awoke with breakfast brain. My mind was like scrambled eggs from all the fragmented images. I sat up, fished a cigarette out of the crumpled pack on the nightstand, and lit it before trying to put Humpty Dumpty back together again. Once the pieces began to coalesce in my mind, I realized I'd had two different dreams, and they were worlds apart.

CHAPTER SIX

Driving around the city's run-down neighborhoods looking at old, distressed warehouses was about as fruitful and delicious as anthrax-flavored ice cream after a tonsillectomy at the Lighthouse for the Blind. I could only hope I'd recognize it in its bare-bones condition. The dream had been very specific. Unfortunately, it only revealed the project finished.

It made me nervous and excited to think that I was about to purchase my very first home. I was finally going to be living the American dream, more or less. I would have to pay cash, of course. It seemed highly unlikely any mortgage company would give me a loan, no matter how steady my employment had been as a third-shift gravedigger.

Meanwhile, I kept writing. One night, I wrote a poem that seemed to magically spill from my pen. *Wow, this is good stuff even if I did write it.* The story was about a teenaged boy being molested by a minister. It was powerful, moving, and I wanted to share it. Of course, at the time, I wasn't connecting the dots; I simply loved the prose.

Settling, albeit nervously, on a venue downtown for my debut, I really wanted to see if the piece would strike the same chord in others as it had in me. I went to the club and signed up to read in the open-mike session. I didn't know anyone there, and began thinking maybe I'd made a mistake until I heard the first few poets reading their work.

Some of them were wonderful. Once I began listening with my heart, it was transformative. Losing myself in the heavenly magic of the words, I felt as if they were speaking in tongues. Then one of the tongues uttered my name, out loud.

BLOOD: THE SANGUINE PRINCE

It took a moment before realizing I was trapped. I had little choice but to flee or take the stage. Unlike Sally Field, I hadn't a fucking clue whether they'd really like me or not. *No rotten tomatoes yet.* I was almost at the microphone. *No one's laughing or pelting me with milk-sodden toast. Maybe I can do this.* While I was busy having an out-of-body experience, the paper managed to unfold itself and I heard someone shakily begin reading to a packed house. There were four pages in my trembling hands and I'd made it maybe halfway through the first one when I noticed a flurry of movement in the crowd.

Oh, that's fucking great. I've already lost the audience. Everyone's attention had shifted to the balcony. Looking up, I thought my mind must be playing unusually cruel tricks on my senses. It wasn't possible. It simply couldn't be. I tried starting again, though my eyes would barely focus. They were being torn from the page, ripped away by the taste in my mouth, his smell in my nostrils. No words could convey…

Where did he go? He was just there. I couldn't see him, the stage lights were too bright to make out much of anything, but everything in my being could feel him. I knew him. He was there, somewhere. *Just finish the fucking poem and go find him, you idiot!*

Centuries seemingly passed before I heard the sounds of thundering applause and paper being refolded. The people standing and cheering would have been marvelous in another circumstance. But given the fact that I unexpectedly had a date, or so I hoped, it was nothing more than noise and unwanted distraction as I hurried from the stage only to be accosted by some drunken idiot heaping praise and shoving a drink in my face.

My inebriated admirer was prattling on about subjects that I will never recall when I spotted him again moving through the crowd toward me. *It can't be. It isn't possible. Keep telling yourself that, dumb ass. He's heading straight toward you.* Gliding almost on air, he smelled like a slow-moving Ferris wheel at the state fair. One moment it was this, another it was that. Apples, blood, oranges, tobacco, and cinnamon, even me. I could smell myself on him, in him. It made me want to laugh and cry and jump up and down like a child. Fighting the urge to rush forward and fling his smallish frame into the air, somehow I managed to restrain myself and let him approach. He was the strangest stranger I'd ever met, and, just like me, he wasn't human.

With his kind smile and infinitely patient, twinkling eyes, he was a fanged Santa without beard or belly and I was in awe of his cape, the fedora, and his cane, especially the cane. It looked capable of granting dispensations or banishing malevolent spirits. He was signing autographs when someone handed me his gold foil, embossed card. He wasn't Frank Lloyd Wright, or even the Pope. His name was Sir Charles Hansworth Belmont, and, although I'd never heard of him, he was the grandest person I'd ever met.

One of the autograph seekers excitedly informed me that Sir Charles was a celebrated author and poet from Great Britain. She had no way of knowing that I was more keen on his fangs than fame. One of the bar's staff attempted to separate His Wholly Otherness from the thronging masses by putting his hand on my arm. The cane came out of nowhere, tapping the man's hand. The bouncer let go of my arm and moved between me and the overly informative groupie girl, saying, "That's enough, folks. Let's give the man some air."

Once the herd was sufficiently thinned, the same drop-dead gorgeous redhead who'd handed me the embossed card was finally able to make introductions. She already knew my name, which I suppose should have been more shocking to me at the time, but I was already on sensory overload and barely took notice. The only thing I remember with any certainty was his final statement. "Don't worry, my boy. We'll be here another few days. I'll send someone for you."

I was about to reach into my jacket for a pen to jot down my address when the cane's handle indicated I shouldn't bother. Since he knew my name without asking, my address probably wasn't much of a stretch either. I imagined him designing and then leaping over tall buildings in a single bound as his entourage whisked him away into the night and left me standing there with my mouth agape and my mind aflutter.

An elated wreck, that's about all I amounted to for the next twenty-four hours. I could hardly sleep or function. I'd been reduced to a manic border collie with a bad case of separation anxiety. All I knew was that for the first time in my life, I wasn't alone, and I couldn't stop pacing or panting about it. I didn't give a flying gnat's ass if he wore a cape, had super powers, or twirled a baton—he was just like me. The mere thought of it took my breath away.

That's exactly the way I answered the door that afternoon—breathlessly. I didn't know whether to tip or hug the courier who handed me the embossed envelope.

"We request your presence…blah, blah, blah." I couldn't rest so I fixed myself a cocktail, gave myself a facial, overdressed, and drove round and round the Mansion on Turtle Creek until nine o'clock that evening. I was a nervous wreck as I knocked on the door of his suite. A young, handsomely dressed man answered and ushered me inside. He silently poured two glasses of wine, bowed ever so slightly, and left the room without ever uttering a single syllable.

I was pretty damned speechless myself when Sir Charles came floating in from another room, offered me one of the glasses, and motioned toward a comfortable-looking sofa. I took a seat as he effortlessly glided into a nearby chair. If one were to say that his mannerisms had the affectations of royalty, it would have been an understatement by several degrees of magnitude.

Silently, carefully, he opened a small sterling silver box on the Chippendale table and offered me a cigarette. I declined as he placed one in a small silver holder and lit it from a matching table lighter. Raising his head, he blew a cloud of smoke into the air. Looking at me, he smiled and paused before speaking. "My dear boy, I'm sure you have a million questions, some of which I can probably answer. But first, tell me, how have you been getting on? I must admit I was somewhat disappointed to learn you'd left University."

"You mean Boulder? But how do you know about…"

He waved his hand to cut me off. "I make it a point to concern myself with all my children. I'm sorry, I thought you understood that I am your maker's maker." I was stunned. He could probably tell by the dislocated jaw in my lap, but was kind enough not to point it out. "I'm aware of the circumstances of your transformation after your game of, what is the term you use...? Goofy Golf, yes that's it."

I sat there completely dumbstruck, wearing what must have been the companion facial expression. He could probably tell I was ill equipped to speak at the moment. "Alas, but I must admit that in converting your maker, I acted somewhat hastily and have lived to regret it evermore. Even still, at the time, I thought it the right thing to do given the tragic circumstances.

"Although it seems like yesterday, it was actually 1953 and I was leaving a late-night party outside Milan. I'm afraid I'd had entirely too much to drink and shouldn't have been driving. Our cars collided coming round a curve and he sustained massive injuries in the wreck. Even bloodied and bruised beyond repair, he was still a beautiful young man. Words cannot describe how terrible I felt standing there watching the life ebbing away from his broken body. Whether out of drunkenness or shame, I restored his health and we've both lived to regret it until this day."

He looked at me, took a deep breath, and sighed. "But what's done is done and there really is no going back, I suppose."

On hearing the story, I couldn't help but wonder if he considered me a mistake and whether I was going to die as a result. He must've seen the concern in my face. "Oh my. I do apologize. I'm afraid I'm being a terrible host. I've upset you with my incessant chatter and not let you speak at all. Where are my manners?"

Hearing the door open behind me, I turned around hoping to discreetly memorize any and all exits. The same guy with the killer suit came back in carrying a small tray. (You don't need to ask: of course, it was silver and perfectly matched to the other pieces on the table.) He set it down in front of me, refilled our glasses, and left silently, the same way he'd come.

Seriously, I could get used to this if I don't die from it first. Sitting before me was a tray of coke set out in precise, neat little lines with a small silver straw to one side. My host smiled knowingly as if saying something about today's youth. I didn't dare offer him the tray when I was done. I just set it quietly, politely, back on the table.

BLOOD: THE SANGUINE PRINCE

We talked until nearly dawn. We talked about everything. No subject seemed too small or unassailable. He explained how our kind are as unique as humans, with differing degrees of talents and proclivities. No two are the same. He, for instance, is extremely sensitive to sunlight. My own tolerance is much greater. Some have pronounced physical strength. Others read minds, both human and vampire, with greater ease and precision. Charles, I strongly suspected, belonged to the latter group. Some of the older ones, or so he claimed, could supposedly turn to vapor and then rematerialize. We didn't play show-and-tell, much to my disappointment. I would have loved a demonstration of that particular skill.

The bat thing was not going to happen, I learned. No werewolves or flying sheepdogs were in my future either. "This night has certainly lowered my expectations," I drunkenly confided, "but on the bright side, I guess I'll save money on the veterinarian bills."

After we exchanged a few "Worst Mirror Moments," I asked Charles about his own conversion. Since he knew all about mine, naturally, I was curious about his. Henri d'Artois, the grandson of Charles X, king of France, had been his maker. Childhood friends, they'd grown up together in the Bourbon Court. Henri had even been king for seven days in 1830. There were apparently a number of our kind in the French Court during that tumultuous time. After several failed assassination attempts, the stakes were growing sharper, and, before getting the proverbial point, Charles took the hint, leaving for England in 1830.

It was nearly five o'clock by the time I'd finished consuming his story and enough white powder to qualify for the Winter Olympics. Even in my abominable state, I could tell Charles still had something on his mind we'd yet to discuss.

"Why don't you tell me about the young man with the polo ponies?" I nearly swallowed my own tongue. Suddenly, the evening's pleasantries had all evaporated, along with my high. I felt naked, coked up, on trial for crimes against humanity (at least one of them anyway), and extremely guilty. Who, honestly, could have asked for more? It was absolutely the most awkward moment of my life, either of them, in fact.

"I know I really messed up. I just couldn't deal with it. It made me sick to my stomach, the whole goddamned thing. I couldn't even look at him anymore. Everything about that whole situation…He was such an arrogant fucking prick."

"Show me the man that isn't. But more importantly, did you love him?"

"You seem to know everything else, Charles. Why do you need to fucking ask?" Tears were welling in my eyes as he said softly, "It's not that I need to ask, dear boy. It's you who needs to say it."

"Fine. Then have it your way. Yes! Yes, I loved him. I still love him, and I hate him because of it. You want the truth? Here it is. I was, and still am, in love with another man and I killed him because of it. And now I wish I could bring him back, but I can't. Sometimes I miss him so much, it nearly destroys me."

Once I heard myself say the words, the lump was so pronounced in my throat, I thought I might faint. I couldn't hold back any longer and the bloody tears began flowing down my face making an awful mess. I didn't care anymore, so I just kept on crying until Charles sat beside me on the sofa, offering a handkerchief and his arm around my shoulder. I'm not sure how long we sat there.

His tone was softer when he spoke again. "My child, I'm not here to judge you. You've only to judge yourself, but be kind when making judgments about yourself as well as others. They're not easily taken back, once rendered. You no more asked to be born who and what you were than how you find yourself today. Learn to embrace the life and gifts you've been given. Your own maker, it saddens me to say, has yet to do so, even at his own peril." Charles took the hanky from my hand, dabbing it at the corners of my rapidly crusting eyes. "Why don't you go and wash your face now? It's time to let an old man get some sleep."

He was waiting for me by the front door when I came out of the bathroom. "Here, I almost forgot to give you this. Wait until you get home to open it." I thanked him and stuck the envelope in my pocket. Taking my face in his hands, he wiped his thumbs under my eyes, stood on the tips of his toes and kissed my forehead. "Goodnight, my beautiful boy. We'll talk again soon. I promise. Until then, try and remember what I've told you. Be kind, even to yourself."

CHAPTER SEVEN

I made it home shortly before six. Too tired to even shower, I fixed a drink, put on George Winston, and readied myself for bed. Hanging up my jacket, I remembered the envelope in the breast pocket. I collapsed onto the bed and tore open the now-familiar gold-embossed seal stamped CHB. Inside was a note wrapped around a cashier's check made out in my name for twenty-five thousand dollars. The note simply read, "Have a gay and glorious time in your new home. I'm sure it will be lovely. I've sent a small gift to 714 Tyler Street. I hope that's the right address. It should arrive shortly. Let me know how it works out. Best wishes, Charles."

I slept soundly that day, maybe it was two. I'm not really sure. When I finally did wake up I felt rested for the first time in months. After making coffee and getting dressed, I drove straight across town to Tyler Street. I knew exactly where it was. I'd been searching in that area. It wasn't much to look at, but it was there—and for sale. I closed on my little slice of hell two weeks later for twenty-six thousand dollars.

It was an unmitigated disaster of a place, but it was mine. Originally, it had been built as a dry-cleaning plant in the 1930s. Today, it was neither dry nor clean, but the weeds from the cracked concrete appeared to be flourishing. Sometime in the sixties it had been used as a Volkswagen repair shop. I didn't even want to venture a guess as to what it had been used for recently...

It was a single-story, ten-thousand-square-foot, cinder-block affair around the corner from the Texas Theatre, where Lee Harvey Oswald had been arrested after the Kennedy assassination.

I tried cleaning the place up myself. After three days, my cheeks had taken on a rosy, healthy glow, leaving me near death, and not in the good way. The sunlight was just too much, so I hired some help. We began by painting the outside of the building flamingo pink. It's not really one of my colors, but Charles had paid for the paint and said it should be gay. It was. Unclear on how many flamingos it takes to make a gallon of that particular shade, I imagine we'd pretty much decimated the wild population of the poor birds in North America by the time we were finished.

One of the guys in the crew was named Kelvin. He explained that he actually wasn't a painter, but an acoustic drywall specialist. That meant he hangs Sheetrock. And Sheetrock was not all that he was hanging. It was summer and he wore frayed Levi's shorts to work every day. They left absolutely nothing to the imagination, except troubled sleep. He was also an *extreme fighter* in his spare time. He knew a great deal about martial arts and was, generally speaking, an all-around kick-ass dude. He had muscles in places even anabolic steroids were afraid to tread and wanted me to notice them all. I did. After we finished painting I hired him to hang my Sheetrock. He was kind enough to drive me to distraction for free.

He had a big monster truck, of course, and insisted on helping me move in. I should have put up a fight, but in my weakened condition I didn't have the strength to refuse. After the last load he collapsed exhausted, breathless, onto the couch. I plopped down next to him on the cool concrete floor. We sat there huffing, puffing a joint, and drinking ice-cold beer. Nine Inch Nails was screaming from the stereo when one of his legs slid off the sofa, coming to rest like a boulder on top of my shoulder. Neither of us moved until I reached over absentmindedly in a stoner's haze and began rubbing my palmed hand lazily along his muscled calf.

He got the message and so did I. "What the fuck are you doin' man? I ain't no fucking faggot!" He jerked my hand away, looking like he wanted to kill me, or be killed.

He still hadn't let go of my hand when I said, "Kelvin, I'm sorry. That was stupid. I misread the situation. I would never do anything to offend you. I really am sorry."

Once he realized he had my hand in a death grip, he let go, swung his leg over my head, and stood up to leave. "It's okay, Dude, but I gotta go." He sat his beer down hard and walked out without shutting the door. I felt like a complete ass-wipe, dick-headed loser. Obviously, the gay thing wasn't going to be that simple or easy. Simple would have been persuading him to stay for dinner, but Charles had made me promise to be kind…

Not everything works perfectly at first, especially in a new house. During the first two weeks, it was mostly hit-and-miss. Inadvertently, I nearly achieved both, backing out of the garage one morning. Not paying enough attention I nearly cost the postal service one of its finest. The screaming was marginal. He was hardly even limping when he handed me the package, still cursing under his breath. It was from Charles. Inside the box sat a small grey gargoyle—legs crossed, long-chinned impish grin, clawed hands neatly folded in its lap. It was devilish piety cast in stone. The note tied around its neck held only one innocent sentence, "Take good care of him, My Pet."

Above my bed he flew, perched on an unseen pedestal screwed to the wall. Using not-so-fine-tipped markers and an overhead projector I was drawing him into a large, circular Celtic knot when Kelvin came calling.

"Hey Dude, whatcha doin'?" He was using his relaxed indoor voice and I'd fed recently. It seemed harmless enough sliding open the meatlocker door, one of my favorite features inside the new loft. I'd bought it in a demolition auction at the old Hormel meatpacking plant. Fashioned from industrial stainless steel, it was timeless and built to last.

First, it was my breath, smothered by his lips. Without additional warning or foreplay, my knees buckled and I found myself caught up in his arms. His kung-fuck-you was strong and my body felt weightless, feather-like, as he carried me into the bedroom. Kingdoms could have been bought and sold with the film rights if I'd only had a video camera.

Between semi-loads of naked wrestling matches he confided how he'd always wanted to secretly get fucked—by his own cock, of course. He couldn't imagine getting fucked by anyone else's. Briefly, I considered indulging his narcissistic fantasy after he ripped my favorite pair of underwear right off my ass. Then he got rough.

I felt sorry for the girls he loudly recounted while wailing away at me with swollen madness. Everything was thrust and parry, monotonous motion, the kind of pent-down friction that inevitably gives way to blood. Somewhere between the sheets, incessant cursing, and frothing sweat, I could smell it, and it was driving me crazy.

Don't get me wrong; I wanted to kill him right then and there. If not for myself, then for all the girls ever bludgeoned by an erection lasting more than four hours. It took everything I had, but, goddamn it, Kelvin was the first man I'd had openly gay sex with and no one was going to die, except possibly my asshole. I could only pray it was as immortal as the rest of me.

After giving as good as I'd gotten, I sent Kelvin packing. His strides were not nearly as long as when he'd walked in that evening, but he did remember to close the door behind him. I was still sore the next day and not just about having to toss the bloody sheets and my favorite boxer briefs.

I was on a ladder behind the bed trying to finish drawing the Celtic knot when the doorbell buzzed. *Please don't be Kelvin.* After opening the door, I wished it had been. Two police detectives were standing there looking very officiously solemn. I didn't recognize either of them. After introducing themselves, they asked to come inside. I apologized for the chaos and explained that I was still moving in. They told me how they'd been newly assigned to a missing person's case and wondered if I could answer some questions. It was the third or fourth time I'd had to give a statement, and it was starting to get old.

"Where were you on the night of…? What was the nature of your relationship…? How long had you known…?" I tersely explained that I had already answered the same questions multiple times. They apologized, saying there had been no new leads. More detectives had been added to the case because of the political pressure from Pretty Boy's family. They were just trying to do their job and see if anyone had overlooked anything previously in the investigation. "Were you aware of any behavioral changes or emotional problems with the victim?"

"None that I'm aware of. But why are you calling him a victim? I thought this was a missing person's case."

"Since there's been no contact for more than three months and no ransom demand, we're assuming that foul play is probably involved."

The taller detective asked, "Were the two of you in a sexual relationship?"

"Excuse me?" They were really starting to piss me off. "Of course not. I assume you're aware he was engaged to be married."

"Yes, sir. We've spoken with his fiancée. But we've also spoken with a number of other people, as well. Some of his friends seem to think he preferred the company of men at times. We have to consider the possibility that if he has met with foul play, it may have been a crime of passion not involving Miss Danforth."

"I see. I'm afraid I can't be of much help in that regard. I know nothing about his sex life at all other than he seemed very happy with Kimberley. I played polo with him at the club and we occasionally played tennis together. That's about it. Now if you gentlemen will excuse me, I've got a very busy day I need to get back to."

I walked them to the door. The shorter one, Detective King, handed me his card and asked me to please call if I happened to think of anything else that might help. He also shook my hand, looking me straight in the eye thinking, *I'll bet you're a lying little cocksucking faggot with those pretty lips of yours.*

Sticks and stones might break my bones, but not before I can rip your fucking throat out through your asshole, Buddy. I shut the door hoping he'd read my mind, as well as I'd read his.

Back up the ladder I went, only to have the phone ring. *This goddamned mural is never going to get finished.* I answered with, "Hello, County Morgue. You stab 'em. We slab 'em." Caroline laughed on the other end. I was still fuming about cops.

"I haven't talked to you for a while. How are things going at the loft? Are you getting anything done?"

"Yes, but I think I could use a break. I'm waiting on some fabric I ordered from San Francisco for the dragon wings. After it comes in I think I'm going to split for a few days."

"Dragon wings? What on earth are you talking about?"

BLOOD: THE SANGUINE PRINCE

"Remember the exposed air duct in the living room? I hate it, so I'm turning it into a thirty-foot flying Chinese dragon. I swiped a pulley motor from a potato-chip display at the grocery store so his wings can move up and down. Except for the fabric, he's nearly finished." I assured her that, as fearsome looking as his teeth might be, he was really the nicest fellow. He even had a long, forked, red ribbon tongue that flickered when the air was blowing.

I asked Caroline if she'd spoken with Kimberley. She had, and, of course, I immediately regretted asking the question and quickly changed topics. I could tell I was starting to get irritable and stressed because I hadn't fed. Kelvin may have snaked my pipes, but he'd left me completely drained in the process. Between that and my recent crying jag on Charles' sofa, I was running a few quarts low. I could still smell the bloody sheets in the kitchen trash and that wasn't helping matters, either. Once I'd gotten Caroline off the phone, I tossed them in the dumpster across the street and went out to pick up a quick bite.

I wasn't in the mood for anything in particular. I just wanted to grab something and bring it home. There was a park near the house. I'd heard it wasn't supposed to be safe after dark, so it was, at least, worth checking out. I cruised over in the Caddie and went for a stroll. The pickings were slim. After ten minutes I'd only encountered one scruffy-looking stray dog. *No thanks. I'm hungry, not desperate.* I was about to give up and go in search of darker pastures when I saw a guy coming toward me from the basketball courts. He was wearing a heavy, hooded, zippered jacket. It was midsummer in Texas. I thought I might possibly be in luck.

Taking a few more steps toward him until I was certain he'd seen me, I stopped abruptly, turned around, and started back toward the car. Head down, hands in pockets, I quickened my pace. There was no point in carrying him all the way to the Caddie, since for the moment, anyway, he still had two perfectly good legs.

I could hear him closing the gap between us as I fumbled for my keys. I could smell the beer on his breath and the odor of crack on his unwashed clothes. I was opening the door when I felt the sharp point pressing against my back, his heart thundering in my ears. He was young, Hispanic, and deeply afraid. I almost felt sorry for him.

"Gimme me your money and your keys, *pinche pendejo.*" His English was nearly perfect; he was, obviously, American born. I'd never had Tex-Mex before moving to Dallas. After turning around, I saw he was surprisingly cute, but I was in no mood to dick around with dinner.

He must have been reading my mind. His last words were, "I'm not playing with you, *pinche puto* motherfucker. Give me the money!"

Instead, I showed him my teeth. They were longer than usual that night. I wasn't trying to be a show-off. I was just really, really hungry.

The moon perfectly reflected the fullness of his big brown eyes. They were enormously surprised. When it began to register in his mind that he'd lost his high and, most probably, his life, the look on his face changed to one of simple terror. It was always the same familiar expression, regardless of race, nationality, or sexual orientation.

Fright, fight, flight. It's nearly always in that order. Catching his wrist as he tried to stick me, I took the knife from his trembling hand, closed it, and put it back in the pocket of his chinos. He tried desperately to break free of my grasp. I allowed him to pull us both toward the trunk of the car. He was amazingly strong with all that speed-laced adrenaline pumping through his body.

Picking him up by the throat, I let him flail himself unconscious. The trunk popped open and I laid him inside, hoping he'd sleep until we got home. He was still quiet when I pulled into the garage so I went in and mixed myself a before-dinner drink. I put Filter's *Short Bus* on the stereo, cranked up the volume, and went back to the car.

He was awake and bright-eyed, if not bushy-tailed, when I opened the trunk. His expression reminded me of that first frightened fawn I'd taken down all those years ago in the woods behind my parent's house. It made me smile.

He'd fished the knife out from the pocket of his pee-stained pants. It wasn't even open as he tried making meager little thrusting swipes in the air. After brushing the hair away from his frightened face, I stroked his chest gently. It seemed to help, if only slightly. The sobbing softened into whimpers and his breathing quieted as I took him into my arms.

Later, I lay in bed finishing a second glass of wine. It wasn't my usual drink of preference so late at night, but I was still trying to get the taste of methamphetamines out of my mouth and his tear-streaked face out of my mind. No doubt, I'd been impacted by my conversation with Charles. I'd really looked further, deeper, into the boy's eyes than I'd ever allowed myself to do with any of the others. It wasn't so much pity I felt toward him as understanding. It hadn't been all that long ago since I'd been on the same track of lonely terminal terror. In the past, I would've never considered how much I might have in common with a crack-headed, carjacking, Hispanic kid.

CHAPTER EIGHT

"My dragon will fly before the dawn!" I exclaimed loudly as I unwrapped the bolt of jewel-toned fabric and discovered the watermarked pattern looked exactly like tiny feathers. After laying out nine yards for one of the wings I went in search of scissors. One CD of tribal drum music and a cold beer later, I'd fashioned a twenty-seven-foot cape and found myself dancing around the living room as if it were Salome's last performance for King Herod. Almost overnight it seemed as if I'd become a complete faggot of Biblical proportions.

Someone needed to stop me before I entered the swimsuit competition, so I calmed my happy ass down and called Caroline. She agreed to come over and help me give wings to Ad'ragon DeMellow. That was his name, by the way. He was turning out to be very chill, especially for a dragon.

We drank, danced, and hot glued until well after midnight. We were both getting a bit sloppy and sleepy when she bolted upright and said, "Oh my God! I knew there was something I wanted to tell you. There's going to be this incredible music festival in Dripping Springs in two weeks. You've got to come with us. It's a five-day campout called Drum Quest. Something like seventy-five bands are scheduled to play. Say you will. Please, please, please, pretty please?"

"Is it at Recreation Plantation?" I asked.

She looked at me pouting. "You're such an asshole. You always know everything. How the fuck do you know about Recreation Plantation? I've only been there once."

"I've been a couple of times. Remember that guy I borrowed the drum from at the Just Off Greenville Bar? Seth is Sumerian, whatever that means. I went down there with their tribe or posse or whatever they call themselves. I like Seth, but, honestly, some of those people are just too fucking strange for words. They take all that shit way too seriously." I looked up and asked Ad'ragon what he thought. Raspberries seemed to be his answer for everything.

Caroline was delighted when I agreed to go as long as I didn't have to participate in any bizarre rituals involving small-animal sacrifices of any kind. I confessed my disdain for rodents and made a comment about once having had a substance abuse problem with cats. It was the first time I'd ever made a joke about it, even if she didn't fully appreciate the humor.

Two weeks later we were traveling down past Austin to the hill country in a convoy. The only thing missing was a gaggle of hippies and the requisite Volkswagen Bus. There were several BMWs, a couple of SUVs, and my Seville. I felt almost ashamed without so much as a single Whirled Peas bumper sticker between us. I hoped they'd let us in the gate.

The countryside was beautiful after we left the main road and started crisscrossing back and forth over Onion Creek. Along the way, high-fenced exotic-game ranches were shaded by towering ancient oaks and populated by strange-looking animals with even stranger names. I was drinking in the fresh air when the wind changed direction and I got a whiff of an unusual antelope with a rack that wouldn't quit. I thought maybe I'd hit him up for a quick date on the way home. There hadn't been any of those behind my parents' house.

When we finally arrived at the campgrounds, I hugged Stacy, the owner, as we checked in. She was a hearty, robust lesbian with a weathered face and a degree in recreational management. I hadn't known there was such a degree before meeting her. I still like the way it sounds, *Recreational Management*, a life worth living, summed up in two words. I always remembered to send her a Christmas card. She said I was the only one who ever did so, considering most of her customers were pagans.

Our group set up on the edge of the main field with seven or eight tents at one end of the lagoon. One of our happy campers, Mike, had fashioned us a very nice banner on a tall staff. After he'd erected it I feared we'd forever be known as the Thunder Peeple. I wasn't sure exactly what the hell that was, but I was pretty certain it had nothing to do with inclement weather. The banner itself was black and white with a big silver lightning bolt striking through the middle. It had bells and feathers and a genuine, authentic coyote skull perched ominously on top of the twelve-foot pole. I didn't care how cool or scary it was, I was still a stickler for bad spelling. Thunder Peeple, at least to me, sounded like a group of flatulent old perverts with incontinence issues.

It was only Thursday and the sun was supposed to be glaring until Sunday afternoon. I quickly got my tent up and went inside. I stayed there until later in the evening when people from the next camp stopped by to "visit." In case you're unfamiliar with the term, "visit" is code for wanting our drugs, our booze, and any of our women who might not be strongly moored to someone else. In olden times I think those visitors were called pillagers or marauders.

I just called them leeches, all except the tall one, Tobias. He was cute and personable and, apparently, had brought his own provisions, including a friend from a nearby camp. His name was Jarrod. I felt only slightly faint and a bit nauseous during our introduction.

For whatever part of my life I'd tried to pray away the gay, I found myself praying that Jarrod might be a Friend of Dorothy, at least for the weekend. The rampaging butterflies in my stomach agreed wholeheartedly. I suspected I was in love, knew I was in lust, and hoped to be a contender for some prize or another that might include his attention and affection.

He was so incredibly, completely perfect in every way. His body and face were heart-wrenchingly sculpted down to the finest detail. His hair was surely of some previously undiscovered strain of sun-bleached gossamer. His beautiful proportions were precise, correct, unexaggerated—and he knew nothing whatsoever about martial arts. Believe me, it was one of the first questions I asked. Hacky Sack seemed to be his only sports interest and although it included a copious amount of kicking, he swore there were no degrees or belts of any kind involved.

We sat around the fire talking well into the night. Slightly drunk and completely high, I hoped I was only drooling on the inside. Tobias and Brianna decided to quest forth in search of the fabled, and oft-maligned

Porta-Potty. Caroline seemed relieved when Jarrod and I decided to chaperone. Someone asked whether or not I had Brianna's leash. The Slutty One was not amused as we traveled along the creek's bank listening to bawdy bullfrogs telling tall tales to chirping choirs of adulating crickets.

Jarrod confessed how bored he was at Rice, studying urban planning and social anthropology. His dad was president of a major winery and footing the grape-stained bills for his son's misadventures in higher education. He liked to party, spend dad's money, and feel appropriately guilty about all of it later. Instead of counseling or repentance, I suggested recreational management. He'd never heard of it either. Not once during the entire conversation did he ever offer the slightest, remotest hint about his sexual orientation. When I did crawl back into my tent later that night, my only companions were a set of blue balls, an aching heart, and a busted gaydar, which as near as I could tell had never worked properly. Best Buy would definitely be hearing from me when I got back to Dallas. I hoped I'd saved the receipt.

The next day was Forgiveness Friday. I woke up to a completely different tune and some strong, black coffee. The music had already started and it was primo. Not too loud, heavy, or fast, it was kind of like a distant cousin of Phish, only with more chords. The air was thick and humid beneath an overcast sky and I could hear the creek calling my name. I answered by casting my clothes and cares aside after laying a beach towel in the shady spot under the giant oak that I considered God's answer to sunblock. Its merciful arms even extended out over the spillway for those of us uninterested in crispy, caramel-colored skin.

I was stepping behind a titless blonde girl sitting on the edge of the dam dangling her feet in the rushing water when I slipped on a patch of moss. Awkwardly, uncontrollably, my arms flapping futilely, I found myself flying backward through the air with the greatest of unease. For what it's worth, even if you're immortal, you can still see your life flashing before your eyes.

"Oh fuck!" is about all my mouth could manage to shriek before filling with cool, spring-fed water as my back slammed violently into the shallows on the low side of the spillway. I was hardly wet, yet completely humiliated, when I felt someone's arms scooping underneath my body, lifting me off the rocky bottom.

When I surfaced, it was Jarrod holding me. He was smiling, beautifully wet, and scared shitless all at the same time. Everyone else was laughing hysterically and clapping. Once he'd towed my wounded ego back to shore, I took his hand and bowed. "Thank you! Fuck you. Fuck you all very much! The next show is at noon. Get your tickets now!" I shot the bird at our flock of fans in a wide, sweeping gesture. In a surprising move, my glistening savior kissed my hand and bowed comically to a roaring, adoring audience as we made our way clumsily back up the bank.

No one seemed to be listening to the band when Jarrod brought his stuff over and spread it out next to mine. Some idiot was walking around naked holding a tray and yelling, "Get yer bacon. Get yer bacon while it's hot and free." *Asshole, you better not be talking about me.*

We were lying on our stomachs when I felt fingers lightly stroking up and down my spine, gradually increasing in pressure. I turned and smiled when he asked, "Are you sure you're okay? You fell like twenty feet and that water was only a couple of feet deep. It would've killed me. I'm surprised you're not dead."

"Me too. I think I must have hit it just right."

"I'll bet your ass is going to be sore tomorrow," he ventured.

"Is that a prediction or a promise?" I queried while willing him to make it so. My face was beaming at the prospect and I'd stopped caring whether I was being too transparent somewhere between the seventh and eighth vertebrae.

Rush to Judgment was coming on stage in half an hour and the girls couldn't decide what, if anything, to wear. One of the marauders was naked, too, only he was passed out, drunk and semisubmerged, at the edge of the creek. He'd been extolling the wonders of his "enormous foreskin" in a poorly reprised Scottish accent the entirety of the afternoon. I was sitting in a lawn chair smoking a roach when Tobias and Jarrod came round to collect his carcass.

Pulling his withered remains from the murky water, it became evident that Mike the Marauder's claims were greatly exaggerated. Expeditious mercy and a few good men transported him back to the wild band of heathens from which he'd come. I was glad to see our prisoner go. I'd been tempted earlier to violate the Geneva Convention and circumcise him myself just to shut the bastard up, but catch-and-release had never been a sport or political philosophy I'd fully embraced. Practically anyone with a degree in recreational management understands how essential culling the herd is to a healthy, happy animal population. Fortunately for Mike, I was on vacation and not playing the role of game warden.

The show was already in riot mode by the time we made our way into the crowd. It was insanity by chaotic design. The band was a dazzlingly bizarre blend of the Electric Light Orchestra and the Grateful Dead. There must have been fifty performers between those on stage and their crazily costumed counterparts running through the audience. Fire and flutes, electric oboes, and fluorescent flags swirled through the DayGlo mass of writhing revelers rushing out into the night and circling back again in an endless parade of communal madness. Topless girls waving giant fans chased feathered nymphs and horny goat-legged boys misting the crowd with intoxicating aromas making the air as confusing and complex as the music.

Underneath the chaos a deep, unseen techno thump drew us down into the wormhole of violins, trumpets, and a cello crowded in behind guitars and synthesizers. The stage had been taken by a storm of strings and blaring winds. More psychic surgery than musical performance, the Ecstasy we'd taken earlier seemed almost superfluous in the sensual sea of bodies undulating around us in wave after wave of blissful discord.

Fantasia on the Prairie was in full swing and I was Mighty Mouse with my chin resting on Jarrod's shoulder. We were rambling about what Disney movies might have been like if Walt could have tripped on the shit we were taking when the nymph-o-lectric train ran between us with Billy Goat in heated pursuit. Until the moment she was gored, Caroline had been standing on a green-resin stacking chair trying to see the stage. Gymnastic genocide in stopgap animation slowly ensued.

Once we'd quit laughing, Tumbelina tried standing up but quickly found herself a part of the unnatural landscape again. I was high, she was low, and before I knew it, I'd whisked her off the ground and perched her atop my shoulders. It was *Dancing with the Stars* on PCP and we'd won the Mirror Ball trophy from Jarrod's perspective.

Voluminous eyes gazed at me, moving up and down with completely stupefied astonishment. "Damn bro! You must be some kind of seriously strong. Where are you hiding all those muscles?" Reaching for my bicep, he squeezed and laughed saying, "Funny, it doesn't feel that big."

"You're looking in the wrong place. My hands are full right now or I'd show you myself. Keep searching. I'll let you know if you're getting warm." Poking him in the stomach, I walked away hoping he'd take me up on the challenge.

Between the drugs, alcohol, and rocking motions from sitting on my shoulders, Caroline was nearly asleep by the time we got her back to camp and in bed. Jarrod stoked the campfire while I found us a couple of beers and tried rolling a half-assed excuse for a joint. We smoked and joked around while he played with the flames. He was on one knee when he turned his head toward me and grinned in a way that can only be achieved on Ecstasy. I smiled and said, "You know you'll pee in the bed if you keep playing with that fire."

He boyishly asked, "Can I pee in your bed?"

"Only if you sleep in the wet spot." We finished the joint and our beers before turning in. Much to my relief, he chose to go behind the tent instead.

It was mesmerizing watching him undress by candlelight. I don't think I've ever seen anything more beautifully sensuous. He must have been reading my mind as he pulled my hand away from the button on my shirt. "Here, let me." Two buttons later he asked, "Do you have any idea how beautiful you are? When we met yesterday, I thought you were the most handsome creature I'd ever seen. When I look at you, it's hard to imagine I'm even looking at someone who's human. You're just too perfect."

"Yeah, I get that a lot," I joked while pulling the shirt over his head. "Sorry, I didn't mean to interrupt. As you were saying..."

From what I could see, we'd both boned up, studied each other hard, and were about to be initiated into the Mutual Admiration Society of America. It may have only been the drugs talking, but I sure liked what they were saying as he pushed my shoulders back and slid on top of me in a snaking dance electrifying my flesh, enflaming my body with his tongue and lips. His was the gentlest, most tender touch I'd ever known. That was the night I finally came to understand what could be, what ought to be, as his body slid slowly down my stomach until I was completely inside him. I'd waited two lifetimes to feel, to know such perfect union.

Long after the drugs wore off we were still in a state of completely ecstatic bliss until Jarrod collapsed exhausted, falling happily asleep on my chest. I didn't want to ever move again. I lay there listening to the concert of our beating hearts mingling with the misty sounds of morning until I dozed off sometime after dawn.

I'd been dreaming in fragmented snippets when I felt Jarrod crawling across my chest. He was sitting on top of me when my blurry eyes opened. He smiled, stretched, and yawned before kissing me and saying, "Good morning handsome."

I smiled back with, "Fuck you, dragon breath. Like the girls from Arkansas say after a long night of hot sex, get off me, Daddy. You're squishing my cigarettes." I was trying to tweak his nipples as he swatted me away and unzipped the tent. "Fine. Run, you coward. Those stubby-dicked asspirates at your camp can't give you this." I waved nine inches of morning wood at him saying, "Sure you don't want to stay? I'll even shower you in gold. Here, let me…"

Watching him dashing across the field, yelping and diving headfirst, naked, into his tent was possibly the cutest thing I'd ever seen. *The quick little fox.* Falling back asleep, I hugged his pillow realizing it was the first time I'd ever had sex without wanting to kill someone.

Sweltering heat and the smell of strong black coffee taunted me out of the tent several hours later. Groggy, foggy, and soggy were three of the five brain cells still on active duty in my mind. Some nameless, faceless entity handed me a cup of coffee that consumed the fourth. I felt fucked with, over, under, and around. The sun, scorching as it was, seemed mild compared to the bread-making heat inside my tent the night before. I'd never had a yeast infection, wasn't sure what it was, but had always assumed it came from nasty, sweaty, prolonged sex. I could only hope that if Jarrod had a bun in the oven, it wasn't growing mold already.

The thought and image combined were too much for my one remaining cellular event. Choosing the nuclear option, *Fuck it*, I snagged a beer and wobbled off toward the water hoping I'd missed last call for bacon. Caroline was on the bank soaking her ankle in the icy creek. I jumped in beside her and let myself sink into consciousness. When I emerged, she'd opened my beer and lit a cigarette. Crawling appreciatively from the muddy depths, I took a long drag and collapsed onto the cool grass until the ghost of debauchery past cast a long shadow over my watery grave. As if he wasn't beautiful enough in his ordinary state, he was absolutely radiant in his new freshly fucked look.

He'd brought along brightly bejeweled accessories named Robert and Terry. Obviously a couple, they were from Houston, too. I only thought I felt out of season until the Baconator came calling. Lunch service was apparently a more formal affair than breakfast. He was wearing a loincloth which proved a nearly endless source of delight and fascination for the two frisky fashionistas.

Wrinkling my nose at Jarrod and the plate, I said, "I prefer my pork pulled, not fried." According to the churlish look painted across Caroline's face, she'd formed an aversion to humor and meat sometime that morning for a reason unbeknownst to the rest of the world. In a fit of decency, Bacon Boy began blushing and walked away sporting a tepee in his Tarzan attire, but somehow I suspected he'd be back. Saying as much, I had no idea I was changing the course of history.

With sweeping gestures and vocal flourishes fit for the stage, Terry began telling us about the authentic teepees he and Robert built for a living. I admitted my ignorance regarding the demand any longer for that particular type of housing. He was more than delighted to fill in my gaps of knowledge. "Oh yes!" he exclaimed proudly, "The Boy Scouts are one of our biggest customers."

Okay, I thought. *Here we have two completely flaming faggots selling teepees to the Boy Scouts and people think I'm strange.*

When they asked what I did for a living. I could tell from the tone and word choice I was being sized up as a mate for Jarrod. Before I could formulate an answer, Caroline chimed in. "Don't ask. He's a trust-fund baby. The rest of us have to dance for a living. Will somebody get me a beer?"

Robert handed her an Anchor Steam and Jarrod lit a joint, passing it cautiously in her direction before they turned their attention back to me as if I hadn't finished my story. The loft was the only thing I could think of for show-and-tell since I wasn't wearing a loincloth.

They inquired about the size of my building, but seemed infinitely more interested in scrutinizing my other assets. Jarrod was highly amused by their poorly disguised attempts to appraise what I considered my private property. Trying to steer their attention back to the story that wouldn't begin, I offered, "It's about ten-thousand square feet. I'm using half, not including the six-car garage. I'm still working on the other half. When it's finished there'll be two other live/work spaces. It has a nice yard along one side, but the real reason I bought the place is because of the roof. It's completely flat and has a killer view of the Dallas skyline. I haven't figured out what I'm going to do with it yet…"

The unambiguously gay duo high-fived each other, answering in unison, "Ohhh…we know. You need a teepee!" They'd obviously done too much early morning wanking-and-baking. Tarzan's bratwurst had gone to their heads and I needed to get a grip before they started pulling permits or worse.

Countering their offer, I claimed, "I'm not sure about the teepee, but I do need to peepee. I'll be back." Jumping up, apparently not fast enough, Jarrod was at my side instantly. I'd hoped to go alone because I didn't really have to go at all. Being a vampire, among other things, means you'll never have to hear one of us saying, "Can you pull over? I need to pee."

By the time we returned, I'd changed most, if not the entirety, of my mind. *It's hot as fuck up there. I'm going to have to come up with something for shade. Why not? It isn't like everybody has a genuine authentic teepee on his roof. It beats one of those tacky pop-up canopies.*

I still remember the words. I'd just waded back into the water when I shot off my mouth. "Boys," I said, "fuck it! Let's build me a goddamned teepee. If you build it, they'll come, right?"

Diving into the lagoon over Caroline's head I could hear Jarrod yelling, "I know I will!' as he splashed into the water beside me. Seconds later I felt legs wrapping my waist in a scissor lock as jubilant arms furled round my neck and he emerged from the mossy depths, a queer monkey on my back babbling some sort of gibberish about having fun the night before. Caught up in the dual spirits of recreational management and animal husbandry, I was forced to baptize him in a rancorously loud display of drive-thru sainthood.

Without shame, mercy, and only minimal moss, he arose breathlessly triumphant like a newly minted god gasping for air and kissed me so fully on the lips in such a way that anyone watching had little doubt as to his denomination while sucking the air from my surprised lungs. I'd created a monster without so much as a single bite. Like a man possessed, his tongue twisted around my own in an eye-popping display to a widely appreciative audience. Unfortunately, Caroline had a front row seat for our lip-locked, tongue-tying extravaganza.

Her ankle was angry, swollen, and purple, the color of an irate eggplant; her face wasn't many shades behind and, from all outward appearances, was catching up rapidly. Sensing that *Boys Gone Wild* wasn't on her favorites' playlist, I decided against an encore and asked if she was ready to go.

"Home. I need to go home. This fucking ankle is killing me!" Straining appropriately, I plucked my pouting princess from the bank and carried her back to camp. While loading the car I managed a quick goodbye and exchange of numbers with Jarrod. My eagle-eyed eggplant caught our kiss, of course, which made the scenic trip along Onion Creek an affair to remember.

Hoping she'd forget was a pipe dream on my part and the offer of a joint didn't seem to appease her either. Passing around a curve I spotted the antelope I'd seen on our way in and thought, *Fuck it. She's being a bitch. I'm hungry and I'm sure as hell not about to eat her angry-looking Barney ass.* After pulling over, pretending the need to take a piss, I walked around the bend and jumped the fence. The antelope was somewhat more standoffish and not nearly as tasty as Jarrod. Disappointed, I let him live to tell a long-toothed tale. I'd read somewhere that chupacabras were rumored to inhabit the area. I enjoyed the thought that, in some small way, I might be adding to the rich fabric of local lore. Every legend has its beginnings someplace, I suppose.

Normally I don't drink and drive, but antelope, I discovered, is some seriously nasty-tasting shit and after I got back in the car I knew I was about to eat another bowl of it, courtesy of Caroline. I'd barely popped the top off my beer and pulled back onto the road before she started in. "I saw Jarrod crawling out of your tent this morning."

"Now that you mention it, I think I did, too."

She wasn't laughing. "He didn't have any clothes on."

"So it would have been better if he'd been wearing a tux?" I asked sarcastically.

"Don't be an asshole. You know perfectly well what I'm talking about."

She was right. It was not the time to be an asshole. *Clock it back, dude. Just let her talk.*

"It's not like I care or anything, but as long as we've known each other… you could have at least told me you're gay."

Wow. I hadn't seen that one coming. It was the first time anyone had ever said those words to me and meant it. It felt completely alien hearing it out loud. I needed some fast footing and knew damned well I didn't have a leg to stand on. Denial was as good a place to start as any. "Would you believe me if I said that was the first time anything like that ever happened? Caroline, come on. We were all high as shit and I'm not sure I even remember half of it."

"Bullshit." She crossed her arms in a huff, turned, and stared out the window. That answered one question. Clearly I was no Bill Clinton. I'd always wondered why lies sounded so much better when they came from his mouth. We drove in silence until she'd percolated enough to build up another head of steam. "When he kissed you goodbye back there, it sure as hell looked to me like you both remembered a whole lot of something.

I still can't believe after all this time you thought you couldn't tell me about…about any of this."

"Caroline, why, how would I tell you about something that's never happened before? What was I supposed to say exactly? Oh, by the way I'm planning on doing it with some guy I've never met sometime next week and I thought you'd want to know because you might think it's kind of gay when it happens." That seemed to shut her up, but only briefly.

"You know the police asked me if y'all were lovers. I laughed at the time. Kimberley even said something about it. I don't remember exactly what, but I could tell they'd asked her, too."

Swallowing my tongue, shitting my pants, and driving the car all at the same time seemed improbable. *Fuck, this thing is going to outlive me. I have to do something. If anybody ever connects the dots…*I'd been taught how good confession can be for the soul, and, since no one knew I didn't have one, it seemed worth a shot.

"Caroline, this is so hard for me, but I have to tell you the truth. For a long time, I've wanted to tell somebody. Whether you believe me or not, last night is the first time in my life I've ever done anything like that. I've always known I had those kinds of feelings. I thought everybody else did too. I don't know, but until now I've done a damn good job of keeping them buried because I didn't want to look at them and I didn't think anyone else would either.

"Last night, none of that mattered. How am I supposed to know if it was the drugs, or Jarrod, or both? When he looked at me the way he did, I said the same thing I've been saying all weekend. Fuck it. Just fuck it for a change! And that's exactly what I did, or at least I think I did. Either way, I'm guilty of something. I must be. It's hard enough trying to figure this out for myself right now. You're the first person I've ever talked to, and I'm a little confused in case you couldn't tell. I'm begging you, can we please keep this between us for now?"

My sister looked at me with sad, pitiful eyes. Although hoping for something more conspiratorial, I was obliged to take what I could get under the circumstances. Considering the lack of screaming or use of the word "fag," I felt she might benefit from another dose of semi-real Taxi Cab Confessions.

"You can't imagine what it was like growing up in my family. They always looked at me weird because I had better taste than my parents by the time I could dress myself. When I was ten, I didn't even get a Christmas present. They gave me a fucking card with money and a note. 'We weren't sure what to get. Buy yourself something nice.' What kind of parents do that, Caroline?

"I was always smarter than the other kids in my classes. I was good at nearly everything, except girls. Other than you, I've always been more comfortable around guys. I don't see why that has to make me gay.

"I don't want to be gay; I want to be like everybody else. Whatever happened last night, if that makes me gay, then fine, I'll deal with it, but I can't see how being high and messing around with some guy once in my life means I have to be a fag forever. Fuck if I know. I just never felt like I could talk to anybody about this kind of stuff before. Thank you." I took her hand and smiled. Truthfully, the speech even choked me up a little.

"You know..." she said in a whisper, "I thought you and that guy from school last year would have made a great couple. I remember thinking the two of you looked really hot together."

"I'm not playing dumb, but you must be high. Who the fuck are you talking about?"

I honestly hadn't a clue until she said, "Trevor, remember? He was that über-hot lacrosse player. I wonder whatever happened to him."

"I hate to be the one to tell you, Princess, but you're dreaming shit up now. Somebody told me he was hiding out in Mexico from his parents. He was supposedly flunking out of school and they were about to kick him off the lacrosse team." My life was flashing before my eyes for the second time in a weekend. Jesus fucking mother of God, if she, or anyone, ever pieced that puzzle together, I could probably kiss my ass goodbye and some guy named Guido hello. Spending the rest of your life in prison is one thing, but given my age and circumstance that might take a while.

Dropping Caroline off at her house, I apologized profusely to her parents for not taking better care of her. My hope was that she'd be preoccupied enough with the ankle to not dwell too much on the rest of the weekend's mounting revelations.

I drove straight home and was damned glad to be there. Getting out of the car, I noticed something shiny on the floor just inside the front door. The gold embossing was a dead giveaway.

Drink in hand, Rufus to the rafters, I sat down to see what Grandvamps was up to. He was mercifully short, omniscient, and pointed. "Hope you had a lovely weekend with your lovely. Much is happening here. Have your passport at hand. We'll talk soon.–CHB"

I'd never been much for surprises, even as a kid. *Curiosity kills the cat*. I could hear my mother, who thought she knew everything, saying it again and again. I was in no mood for mysteries or lectures. *Fuck it. I'm way too tired*. Ad'ragon was left in charge of all things suspenseful. He needed to start earning his keep somehow, instead of sitting there silently pooh-poohing everything all the time.

CHAPTER NINE

The next few weeks were almost normal, at least as normal as it gets when you're dead and dating. Jarrod called enough times for it to slowly dawn on me that he considered himself my boyfriend. I didn't particularly hate the idea, but I wasn't completely comfortable with the whole concept either. As I grappled with the notion, I realized it was more about Jarrod than the thought of having a boyfriend.

Don't get me wrong. I really liked him—and the sex, undoubtedly the best I'd ever had. Even in the fiery-hot passion of the moment, I'd had no desire to drain him. Still, there was something missing. Without question, he was one of the most breathtakingly handsome young men I'd ever encountered, yet, in many respects, he was still a boy. He lacked ambition, purpose, and direction. In coming to grips with my own sexuality, I realized that those were important qualities for the man of my dreams. Hell, who was I kidding? I'd never allowed myself to even think of another man in those terms. Nevertheless, I hungered for something more. Beautiful as he was, instinctively I knew he just wasn't it.

About the time I'd decided to have *the talk* with Jarrod, Robert called from Houston to let me know the teepee was finished and they were planning a trip to Dallas. He said they'd bring it up on their trailer. I asked why it needed to be hauled on a trailer. I shouldn't have.

"Are you insane? Twenty-four feet is like two-and-a-half stories tall. That's as big as a fucking house!"

Terry chirped in on the other line, "Not really...Okay, maybe a tall, skinny house. Think of it as a tract house. It's only twelve hundred square feet."

Oh great! Two flaming homos were bringing me a teepee big enough to be seen from downtown. *Honestly, how do I get myself into this shit?* They also intimated that they were bringing me a surprise to go with the teepee. *Fan fucking tastic!* For a dead guy, my life was full of wonder. They arrived the following day with teepee and said surprise in tow.

Wearing a very skimpy loincloth and feathered headband, Jarrod popped out of the teepee like a stripper at a gay sweat-lodge party. I know they meant well, but I had serious reservations about their sanity and desperately wanted to get Jarrod in the house before anyone got a look at my flaming, squawking Indian dancing around nearly naked in the street.

Robert and Terry had a room at the Melrose Hotel so they could be close to the bars. Tonto wanted to stay with me, naturally. I couldn't very well say no to a nearly naked savage. But I did ask the white party boys how, pray tell, were we supposed to get the world's tallest teepee on the roof? The two of them leapt off the sofa and gave each other another well-rehearsed high five. "We'll manhandle it!"

Tonto could tell Ke-mo sah-bee was anything but amused. Squeezing my bicep, he reminded everyone how strong I was. I'd been cornered by a Comanche and I knew it. "Okay, you faggots, I guess we can at least try."

Miraculously, we managed to muscle it off the trailer without a hernia or hemorrhoid between us. I sent the three of them up to the roof while I pushed from below. Like most things, it looked harder than it actually was. Standing the damned thing up and staking off its enormous ass was far more difficult. By the time we'd finished, I was so exhausted and weak I admitted to Terry that he was right. It was only the size of a tract house—a very nice three-bedroom, two-bath, with a double-car garage and spacious suburban lawn, but still, a tract house.

The boys put their trailer in the garage while I fixed drinks. We smoked a joint and let Ad'ragon cool us off. Robert observed that not only did I have the world's tallest teepee, but I also owned the biggest ceiling fan on the planet. He and Terry invited us to come downtown with them to the bars. I declined, which made Jarrod deliriously happy. Far less certain regarding my own happiness quotient, I knew Tonto wanted the grand tour. After they left, I gave it to him all night.

He really was very sweet and that was part of the problem. I was discovering I'm not that keen on sweets. We carried blankets and pillows up to the teepee sometime after dark. Iced beers, a couple of joints, and an occasional star lit our way. By the time the night was over, my path forward seemed more clouded than ever.

I liked Jarrod. He obviously liked me. What exactly was my problem? I felt like an asshole. Here I was with an exquisitely beautiful young man who was completely smitten. He was educated, well mannered for the most part, and from a good family. It seemed familiarly uncomfortable. It would be a while before I understood why.

Robert and Terry came around the next afternoon with more stuff in the back of their truck, eager to barter the loot in exchange for Bloody Marys. We hauled the crap up to the roof and made a pit inside the teepee. The optional fireplace was exactly what the place needed. I was so happy with my new conical condo, I offered to take them and their Indian friend to dinner at a quaint new restaurant in the Bishop Arts district near the loft. My gritty little neighborhood was beginning to enjoy something of a renaissance. (That always seems to happen when the gays move in…)

We were laughing, drinking, and having a generally good time when it dawned on me that I was in the midst of my very first intentionally public appearance as a gay man, or half a gay couple, or whatever it was. I felt so comfortable, I actually ordered food. Having developed a penchant for exotic species recently, I asked for Chilean sea bass in a béchamel sauce. It was infinitely better going down than twenty minutes later when it came back up.

Once I'd relieved myself of fish and friends, I went back to the table. Terry was in the middle of describing some raunchy detail of his and Robert's three-way from the previous evening when I noticed a couple being seated at a table by the window. The waiter was handing a nicely preserved older woman her menu. Obviously well- and locally-bred, her Texas-sized hair was proudly combed, sprayed, and piled miles high atop her steady head and sturdy shoulders.

I was admiring the architectural stamina of her coiffure when it tilted precariously to the left. She was reaching for her purse on the floor as I wondered in amazement whether or not she'd fall out of the chair. Quite literally, I nearly fell out of my own as her husband came into view. Not very colorful to begin with as complexions go, my face must have turned completely hospital white as I gazed, horrified, into the face of Detective King. Suddenly, uncontrollably, I wanted to kill everyone in the room. It took an immense force of will to remain seated and composed.

Jarrod put his hand on my arm and said, "Babe, what's the matter? You don't look so good." I snatched my arm away and covered my face with the napkin. *Too late*, my mind was already racing to places gruesomely unimaginable. All I could do was sit there feeling sickened by the smell of bloody hearts pumping, one of which I wanted to rip from its chest. Someone needed to die and it wasn't going to be me. I paid the bill and asked that we leave. Of course the asshole was looking straight at me as we walked out the door.

Bombay Sapphire gin and really good weed…they're the perfect accompaniment to an evening of shedding one's murderous thoughts—or any thoughts for that matter. After several prescriptively refreshing doses of both I could feel my moonlight white complexion returning along with the ever louder chorus of begging from the Village People who wanted to go out dancing and wouldn't take no for an answer.

Dallas is a big city. It has dozens and dozens of gay bars from which to select. Somehow they managed to choose the only one named Village Station. The irony wasn't wasted. It was a vast, multi-floored ocean of shimmering, glittering, sweating homosexuals preening, parading, and posing on better drugs than mine. Don't get me wrong, I love the nightlife, but I'm just not that into theatre of the absurd or acid-laced twinkies.

We did manage to dance our asses off. Fortunately, the club was so crowded that Jarrod never noticed, at least in the mirror's reflection, he was dancing alone. Perspiration and poppers permeated the air. Ripped, writhing, shirtless bodies dripped with the stuff of gay boys' dreams. Vampires don't sweat, so every trip to the bar meant another anointing in the bathroom sink. I was splashed to my shoes and sloshed to my liver's content by the time the taxi dumped us at the curb. I'd told the cab driver, "Just look for the teepee."

From blocks away it was still there. Jarrod was slumped on my shoulder softly snoring as the cab pulled to the curb and I pried him from the back seat. Soon he would be falling asleep in my arms again for the last time.

It wasn't the least bit surprising when the police showed up on Tuesday. I'd been expecting them Monday. Detective King seemed to be in a particularly good mood. I didn't think the tall one looked like he got laid very often. They were *in the neighborhood* and wanted to know if I could come down to police headquarters for an interview. I explained that I'd already told them everything I knew and couldn't imagine what else I might have to offer. They were very insistent. I asked if I needed an attorney.

King smirked while he let Detective Drake play good cop. I suspected that's why the big dude probably never got laid. Everyone likes a bad boy in uniform, regardless of stripe. "This is really not a big deal," he offered calmly. "We want you to look at some photos and talk about some statements people have made."

I agreed to meet them Thursday afternoon. Detective King smiled his little self-satisfied, shit-eating grin as they walked out the door. Mentally, I strongly suggested he go home and fuck his wife really well that evening. I'd already decided he wouldn't be able to make our appointment two days later. Walking them to the door, I noted the license number as they drove away in their black Crown Victoria sedan.

I waited in the park across from police headquarters that evening. He drove out a couple of hours later. It was somewhat surprising he hadn't mentioned that we were neighbors. His house was on Twelfth Street, only four blocks away from my loft. It was a very nicely renovated little bungalow with charming period colors and surprisingly good landscaping. The hostas were exceptional. I wondered what his wife's secret was; I'd never had much luck with them.

Painting freshly plastered walls proved infinitely more interesting than watching her garden grow while waiting for morning. The teepee had thrown me off schedule and I was trying to get the other loft ready to rent. The entire affair kept me thinking about Jarrod, wondering what in the world I was going to do with him. I thought about Detective King also, even though I knew exactly what I was going to do with him. Of course

Pretty Boy was never far from my mind. He may have been dead, but he was in no way silent. That particular evening I couldn't turn up the stereo enough to drown him out at all. After cleaning the paint roller, I fixed a drink and went to sit in the teepee hoping there'd be less shouting on the rooftop.

The sum totality of my life was completely fucked as near as I could determine. I wanted to break up with Jarrod because he was too young and soft, beautiful and gay. I wanted to kill Detective King because he was an old, hard-nosed bastard who wanted to send me away. And Pretty Boy…I wanted to bring him back from the dead, if for no other reason than he wouldn't stay out of my head.

Only one of them could be a winner so I choked Detective King the next morning in his driveway at 6:15 a.m. Seconds before he would have died, I released my grip on his throat and laid him on the perfectly manicured lawn. While he was losing consciousness I tried using all my powers of persuasion to convince him that I was a nice guy, not a homo, and certainly not a killer. He would quit riding my ass, and I'd never ridden Pretty Boy's, either. Taking his service revolver and wallet, I jogged back to the loft, tossing them in the dumpster behind El Rancho Mexicana on the way. I could never understand how that place was so wildly popular; it always smelled like nothing but a grease pit to me.

Thursday afternoon I met alone with Detective Drake. I was trying to penetrate his mind with thoughts similar to the ones I'd shared with his partner the previous morning. Having no clue whether any of it was working or not, I could tell the poor guy still hadn't been laid. He was entirely too nice, even when opening the folder and showing me the picture.

His finger was tapping Trevor's forehead. After watching him dehydrate in my closet for months, I'd forgotten how cute he'd been. Beaming smile, brightest of eyes, blonde, blonde hair, the all-American dream…and now, one of my worst nightmares.

"Yes, of course I remember him. He volunteered at the Haunted House a couple of times last year. I'm sorry, but I can't recall his name. I think someone said he was flunking out of school and split for Mexico. We had a lot of volunteers working there at the time. Honestly, I didn't have time to interact with many of them. I wish I could be more help, but that's all I remember."

Shrugging, I looked Detective Drake squarely in the eyes. I'd never been more serious and casual at the same time. He took the slightest of breaths and closed the folder. For some odd reason, I actually felt like the fucker believed me. All I can say with any certainty is that I walked out of the police station under my own steam instead of being escorted away in leg irons and handcuffs.

CHAPTER TEN

The work was coming along nicely on the lofts. I'd finished the second space and almost completed my own. Someone named Theo called about the apartment the second day it was in the paper. As heavenly voices go, he sounded delightful enough on the phone. In person he was angelic, but too lean and lengthy for cherubim status. I'd exchanged my gaydar at Best Buy so I could tell with some degree of certainty he was also straight. A third-generation furniture maker, sometimes musician, and all-around goofball, he was unquestionably charming. Taller than the longest day, hair darker than the deepest night, Theo was a grinner with a huge mouthful of perfect teeth.

His eyes twinkled, his cheeks dimpled, and my heart melted. The guitar, pearly whites, and Waterpik, of which I was jealous, all moved in a few days later. I know it's sick, but in the beginning I actually had fantasies of brushing and flossing together in front of the mirror. They faded with time, of course, as I came to consider him a friend.

Never once did he invite me to dinner and I returned the kindness. It was such a slow, subtle process I didn't realize how much I'd missed having a buddy until I had one again. Theo was in love with the teepee and sawing wood in those days. He also slept a lot, much to my relief, but that was before the start of the war.

It began innocently enough, as do most regional conflicts. Dallas Power and Light ignited the situation by selling off an old building across the street to an artists' cooperative. Children were involved, which only aggravated the situation. Josh, one of the stoned-in-residence artists, came calling one day with a sack full of coonskin hats and feathered headdresses. They'd seen the teepee and wanted to play cowboys and Indians.

Theo and the neighborhood kids, or indigenous tribes—as I liked to call them—outnumbered the Union of Always-Lit Power Workers by three-to-one. After a few weeks of daily skirmishes and sleepless nights I was contemplating taking up the lost arts of blanket weaving and smallpox production when the reporter came calling.

Hillary wanted to do a story on the *darling* but *politically incorrect* cowboy/Indian wars raging in Oak Cliff. Apparently the indigenous people, or at least those under twelve, were going to school, much to everyone's amazement, eager to study American history. Somehow we were to blame, according to parents, teachers, and the woman standing at my door.

"Talk to the teepee guy on Tyler Street. He started it." Those were her precise words. Initially, I was relieved she and the photographer hadn't said, "Sir, you're under arrest. Will you please come with us?"

The article came out a few days later with several photos and a heartwarming story about how much the kids had prospered due to the ongoing war. There was a silly picture of Theo and me in our headdresses and feathers standing back to back, arms folded across swollen, exaggerated chests. He was grinning as usual. I was dashing as always. Looking at the picture I thought I might even possibly pass for an Indian, albeit a lightly complected one.

Ten days later the first letter arrived. It had a forever stamp instead of gold embossing; clearly it wasn't from Charles. The tightly scripted handwriting alone would have been enough to identify the sender without the dove-and-cross, peel-and-stick return address label. It began much the same as the ones that followed. "My son, I know this is you. Marty sent us the picture. I can't understand why you're pretending to be an Indian, or why you've forsaken your father and me? What could we have done to turn you away from us and your Lord, Jesus Christ? We still love you whether you're an Episcopalian or a Navajo. Please come home. Your father has taken up smoking again. Who knows how long he has? No one lives forever, except our Father who art in Heaven. Hallowed be His Name. Through Him all things are possible."

Biblical references aside, *fuck me and fuck you too, Marty*. The meddling old bastard had picked up a copy of the *Dallas Morning News* on a layover at DFW and sent the article to my folks. Running away seemed almost instinctual, but I'd already done that and I had enough problems without being redundant or paranoid.

The letters kept coming, each more tearful and bizarre than the last. She was breaking my heart even if she was single-handedly keeping the U.S. Postal Service afloat. I finally stopped opening or accepting them. Without paying attention one day, I almost marked *Return to Sender* on a letter from Charles until I noticed the Australian stamp. Courier pigeons and gold initials can be easily mistaken for doves and crosses, but this envelope was typed and devoid of the usual gold-embossed seal.

The instructions and airline ticket indicated I was to meet him in Sydney. I got the distinct feeling he wasn't asking me to join him on holiday. I could tell he hadn't written the letter himself. It was curt, business-like, and to the point, unlike Charles' usual, gushing prose. My accommodations had been made, someone would pick me up at the airport, and there was no ticket for, nor mention of, a return flight. Under the circumstances it sounded like an offer I could hardly refuse.

Theo agreed to hold down the teepee and keep the white menace across the street at bay while I expanded the empire beyond our immediate shores. My grandfather had fallen ill, was in the twilight of his life, and wanted me by his side. When told, the story slipped so effortlessly from my lips, I had no idea what I'd even said. The lie, the fiction, the truth—sometimes they're so close to each other, hardly anyone can tell the difference.

Business Class and Quantas nearly killed me. Between flight delays, connection problems, and time on the tarmac, I spent almost thirty hours chasing the sun. I was burning up by the time the plane touched down in Sydney. My stomach was roiling, my blood was boiling, and I was virtually staggering as we debarked. It was too risky to even think about feeding inside the terminal. Stumbling toward customs, I must have looked like death warmed-over; I felt even worse, if that was possible for someone in my condition.

Dangerous, dizzy, and nauseous were my first, middle, and last names when the inspector took my passport. *Drug mule, rock star, flu bird—I don't give a flying fuck. Just stamp the goddamned thing before I do something we'll both regret.* Either the Vulcan mind-control shit worked, or he was afraid I was going to blow chunks on his jacket. He popped the rubber seal of approval on the damned thing and slid it back in my direction, which didn't much matter by that point—nothing did. The left half of my upper and lower lips smiled and thanked him. The other parts of my face were busy stroking out in mini-convulsions as I snatched the passport off the counter and listed to the right.

Forward momentum and a fast-talking redhead saved me. My one usable hand was clutching the counter as I fell farther toward the ground with each stumbling, staggering step, knocking people out of the way. Once I'd run out of counter space, I was nosediving for the floor when I felt fingers wrap firmly around my dangling, useless arm. Swimming in and out of consciousness, I said, "Hey, I know…" Black, then back around, "You're that chick…"

Somewhere from within my death-defying scrabble as a palsied stooge I heard her say, "Let's get you to the car. We have to hurry." She wasn't telling me anything I didn't already…

Black had suddenly become my new go-to color. Buckling knees, someone trying to lift me, broken voices saying "diabetic brother" and "home insulation"—those were the last of my memories as something unseen propelled me forward into complete darkness and ever more comfortable unconsciousness.

Her wrist was a wreck by the time I felt the car moving. I'd been sucking and slurping like a crack baby on methamphetamine formula until I saw her wincing from the pain as she pulled her arm away. "You'll be feeling better soon. My name is Vanessa. Do you know your name?"

While slurring the words "Dizzy Giuseppe" and trying to make light of the bloody mess I'd made of her pink skirt, I felt my head being urged back down into her lap.

"That's right. Now why don't you try to get some rest? We'll be there shortly." She'd pressed a tissue against her wrist as if it were only a minor scratch while I was left to grapple with the blood in my mouth and nostrils mixing into distinctively unfamiliar tones along with the dry cleaning fluid on her skirt and an assortment of feminine washes, lotions, and potions.

As our car pulled underneath a sprawling hotel complex, my still-extended fangs chattered away when we passed over several speed bumps. I only dared raise my head when I heard a metal door ratcheting up and saw the bright red warning signs: *One Way. Restricted Access. No Exit.*

I took it to mean we'd arrived, considering the guy greeting the car was dressed as an organ grinder's monkey and pretended not to notice the blood on my face and our clothes while unloading the luggage. The dimly lit elevator had only four buttons, B, twenty-four, twenty-five, and twenty-six.

Room 2525 was so dark when the porter opened the door a bat could've gotten lost inside, and I'd neglected to pack my coal miner's hat. "Jeez… Can somebody turn on a fucking light?" I asked.

Vanessa started laughing. "I can tell someone's feeling better. Rafael, you heard the man. Open some curtains and, unless I'm mistaken, bring a bottle of gin with some tonic and ice, and shake your ass about it."

I love literalists. He actually did a bunny wiggle on the way out which I found hysterical. Laughing, I yelled, "Limes! Bring some limes!" Vanessa was right. I was feeling better.

Raising his arm above the brightly festooned fez, Rafael formed a circle using his thumb and forefinger without ever turning around. I wondered whether he was mute or just a fan of Charley Chaplin movies. Either way, he was back in a silent flash and didn't seem interested in waiting around for a tip after depositing the drinks on the desk.

Vanessa had already vacated the premises, saying only, "Sorry I have to run, but I need a transfusion and I have a hair appointment in an hour. Please get some rest. I'll let Sir Charles know you've arrived." Mixing myself a drink, I could still taste her in my throat. Although human, she was a force to be reckoned with nevertheless, something told me. From what little exposure I'd had to the mysterious sex, I knew I preferred them straight and strong, rather than shaken or stirred.

BLOOD: THE SANGUINE PRINCE

After getting sufficiently cocktailed, I fell out of my clothes and into bed. Not knowing how long I'd slept, I awakened to the sound of someone knocking. Garish light and a very handsome, mid-twenties-looking man greeted me as I opened the door in boxer shorts. He was anything but human and smelled surprisingly like Charles as my eyes and senses tried to swim into focus.

The Armani suit was obviously hand-tailored. His hair was incredibly blonde, almost too blonde for the airbrushed tan. Behind his inquisitive watery-blue eyes I could see the murkiness of the ages. Smiling effortlessly and without introduction, he said, "I hope you don't mind that I ordered drinks. After hearing of your harrowing experience, I thought you could probably use one." I gathered that, even though he was holding a tray, he wasn't from room service.

"If you're feeling up to it, Sir Charles would like to see you downstairs..." he paused mid-sentence, looking me up and down, neither approving nor disapproving, "...when you're ready."

"In that case, won't you come in?" *What an asshole.* "I'm going to take a shower. Please make yourself at home. I'll be out in a moment." In other circumstances, I might have been more willing to see his hole and raise him a prick, but I wasn't in a poker-playing mood. I needed a Calgon moment and he was probably too old for me anyway.

I came out of the shower in a towel and found him sitting in a club chair smoking a gold-rimmed black cigarette. Two untouched cocktails and a glass of wine sat melting on the table beside him. The whole, if not quite wholesome, scene struck me as a photo shoot for *Town and Country* or *Esquire* magazines. *GQ* would have been beneath him at any rate.

With me nearly naked, he stood up, adjusted his trousers, and handed me the one glass of vino. It felt awkward, to say the least. Heavy, thick, and warm to the touch—clearly wine wasn't the main ingredient. Smirking at the look of hesitancy on my face with what would normally pass for a smile, he said, "I thought you might like a little pick-me-up. I imagine your trip must've been somewhat draining...having to fly commercial all that way."

I'd never tasted blood other than straight from the tap. I wasn't sure whether to sip or slam it. I didn't want it to get cold, but at the same time

I didn't want to appear as if I were playing with my food. Tentatively I took a sip. I'm not going to lie—it was just plain weird, so unnatural, so affected. *So sexless.*

"Drink it. I assure you it's quite fresh. We blend it ourselves." Unlike anything or anyone I'd ever tasted, it was, surprisingly, not the least bit gamey. After another longer sip I realized there may have been no copper aftertaste, but I was still standing there in a damp towel sipping blood from a glass. His eyes had only managed to travel as far back up as my chest by the time he finally got around to introducing himself. "Ziegfried Hammell, at your service. Welcome Down Under."

Bowing only slightly from the waist, he was offering a salutation or asking permission to board—I couldn't be certain of which. Thinking he sounded vaguely German, I fought the urge to curtsey and turned to the dresser where I'd left my bag—only it wasn't there. I opened the closet door and found three carefully crisped jackets hanging next to my own clothes, which I hadn't unpacked.

I was admiring one of the suits when he said, "Try the blue one. It weighs almost nothing. Sir Charles asked me to fetch you some lighter things. I hope you'll fancy them. The heat here can be brutal this time of year." Sitting back after loosening his own tie, he watched me dress, with some pleasure, I suspected, from the slightly nervous tic at the corner of his mouth.

Borrowing his cigarette, I took a long drag and dropped it in a spent glass as he fluffed the front of my jacket. "There, that's perfect. Are we ready?" he asked.

"As perfect and ready as we'll ever be. Lead the charge. I'm right behind you."

Rather than walking out the door, Ziegfried picked up the phone and spoke to someone. "Would you please let Sir Charles know we're on our way? Thank you." He turned back toward me and said the car would arrive shortly.

I thought I understood what he meant until the wall started humming an unfamiliar tune. When the panel slid open and he ushered me into the elevator, all I could say was, "Wow."

"Occasionally, our guests have privacy concerns. This is one of the ways we meet their needs."

There were no buttons to push as we descended quickly and quietly in the carved wood paneled box equipped with ornate sterling silver handrails. It looked as if someone had taken a coffin and flipped it inside out.

I couldn't help but observe, "Either old habits die hard, or somebody has a really wicked sense of humor."

He replied dryly without a hint of a smile, "Around here, I suspect, it's a bit of both."

CHAPTER ELEVEN

Ziegfried should have warned me before the elevator door opened. I'm uncertain what he was supposed to say, but he should have warned me. I must have looked like the dumbest rube in the world as I stood there, slack jawed and speechless. The room was something of a cross between the garden room in the Biltmore mansion and the captain's bridge of the *Starship Enterprise*. Someone had also plundered the Getty Museum for good measure.

The ceiling of the immense rotunda soared up to dizzying heights. The art and furnishings were beyond breathtaking. Light from some unseen source illuminated and bathed everything without a single window. It was the Lost World and I felt like a very lost little boy, afraid to step off the elevator. Ziegfried took me by the arm. "Don't worry, I'll give you the grand tour later. It's always like this the first time."

Directly in front of us sat a beautiful brunette woman behind one of the most stunning desks I'd ever seen. She said, "Go right in, he's expecting you."

"Thank you, Elena," he said. Passing beyond the desk he explained that I'd have to stand very still for a moment while I was being scanned. A door opened and he ushered me inside a rounded clear-glass tube, like the kind they use at a bank drive-thru, only large enough for a human to stand inside. I was wondering if I'd be sucked away when the damned thing started humming.

In a few seconds the chamber filled with bright blue light and I heard a buzzing noise. Green lasers scanned up and down my body. When the noise stopped, the lighting returned to normal and the tube rotated open on the other side, leaving me feeling like a hamster in a Habitrail. Ziegfried was waiting, smiling. "Sorry for the inconvenience. You won't have to do that again. If you'll come this way, Sir Charles' apartments are right around the corner."

"Charles has an apartment here?" I asked.

"Of course, everyone on the High Council has apartments in The Havens. As far as I know, we have the world's only underground zip code."

The sound of our heels echoed through the marbled halls, otherwise the place was deathly quiet. I was thinking some nice rugs might make it seem less like a mausoleum as we turned the corner and encountered a set of oversized, heavily-carved, double doors. I was almost certain I recognized the man standing beside them as someone who'd been with Charles' entourage that night in Dallas.

He nodded slightly as he opened the door. Inside, the difference was like night and day. All the harsh light was completely gone. Evening ambiance filled the cavernous room as softly jeweled colors washed the walls from Tiffany lamps and the dancing flames of candlelight. I wasn't sure if the room was two or three stories high, but the upper walls were lined with books. Elaborate spiral staircases flanked each end of the room divided by an enormous see-thru fireplace roaring in the middle.

Just as my eyes were beginning to adjust to the twilight dimness, I heard his voice. Charles was beaming as he came out of an adjoining room and grasped my shoulders. "It's good to see you, my boy. It's so good to see you. My, but don't you look smart! I hope the suit is to your liking. I must say, you look quite the picture in it, at least to these tired old eyes. Here, turn around and let me see you." After spinning me completely around, he gushed, "How handsome, so very, very handsome you are, even more than I remember!"

Turning to Ziegfried, he said, "Thank you very much for all your help. I'd have gone up to meet him myself, but, as you know, there is much to attend to right now."

My handsome blonde friend bowed slightly and shook my hand. "It's been a pleasure meeting you. If there's anything you need at all please don't hesitate to call. My number is in your pocket. Now if you'll both excuse me, I'll take my leave. I'm sure you have much to discuss. I'll see you both later tonight." Then he was gone. Not as in "walked out the door," he simply vanished—the fucker just up and disappeared. Charles didn't seem to notice.

We sat in two overstuffed chairs in front of the fire. Charles apologized for the flight fiasco and assured me that other arrangements would be made in the future. We drank wine and made small talk. When I got around to thanking him for his gift toward the loft, he asked about my newly acquired, massive erection.

Perplexed and embarrassed, I looked down at my crotch. *Nope, not there.* He shook his head and chuckled. "No, silly boy. I meant the monstrosity on your roof."

"Oh, you mean the teepee. Yeah, I have to admit I think they overdid it a tad."

"Yes, I saw the newspaper photos. I must say it's quite an eye-popping, attention-grabbing get-up. I understand your parents saw the story as well. How are they?"

I swallowed hard, downed the remainder of my glass, and said, "Bewildered."

"Precisely, which brings me to the next subject. In our peculiar state, almost every kind of notoriety or public attention can be harmful, if not fatal. In my case it's been a rather slow, steady death. Nevertheless, my time has come, and that's at least part of the reason why I've sent for you."

"I'm not sure I understand, Charles. How can this all end? Being reborn means you live forever. You can't die. I can't die. I thought immortality was the bonus for having the life sucked out of you in the first place?"

He paused for a moment before forming a response. The weariness on his face was palpable when he spoke again. "Walking down the hall moments ago, you called The Havens a mausoleum. That was a very astute observation, by the way. This is a tomb, an elephant graveyard of sorts, really. Those of us who live too long, come here to die. And the time has come for me to say "Au revoir."

"There is much that needs attending before my send-off. To the world above I will be dead in a matter of days. Given how much fanfare there will be in the press, I cannot emphasize strongly enough how important it will be for you to avoid the spotlight at all costs. You cannot be a part of this in any way. Am I understood?"

He didn't wait for a response. I nodded anyway.

"You will be safely at sea on the *Empress de Luna* during the media onslaught. I regret not having more time to prepare you, but when are there ever enough hours in remainder at the end of one's days?"

While I was busy conjuring up images of vampires running back and forth frantically wringing their hands, he kept piling on the morbidity. "I've had an attorney appointed to administer the estate in England. You'll have a lovely home in Gravesend, and an endowment to cover your living expenses."

As he reached to hand me the attorney's card, I could see faint worry lines at the edge of his eyes. "Charles, please tell me you're not really going to die, are you? And why, for God's sake are you giving me money and a house in England? You've already paid for the loft in Dallas and I've barely moved in. What's really going on here?"

"No, of course I'm not going to die, except to the world above, though I must, of necessity, remain here in The Havens for many years to come. My boy, there are not many I trust and even fewer upon whom I can rely. You've yet to be contaminated by the viral greed and hubris that possesses and afflicts most of our kind. That's why I've kept you insulated from all this until now." His eyes swept the vastness of the room in an unmistakable indictment of everything he surveyed. "You've yet to develop a disdain for humanity. My sincerest hope is that you never will.

"Our relationship with mortals is not one of overlord and servant. It is symbiotic by its very nature. We protect them from harm as best we can and they sustain our lives in return. I'm more than certain all meaningful life, including our own, would quickly perish were this delicate, fragile relationship to become unbalanced. Yet sadly, there are many among us who struggle mightily toward that very foolhardy end.

"My boy, I've waited more than a hundred years for your arrival. Now, at last, the time has come for me to concentrate on my work here with the Council while you tend to the world above."

I hesitated, considered bolting, and in the end settled on balking. "I'm flattered, Charles. I really am, that you think so much of me, but I'm not sure your confidence is well placed. Surely you have to know I've always been a slacker at heart and I don't know the first thing about world affairs. Remember, I went to public school in America? Honestly, I never paid any attention to politics, much less vampire politics. Frankly, I didn't even know there was such a thing, if that's what we're really talking about. Basically, you're the only vampire I know other than the asshole who bit me on the golf course.

"Oh wait, I'm sitting here lying. There's one more, the blonde guy who disappeared a few minutes ago. Let's not forget him." I pointed toward the door for emphasis. "Charles, I don't think you realize—the only thing I'm good at is killing people. And if I understand you correctly, now you're asking me to save them?"

He smiled broadly, and the fucker actually put his hands together like he was going to start clapping or something. He was elated. I was confused. "Precisely, my boy. You are as intelligent as you are handsome. Have no doubt, you will learn, and quickly. Our survival depends upon it. In three days you sail for England. I've arranged not only your passage but your tutelage as well. You'll have sixty days between Sydney and London to find and cultivate your gifts, which are greater than you can possibly imagine. The very blood coursing through your veins is no mere myth or accident. It is your destiny as you shall soon discover."

"Gifts? How can you possibly say that, Charles? I don't even have a soul."

"Don't be foolish, my child. Of course you have a soul, a beautifully incomprehensible soul to those foolish or ignorant enough to deny the truth. As to your gifts, remember our last conversation? Like I told you, we all have them to some degree or another. I'm already aware of two that you possess. Your tolerance for sunlight would kill most of our kind long before you even begin to weaken. That gift alone tells me I'm right. The other, it seems, is that remarkably lovely nose of yours. It really is extraordinary if one stops to think about it…

"Do you remember the night we met when you were reading your poem?"

I nodded.

"You smelled me long before you could see me. Even though you'd never met another of us, you knew I was there. Through the musky bodies, smoke, and liquor, you were able to distinguish me from the rest of the building's odors. As I recall, the experience was quite distracting for you."

He seemed quite amused at the memory. In retrospect, I had to admit it had been pretty funny, but I wasn't in a particularly humorous mood at the moment.

"It would appear that your sense of smell is so pronounced, it even seems to serve you at the molecular level. With the proper training, I imagine you can even learn to detect emotions and intentions. The mind, even consciousness itself, is capable of masking, burying itself away from those who might try to pry. If you let it, that beautiful nose of yours will learn to unearth the truth, strip away the masks no matter how deeply they're buried or how long they've been worn. That, my son, could be a very useful trait should you find yourself in a pinch.

"I can only hope that genetics and your bloodline will bear you out to be something of an empath as well. That trait, along with the wait for your arrival, have sustained and served me for two centuries. However, I lay no claim to that sunny disposition of yours. It most assuredly comes directly from your maker. I can begin withering at the mere thought of a bright, cloudless afternoon.

"For now though, I think you've had quite enough of an old man's ramblings. Why don't you run upstairs and freshen up? I've planned a little party in your honor this evening, then a night on the town. After all, what kind of boorish host would I be if I let you come all this way and didn't show you the sights and sounds of Sydney?"

Rising from his seat, he placed his hand on my arm and walked me to the door. I noticed the shadows we cast in the firelight looked exaggeratedly large and ominous. His gaze never left me. I could feel the weight of presumptive burdens pressing, dressing me up and down. At that moment I think I would have been more comfortable naked than mythical.

On cue, the doors opened wide and unearthly light assaulted the room as well as my vision. When my eyes adjusted, there stood Ziegfried again, hands in ticking-striped seersucker pockets, with a big smile stretched wide across his waiting face.

Charles instructed, "Ziegfried, take him upstairs and make him even more handsome. I know that may be difficult, but I'm confident you'll come up with something. We have people to see and places to go. Now, off with the both of you." He grinned impishly and shooed us away as the sentry closed him back into the solitudinous twilight of his own making. As we made our way down the hall, I wondered whether it might be a dungeon adorned to resemble a palace? Exactly what was it I was supposed to be inheriting? I'd already discovered on my own that immortality wasn't necessarily all it was cracked up to be. Now I was being told even *that* may not last forever.

CHAPTER TWELVE

Ziegfried must have sensed my apprehensions and tension in the elevator. He began rubbing his hand against the back of my neck, working his way down between my shoulders by the time the elevator door opened. I'd been trying to melt into the floor, but somehow we'd ended up back in my room with him asking how my visit with Charles had gone.

I was already in the process of slipping off my loafers in order to throw myself onto the bed when I noticed the tux all neatly laid out in the place I was hoping to deposit myself.

"You like?" He picked up the jacket and held it against me. "Smashing, absolutely smashing!"

"Yes it is. I'm sure I'll turn all the boys' heads tonight."

"Let's hope not, human necks are very fragile. They snap so easily. Mine is a bit more durable. And I must admit, you've already turned it."

Unlike with Charles' eyes, there was no mistaking the look in Ziegfried's. He was pure predator. The guy was fast, smooth, and incredibly handsome. Looking beyond his broad shoulders I noticed two cocktails and a couple of glasses of blood. They could call it *red* and blend it with wine all day, but for me, it was still going to be an acquired taste…

Several stacked pillows later, I grabbed a glass of the stuff and landed sitting up on the bed. "Red" doesn't slosh much in the glass. It's very viscous, and at that point I didn't find it remotely delicious. Eating out had always been my preference, but, when in Rome…I raised my glass, anyway, in a flagging salute and, before I could blink, Ziegfried was sitting beside me on the bed, glass in hand, flashing fangs and looking ready to pounce.

From the tenting of his trousers, I could tell his hopes were up and, being something of a people pleaser, I hated to let him down.

Handing me his glass, he asked, "Would you be a lamb and hold this for me? I'll be right back." I took his drink while he took to my zipper. Once my pants were down around my knees, I sensed I wasn't the only one eager to please.

Looking and sounding completely vampish, he reminded me, "Charles said to make you even more handsome. I'm not sure that's possible. This is the only thing I can think of. I hope you don't mind. Now where was I?" Within seconds he was inflating more than my ego.

Can you imagine getting a blow job from a saber-toothed tiger? I couldn't either—until it happened. Ziegfried was less hairy. Of course, he's German. *Oh fuck! That feels so good. Please don't stop.* He had my stiffening cock between his already swollen fangs, urging it up, licking it down. He was jerking me off with his teeth! My eyes were shut as I began unbuttoning my shirt. I'd had guys go down on me before, but never at fang point. *My balls! My God! Oh yes, lick me. Lick me just like that.*

When I couldn't take it anymore, I flipped him over on his back trying to control the pace. Even pinned down, he didn't miss a stroke. My cock was sliding all the way down the back of his throat. His neck hadn't appeared nearly that muscular from the outside. Picking up speed and one of my legs, I slammed myself into his eager, hungry face. He was taking it to the tonsils in ever-quickening strides and I was about to explode when he let go completely, unexpectedly. In a blinding flash I felt fangs piercing the soft, tender, ecstatic flesh of my ball sac.

One good tug and several epileptic seizures later I'd spewed my life's savings across the room and collapsed in an exhausted heap, nearly dead and much appreciative for the skillfully articulate execution. Unlike a mouthy, noisy rattlesnake, Ziegfried was more than content to lie there afterward, quietly licking at my wounds and his winnings, which were still oozing from my twitching, spasmodic body.

"Oh my God! That was manslaughter," I laughed breathlessly. "I'll bring you up on charges!"

BLOOD: THE SANGUINE PRINCE

He hopped from the bed, dropped his trousers, and said, "Too late, I'm afraid." Pressing himself past my lips, he said, "Suck on that, Your Magistry. Yes, His Honor likes that, doesn't he?"

In my limited porn-film-viewing experience, why does it always seem so much hotter when the guy's talking really dirty? Ziegfried speaks German, which made it sound all that much nastier. While he was pummeling my face I began enjoying something of a renaissance, busily stroking away at the fiery passion that found me once again fiercely in its grip.

Despite a lack of schooling in oral examinations and absolutely no vocal training whatsoever, I started growling from deep within my throat. Before long I was a gulping, operatic gondolier, steering Ziegfried watery eyed to the point of no return. The vibrato of my lowest notes really seemed to float his boat. After barking a few more orders, obscene commandments, and phallic-laden profanities, he was bursting with Wagnerian enthusiasm to an overpacked, appreciative audience of one. Within minutes I had German dripping from my lips without having understood a single word, which I suspect is often the case with opera.

Singlehandedly I'd been giving myself a good drumming the whole time, trying to stay in tune and tempo, when, just like a foreigner, he stole my job at the last second and finished it himself. Considering the recency of my last outburst and his undocumented status, it was a wonder he got paid at all. All truth be told, I'd been feeling overtaxed and overworked until his German ingenuity came into play and brought me back, hand buffed and spit shined, from the brink of mediocrity to a highly polished, explosively brilliant finish.

Fascist facial or Bavarian cream pie, call it what you will. Either way I relaxed afterward and watched him hungrily lap away the evidence of our war crimes and misdemeanors. The scene was so clean by the time he'd finished, I no longer needed a shower. Diplomacy dictated I take a bath anyway. Fortunately, Calgon comes in powdered form and wasn't on the list of banned substances.

Still smoking, hot, naked, and in bed, Ziegfried had an ashtray perched on his chest when I emerged from the tub. He made smoking look more glamorous than anyone I'd ever known. I asked him to light me one, although I knew not to make either of them a habit. One was potentially lethal and the other would probably yellow my teeth.

Blowing smoke rings casually into the air, he asked, "So how did it go with Charles today?"

"Fine, really. Let's see. He's going to die soon, or at least take early retirement in The Havens. Three days from now I'll be stuck on board a cruise ship for two months headed for someplace in England called Gravesend. How charming does that sound? I've inherited a house along with buckets of money to keep up the landscaping and pay the help. I'm supposed to avoid the press at all costs, and, lest I forget, study ever so hard because I have to save the world from itself and evil vampires at the same time. I think that pretty well sums it up."

"Yes, that sounds about right. He has been rather grumpy lately since deciding to take a powder. I imagine he's going to miss Europe and his friends. I suppose I would, too."

While spit shining each other's knobs, we'd also managed to polish off the rest of the gin. Another simian-suited bellhop brought more booze and carried away the empty tumblers along with my mostly untouched glass of wretched red. Watching him walk out the door, I wondered if they might not have some sort of recycling program downstairs in The Havens. Leftovers had never been a problem for me personally, but I still hated seeing things go to waste.

Once the door closed, Ziegfried casually asked, "Did he speak to you about Sebastian?"

"I don't think so. Who's Sebastian?"

"Your maker, of course."

"To be honest with you, I didn't even know his name. But yes, I guess Charles did mention him. Something to do with my high tolerance for sunlight. Why do you ask?"

"No particular reason. Just curiosity. Now if you'll excuse me, I need to go home and change while you get your own handsome ass dressed in that exquisite new tux. Thus far, it seems we're much better at taking each other's clothes off than putting them on, and we can't very well afford to keep your guests waiting, now can we?"

Being blown is one thing. Being blown off is an entirely different matter. I smiled sarcastically and shot back, "I don't know about you, but I can afford to keep them waiting. Haven't you heard? I'm a trust fund babe." Before I could say anything else, he kissed me lightly on the lips and vanished into the hallway. That answered one of my questions. He wasn't staying downstairs in the dungeon, I mean The Havens.

The tux fit perfectly. Its midnight blue silk was undoubtedly the finest fabric to ever grace my astounding derrière. Without a doubt I would have gladly drained a hundred German sailors in a U-boat for a moment of self-reflection as I toyed with my trousers and grappled with the question of whether or not to put on underwear. I still hadn't decided by the time I heard the knock at the door that completely squashed my narcissistic free-balling fantasy.

At least it's not another flying monkey, although he is one hell of an organ grinder, I thought as I opened the door, *the Wizard of Knobs.* I was trying not to laugh at my own silliness or in his face. He'd brought a bucket of ice, which I sorely needed, and he was dressed to kill. Dying of thirst and ready for a little mayhem myself, I stepped aside and let him in.

I suppose that's the way it always begins—by letting the wrong one in. Why do the dangerous ones always have to be so fucking handsome? While I was lost in movie-marquee thoughts about bad-boy vampires, he'd already fixed us each a drink and was in the process of whistling while spinning me round and round. Going through the gyrations, I couldn't help but notice how both our Trojanless horses were already rearing admirably, gearing for battle.

Laughing, I pushed him away. "Down boy! Haven't you had enough for one night?"

"Sorry mate, I've never been much of a clock watcher. Now cock, that's a different story. And just look at yours in that getup!"

After I had swatted his hands away several times, he could tell the horseplay had worn thin on my nerves and patience. "My apologies, but you do look like a million bucks!"

Without thinking I snapped back, "So do you. I may not be used to it yet, but if I'm allowed to keep my clothes on for a moment, I'm sure I'll learn to dress the part."

Unfazed, he calmly replied, "We all do, Sir Nicholas, we all do. And thus far I'd say you're succeeding wildly."

"Nicholas? And what's with the 'Sir' shit? You know that's not my name."

"It is now. Again, my apologies, but I assumed Charles told you as much." Reaching into his jacket pocket, he handed me an envelope, and (before you ask) yes, it had the gold embossed seal. "I'm sorry, I would have said something earlier had I known. I can tell I've upset you, but why the frown? You're a new man, and an incredibly handsome one at that, I might add."

"Excuse my lack of giddiness, Ziegfried, but I'm supposed to go downstairs and meet a bunch of strangers right now while pretending to be someone I've never heard of until this moment? How the hell am I supposed to do that when I don't even know who the fuck I am?"

Brushing aside my theatrics, he asked, "Have I told you recently how beautiful you are when you're mad, Sir Nicholas?"

"Considering I only met your ass today, it's highly doubtful." I bared my fangs at him and snarled as convincingly as possible.

He snapped back, fully fanged, giving him a lisp as he tried to speak. I can't even recall what he said, I was laughing so hard by the time he'd finished, tears were welling in my eyes.

It was a moment of comedic, pubescent genius and exactly what I needed. I couldn't help myself. Mimicking his voice, I asked, "Are thu twyin to twalk pwitty to me? Thwat's swo hot."

"Bite me, asshole. I can't help it if mine are longer than yours. You won't think it's so funny when you're my age.

"Now will you just open the goddamned envelope? We may be immortal, but we don't have all night. Besides, the suspense is killing me and despite rumors to the contrary I'm still too young to die."

I ripped it open and took out the passport first. As is nearly always the case, a picture is worth...*Damn!* I had to admit, I was quite handsome. And indeed, my name was (and still is) Nicholas. Nicholas Adrian Wellstone. It seems I was born in Leon, France, on February 6, 1986. *That makes me an Aqueerious!*

I didn't bother to explain why I was still laughing. Instead I bowed and extended my hand. "Sir Nicholas Adrian Wellstone. Pleased to make your acquaintance. I seem to be twenty-four years old and according to the most recent records available, my newly acquired penis is a mere half my age in length, but considerately more robust in girth as a result of an aristocratic birth. Here, let me show you what good breeding can do."

"That sounds both satisfying and salacious, Mr. Wellstone. Truly, I can hardly wait. In fact I shall savor the moment when we might find the opportunity to visit at some length and explore the depths of such a broad topic clearly of such mutual interest and benefit." Farcically, he stooped over in a palsied manner like there was a two-by-four sticking out of his ass. "Ziegfried P. Hammell, my good girthsome Sir, at your undying service." He was so into character, I had to help him stand back up after his decimation of and defecation on the name and likeness of Colonel Sanders.

Changing expressions from gored to bored, he asked, "Don't you think we'd better be pounding the pavement instead of my ass if there's any hope of getting downstairs sometime in this century? Will you please finish reading the fucking bio and let's get out of here?"

"Let's see. I'm a financial analyst at Dunston, Brown, & Whittlesby, LLP. I hope they don't find out I'm terrible at math. I have an MBA from Stanford even though I've never been to California. I guess that makes me smarter than I look. I went to some hoity-toity boarding school in Massachusetts for the super-rich. My roommate was some kid named Abdullah who's now the King of Jordan. Seriously, Ziegfried, who are we supposed to be kidding here? I thought Jordan was some river from a Bible song. Now you're telling me it's a fucking country, too?"

I wasn't about to wait for a response. I was on a dramatic roll. "My mother, Primrose, God rest her soul, was Charles' sister who died tragically in a boating accident in the south of France when I was twelve." One sweeping gesture of hand against forehead later, I took a breath, swooned and went for Act Two. "She was murdered, I tell you, just like Diana! No one believed me at the time. They said I was too young to understand, but I knew all along it was my father, Harold. That bastard never came home from his hunting trip in Kenya. He's probably still there with his black mistress and her huge tits, living off my trust funds. I knew he never loved us. I tried convincing Mummy. Really I did, really. You've got to believe me, Uncle Ziggy! I know that's why she threw herself overboard without one of those long pink floaty things!"

"I'd like to, Scarlett, you know I'd like to believe you. It's that damned fever you had as a child. It made you not right in the head. Sometimes you confuse things. Why don't we go downstairs now? You can finish coloring in the family photo album when we come back, I promise. I even bought you a new box of big, fat crayons."

He was grabbing at his crotch while I laughed my ass off. "There'll be dancing. And ice cream. Remember how you love to dance, Scarlett? Here, give me your hand."

Not missing a beat he danced and twirled me out the door and into the hallway. Smooth as the underbelly of a young snake after shedding its first skin in a warm summer rain he glided us to the elevator and pushed the button without my ever noticing we weren't heading to The Havens far below Sydney's noisy, traffic-filled streets. We were staying in the hotel.

When the ballroom doors opened there was blood everywhere. Human blood, I could see it, smell it, taste it, beneath sequined gowns and penguined tuxes, pumping away like a pipeline. I'm not sure exactly what I was expecting, but that sure as hell wasn't it. I hadn't eaten a decent meal since leaving Dallas and spread out before me was a bedazzling buffet of all-you-can't-eat. It wasn't a party, it was a torture chamber, and I was the guest of honor. Ziegfried saw the bewildered expression on my face and asked if I was okay.

"I'm not sure, I think I was expecting more vampires. Capes, fangs, pasty faces, minuets. Fuck if I know. This is nothing but a bunch of fat, old society bitches and their bored, rich husbands. If life is a truly a banquet, this looks like an ATM to me. Let's make a withdrawal and blow this hole."

He was about to scold me when I spotted Charles walking toward us with two exceptionally pretty young women draped around either arm. As they drew closer I realized I wasn't the only hungry maneater in the room.

Ziegfried was playing demurely in the shallow end of the shark tank so I was forced to dive in first. I'd already tasted one woman that week. Eating a couple more might be anticlimactic, *but a man's gotta do what a man's gotta do,* given the circumstance and opportunity, of course.

Was that Barney Rubble from The Flintstones? *Seriously dude—get a grip.* I decided to change stations and broadcast my newly scripted aristocratic chin. "Uncle Charles, it's so delightful to see you. Thank you so much for all this." One small hand gesture and a quick sweep of eyes around the room, I rested my gaze on the two spellbound lovelies before me. Cooing theatrically, I said, "And thank you for this, and this," nodding toward one, then the other.

Charles, looking less than amused, said, "Allow me to introduce Cassandra and Tiffany."

Since her baubles were much more expensive, I took Cassandra's gloved hand to my lips and said, "Encantada." Considering how rusty my Spanish conquistador was, I hoped I hadn't ordered raw fish on a crisp tortilla.

Nearly certain Ziegfried was about to drive a stake through my heart, I stepped out of striking distance, leaving him to grapple with the more shabbily-jeweled Tiffany. He hadn't been nearly so stingy with his kisses earlier, I thought, as I watched him stiffly bow and delicately clasp only the tips of her white-sheathed fingers.

Charles interrupted our little game with further introductions. "Ladies, may I present my nephew, Nicholas, and his equally inebriated friend, Ziegfried."

Ouch. Don't fuck with the old guy when he's swimming with sharks.

Charles dragged us and the Fräuleins along to meet the rest of his imperiled court. Unrealized blonde ambition seemed to be the theme. The camphorated gases emanating from their overly lacquered hair and haughty husbands were repugnant. Any semblance of testosterone was overwhelmed by the malodorous smell of cigars and Bengay. Many of them, I suspected, still were. I'd never felt more like a vegetarian politician stumping for votes at an ugly-baby convention where the only thing on the menu was oversmoked, highly sauced barbeque with all the trimmings preapplied.

Clinging to me like kudzu vine or some other invasive species, Cassandra was at risk of being drained to her peroxided roots when Vanessa walked in.

I shot Ziegfried "the look" and said, "Excuse me ladies, but an old friend has just arrived and we really must speak to her. Don't you two run away." It was like trying to back out of the fiery gates of hell without rankling the hackles of Cerberus, the dual-headed demon dog.

"Vanessa, you look absolutely radiant. Please save us from these high-flying predator drones. We promise never, never to be bad ever again," I pleaded with heartfelt sincerity.

Her shoulders sank as her incredibly ruby red lips turned pouty. I thought for sure we had her when she grabbed my chin and said, "You poor thing, I've already saved you once this week. I'm afraid you're out of luck. Suffering builds character. You both look very handsome tonight by the way. Now back to the leeches."

"And I thought we were the blood suckers," I whispered in Ziegfried's ear.

"Hardly," he quipped very dryly while navigating me expertly by the elbow toward the men's room. Once we were safely inside, he instantly pinned me against the inside of the door. There was no time to react before his lips and hips were pressed against mine. Smiling in a devilishly relieved grin, he was teasing, groping, and grinding away at my crotch. "Calling number nine, number nine."

Rudely, someone slammed open the door with something nearing blunt-force trauma, making a manwich of us between bent hinges and the newly cracked wall. Charles peeked around the door's splintered impression of Ziegfried's back, saying, "Boys, let's not piddle. Vanessa has had the car brought around. It's time to go."

I looked for any sign of amusement on Charles' face. If there were any, I couldn't tell. I'd lost my hard-on and loosed a couple of teeth by then anyway, so we obediently followed Grandvamps through the crowd, offering sincerely two-dimensional goodbyes. When the lobby doors slid open, I was suppressing the urge to kick off my shoes and make a run for it until I saw Vanessa standing beside the most beautiful Rolls Royce I'd ever seen. Actually, it was the first Rolls I'd ever seen, at least up close. Once we were inside and moving, I told Charles how exquisite I thought the car was.

"Yes, it is quite lovely. So is its cousin parked in the garage at Gravesend. Nicholas, so help me, if you put even the slightest of scratches on her, I'll drain you personally." He smiled warmly, the way I imagine Satan might while bouncing his own screeching grandchildren on smoldering knees. "Not to worry, my Boy. I'm sure you wouldn't want an old man to travel all that distance for a couple of pints, now would you?" He gave me the evil clown eye once more and tapped my knee with his cane. Someone's mood had improved noticeably.

"I must say you boys were the toast of the ball tonight. My first rule has always been to leave them breathing. The second is to leave them talking. You did quite nicely on both counts."

We were pulling up in front of the Sydney Opera House, not into a parking lot or garage, but at the main entrance. Lasers were bouncing all over the harbor as our entourage emerged from the Rolls to thronging masses of screaming onlookers. Hundreds, if not thousands, of cameras flashed like blinking strobe lights. I was a blinded, ascendant rock star climbing the storied steps toward fame, fortune, and…disappointment when I realized they weren't there to see us, but the passing of the Olympic Torch.

I'd forgotten Sydney was hosting the Summer Games. People had come to watch Andrea Bocelli, the blind opera singer, pass the undying flame to pop diva, Olivia Newton-John. His searing, soaring rendition of Verdi's "Di quella pira" brought tears to my eyes as she took the torch from his hand and passed it to the final runner. The irony escaped me completely until Charles leaned in close and whispered in my ear. "What a perfectly splendid evening to die."

Apparently it was, according to the hundreds of media outlets reporting it all over the news in the days that followed. Peacefully in his sleep he'd passed, a great man of letters, philanthropist, and much beloved patron of the arts. I even saw Mick Jagger saying, "I've lost a dear friend today."

Sympathy for the devil, indeed…

Ziegfried and I were watching the purported news on one of Murdoch's stations, propped up in bed, sipping a little red, minding our own and each other's business, when the phone rang.

He spoke briefly and set the receiver down. "Well, I hope you're prepared to meet your maker. We need to get dressed and go downstairs now. It's showtime and you're up next."

Somehow, in order to survive, I'd convinced myself he only existed in the nightmarish realm of my dreams. Now he'd been given a name and was about to become flesh once again. Why, after all this time, was I being asked to bring my monstrous creator back to life?

CHAPTER THIRTEEN

The flipped-out coffin and Starship Mausoleum were no dream. The Havens was real, only this time it didn't seem so much like Disney after Dark. I felt more like St. John tripping in the techno-cave at Club Patmos to some completely fucked-up Revelation remix. The same undeadened sound of our soles, at least to my uninitiated ears, echoed through the stratified hall. Immutable, unidentifiable, lost to an outside world, the corridor seemed to go on forever.

Ziegfried, without losing step or stride, was clearly reading my marble-strewn mind. "It helps keep down the maintenance costs in the long run, even if it is a bit noisy."

Making one final turn we happened upon not one, but two sets of colossally oversized double doors with pairs of equally no-nonsense-looking fanged sentries flanking each set. Searching for pulleys, rollers, or some other mechanical device, I watched in awe as the massive, multi-storied doors swung open, allowing us entry into the Great Hall. (No shit, that's what it's really called. I was impressed enough to ask.) My eyes and mouth were both agape as we stepped inside.

New York Public Library, I'd like to introduce you to the Palace of Versailles. Obviously the architects had been given no budgetary or design constraints of any kind. Without question, this was the deepest, largest, marble-clad tomb ever constructed or conceived, and thousands upon thousands of pasty-faced, semi-living bodies occupied nearly every seat in the massive chamber.

So absorbed by my surroundings and the hall's congregants, I almost fainted as we neared the front. *He'd been staring straight at me the whole time.* Taking those last few steps and sitting my ass down in that chair required more restraint and courage than anything I've ever experienced. *I may have been born gay, but I wasn't born a viper.*

Gazing, for the second time, into the eyes of the deadly, deathly serpent who'd pumped me so full of incurable venom and drained the expectancy of my life, I knew nothing and everything had changed. When abandoned there beyond death's redemption in a pool of my own blood and ripped-apart flesh, decaying and filthy with only maggots left to vie for my attentions, I'd had to hate something, someone, in order to stand.

Only by that hatred was I able to summon the strength, the will, to right myself and walk away from the death sentence he'd rendered so recklessly with the rabid abandon of a frothing, diseased animal. I could smell the intensity of his rage from across the cavernous room as I stared uncomfortably, hypnotically into the burning fire of his emerald eyes, the inferno of his face, the face of a thousand nightmares, my dream demon come again to life.

He was more handsome than my memory allowed, and his blood was still boiling at a fevered pitch—just like the night we'd met. Angry and passionate, an immortally furious god...*Beauty and the Beast.* I wondered how many might say the same about me?

Extreme discomfort turned my gaze and thoughts elsewhere. In surveying the room I couldn't help but notice the cloistered groups of ashen faces gathered and scattered around the sprawling, massive hall staring at me, and only me. Quickly it became apparent they were there to see *me,* not my maker. It wasn't a funeral insomuch as a viewing. Unlike the previous evening's flashing bulbs, blinded stars, and glittering gowns, there was no mistaking that these whispers and sideward glances were being cast in and around my direction.

Rapping the better part of his cane against Ziegfried's shin, Charles thoroughly squashed any newfangled notions regarding decorum of the undead. I sat rigidly upright, hoping to avoid a similar fate as two men and one very singularly pronounced woman entered the now quiet chamber, echoing heels of thunder in their wake. Each took seats behind a heavily carved, gold-gilded table with my maker shackled and suspended crucifix-style in the air behind them, sans the spikes and crown of thorns. The similarities were obvious. The differences were, too.

My Lord was a beefy, hunky blonde who'd committed many, many crimes. Bloody wounds were his gift to man instead of the other way around. The grimmest of reapers, his only dispensation was death, and in my case he'd managed to muck even that up nicely. Looking in his face I could see recognition, not of the wounds he'd inflicted, only of the meal I'd been and the threat I now posed.

None of the judges seemed to be shedding a tear for the monster who had stolen my life and my innocence and brutalized me beyond death. Hanging behind the three of them with his neck, arms, and ankles locked in silver stocks, his head, hands, and feet moved in jerking, fitful spasms. The rest of his body was bound, wrapped round and round by heavy silver links woven together. I couldn't decide if they were chains meant to bind or chainmail meant to protect him from me. Had he not been wearing it, I would have been sorely tempted.

Turning to the judges, I was completely transfixed by the woman's eyes, and hardly listened when the man sitting at her right spoke. Barely blinking, she slowly surveyed the room, sleepy-eyed as an ancient cobra. When her gaze came to rest on me, those eyes seemed older than time itself, and she didn't appear interested in wasting any more.

Once the man had finished speaking, she slammed an ear-shattering gavel on the table bringing the proceeding to some kind of order. Thankfully the roof held as the echo died. The place was already quiet as a church mouse and I found the whole banging thing completely unnecessary, even if I was seated before God and she was about to get all judgmental on us. Squirming in my seat, I could only hope she knew of my tireless efforts on behalf of the March of Dimes.

Maybe she was exhausted from all the power hammering, but her sidekick was doing all the talking, and he damn sure had no need for a microphone. "Today is the first time in more than twenty years the High Council has been convened for this purpose. I am greatly disappointed at the necessity of having to do so again." He paused, looking out across the audience and cleared his throat. "Sebastian Phillipe Badeau, your actions have continually brought disgrace and danger to our civilization as well as to that of mankind. More than once you have created, and we've had to destroy, abominations."

Admittedly, my imagination tends to run a bit wild at times, but I sure as hell hoped they weren't talking about me.

"You do not feed in order to live. You feed for no other reason than to wreak havoc and create chaos. You are not vampire. You are a merchant of death, bent and twisted in your desire for, and accomplishment of, wholesale destruction. Ample though our warnings have been, no regard for our laws is in evidence here today, quite the contrary. Very well do you know that none of our kind should ever transform any human to that which we are without consent and careful consideration. You have no regard for either precept. Therefore, it is the decision of this Council that you must be banished to the desert at dawn. Do you have any final words before you are remanded unto the Sun?"

It seemed like the longest, most uncomfortable pause in all of history as he surveyed the room. Finally, with his gaze fixed upon Charles, Sebastian began to speak. "My maker," he snarled, spitting venomously on the floor, "I owe you nothing, neither word, nor deed, nor allegiance. You are surely no Prince, and certainly not mine. I asked you not for this fate far worse than any dreaded mortal death. Why could you not leave me to die like any other man?"

The sheer hatred in his eyes was palpable. In some sense, I thought I might understand why there had been such fury in him on the railroad tracks four years ago. Obviously though, time was not going to heal or ease his tormented pain. He'd made that abundantly clear the night he ripped me a new asshole.

He wasn't finished, only pausing for effect. "You," looking across the room, he yelled, "are the true monsters here. I do not hide behind the mask of darkness. I do not pretend to care for or about men." *Sure, tell that to my ass, buddy.* "Humanity is a lie. All of you have seen to it. You sit here sipping from your bloody cups of righteousness, preening, pretending you bring not death to all that you touch.

"I asked not for these appetites nor the fatted calves that feed them. Once, I was a man and you stole not only the innocence of my life, but the dignity of my death." *Damn, he must be my father. He sounds just like me.* "I would tell you all to go to hell, but surely hell itself is nothing more than another of your fanciful, endless fictions. If I am wrong and there might be such sweet relief as the true death, then I gladly welcome the sun to brighten my path and hasten the journey."

The crowd was buzzing until the ancient woman spoke. "Where is the witness?"

Charles pushed me up out of the chair with the head of his cane pressing against my back. Every eye in the room was on me as I reluctantly stood up and met her piercing gaze while trying unsuccessfully to melt, shrink, or otherwise disappear.

She asked, "Did your transformation take place at the hand of this man?" Her eyes never left my own as she pointed above and behind her head as if none of us knew to whom she was referring. I had the feeling she'd done this once or twice before.

"Yes, Your Honor," I said, feeling like the last living idiot from a tribe of retarded pygmies. How the hell was I supposed to know what to call her? I'd never met the woman before and had no fucking clue who or what she was, other than very, very serious.

"Was the transformation without your prior knowledge or consent?"

"Yes, Your Honor."

"Then the decision is final. Sebastian Phillipe Badeau, you are hereby remanded unto the Sun at dawn. Remove him from The Havens."

The third man never spoke, but he was the first to get up and walk out. Charles, Ziegfried, and I left the still chattering room right behind him. I was speechless and in shock, but I'd obeyed Charles' second rule and left them talking. I wasn't so sure about the first. It seemed questionable as to whether or not some of them were still breathing. Sometimes the line between death and death warmed over can be rather blurry.

As soon as we were behind closed doors I asked Charles, "Why the hell didn't you tell me that was going to happen?"

"I couldn't afford to taint your testimony. I truly am sorry it had to be that way. It was unavoidable, Nicholas. If I'd warned you at all, they would have known."

Ziegfried was making cocktails. I was tempted to ask for the bottle and a straw. Again, he must have been reading my overtaxed mind; it was pure gin on the rocks. I slumped silently into a chair and must have dozed off with the glass in my hand after downing the drink.

Most of the ice had melted when I heard Vanessa's voice saying, "It's time."

Oh fuck! Not again, who died this time? The words jarred me out my sleepy fog as Charles proceeded to explain that since I was the victim of and witness against Sebastian's extra-amorous crimes against humanity, according to custom, I had the distinct privilege and immortal obligation to be present at his dawn execution. Paint me a pessimist, but I had serious misgivings whether or not a joyride in the desert could cure a bad case of raccoons.

Gee, I thought, *I'll have to remember what a blast Australia is next time I plan a vacation.* Now, as an added bonus for taking a tour of The Havens, I was being given a side excursion to the outback's Desert of Death. The folks Down Under and those way down under sure as hell had peculiar ideas about what constitutes a good time. If I ever managed to find out exactly who my travel agent had been, I'd have to remember to thank him with a handshake and stake to the heart.

Ziegfried and Vanessa came with the driver and me. It wasn't a limo or Rolls, and there was no open bar, or any bar for that matter. *What a cheap bunch of fucking vampires,* I thought. I kept wondering if it would be too crass to ask them to stop for a six-pack.

There were two Range Rovers and I assumed Sebastian was safely shackled in the front one. With the windows so darkly tinted it was impossible to tell. Once we left the city there wasn't much to see except one lonely business in a rundown, clapboard-sided shack with a brightly lit neon sign advertising "Uncle Pete's Psychic Bait & Tackle." I wasn't completely sure what one is supposed to do with clairvoyant minnows in the middle of the desert…

Sometime shortly before sunrise we left the main road, actually the only road, and started into the outback. There was nothing but desolation and dirt. It seemed an oddly appropriate place considering our purpose. We drove for what must have been twenty minutes before coming to a stop near a canyon cliff at the end of Sebastian's world.

Two men, dressed in dark suits and darker shades, came out of the front Rover and opened its right rear door. Under his own wriggling steam, my maker emerged to take his place in the sun. With the exception of too much silver jewelry, he seemed appropriately dressed in a light-colored, breezy-looking, tropical print shirt and slacks. There seemed to be little wind in his sails or in the surrounding air as the men removed the last of his binding ties and retreated to the relative safety of tinted glass and conditioned air.

My maker looked up as if merely checking the weather. I could almost hear the thought in his head. "Hot, dry, and sunny. Today looks like a real scorcher, folks." Turning his gaze toward our vehicle, he stared blindly through the blacked-out windows. Slowly, deliberately he began walking toward our car. I could feel Ziegfried tensing as Sebastian came closer.

Within reach of the passenger side of our vehicle, he extended his hand, planting hardened nails into the coats of paint, puncturing and tearing metal like so many layers of unresisting skin as he walked along the side of the car. Before and since, front to back, I've never heard such a racket. Vehicular manslaughter rocked the car, and, admittedly, my nerves as he passed beyond the window without casting the slightest glance in my direction.

Out of metal and time, I watched him and the waning stars blinking at the morning's first light as the lead car turned in a wide circle, slowly tracing his path beyond our bumper toward the cliff's edge. In the rearview mirror I could see the beginnings of a faint glow about his head. Anything but a saint, he, nevertheless, reminded me of a Russian religious icon bearing a luminescent halo above sinless shoulders.

I'd rather he hadn't, but our driver followed behind the first car bringing Sebastian's body into full view. Tiny, twisting, stingy little plumes rose from his hands and face, dancing in the morning air, dissolving, disappearing him into nothing as if he'd never been. I watched (and still remember) the rising sun licking, carrying away his youthful, glowing skin. Even in the burgeoning light I could see him burning brighter and brighter, until what was left finally began giving off sparks. (Fuck you, or anyone else who says vampires don't sparkle. I saw it myself. They may have to die to prove it, but believe me, they can sparkle like the fourth, fifth, or any other day of July.)

In fact it was the seventeenth of September and I'd seen the lighting of the Olympic torch two nights before. It couldn't hold a candle to what I witnessed in the desert that morning as my flaming father exploded in a pyrotechnic blaze. Ironically, a few years later my other dad would die in the desert too, only he would be clutching his chest and a nine iron on the seventeenth hole of some golf course in Palm Springs.

CHAPTER FOURTEEN

On the drive back to The Havens, I laid my head on Ziegfried's shoulder with the faint hope of trying to get some sleep. My past and future kept colliding, making entirely too much noise for anything remotely resembling rest to come journeying my haggard way.

Back at Hotel Haven I did manage to grab a shower and a few fitful zzz's. As I'd suspected the rambunctious raccoons were as eager as ever to defile my dreams. Between trading blowjobs, star witnessing, and viewing exploding vampires in the outback, I was beyond exhausted. Still, it was a relief when the phone rang, sending the furry bastards scurrying back to their foggy forest hideout in the recesses of my weary subconscious. The newly adopted German Shepherd was on the line asking if I might be up for company. I suggested he stop by the bar and fetch some Type-O Merlot while I made myself presentable.

Still feeling a bit groggy when he arrived with lunch by the glass, I almost didn't recognize him in shorts, boat shoes, and a polo shirt. He hadn't struck me as the casual sort. While we sat sipping and smoking, he asked, "You know the boat leaves tomorrow, right?"

"Yes, I'm keenly aware. Would you like to go on a very, very long date?"

"Actually I'd love to, but Charles has made it abundantly clear he doesn't want any distractions befalling you while you're en route. Apparently, you're going to be a very busy boy."

"Yes, I've heard as much and it bites."

"No my love, it positively swallows. I think I shall not easily endure the sadness of your estrangement for such a long time," he exclaimed with an exaggerated, heavy sigh.

Patting the bed, I said, "Then do come hither so that we might dither if only for a while, before I sail away to the grand old Isle."

He laughed and threw himself on top of me saying, "I haven't been dithered in ages. How thoughtful. Promise me you'll be gentle. Did you remember to bring protection? Handsome as you are, I don't think I'm ready for children."

"Not to worry, I had a vasectomy in the spa downstairs earlier. If we hurry, we may still have an hour before it heals."

Sixty days at sea sounded like an eternity, and Charles had warned me to behave myself. I hadn't read the morals' clause on my boarding pass and wasn't sure whether ass piracy was considered maritime crime or not. To be on the safe side, I dithered Ziegfried's fangs down to about the size of a baby rattler's while playing punching bag with his vocal cords. My first mistake was pulling out. The second was plunging back in. Until his legs were over his head, I would've never pegged him for a screamer.

Don't get me wrong, I like opera as much as the next guy, but not sung in a purely staccato German tenor. I thought it was my ears ringing as we approached the death one way or another. During the final curtain call, I realized it was the phone. We were being summoned downstairs. Ziegfried may have been saved by the bell, but I could say with some certainty I'd lost 70 percent of my hearing and, without question, the room was completely destroyed. The Havens would probably sue for damages. And my German Shepherd? Though in no way neglected, he was definitely beginning to show signs of wear and tear. This could've easily been mistaken for a case of animal abuse. I regretted we couldn't take the stairs down and give him a little more time to get his shit together.

Charles was in a quiet, somber mood when we arrived. Eyeing Ziegfried suspiciously, he asked me without correcting his gaze, "Nicholas, I trust you've sufficiently recovered from your journey to the desert?"

Raising my voice, I replied as if he were nearly blind and deaf. "Yes, Sir. Much better than some." After a pause, slightly louder I asked, "And how are you feeling today?"

"Point well taken." He'd turned his head, smiling. "Still, I am sincerely sorry you had to endure such a ghastly spectacle."

"Actually, Sir, it was much more ghastly the first time I endured Sebastian making a spectacle of himself."

With his back turned, Ziegfried nodded silently from the bar. In my mind I could hear him saying, *like father, like son*. I also noticed the stray hand rubbing his ass when he served the drinks and his choice to remain, tattered, but standing, behind his maker.

"Nicholas," Charles began, "there are other matters, some of which will require discussion…and discretion…preferably before you sail tomorrow." The evil clown had once again possessed Grandvamps. He always seemed happiest when he was biting back.

"Arrangements, of course, have been made for all your needs while on board."

Ziegfried smirked from behind the relative safety of his Prince's shoulder while I considered swiftly purchasing the nearby cane o' chastisement and seeing if I could get a clean shot off. Charles wasn't ducking. Either he didn't understand, or he was making an effort to ignore us. With him, sometimes it could be difficult ascertaining the difference.

"We own the cruise line. You'll have nothing to concern yourself with in that regard. But please, Nicholas, bear in mind there will be thousands of humans aboard. You are to keep yourself in check at all times. And, as I said before, have absolutely no interaction with the media. They're like cockroaches. You can never kill them all. They love lurking in dark corners, waiting to nibble away at the edges when they think you're asleep."

The irony didn't escape me. Charles scowled unappreciatively, which seemed to amuse Ziegfried more than my mental sarcasm. Momentarily I flashed on the clairvoyant minnows, since we were all interacting, but only one of us was actually speaking.

My pet with the inflamed prostrate seemed to get the message. He took my glass and retreated thirty paces to the bar.

"Speaking of small fish in a big pond," Grandvamps observed, "let's conclude this nasty business about Sebastian. Nicholas, there were many things which caused the Council to take the action you witnessed yesterday. For decades I had intervened on his behalf, cleaning and covering his sordid affairs. After all, he was my progeny and, as I saw it, my problem. I held out hope until the bitter end that such a beautiful, powerful creature as he might…Ah well, what's done is done. The whole affair would weigh forever heavily on my heart were it not for you, my boy…truly the only good thing to ever come of his making."

I could tell Ziegfried had heard the story many times. He waited for the pregnant pause, inserted the cocktail in Charles' hand, and squeezed his shoulder sympathetically from behind. Smiling, he held up two fingers, indicating that we were now ready for the second verse of the same sad song. I assumed it would be a long one because he came around and took a seat.

"Sebastian's fate, like everyone else's, was inescapably informed by his own character. Transformation allows us to evade the human death for centuries, or even millennia, but there is no power in the universe that can alter the composition of one's character. Immortality only serves to amplify that which is already present."

I asked, "So, if I understand you correctly, what you're telling me is that a leopard doesn't change his spots. The tiger must live with the stripes to which he is born?"

Charles stopped long enough to notice Ziggy the overworked, or worked-over, shepherd boy nodding on the job. "Mein Herr Hammell, I hope we're not putting you to sleep?"

Jerking upright, Ziegfried said, "No, not at all. You were just about to discuss the problem of our little menagerie of evil in the age of modernity. Forgive me, my Prince, I haven't had a chance to show Nicholas around The Havens yet. Zoology isn't what it used to be, is it, Sir?"

It was my turn to fix the drinks before things turned ugly. I was looking for the larger glasses when Charles said, "It is true that many of our kind are completely bent on, and have every intention of, enslaving humanity by giving mankind the ability to destroy the planet and every living thing upon it. The fallacy of this deadly brinksmanship is that somehow we'll come in at the eleventh hour and save the world from absolute annihilation. Humans will finally, at long last, revere us as gods instead of fearing us as monsters."

Ziegfried added, "Of course, for this crazy plan to work, man could never know that we were the ones who poisoned the well in the first place."

Always eloquent, I asked, "Don't get me wrong, I love being on top as much as the next guy, but who the hell could be that evil and stupid at the same time?"

Unlike Robert and Terry, Charles and Ziegfried were able to look at each other without high-fiving after every joint statement. "My boy, if you haven't already, you'll meet them soon enough. Their names are hubris, greed, and unbridled will to power. They're all around us, and they will stop at nothing."

I knew exactly where he was heading, and I was being shoved in front of the speeding train. At least Sebastian had left me for dead on the side of the tracks…This time I wasn't slipping down the rabbit hole. I was being pushed.

Charles seemed less than interested in attending my pity party. "Nicholas, I'm sure you've heard the expression, 'For of those to whom much is given, much is required.' Now is the time for your generation to pick up the torch…"

"And light the way," I interjected. "Charles, I'm a vampire, not a Kennedy. I don't have a death wish, especially considering that, to hear you and Ziegfried tell it, evil has its own zip code." Waving my hand in a grand sweeping gesture like Vanna White on *Wheel of Misfortune* did nothing to dissuade Grandvamps. Playing the game by his rules, Manifest Destiny was the right answer. Playing by my own, it was Good Time Charley.

Shaking his head, he took a deep breath. "Nicholas, I know you've asked for none of this, and how reluctantly you must come to these tasks, but, my boy, you can and will do greater things than you could presently know. Your heart is good. Your mind is sound. You have the strength of character to overcome any and all obstacles foolhardy enough to stand in your way."

I was about to object to this view of my own character on moral grounds, but Charles wouldn't shut up long enough. "My son, life is an imperfect proposition at best. It always has been, but look where it's taken you already, Nicholas. Even death itself dares not speak your name."

It seemed like the perfect time to bring up Sebastian, but I hated eating, or beating, dead horses. Regardless, I had the distinct feeling a profuse amount of smoke was being blown up my ass. Yet what choice did I have? Assassinate my own character, give up millions and the mansion, not to mention the Rolls? Fuck, even the town, Gravesend, was named after our family.

If I balked and walked, I knew I'd spend the rest of eternity alone, and for what? Go back to Texas, choking my chicken and the remainder of Dallas' detective squad? I was screwed either way. Knowing the gods, even on a first name basis, can't always get you what you want, but I suspected I was better served dying in the back seat of a Rolls than serving life in a Texas prison.

CHAPTER FIFTEEN

Handsomely scrubbed, well-pressed, and dressed head to toe in the whitest of whites, Peter, the chief purser, greeted me on the dock. "Welcome aboard, Sir Nicholas." Without a doubt, I was developing a reflexive cringe to the sound of that name. I was neither fat nor jolly enough to go through life being referred to as Son of Santa, and that's exactly the way it made me feel. He'd also called me *Sir* and it was much too early in the day for that.

"Thank you, but I'd prefer to be called Adrian. Can you do that for me, Peter?"

"As you wish, Sir. I mean Adrian. If you'll allow me, I'll show you to your stateroom."

He was still blushing as we entered the elevator. His eyes looked straight ahead as I admired his long lashes and perfect skin. I forced myself to stop the admiring at his chin. I'd promised to be on my best behavior and wasn't about to spend the next two months regretting not having negotiated a more lucrative deal on the morals' clause in my contract.

The elevator stopped on the fifteenth floor. I followed Peter to the end of the hall where he opened the door and led me into the suite. "I hope you'll find your accommodations suitable, Sir. Excuse me, Adrian. Sorry about that, I guess old habits die hard."

"I wouldn't know, Peter. I've never been a retired nun."

Blushing and laughing with his head thrown back, I thought how cruel life can be at times. Nothing would have made me happier at the moment than to jump right in with both fangs. After a few seconds I realized he was speaking again. "...steward's name is Carlos. He's been with us a long time. His number is on your phone and he'll be around shortly to help you get settled in. If I can do anything at all to make your voyage more pleasant, here's my personal number." By the time he'd handed me a business card and left, I was in dire need of a gin and tonic smoothie with Valium sprinkles.

Sixty days at sea, I thought, and my cabin steward is a geezer, an ancient mariner. I was definitely going to have to get lawyered up before the next round of contract negotiations. But at the moment getting liquored up sounded more profitable.

Until my search for the bar, I hadn't paid an ounce of attention to the room. It was beyond beautiful. Even without the grand piano, it was enough to bring Liberace back from the dead and kill him all over again. The view itself was heart stopping. Solid glass walls, floor-to-ceiling, wrapped around the corner balcony at the back of the ship, making for a very private floating penthouse on top of the world. The place screamed money, and I could hear my trust fund being drained away one nautical mile at a time.

Watching the million or so stars beginning to dim in the distance, I found the bay breathtaking. Standing on the balcony, the doors open behind me, I could see the faint promise of the sun trying to rise out of the darkness. Leaning against the rail, I let my senses fill with the intoxicating smells of the ocean. They were dizzying, exotic, and otherworldly, and somewhere, someone was knocking at the door. Tripping over my own feet as I came back inside, I realized I was probably high on diesel fumes.

Still a bit giddy and lightheaded, I fumbled the door open. *Ancient mariner, my ass. Well hellooo...* I didn't even say it out loud, and it was still embarrassing. *Definitely high on diesel.* It wasn't Peter, the pansexual purser. Rather, he was tall and dark, with deep green eyes; this man had probably never blushed in his life, or lives—either of them. I'd heard the Mediterranean diet was all the rage, and I could see why. Between the overdose of eye candy and diesel fumes I was going into anaphylactic shock. No ifs, ands, or perfectly rounded butts about it, I was nearing death's door. I thought if I could just reach out and grab a fistful of those soft, black, lazy curls of near-shoulder-length hair, I might be able to pull myself back from the brink.

I try to never have delirium tremors before I've had my morning coffee and squeezing my eyes shut didn't help a damned bit. When I reopened them, he was still there and, yes, still gorgeous. Being over six feet myself, there aren't many people I look up to, but in his case I felt an exception was warranted. By the time I'd come back down the mountain and regained the power of speech, I heard myself saying, "I'm sorry, please forgive me. I was expecting someone else."

"My apologies for intruding, Sir Nicholas. I'm Carlos, your cabin steward. If this is an inconvenient time, I can come back later…"

I'd never had the urge to lick someone's eye, but both of his were so luminescently emerald it was difficult to believe they were real. Stepping awkwardly aside, I ushered him in. Using both my hands to shake his, I said, "Carlos, nice to meet you. But please, call me Adrian. My Uncle Charles' name was Sir."

"My condolences, Adrian, on behalf of the entire Crown Jewel Cruise Line family. We were all very sad to hear the news. He was a great man. I have nothing but wonderful memories of our travels together."

"You knew my uncle personally?"

"Of course. I was his steward any time he traveled abroad. I last spoke with him only a few days ago. He called, personally asking me to take care of you. If you'd like, I'll come by later this evening and give you a tour of the ship. Until then, please let me bring in your luggage and show you around the suite."

"Sounds like a date. I'll look forward to it. Now how about that show and tell?'

We *toured* the bath after he set the suitcases on the bed. Only slightly less than straight out of another of Liberace's wet dreams, it was perhaps a bit over the top for me. Opulently appointed, the room featured a colossus-sized round Greco-Roman jetted tub of alabaster marble in the middle, and was replete with columns and a chandelier so vast it could have only been assembled on-site. And a sight it was, but God bless a decent decorator's soul, at least nothing was pink or gold or in the shape of a swan.

I was compelled to ask, "Theoretically, if I were to take a bath in there, would it count toward my scuba certification? What about lifeguards? I don't see any signs posted."

The laugh alone was torturously sexy. "I'm afraid not, but if you'd like, I'd be happy to stand watch. I'm told you have a great fondness for Mr. Bubble baths. Would you like me to draw you one?"

What the fuck? Mr. Bubble? Oh screw it, that's close enough. "Not right now, Carlos, but out of curiosity, where did you hear…?"

"I hope you don't mind. I asked Mr. Hammell for a list of things you might enjoy to make the voyage more comfortable."

"So you know Ziegfried, too? Why am I not surprised?"

"He's been a personal aide to Sir Charles for many years. We've traveled together extensively. He also mentioned that you prefer Bombay and coke."

"Actually, it's tonic and lime."

The sexy was back and he was killing me with it. "No, I'm sorry, Adrian. Sometimes my English gets ahead of itself. I didn't mean Coca Cola. I meant the powdered kind."

I could've easily wept at his words. "Carlos, I can't express to you how much that means to me. I'm truly touched by your clarification. Would you happen to know where I might find a straw?"

"I think I have just the thing you're looking for," he said more than splendidly without a hint of sarcasm. "Here, let me show you."

My dreams were crushed during the long, arduous trek to the salon. I was hoping for a layover in the bedroom, but he had a more artistic destination in mind. It was a beautiful abstract rendering of the famous eighteenth-century Gainsborough painting, *Blue Boy*. Livelier than the original, it revealed a certain spirit—in fact, two glasses of reddish spirits, along with a mirrored tray. Between the neat white, powdery rows of pharmaceutical grade bliss, I could see the reflection of Carlos' unmade bed. Not wanting to dwell on that too deeply, I tried focusing on the positives, dozens of them, right under my own nose. In counting those blessings, I found them plentiful enough to keep the raccoons at bay the rest of the day.

Rolling up my sleeves, I grabbed a straw and set about the difficult task of boosting my own morale since Carlos wasn't willing to lend a helping hand. Two, maybe four lines later, I was skyping with Jesus when the object of my wanton desires walked across the room and bent over in front of a console cabinet. He could have knelt, squatted, sat down, or any number of other things, but he chose to bend from the waist. It was a long way down and I admit I'm weak, even in the presence of God.

Since I'd only been chatting with the Lord and we hadn't signed anything binding, I was all about the falling from grace. It wouldn't be my first time, but if I hurried there might still be time for our cocks to crow on the patio before morning. I'd never done it fifteen floors up. My old high rise in Dallas didn't have a balcony.

I should have waited. Thirty seconds later it became evident I'd sold my soul for nothing—again. He hadn't been reaching for his ankles, he was opening a safe, the contents of which proved to be far less inspiring than Blue Boy's trove of treasures. Better at busting balls than moves, Carlos handed me defeat and a pile of musty, tattered papers. I'd been served as close to breakfast in bed as I was going to get apparently.

"This is your itinerary, my friend. And your plate appears to be quite full."

"On some level I suppose that's good, because I've almost finished this one." Offering evidence of my dedication, I showed him the demolished coke tray. "I hope this is one of those all-you-can-snort cruises. That's some seriously good shit. Care to join me?"

"Thanks, maybe later when I get off." Somehow he managed to make even rejection sound beautiful. "Take a few minutes to look over your schedule. I'll put your things away."

Looking Carlos over sounded more fun, considering I was all coked-up with no place to go. Following him to the bedroom, I opened the balcony doors and sat in a nearby chair watching him unpack the suitcases. While I was blathering away, I noticed how he kept glancing over my shoulder. Finally I asked, "Carlos, is something the matter?"

Looking relieved, he said, "The dawn is breaking and I need to shutter the windows."

I felt like an ass. "I'm sorry, you should have said something." I got up and closed the balcony doors as he hurried over to the bedside table, pushing a button on the remote. Louvers extended down over the doors and windows as the room's lighting slowly changed.

All the amusement had been sucked out of his face and the atmosphere as we lost the morning sun to the evening's gloom. Without question it was the fastest onset of seasonal affective disorder I'd ever seen. His voice had changed completely when he next spoke. "Adrian, may I ask you a question?"

"Ask away."

"Is it true what they say about you, that you can stay in the sun for long periods of time?"

"Yes, I suppose it's true, at least to some extent."

"That must be marvelous. This morning," he said, pointing toward the shuttered doors, "is the closest I've come to a watching a full sunrise in forty-seven years."

I could see the longing in his eyes and smell the lamentation clinging to his skin in place of sweat. Five years without perspiring had been rough enough, I couldn't begin to imagine five decades. Trying to lighten the mood, I joked, "So shuffleboard this afternoon on the Lido Deck is out of the question, I guess?"

"Sorry, today's laundry day and my room's a mess." When he paused I could see the luxuriant wheels rotating slowly in his head until he happened upon the right gear. "Ziegfried warned me…but only about your beauty. I'd better take my leave and let you study, if that mind of yours has any hope of ever becoming as sharp as those fangs—which are showing, by the way."

By the time I could adjust my grill, he'd ducked, run, and returned. Unwilling to risk his neck, he allowed only the upper portion of his head to peer round the doorframe. "I almost forgot. Captain Stillman wanted me to invite you to his cocktail reception tonight at seven."

I almost considered it for a moment. "Please offer my thanks and regrets. No offense to the captain, but I already have a more attractive engagement this evening. Maybe another time. By the way, when do you get off?"

"Any time you'd like, as long as it's after dark. The *Empress* is much prettier at night."

We'll see about that, I thought closing the door behind him. Gathering a stack of papers, my wits, and a stiff cocktail, I promptly proceeded to fall asleep on the sofa, never hearing or feeling a thing when the ship sailed.

I awoke that evening feeling completely refreshed. Rest can do a body good, even when you're dead. No Ziegfried, no trials or trails, no Havens, and nothing else weighing me down except the folio still perched on my chest. I'd glanced through it and Carlos was right. It read like the entire course catalog of some esoteric liberal arts college in Oregon. How the fuck anyone could or would expect me to study, much less learn all those subjects in sixty days was a bit difficult to imagine. The why of it all was another question entirely.

Searching for wakefulness and coffee I came across the remote. When I opened the louvers and balcony doors, the wind felt wonderful on my face. The sheer power of the giant ship throbbing beneath my feet as it cut effortlessly through the water was like nothing I'd ever experienced. Standing on the balcony listening to the mélange of wind and wave crashing into the ship, for the first time in years I heard only a singular sound.

I went back inside with the intention of drawing a bath. The phone rang as I was passing through the bedroom. It was Carlos. His only words were, "Please, allow me."

"Thanks. That would be very nice."

Before I could finish unbuttoning my shirt, he was there flashing the smile of an Argentinian or Castilian soap star. All the Latin daytime demigods look somewhat similar in my opinion. Regardless of his roots, I was rabidly become his number one fan, virtually drooling with anticipation at the thought of another exciting episode of *Beguiling Knights*.

"It's good to see you well rested, Adrian, but you look hungry."

You're right, of course, but for all the wrong reasons, I thought. "Now that you mention it Carlos, I'm starving. Cramming for finals is such hard work I think I could drain a Clydesdale right now."

"That surprises me. Isn't he a little old for you, or do you have a thing for bankers?"

"Carlos, what in the fucking world are you talking about? A Clydesdale is one of those giant draught horses in the Budweiser commercials. I know you've seen them."

Coming back from the salon, he laughed hysterically. "Oh I see. I though you meant the banker from that American television show with the rich country people. You know, the one with the abuelita, 'Granny.' They live in the big mansion in California."

It took me a moment to realize he was referring to *The Beverly Hillbillies*. "No, you beautiful imbecile, that's Mr. Drysdale, and you're right. He's way too old for me."

Laughing my ass and shirt off at the same time, I handed him the latter in exchange for a glass of dinner. The first I was hoping to save for debauched dessert on the balcony. When my program began, the lead actor picked up the phone, punched a few buttons, and set the receiver back down. "Now there will be no interruptions. Why don't you go out on the balcony while I draw your bath? I'll join you in a moment."

He was far too late. The show was already a hit, and with no commercials, I could just feel...*fingers on my shoulders*. I hadn't even heard him walk outside.

"If I may," were his first words.

Mine were, "Please take whatever you like, just don't hurt me."

Strong hands and long fingers traced the tensions from my upper body, exorcizing demons by the dozen and casting them into an unforgiving sea. Knowing I was praying in futility, I still hoped they'd be swept back to the shores from which they'd come. Deep, down under...*my arms, my hands, my fingers*...he was coaxing my being out of complacency, pointing me toward the vast unknowable darkness of a star-filled sky. Melting, I took one last breath and exhaled a dreamy sigh of relief deeper than the ocean's floor.

As is customary in this cruel world, when I'd melted into a glutinous mass all over the balcony, I began hearing voices. They were trying to collect the remnants of my dead, or almost dead, lifeless body. Warm butter would have had more substance and stamina.

"Adrian, Adrian, where are you? Why don't you get in the bath? I'll fix us a drink."

Having never heard such cruel words, I floated toward the tub in protest, with Rufus Wainwright crooning something about the valleys of life and shadows of love. Nirvana had never sounded so sweet as my clothes falling quietly into a careless heap on the bathroom floor.

I'd only managed to get one leg in the tub when Carlos came in bearing ginned-up gifts and an Etruscan grin. "Adrian, forgive me for saying, but your body is fantastic. It's so...so exquisitely proportioned. You are ever more beautiful than I imagined."

"So, you've been imagining my body?"

He smiled, looking me directly in the eyes, and said, "We all have dreams, don't we?"

"That we do, my friend. That we do. Would you care to join me in a tub of bubbly?"

"Perhaps...another night. If you don't mind, I think I'd rather wash tonight."

Deflated, I sank into the shallow depths of warm, sudsy despair and stayed there drowning in Rufus' soulful voice as my would-have-been soap star chastely tried washing the sins from my irredeemable flesh. No longer able or willing to struggle, I died all over again in the tub that night. Using only his bare hands and a loofah sponge, Carlos caressed the life right out of me. With absolutely no reservations, I can say that passing away was infinitely more pleasant the second time around.

My fingertips were not the only shriveled raisins dangling from my body when I grudgingly hoisted my happy ass out of the water. My embarrassment of bragging rights had become a sad search for survivors. In the freezing-cold air conditioning, I could've used a fluffer, but had to settle for a fluffier towel. Still, *the boys* weren't buying any of my bereavements. I'd let them drown in the prime of their afterlives and they were in no mood to cooperate.

Walking out of the bathroom contemplating the pleasures of emergency resuscitation by Peter's pursed lips since Carlos was intent on keeping his zipped, I noticed an outfit of clothes neatly arranged on the bed. As had been the case with so much of my life, I hadn't chosen or paid for any of them. As I dropped the towel and stepped into the slacks, the thought flashed through my mind that were I to live long enough, maybe people would eventually stop trying to dress me to suit themselves.

With some trepidation, I agreed to take the elevator to the main deck. Between my recent ups and downs in The Havens and my earlier wisecrack about shuffleboard on the Lido deck, it was neither my preferred method of travel nor favored destination. I'd paid scant attention coming on board, but the ship was a sight to behold when we got downstairs. The second-largest ocean liner ever built, the *Empress de Luna* was sixteen stories tall, more than four football fields in length, and had ten thousand people on board. I was almost as impressed with the ship as I was with my star-studded tour guide.

In its main lobby hung the world's largest painted canvas. Stretching three stories, it was an exact-to-the-brush-stroke replica of Van Gogh's *Starry Night*. Breathtakingly beautiful, the painting gave me the feeling of being under water. Considering we were in the middle of the ocean on a boat, I thought I might have chosen another, less undulating work by someone in calmer possession of his faculties and both ears. Otherwise, it was spectacular.

Turns out we owned six ships, all in near continuous motion around the world. Not as hurried as his human counterpart, a vampire's preferred method of travel is cruising, Carlos explained. I would have agreed wholeheartedly were it not for the plates of food in seemingly everyone's hands. Briefly I found refuge in one of the galleries with a docent and signs saying "No Food or Drink Allowed." The entire room was brimming with Impressionist masterpieces I would have thought to have been reserved for the world's great museums.

We were salivating over a Toulouse-Lautrec when a purser approached us. Sadly, it wasn't Peter saying, "Excuse me, gentlemen, but the captain would like to see you in his quarters as soon as is convenient."

Carlos replied, "Tell Captain Stillman thank you, Johan. We'll be along shortly."

"As you like, Sir," the young man said before spinning on his heel and walking away briskly.

"What was that all about?" I asked.

"I told you he wanted you at his cocktail reception. I suspect he's been given quite specific instructions about your presence on the ship. He is very much, how do you say, a *tight ass*. Let's go make him happy for a few minutes, then we can finish our tour."

I followed silently as Carlos led us up several floors, past a security lock, through another guarded door, and into the captain's quarters. I got the impression that particular hallway didn't see much traffic.

I was going to ask about the high security when Carlos volunteered, "This ship cost more than two billion dollars to build. Knowing our clan, I doubt they'd leave it in the hands of any mere mortal. Trust me, Captain Stillman is neither."

Expecting a vampire, I was taken aback when the door swung open and a large, but very human, barrel-chested man came lumbering up to us. "Sir Nicholas, welcome aboard. It's a privilege to have you sail with us. I'm sorry you couldn't join us this evening. I trust you're feeling well?"

"Quite well, Captain Stillman. I did get some much needed rest today and Carlos is being gracious enough to give me a full tour of the ship tonight."

"Thank you, Carlos. I know, as always, I can leave the needs of our most important passengers in your capable hands. Now, if you'll excuse us for a moment, I need to speak with Sir Nicholas. I'll return him to you shortly."

Carlos winked at me as he backed out of the room, saying, "As you wish, Captain. Sir Nicholas, I'll see you in a few moments." He bowed slightly before closing the door.

"Sir Nicholas…" the captain began.

"If you don't mind, sir, I prefer to be called Adrian," I tried giving him my most charming, disarming smile. The look on his face made it perfectly clear he wasn't taken in by any of my once formidable, considerable charms.

"Look, son, it's my job to keep everyone safe onboard this ship. Your grandfather told me in no uncertain terms that, in addition to commanding this vessel, you are to be my number one priority for the next sixty days. And since you are my responsibility, I would appreciate your cooperation at all times. Are we clear?"

"Quite clear. Only Sir Charles was not my grandfather. He was my mother's brother."

"Let's cut the bullshit right here and now. I've been around a long time, son, and I can assure you I know where most of the bodies are buried, and where they're not, for that matter. Your grandfather's is most assuredly among the living, unlike your maker's.

"In case you're curious how or why I might know this particular piece of information…I gave a deposition at the *liber indiciorum* trial against Sebastian. On my ships alone, in just the last twenty years he drained one person and turned another. I'm sorry for your loss, but I can't say I was sad to see him fry. Your maker was a real pain in the ass."

Ouch! What a fucking jerk! Something told me he was not a part of the all-you-can-eat buffet, and I had absolutely no clue how to steer an ocean liner. *It's your lucky day mofo.* "Well, since we're dispensing with the niceties, let me be clear with you, Captain Stillman. My grandfather gave me two marching orders. Avoid the media. Stay out of trouble. I intend to do both. While I would greatly appreciate any help you might be able to offer with the former, in regard to the latter, Sebastian was my maker, not my fucking role model. I can also assure you he was more of a pain in my ass than he ever was in yours. Now if you'll excuse me, I have a tour of your marvelous ship I'd very much like to continue. Good night and good sailing."

CHAPTER SIXTEEN

Dawn came way too bright and early for my weary, undead ass that first morning at sea. Exhausted, I was more than ready for bed. My typical *all-nighters* had never been so draining, at least for me anyway. I'd pulled all the manuscripts and books out of the safe and had them scattered across the living room floor when I first felt the sun's heat licking at my lazy, fatigued eyelids. I shuttered the windows, turned the air down, and considered the impossibly steep learning curve. The little I understood seemed overwhelming and the rest made no sense whatsoever.

Interspersed with all the history and politics was something about which I had no clue. Nadir Assessment; Nadir Training; Nadir Purposefulness. *What the fuck is Nadir?* Amazingly enough, it was in the dictionary. Turns out it's an astronomical term meaning "directly below the zenith, at the bottom point." *Okay great, thanks, Miriam. That explains everything, Webster.* I thought of Underdog and wondered if I'd need a mask and cape along with my gym shoes? "Adrian Takes a Bite Out of Vampire Crime." I could see the headlines. When I'd decided that Undead Dog sounded better for my superhero name, I knew it was time to step away from the books and get some shut-eye.

The knock at the door was right on schedule at six p.m. sharp. Not the best way to begin the first day of school, I was neither awake nor dressed. His name was Camuel, Camuel Beau Pre, and he was to be my history tutor. Even coming out of a coma, I could tell it was going to suck majorly. I'd never liked school much to begin with and portly professors were not my cup of tea, either. Professor Beau Pre smelled, if possible, mustier than his dusty old books. He was the first fat vampire I'd ever met, but, then again, I supposed he wasn't terribly concerned about diabetes or heart disease.

The Draconians and Visigoths nearly put me back in the coma, and I had doubts that the ship's bookstore would have the *Cliff's Notes*. With no real comprehension of, nor appreciation for, the wars that had raged for millennia between our clans, I genuinely thought the stories were nothing more than relics of ancient fiction. The books were boring, and the myths they contained were easily as tired as Beau Pre himself. In reality, I should have been paying more attention. Soon, very soon, I would come to understand how the past and present are not coolly distant relatives, but smoldering hot, incestuous cousins instead. The world, then and now, is much more fluid than I could've imagined.

Carlos came around later in the evening and we had dinner on the balcony. When I asked him about the Nadir training, he told me what little he knew. It was supposedly an ancient form of vampiric martial arts. He'd never seen it used by one vampire against another and had only heard rumors of its actual existence. Regarding humans, it had no purpose at all.

"What would be the point? We're faster, stronger, and more agile than any human. We heal quicker and have a much greater tolerance for pain. I doubt even the greatest Kung Fu master would stand much of a chance in a serious bar fight. That shit is strictly for movies.

"By the way, you have the gym reserved every night this week at three. I've never met your instructor, Alaric, but he's supposedly very, very old."

At least it sounded more interesting than Professor Dumbledore and Musty Mythology 101. I'd never thought about fighting another vampire. I'd met so few, and thus far, with the exception of Beau Pre, fucking them seemed like much more fun.

I asked Carlos if he'd like to take a bath with me after dinner. He said yes, but thought instead I should probably save my energy, lay off the coke, and take another crack at the books.

"You've only been alive, what twenty-five years or so? Our history spans thousands and thousands of years. I suspect you have a lot of catching up to do. Your grandfather and the Dorians are investing a great deal in you and 'There are more things in heaven and earth, Horatio, Than are dreamt of in your philosophy.'"

"Thank you for sharing, Carlos. Although I love hearing you quote Shakespeare on a moonlit terrace, I hope you realize it just makes me hornier than I already am."

"I have little doubt, Sir Nicholas, that your affections are both everlasting and lethal."

"Thank goodness. I was afraid I'd lose my mojo horno over the centuries." After we'd quit laughing, I asked, "You do realize you called Charles my grandfather just now? Since even Captain Stillman seems to know, I guess there's no point in pretending. Does everyone know?"

"Adrian, I doubt there's a vampire on the planet who hasn't heard of you. And yes, everyone who needs to knows Sir Charles isn't dead. Since we're on the subject, please try and play nice with the captain. He's a loyal and trusted ally to our clan. As your grandfather would oft-times say, we need humans more than they need us."

"Carlos, what I need right now is to see you naked. If I don't, my face will in all likelihood break out over this. Sexual frustration is very bad for my complexion."

Stroking my hair instead of my cock, the bastard said, "Poor thing, you are looking awfully cold and pale. I'll run you a warm bath and find some Clearasil."

When I heard the water running, I went in and poured us each a glass of champagne. We didn't seem to have any rat poison, so I put on the Broadway musical *Cats,* arguably the next best thing. "Memory" wafted through the suite, "Touch me. It's so easy to leave me, all alone with the memory, of my days in the sun..."

Handing him one glass, I set the other on the edge of the tub and slowly began undressing. He was helping me with his tortured eyes. "Adrian, do you know how incredibly beautiful and impossibly irresistible you are?"

"Was Ziegfried?" I asked, as I lowered my perfectly pissed ass into the tub.

He thought a moment, smiled slyly, and said, "I didn't try. He's hard and treacherous. He'd lost any semblance of humanity years before I met him. He deserves and wants to be fucked like a dog. I simply obliged. You, however, are still a thing of beauty. I want to savor everything about you, slowly."

Ouch. I reached out of the tub and touched my glass to his. It was one of those perfectly embarrassing moments. I'd just had my throat slit by a silver-tongued soap star. Everyone should die that way at least once. Since he was up already, he reached over and laid a towel by the tub. "Go read about your ancestors. Some of them may be more interesting than you think." Kissing me softly on the lips, he walked out of the room and into my heart.

I toweled off and tried stuffing my screaming erection into some jeans. It was determined to make life uncomfortable. I gave up the struggle, wrapped it back in the towel, and grabbed some Musty Mythology. If that wouldn't drown its demands, it couldn't be killed.

Finding I'd fallen out of favor with Blue, I turned to snorting dust, and actually cracked open one of the books in the process. Somewhere around the third page, I was wishing I'd waited for the graphic novel. By means unknown, space alien vampires had come to Earth from a planet called Marduk, which had exploded and formed the asteroid belt in our current solar system, giving us the moon as well. Marduk had a rotation around the sun in a 3,600-year elliptical orbit, giving its inhabitants a very, very long life span.

Once upon a long time ago, Anu and Enlil, these ancient Sumerian gods, or space alien vampires, came to Earth in search of rare minerals. While here, they bore children who seemed very fond of sexing it up with humans. I could at least understand that part…

When the genetic pools became mixed, it had the unintended consequence of near immortality for humans. This severely pissed off the eldermost of the ancient vampire gods, who, at their age, probably weren't getting any in the first place. Out of spite, retribution, or just plain old-fashioned jealousy, they flooded the earth to wipe out the monstrous scourge their children had so happily created. Hence the Diluvian stories, such as Noah's ark, scattered throughout early human myths. Parents can be such a buzz-kill, I thought.

Naturally, things didn't go as planned. Some of the humans and ghastly human-vampire hybrids both survived. Mom and Dad were outraged. *Another family vacation ruined by horny teenagers.* They gathered their ill-behaved, libidinous children and the family dog, Astro*pithecus*, together, jettisoning everyone's not-so-happy asses back to Marduk. (Okay, I admit making up the part about the dog...)

I'd had enough. *Honestly? This shit's crazier than the* Bible. Scratching that one off the list, I picked up another text and thumbed through it. From ancient Greece, this character's name was Draco, and at least he was verifiably real. He'd been someone's great, great, great grandvamp. I had one myself, so I knew it was possible.

Somewhere around 621 BCE he *persuaded* the Greek Senate to ramrod through some pretty tough laws requiring the death penalty for everything he found offensive, even idleness. No joke, even lollygagging on a street corner carried a punishment of death under his brand of merciless, bloodthirsty justice. Of course, these "criminals" hadn't committed any serious crimes for the most part, they were just a food source—and the dead, humans at least, tell no tales. I was shocked to find out the whole Dracula franchise hadn't begun with Vlad the Impaler. In actuality it had come from one of my own relatives, Draco.

Thus began my education in history. I quickly discovered that vampires were, and still are, world-class revisionists. All of human history had actually been written or rewritten by them in pursuit of their own purposes. I wasn't sure whether to be excited or afraid. As I recall, I was quite a bit of both that night. It was a lot to absorb in an evening. Overwhelmed, I did what any young gay creature of the night would do. I put on some old disco.

"At first I was afraid, I was petrified..." Gloria Gaynor was belting it out while I twirled in a towel on the terrace. That's when Carlos came calling and shut down my fifteenth-floor Copacabana dance party.

"Sorry to interrupt, but it's one o'clock in the morning and I suspect the neighbors may not be as enlivened by Ms. Gaynor at this particular moment as you are. Why don't you put some clothes on? Let's go for a walk."

Slightly embarrassed, I grudgingly agreed and got dressed. Walking into the hall, Carlos suggested we take the stairs. He held the door for me, which I thought was sweet. I'd gained the first couple of steps when he swept by me in a blinding flash the same way Ziegfried had done in The Havens. In deciding to chase my soap star's bubbled butt down the stairs, I'm not sure how fast I was going when he grabbed me and yelled, "Gotcha!"

He literally snatched me out of the air, squeezed me into his arms, and kissed me deeply. Since I hadn't yet started my Nadir training and knew no vampiric martial arts, I thought it unwise to resist his soft, passionate lips. Instinctively, at the same time I knew the game had other meaning. I was beginning to understand everything vampires did had multiple meanings.

"That was just a kiss for luck tonight in your Nadir assessment, whatever the hell that is."

"I hope it's at least a pass or fail grade. My parents hated when I brought home C's."

Carlos opened the door for me again as we walked out to the deck and found ourselves under a beautifully chilling moon. Rubbing shoulders, we were walking in lockstep beside the rail when the camera started flashing in our startled faces.

My first instinct was to shield my eyes, then drain the asshole. Carlos took the less terminal route, reaching out with his long arm to pluck the camera from the photographer's hand.

"Hey man!" the asshole protested, "You can't do that. Gimme' my fuckin' camera back!"

Carlos simply smiled, towering over the man's much smaller frame, like Wilt Chamberlain preparing to play midget darts with a dwarf. The idiot was about to object again when Carlos took one giant step forward, nearly touching the shutterbug's toes with his own. The previously unheard, deep, gravelly voice sounded quite convincing to me. "You can pick up your *fucking* camera tomorrow morning at the Purser's desk. Ask for Peter."

Carlos slid the camera in his pocket, extending his free elbow in my direction as we turned to continue our stroll. Before we'd taken two steps, the foolish, foolish man tried reaching into Carlos' jacket pocket. Somehow the guy's face inexplicably careened into Carlos' free elbow. High wind, humidity, and a wet slippery deck? Or sloppy inebriation? It's hard to say.

BLOOD: THE SANGUINE PRINCE

We moved on and finished our stroll in blissful, assault-free silence. Passing behind one of the sports courts, we found ourselves alone at the rear of the ship. The *Empress* was quiet as Carlos slid his arm round my shoulder. Already happy on top of the world with my penthouse suite, I could tell I was about to get another upgrade in my package when he leaned in to kiss me again…and again.

CHAPTER SEVENTEEN

Taking the stairs down to the second floor heading for the gym, I could hear my heart pounding and feel the blood racing through my veins. Both were obnoxious and distracting. It was like *hitting the showers* in high school all over again. Nervous, excited, jittery as an alley cat in heat, it was easier blaming Carlos than facing the truth. I was afraid.

Alaric was waiting. He looked to be about forty, maybe a bit leathery and tanned in the face, but certainly not four thousand. Sporting a closely trimmed beard and sharp features, he was nothing at all like the hunched-over, ancient Kung Fu master I was expecting. Very casually he stood up behind a banquet table and extended his hand. "Sir Nicholas, welcome. I am Alaric. From the look on your face, you were expecting something or someone quite different, no?"

"Honestly, yes. I was told you were very old and that Nadir training had something to do with martial arts for vampires. I'm afraid I've let my imagination run away with me."

He took my hand in a crushing grip, saying, "Not at all, you are right on both counts. It is true. I am older than dirt, and, if you are able,...you will learn the ways of the Nadir."

Due to the bone-crunching demolition noise in my hand, I had to struggle to hear him. "I was born in the year, as you would know it, 370 BC on an island in Romania. My conversion took place in 325 BC on a conquest in northern Africa. So, yes, I have been around quite a long time. Actually, I've been resting since about the time you were born, so you'll have to excuse me if I'm a bit grouchy, because these old bones are just not what they used to be."

No shit. I feel your pain, I thought. *On top of everything else, now I can look forward to twenty-five-year power naps.*

"Your grandfather and Queen Ana convinced me that Nadir training was necessary for you. And, honestly, I haven't been abroad since your maker was in diapers. I think the sea air might do these old lungs some good. I used to be a smoker."

He was laughing heartily, when, out of nowhere, he slapped me across the room. I didn't even see him move before I was airborne, slamming hard into the back wall of the gym.

"What the fuck?" I yelled in midflight. *This motherfucker isn't cranky, he's crazy.* After shaking my head thoroughly in an attempt to unscramble my brains, I scraped myself off the wall and stood up, fangs bared.

"Just testing your reflexes. Not bad, they'll get better. Relax. Now come sit down and tell me what I'm thinking."

"This better be pass/fail or somebody is seriously getting their ass kicked," I mumbled under my breath, walking back to the table. I hoped the old motherfucker could read my mind.

I don't know why, but suddenly rigatoni popped into my head as I took a seat. I could see the plate and smell it, too. It smelled really good. I looked at him saying, "Rigatoni, I smell pasta."

"Very good, young man. It was actually cannelloni—in 1897, I think. Tasted delicious, but made me sick as a fucking dog. I haven't eaten since."

I really was beginning to think he was crazy when he pointed toward the corner and told me to "go pick up those weights."

I walked over and picked up the barbell. He screamed, "No, no, no! Pick the whole goddamned thing up!"

Clumsily, I gathered and lifted the bench, all the weights and harness. Don't try it at home. It was fucking heavy as shit.

"Now drop and give me twenty."

I just looked at him, seriously unamused.

He started laughing and said, "Sorry, I saw that in a movie once and I've always wanted to say it to somebody. That was pretty good. I'd guess about three thousand pounds.

"Now jump."

"Excuse me?" I asked.

"Jump. How high can you jump?"

Before I could respond, he was swinging from a light fixture on the ceiling. I joined him.

"Excellent. Good reflexes, too. Maybe a bit slow, but we can work on that."

He was still hanging from the light fixture like some kind of crazed monkey when he nodded toward a set of parallel bars. "Try walking on your hands."

I dropped down, went over to the bars, and hopped on. After walking the length of them, I bent down and hoisted my body into the air in a feeble attempt to walk on my hands, landing straightaway on my ass instead.

Laughing, he remarked, "Well, at least you won't be defecting from the House of Dorius to join the Russian gymnastics team. I thought you pretty boys were supposed to be good at that sort of thing. Shows what I know. Now, come with me."

He simply vanished without a trace. Like so many of the men in my past, he just disappeared. I thought I might've felt the slightest breeze when he left, but I wasn't even sure about that. I looked all around the ship for him to no avail. Finally I gave up and went back to my room. Naturally the old fucker was sitting there on the sofa sipping a glass of red when I walked in.

"How did you…"

"Carlos let me in. Nice fellow. You looked hungry when we were downstairs. I thought it might be affecting your concentration. Come sit down and we'll take a little break."

I took a glass from Blue Boy and sat on the sofa next to him.

"Had we been on dry land, you'd have probably been able to follow me here using your sense of smell. I purposefully went out to the deck to throw you off my scent.

"In the gym tonight, you were not so much reading my mind as smelling my memory of the food. Your olfactory senses are remarkably good. They will serve you well. I suspect it's either innate or else you inherited it from Sebastian. You certainly didn't get it from Charles."

"You knew Sebastian Badeau?"

"I never met him personally, but his insatiable appetites were as widely known as his ability to withstand direct sunlight. I understand you're even more remarkable in that respect. You will learn to use the Nadir for drawing your enemies out into the sun."

"I wasn't aware that I have any enemies."

"You'll have to talk with Charles and Queen Ana about that. I don't imagine they would've awakened me were there no vipers slithering about beneath your bed.

"Once, a great many years ago, I, too, was a king. My conversion relieved me not only of the mortal coil, but also of responsibilities for the affairs of state. I doubt very much has changed since I sat on that throne."

"I'm not sure I get your point, Alaric. I'm certainly no one's king. I sit on no throne, and to my knowledge, I'm not in the habit of making enemies."

"Son, gravity can be your enemy. Ask a frog how it feels about bumping its ass every time it hops. I think you're smart enough to know how much fuss and commotion is being made over you. Don't be coy about it. Your destiny may not be completely determined at this point, but the trajectory seems pretty goddamned obvious to me, and, I suspect, to a lot of others as well. If my guess is correct, any number of these bloodsucking motherfuckers would be more than happy to take your place, given the opportunity.

"Like I told you, they didn't take me out of mothballs for nothing, so let's cut the shy crap and get down to business."

Alaric headed away from the gym when we went back downstairs.

"Where are we going?" I asked.

"To get some fresh air and check you for speed and balance. Only, this time I'd rather you didn't try walking on your hands if you don't mind."

We went outside to the Lido deck. It must have been around four-thirty and there was a swabbie mopping the teak floor.

"Excuse me for a moment," Alaric said. He walked over to the man and explained, "My good sir, my young companion and I are going to hop up on the railing and walk along the edge. There is no need for you to be concerned or call anyone. You will not even remember we were here. Have I made myself clear?"

"Yes, sir, as you wish. My name is Dmitri, if I can be of service." The guy went back to mopping the floor as if nothing at all had happened.

"That was pretty fucking cool, Alaric. I tried it on a Mexican in the trunk of my car once. I wasn't sure whether it worked or not. I thought maybe they just made that shit up in the movies."

The next thing I knew he was standing on the stainless-steel railing on the side of the ship. He motioned for me to join him. "Follow me and do what I do. If you must fall, please, by all means, fall to the deck. I never cared much for swimming with sharks."

Hopping up behind him, I felt a bit disconcerted at first trying to follow along. I quickly figured out if I didn't look six stories down to the water, my stomach didn't churn with the waves. He walked faster and faster as we made the perimeter of the ship. Laughing to myself, I thought the video would have been great: *Power walking for vampires…*

Snapping at me, he yelled, "Will you please stop that jabbering and pay attention!"

I was about to apologize when he broke into a trot. It was amazing I could keep up without falling off. When he started running, I felt like I could have passed him at one point, but there was no passing lane. Nearing full throttle we were moving so quickly, I doubted any human could've seen us in the blur of exhilaration.

After six or seven speed-laps, Alaric slowed down and jumped off the rail. "Excellent, young Sir. If I didn't know better, I'd say you've been on the rails before."

"Actually, you might say I was born there," I smirked.

Not getting the joke, he walked over to the same doors we'd come out of and held one open. "See you tomorrow night. Make certain you're well nourished and rested. You'll need both more than you think." Then the old fucker vanished in a blur. Seriously, that trick I was more than eager to learn.

Feeling exhilarated about how the night had gone, I decided to take the stairs. As I made the corner at the eighth floor, Carlos was crouching around the bend. This time I smelled him and tried silently sneaking up the rest of the way. Unaccustomed to stalking soap stars, I blew it by bursting out laughing before I could capture my prey. *Crouching Vampire, Laughing Ninja*, I thought. Carlos must have read my mind. He was still snickering as we passed the "Level 10" sign.

"So how'd it go tonight, you hot, sexy warrior?" he asked in feigned seriousness.

"It was great. You should come for a rail run with me some night."

"No thanks. I was watching from the balcony and I think I prefer a wider berth. Speaking of berths, I ran us a bubble berth and uncorked a rare bottle of red I think you'll like."

"Us?" I asked as he opened the stairwell door. I could hear Roberta Flack's "Killing Me Softly" from the hallway.

We were beside the tub slowly undressing and kissing each other, when it dawned on me I'd never seen Carlos naked. The more clothing he shed, the more amazing he became. Grecian marbles be damned, he was more muscular and simultaneously sinuous than even Michelangelo, who knew a thing or two about hot Italian men, could have envisioned. The graceful waves of his hair defined the features of a near-perfect face punctuated by those shimmering emerald eyes in which I kept getting lost and found over and over again.

If it's true that clothes can indeed make the *man*, nakedness made Carlos a *god* of unimagined proportions. He and the statue *David* deserved to be naked for a reason. In comparison, Carlos' hair and cock were considerably longer, with the latter growing by the minute. My own resolve had stiffened to the point of becoming a quivering arrow by the time he swept me off my feet and stepped into the tub.

My arms fused around his neck, I was completely relaxed as he lowered me into luxurious suds. I'm sure I woke the neighbors as I screamed back out of the tub, setting what must have been a land-speed record. "Fuck! That water's hot! Goddamn it, Carlos, I'm a vampire, not a fucking lobster!"

Never let anyone tell you that cold alabaster marble doesn't have mystical healing properties, especially when your ass is on fire. I was saying,

"Ahhhh," and simultaneously hoping my skin wasn't the peel-and-stick variety as he tried to apologize.

"Adrian, my sweet bonnie prince, I'm so sorry," he cooed soothingly, while trying to kiss one of my blistered toes.

I must've shot him a murderous look. He seemed completely confused. "I know I've boiled you in Mr. Bubbles, but did I say something wrong?"

"No, I'm just tired of all the *Sir this* and *King that*. Fuck them, their thrones and their goddamned expectations." Hearing my own whining, I realized I sounded like a royal brat. "Sorry for the tirade, Carlos. I shouldn't take it out on you. It's not your fault. If I remember correctly, you were kissing my toes. Please carry on."

"Come here, my perfectly poached little peasant. Let me soothe those overheated expectations out of your exquisitely scalded body."

While he unfolded his arms and long, muscular legs, I eased myself back into Hell's hydro-spa and nestled between his Davidian thighs. Before long the water had cooled enough that I was able to stop wishing he'd been chiseled from marble instead of the rock-hard flesh pressing insistently at my backside. We made steaming hot love in lukewarm water until long after the sun came up in the windowless room.

The last thing I remember was drifting off in his arms. He must have crept away sometime during the day because at some point the phone rang and it was him saying, "Good evening, I was wondering about the visiting hours in the burn unit?"

"Tell nurse Blue Boy to bring my pain meds. Then we can talk."

Getting dressed, I heard the familiar snapping of the magnets and the painting swinging open in the salon. Upon investigation I encountered two long disembodied arms protruding out from the wall, one with the mirrored tray and the other holding a glass of red. *Cute, undeniably cute*, I thought. I'd probably passed away sometime during the night from my injuries and had only made it as far as *The Addams Family* level of purgatory in the process.

Carlos' scrunched face and lips were pressed into the opening trying to say, "Good evening. This is the last glass of red from our bottle. I saved it for you."

"Uncle Fester, I think it and you were both the best I've ever had." Taking the glass, I said, "This one tastes like pomegranates, but I much prefer the other nectar I tasted last night. If you can get yourself dislodged from the wall, I'd like to try it again."

Pulling his arms back through the portal one at a time, he explained, "Actually, it is pomegranates. She's a donor; her name is Selene. The family has a vineyard on a small island in Greece. When she knows they're shipping me a case of wine, she eats almost nothing but pomegranates from the orchard for a week, and sneaks a bottle of red into the case. I'd love for you to meet her some…"

Knock, knock, knock. Someone was at the door. Carlos seemed amused in a kissing-gourami, bubble-eyed-fish sort of way with his head still compressed in the wall. "Must be Beau Pre," he laughed distortedly. "Gotta go. Have fun." One of the arms reached back through and slammed the painting shut, leaving me holding the drugs. *Not cool, Uncle Fester. Totally not cool.*

After stashing the stash in the bedroom, I answered the door. "Welcome, Professor Beau Pre. How nice to see you again. Won't you please come in?"

"Thank you, Sir Nicholas."

I cringed at the sound of those words, especially coming from his antiquarian lips. "Please, if you would, I'd prefer you call me Adrian."

"As you wish. So tell me, how've your studies been coming since we last met?"

"Very well, actually. I've gotten through the Sumerian period and into the early Greeks. I've read about Draco and the first-written laws. I'd always heard the word *Draconian* but had no idea as to its origin. He and his boys were apparently some bloodthirsty motherfuckers."

I can't believe I just said that. From the look on Dumbledore's face, he couldn't either. I hadn't had enough sleep or coke. Since one was out of the question, I excused myself momentarily, went in the bedroom, and proceeded to powder my nose and numb my tongue.

When I emerged, Beau Pre asked, "I've heard that Alaric has been awakened and is on board?"

"True. Your sources are correct, good Sir. I met him myself only last night."

"Marvelous, I'll have to plan dinner with him and do some catching up. I think the last time we saw each other was during the Middle Ages." He let out a big belly laugh and said, "Bubonic plagues, rats and all, those were ghastly times as I recall. I shouldn't want to revisit that period ever again. We nearly starved and what little there was to eat tasted like diseased vermin. Terrible times I tell you, terrible times. But that's enough of an old man's ramblings, my young Prince."

Excusing myself, I took a nosedive and made a quick trip to the makeshift medical station set up on the bedroom dresser. Thanks to nurse Blue Boy and Uncle Fester's modern miracles of pharmacology, I returned no longer feeling the compulsion to drain an old fat guy and cut class for the rest of the evening.

Dumbledore was waiting, ever ready with his *Book o' History* in the salon. "Since you've gotten through the…Draconian period, let's talk today about the origins of your bloodline. Your ancestors, the progenitors of our line, are descendants of an ancient vampire named Dorius. Your clan, or House, as you might think of it in more modern terms, are the Dorians. Your grandsire, Charles, is the Dorian Prince."

Why do I hate that word so much, I asked silently?

"You should have read," he said, looking at me doubtfully, "about the Dorians' conquest of Greece around 1,100 BC. Many scholars erroneously claim they were Greeks, which is absurd. If they were Greeks, they couldn't have very well conquered themselves, now could they? In fact, they were not Greek at all. They were vampire. Tall, blonde, handsome vampires who'd migrated from the area you'd call Albania today. They spoke different languages and had very unusual customs, according to those who witnessed their arrival on the island of Crete.

"Before the migration, during the Mesopotamian period, when the Dorians were still in Albania, they were ruled by a great vampire king called Aryan. We don't know much about him today, only that he was directly sired by Dorius, the only son of Sin, first born of Emperor Anu's heirs.

The Nephilim were the warring class of their planet, Marduk. Dorius was Anunnaki, the bloodline of God and the sole survivor of the royal family.

I asked, "So Dorius was the grandson of the emperor? I remember reading about Anu and Marduk, but who were the Nephilim? I heard Charles mention something about them."

"As I said, they were the warrior class of Marduk. The human Bible refers to them as *fallen angels* in the Book of Genesis. The verse goes something like: 'That the sons of God saw the daughters of men that they were fair; and they took themselves wives of all which they chose.'

"We, my boy, are the progeny of what some would call the *unholy alliance*. Vampires, at least the earthly variety, are an unintended consequence of the Pleiadian Wars. Those soldiers, the Nephilim warriors, went back to Marduk to rest and recover after battling the Pleiadians for thousands of years. Once they returned home, they bored quickly, longing for adventure and the conquest of other worlds.

"Anu, the Emperor, had only recently returned from a less-than-successful mining expedition on the blue planet, Earth. His eldest son, Sin, recruited some of the restless Nephilim warriors for yet another attempt at reviving his family's waning reputation and flagging fortunes. While here on Earth, Sin's wife gave birth to a son, Dorius, who, after his father, would have been third in the royal line of succession.

"The Nephilim, in their extracurricular activities, began cavorting about, siring children of their own, courtesy of female humans. Although none of these *abominations* had a drop of royal Anunnaki blood among them, before long the Nephilim started carrying stories back home of how easily Earth women were parted from their virtues. Word of the easy pickings drew more and more of them here and, before anyone understood the gravity or depravity of the situation, things began to spiral out of control.

"Factions began developing. Lawlessness and petty rivalries ruled the day. Cities were leveled, humans were killed by the score, and these *Earth Wars* began spreading back to Marduk. Anu tried to stop the violence and restore order, but nothing worked. Out of desperation, he even ordered the Earth flooded, but when the waters receded there were still a few *abominations* along with a scattering of humans who'd somehow managed to survive.

"Dorius, now an adult, sent word back to the emperor that some of the Devil's spawn had turned out to be better swimmers than expected. Anu was outraged and ordered everyone home to Marduk. Dorius was left to oversee the evacuation of the planet. According to legend, some of the Nephilim didn't get the memo and missed the last train.

"Since they were so fond of the blue planet, Anu made the decision to let them stay, forever. He had Dorius construct a special prison for the deserters. It was, and still is, called Tatarus. The literal meaning is *total darkness*. He had the remainder of his once-proud warriors rounded up and cast into the blackened depths of eternal hell.

"In the meantime, Marduk's troubles continued. When the Nephilim on the home planet got word of the fate that had befallen their comrades, they turned against the emperor and began warring with the Anunnaki. After several centuries of back and forth, the situation escalated and they began using nukes on each other.

"Legend has it, the Nephilim even used them here in an attempt to free their brethren from the darkened dungeon of Tatarus. The destruction of Sodom and Gomorrah is one such example of how humans have incorporated these events into their own histories.

"When Anu learned of a huge nuclear assault aimed directly at his palace, he chose the final solution and retaliated with extreme prejudice. In the last moments before the annihilation of Marduk, he ordered Dorius to release the remaining prisoners still alive inside Tatarus. The emperor knew it was the only way to prevent the complete extinction of his planet's once-glorious civilization.

"The doors of the Nephilim's hell were cast wide open, and out walked the few survivors directly into the glaring sunlight of Earth. Most had long since perished in darkness and starvation. Those who emerged and survived learned to live under cover of darkness, never again to enjoy the light of day.

"Only Dorius could tolerate the sun. His world had been shattered, lost forever. Alone, starving, and surrounded by enemies, he turned to his only companion, a human called Aryan, for comfort and sustenance. Together they roamed the Earth for centuries, evading or fighting, until they'd finally outrun the enemy and settled in Albania, where, ruling together, they built up a great kingdom. Aryan grew stronger as his human blood mingled with that of the Anunnaki, but Dorius began to weaken and age.

"Emboldened by the light of the newly formed moon, legend has it, their enemies began gathering in numbers and strength. Old and sick, Dorius lay dying while Aryan defended, by the light of day, the kingdom they'd built together. From that point forward, everything we have is nothing more than rumor, conjecture, and myth. That, my young Prince, is your early legacy and, for tonight, the end of our lesson."

Beau Pre could see I still had questions. Rather than answer them, he cut me off at the pass. "I wouldn't worry myself too much about all this if I were you, Adrian. It would seem almost natural, given your predilection for the company of men and capacity for sunlight, that the rumor mill will churn out stories that you're Aryan reborn, or some such nonsense. Furthermore, it does little to quiet wagging tongues with everyone knowing all too well how your conversion took place in the House of Dorius, under the sireship of our Prince. My boy, you may as well get accustomed to it. You are the stuff of legends."

Knowing he'd let his mouth overload his fat, old ass, he offered what comfort he could before making a hasty departure. "Welcome aboard, Sir Nicholas. For whatever it's worth, I promise you'll get used to this eventually. Meanwhile, keep in mind that gossip is the blood sport of immortals."

One door closed and another opened. Uncle Fester was inquiring from beyond the Blue. "Is Dumbledore gone? I thought I heard the door close."

"He is. You did. And here it is again, in case you missed it the first time." I slammed *Blue Boy* into the wall, hoping no one would call Child Protective Services. I was in no mood to play *Hollywood Squares* or watch *The Addams Family* through a hole in the wall.

Though I gave it my best effort, after searching frantically, I was unable to find a hammer, nails, or Super Glue, and had burned through the rest of my medical supplies. Armed with only a roll of transparent tape, things were looking bleak, my resolve was growing weak, and I hadn't eaten dinner.

Peter sounded perfect. I'd come across his card, scanning for building materials underneath the bed. But if my body wouldn't fit, I doubted his would either. Not to be deterred because cruise ships aren't exactly known for their spacious walk-in closets, I was considering the consequences of dumping him after the first date when someone knocked at the door. For once, I hoped to hell someone hadn't been reading my mind. Hungry, hesitant, and only just shy of repentant, I peered through the peephole and breathed a sigh of relief. It was Uncle Fester, the Blue Boy molester from next door, and he had a bottle with two glasses.

In yet another of my many moments of weakness, I invited him in. Having a soft spot for washed-out soap stars, I had to admit he'd done a lot to get himself cleaned up. Where there's wine, there's hope, my mother would've said repeatedly, had she been a drinker. Taking both our dreams and dinner out on the terrace, we were able to find common ground after several heated rounds of negotiations. The cushions from the chaise lounge were instrumental in brokering peace with the floor, which had suffered greatly during our bouts of strife and internal conflict.

By joining forces we thought we had the wind at our backs, but before long we'd plundered each other's treasuries and squandered the wealth of both our nations. Sometime later during the Spanish inquisition, Carlos casually asked, "So how did it go with Beau Pre today?"

"It was torturous. If even half of it is true, it's the most amazing story I've ever heard. Beau Pre loves to lecture, but he sucks at answering questions and I have a lot of them. For instance, when I asked about the Nephilim, he blew me off and told me not to worry about it. That's bullshit. How am I supposed to learn anything if I can't ask questions?"

"You're right, *mon ami*. Maybe I can help. What is it you want to know?"

"Tell me about them. Not the mythical ancient warrior stuff, but who are the modern Nephilim?"

"I've never heard anyone refer to them as modern. Dinosaurs, yes. Modern, no. Let's see…To begin with, they're arrogant assholes who consider themselves superior to every other living thing on the planet. They stink to high heaven, especially the old ones." They resent the Dorians and consider us interlopers.

"We've been, at least nominally, holding the clans together for 2,500 years, and they still call us *pretenders to the throne*, although we've never held the throne. Queen Ana has worn the crown for, I guess, 4,000 years now. Essentially, I'm apolitical. I find it a lot easier to stay alive that way, but I cringe in horror at the thought of Akkad, their prince, taking over if anything were to happen to her. And as I'm sure you gathered at Sebastian's trial, she's no summer chicken."

"Spring chicken. But nevertheless, you're telling me after thousands and thousands of years they still have a stick up their ass because of Dorius? How can they possibly think anyone's blood is still pure today?"

"They don't, except for their own, of course. Masters of delusional thinking and abysmal failures at personal hygiene, that's how I'd describe today's Nephilim. They can't accept the fact that all the gods of old have long since passed away. We, the Dorians, are all that's left of what they seek, and it makes them crazy.

"Not everyone is like that. Take the Chaldeans, for instance. I've met quite a few of them through the years. Musicians, architects, very artsy types, they bathe regularly and tend to dress very stylishly. They've always tipped me well and for the most part have a great sense of humor. Very warm and cuddly as vampires go…"

Leaning back in the chair laughing, I spotted a solitary bird flying by in the night sky. I marveled at how odd and lonely it must feel in the middle of the ocean's vastness with no resting place in sight and such a long, uncertain journey ahead.

Carlos interrupted my thought as he stood up behind me, bent down, and kissed my brow. His fingers were inside my shirt stroking my chest when I asked, "One more question, then I promise I'll quit. Have you heard the rumor that I am Aryan reborn?"

"Of course. Gossip is the blood sport of immortals, in case you haven't heard."

"Yes, I have heard. But what I'm asking is…do you believe it's true?"

Removing his fingers from my shirt, he came around in front of me and knelt on one knee. "I have no idea, but there is something I do know." Looking as serious as I'd seen him, he took my hand and said, "Sir Nicholas Adrian Wellstone, whether you like it or not, your name is neither a curse, nor a cure for the world's ills. Be what you will, but always be true to that beautiful heart of yours. It, and it alone, will lead you away from darkness."

I'm sure he meant well, but the words *heart* and *darkness* conjured up memories of Joseph Conrad's depressing book and the bat-shit craziness of *Apocalypse Now*, neither of which seemed particularly instructive or inspirational.

It was time to get ready for Alaric anyway. At least he was trying to teach me how to handle pit vipers without getting bit.

CHAPTER EIGHTEEN

Vampire politics can be a very draining and depressive subject. I should have known better than to discuss it during dinner. On the way to the gym, in desperate need of a mental makeover, all I could think about were depressing movies, which only added to my apprehensive melancholy. Don't get me wrong, *Titanic* was beautifully filmed and had a lovely sound score, but nearly everyone dies and the fucker still sinks like a rock—not an uplifting film in my estimation. Fear of the future is fine for mortals, but when a vampire gets stuck in a rut it's possible to dig a trench deeper than the Grand Canyon. That's where I felt headed, over the edge and straight to the bottom.

Three tables were set up where the weight bench had been the night before. Aikido Joe Geritol was sitting stoically in a chair six feet away with his arms folded across his chest when he barked his first order, "Break it apart."

"With what?" I asked, looking around the room for something to smash the cinder block.

Before I could even blink, he was out of his chair and shattered pieces of concrete were exploding in every direction. I ducked as one of the chunks whizzed past my face from the thundering impact of his fist.

"Use your hands! They are weapons! Others will use theirs against you. I can assure you of that!"

Dude, seriously, do you have to scream? I knew better than to say it aloud.

I walked over to the second block and tried smashing it with my fist. It did break apart, but only fell into large pieces on the now-cracked table.

"No! No! No! Use your center of gravity. Use your whole being when you destroy the enemy. Nothing should remain. Send his shards to Tatarus!"

I walked over to the second block and smashed it as hard as I could. Shit did actually fly everywhere, much to my surprise.

"Better, but you have to come at the enemy from underneath. That's where your power comes from. Draw it from your feet. The force of your strength will travel up through your body into your arm. That fist is a weapon. Now use it!"

I planted my feet firmly on the ground in front of the third block and tried to feel the strength moving up through my body as I swung my arm with every ounce of strength I could summon. I wasn't even certain I'd hit the block until I felt tiny concrete fragments lodging themselves into my face and upper body.

There wasn't enough of the banquet table left to serve Weight Watchers for one, and Alaric was a bloody, happy mess, standing there choking on dust and rubble. "Excellent! Can you feel the power beneath your feet now?"

"Actually, yes I…"

Before I could finish forming the thought, much less the words, I found myself airborne again, violently slamming into the wall twenty feet away. He screamed and laughed at the same time. "I told you to keep your feet on the ground!"

"Motherfucker, that hurt!" I wasn't sure whether it was my ego or a spinal injury, but before I knew what I was doing, I was up off the floor and running at him with my head down like a charging bull. At the precise moment of impact with his belly, I ducked, dug my feet into the ground, and hit the old fucker with everything I had.

He didn't smash into the wall—he went through it. Shattering porcelain and laughter were the only noises I heard until he yelled, "That's what I'm talking about! Come help me up, boy! I think you ruptured my spleen."

Emerging from the hole in the wall and dusting himself off, he was still laughing. "Somebody's going to have to pay for this…Thank Ana it's not us!"

I suspected Captain Stillman might not agree when water began gushing out behind him onto the gymnasium floor as a result of our shoddy workmanship. I could see the lawsuit: *Imperial Crown Cruise Lines vs. Dukes of Haphazard Remodelers.* While searching for a water-shutoff valve, I called Carlos and explained how we'd had a small accident in the ladies' room.

Hacking and coughing, Alaric suggested we go outside, dry off, and get some less-particulate-laden air. Feeling a bit full of myself and construction debris, I agreed. We encountered two swabbies mopping the deck. Nudging my codefendant in the side, I said, "Allow me." Walking over to the better-looking one, I chortled, "Gentlemen, good evening. My friend and I are going to jump up on the railing and have a jog around the boat. There's no need for you to be alarmed or call anyone. We'll be fine. Have I made myself clear?"

They looked at each other in wide-eyed amazement before bursting out laughing. The hot one asked, "Are you drunk, mister? We can't let you do that. But whatever you're smoking, we could sure use a little. How about hooking us up? That must be some really good shit." I was about to make a second pass when Alaric came over and straightened the matter out. The boys took their mops and went inside to clean up the mess in the gym.

I hopped up on the railing. "Let's go. I'll race you."

"No, tonight is about speed and endurance. I hope you fed well. Take your time, build up your speed, and let's see how long you can go. Pay attention to your breathing and heart rate."

Pacing myself at first, the wind and the water's smell felt and tasted wondrous rushing across my face and into my nostrils. Very freeing—I felt almost like I was flying. Breezing past the small hurdles in my path only added to my exhilaration. Running faster and faster, I'd finally picked up so much speed I could barely feel my feet touching the rail. It seemed as if time and matter were standing still. I was the only thing moving in the whole wide world.

"Calgon, take me away!" I shouted triumphantly with my arms stretched in the air, making delirious laps around and around the ship's perimeter at blinding speeds. I was flying, soaring, probably twenty, maybe thirty feet over the side of the ship before realizing I'd been pushed. Something, someone I'd hardly noticed came at me with such subtle force and exacting precision as I was rounding a curve at the rear of the ship, that several seconds passed before my dopamine-filled mind fully registered that I was actually airborne. The only problem was I didn't know how to fly.

Just for the record, when you're moving at nearly two hundred miles an hour and someone pushes you off the side of a ship six stories above the water, you have a long time to think about how completely, totally fucked you are.

I had a hard time believing it myself, but even over the deafening roar of the ship's engines, I could hear the bones snapping and splintering in my neck and back as I hit the water, bouncing over and over the waves like a stone being skipped across a cyclonic pond. With significant degrees of pain and certainty, I watched as my ship sailed away into the night, calculating the proximate time and causes of my death. Barely buoyant, more than broken, and decidedly non-jubilant, I thought of Ophelia, belting out Shakespeare's bawdiest tunes, only I didn't feel much like singing and couldn't remember any of the words.

Unbeknownst to me, whilst I was in the midst of my first flying lesson, a lovely, older woman named Amelia Crawford was sitting on her rear balcony drinking my personal favorite, Tanqueray and tonic. Screaming at her husband in a remarkably well-rehearsed alto, she yelled, "Oh my god Floyd, I just saw someone land in the water! Do something! Oh my god!"

Floyd drunkenly picked up the phone and stabbed at what he thought might be the button for the operator. He wasn't really sure, nor did he actually care. Surprisingly, someone came on the line and said, "Yes, may I help you?"

Caught off guard, Floyd thought for a moment, before calmly remarking, "My wife, Amelia, thinks she saw a man go overboard."

"Yes, sir. When did this happen?"

Amelia was clutching at the lapel of Floyd's pajamas, screaming. The operator heard her and asked, "Sir, was this at the front or back of the ship?"

"At the back! At the back," Amelia screeched into the phone.

"Thank you, sir. We'll call you back."

The bones in my back and neck were trying to mend themselves while my lungs were otherwise engaged in taking on copious amounts of salt water and seaweed. Under other circumstances, I might have been more concerned about exceeding the daily-recommended dose of sodium, but the ship suddenly slowed. I watched in horror while it lurched impossibly to the right, seeming as if it were about to capsize on top of me. Like some drowning idiot with a broken back in the middle of the ocean, I was attempting to swim away when I saw the first flares and giant, glowing, white orbs being tossed into the water.

Luminarias? That's great. I'm out here dying and they're throwing a fucking party!

The ship somehow righted itself and began turning slowly in my direction as I watched more and more house-sized, glowing beach balls being tossed overboard. Although the atmosphere was becoming more festive by the minute, it was difficult having even the most guarded optimism when my choices were drowning at sea or being run over by the world's second-largest ocean liner.

The diver's heartbeat was much faster than my own as he pulled me from the water into the lifeboat. I would have embarrassed us both, but I was freezing my ass off and barely breathing as he straddled my deflated chest. Someone behind me was putting my neck into some sort of brace. It was probably just as well. I wasn't in much of a mood for a party…

In spite of it all, I was enjoying being manhandled by all those drenched seamen until they hoisted me onto a gurney and whisked me toward the infirmary. Hospitalization and immortality are seldom, if ever, compatible. All strapped-in and no place to go, I was starting to panic when Carlos appeared out of nowhere.

I doubt I've ever been happier to see anyone in either of my lifetimes. With my body bound and the oxygen mask strapped over my face, I couldn't speak. He must have heard me cursively hyperventilating in his head about Hannibal Lecter, how I was about to bite someone and, otherwise, what a generally rough day I was having. He kept removing the mask while one of the medics argued, trying to wrestle it back over my face. Normally, I would've been thrilled to see two guys fighting over me…

Carlos, my beautiful Moby Dick, was trying to unbind the straps when Captain Stillman entered stage left, slamming through the doors like Debby Downer on extra-strength menopause pills going all Ahab on everyone's ass, screaming, "Leave us!" I was more than impressed when they actually did.

After clearing the room he was generous enough to give me a more than ample piece of his mind, although it was my back that was actually broken and in need of donations. "Do you have any comprehension what you've done? Every media outlet in the world is already on board this ship and helicopters will bring more by morning!"

"Someone pushed me," I gasped breathlessly, wincing in pain as the vertebrae in my back tried locating their next of kin.

"You've got to be kidding?" Stillman asked.

(Seriously, if I happen to live ten thousand years…that has always been, and shall forever remain, the dumbest question anyone's ever asked me.)

Four bodyguards, or sentries, or whatever you'd call them, accompanied Carlos and me back to the suite. Two of them went outside on the balcony and shut the door. Carlos locked it from inside. The other two stayed in the corridor. None of them were human. I wondered exactly how many vampires were onboard the ship. I hadn't thought about it until then. I probably should have.

Without further adieu, Carlos went in and ran a bath. After the longest while, he still hadn't returned. I was considering releasing the orbs when I found him floating in the tub, good side up. Two glasses of red sat taunting, mocking me from the far ledge, daring me back into the water. With some trepidation and considerably more deliberation than ever before, I stepped lightly into Calgon's healing waters and Carlos' outstretched, ambulatory arms.

My neck was still incredibly stiff and swollen, unlike my cock, when the phone rang the next morning. I was completely out of it when Charles came on the line.

"Nicholas," he began (which is never the way I like to start my mornings), "How are you, my boy? I trust you're recovering from your impromptu swimming lesson last evening?"

"I think I'll live, but I wouldn't care to offer that same prognosis for whoever did this. I don't suppose you have any candidates, do you?"

"Not yet. We're still going over the passenger list and ship's manifest. Rest assured, we will get to the bottom of this. Until then, we've assigned extra sentries to your cabin and a security detail will accompany you to Nadir training. How's that coming by the way?"

"Except for the water aerobics, so far it's been smashing. In light of last night's revelations, I can promise you I'll be redoubling my efforts to graduate with highest honors.

"While I have you on the phone, Sir, I wanted to apologize. Captain Stillman seems to think we'll be deluged by the media today. He's not very happy with me right now."

"I can only imagine. You were already making quite a splash in the press."

We were both laughing uncomfortably when he added, "I shouldn't worry too much about it, Nicholas. Confine yourself to quarters and they'll move on in a few days. If they don't, we can always give them something else to talk about. In the meanwhile try and get some rest. We'll talk again soon."

The line went dead and I reached over Carlos to hang up the phone. He grabbed me on the way back to my side of the bed. Maybe I wasn't that sore after all...

I woke up that evening after several rounds of bad dreams with someone banging at the door. Dreary-eyed, I pulled on my boxers and answered. It wasn't raccoons, so I assumed I must be awake. Beau Pre was standing there alongside two sentries. "Ah Professor, I'm sorry, I should have called, but I'm afraid I'm in no condition for company this evening. If you don't mind, I think we're going to have to take a rain check."

He was saying, "Yes of course, I heard you had quite an eventful evening..." as some asshole with a camera came down the hall flashing photos of me in my drawers. I would have asked for a set of prints and drained the bastard on the spot if not for the witnesses. Instead I suggested one of the guards deal with it and slammed the door on the lot of them.

Carlos let Alaric know I wouldn't be making it downstairs for water gymnastics either. We were having what was becoming our ritualistic dinner on the terrace when I asked, "Do you think it's possible…we could have a traitor in the House of Dorius?"

Almost flippantly, he replied, "I wouldn't be surprised. Alliances are like shifting sand, my love. Vampires can be as fluid with their affections and affiliations as anyone else. I used to have an old friend who was fond of saying how everyone's always looking for a cheaper whore.

"Like you, I was reborn in the House of Dorius. Others may draw our blood, but no one can change it. Have I been approached over the years? Of course, but I trust my Prince. Charles does a great job herding the bats as far as I can see. Whether a Dorian pushed you or not…that's a question I can't answer, Adrian. Suspicions, they're as bountiful as the seas. But if you want to catch the big fish, keep your eyes open and your nets wide."

I'm sure my tone must've radiated the reassurance I felt from Moby Dickhead's homily. "I'm with you in spirit, brother. But if you ask me, it's starting to sound a lot like the mafia."

There wasn't a hint of facetiousness in his voice when he laughed. "The mafia? You can't be serious? Strictly amateurs. They learned everything they know from the Vatican. That was ours, too. From what I understand, we sold most of our stake in the Church when they started shedding more blood than anyone could consume.

"No one likes liabilities, but, if I had to venture a guess, the obvious choice would be Nephilim. It may only be my imagination, but in all the excitement last night I thought I could smell a faint trace on your clothes when they pulled you from the water."

"Wait. You said they give off a foul odor, right? Last night, when I was making those laps, every time I rounded the back corner of the ship I knew I smelled something. I assumed somebody had taken a shit in the Jacuzzi."

His face wrinkled, laughing. "That's completely gross, but it wouldn't be the first time someone's had drunken bowel syndrome on this boat. Believe me, I've seen worse."

Eager to narrow topics, I asked, "How many Nephilim are on board?"

"I have no idea, although I wouldn't think very many. We don't have any ports of call in eastern Europe on this route."

"So if there were any Nephilim on the ship, we'd be able to recognize them by their smell?"

"Unless they've been converted recently. And it's doubtful the Nephilim are having a membership drive right now."

"Everyone keeps saying my nose is better than a bloodhound's. Let's go walk around and see if we can pick up the scent."

Rubbing my sore neck, he said, "As you like my bonnie, broken prince. And, just so you know, everyone is right. Your nose is much nicer than any bloodhound's."

The elevator doors opened to an onslaught of cameras and microphones. The first reporter was kind enough to fall backward into the crowded field of his journalistic brethren as we made a hasty retreat back to the safety of the fifteenth floor. One of the two security guards was about to give me a stern lecture. I apologized and assured them it wouldn't happen again.

Shutting the door behind us, I made the additional mistake of turning on the television. I didn't appear to be doing any underwear commercials, not at the moment anyway. "Millionaire playboy miraculously saved at sea." They'd used one of the photos from the Sydney Opera House where Charles and I were waving to the crowd with Olivia Newton-John.

"The drunken heir to a great fortune fell from a cruise ship in the middle of the Indian Ocean late last night. Stay tuned for exciting footage of the rescue after this short…"

"…more exclusive details about the story of Sir Nicholas Adrian Wellstone falling overboard from a luxury cruise ship last night. He's the handsome, reclusive heir to millions everyone's been talking about."

I threw the remote at the TV. When the two sentries on the balcony heard the explosion, they spun around with guns drawn. I'd always thought fame and fortune meant you never had to say you're sorry…

After I'd apologized to everyone, including the poor television, Carlos said, "I have an idea," and made a phone call from the quieter confines of the bedroom. I was downing a double when he came back to the salon.

"I had a purser clear the observation deck above us. We can take the stairs. I thought you could use some untelevised airtime. I hope you don't mind, but I invited Alaric to join us. On the phone earlier he sounded worried about you."

"No, that's fine. I wanted to talk to him anyway. I need some perspective, and since he's older than dirt, he's bound to have several of them."

Comfortably seated in the aptly named crow's nest, I decided to get it over with and eat the last serving of shit pie I had coming. "Alaric, I owe you an apology. I know you've gone to a great deal of trouble trying to teach me the ways of the Nadir. Until last night, I honestly thought everyone was making an unnecessary fuss about very little. I guess I had to learn the hard way, and, believe me, I have.

"From this point forward, you have my absolute, undivided attention. No more games. I promise I'll train as hard and as long as my body and mind will allow each and every day until you tell me I'm ready."

"Good. Then we begin with your training tomorrow night. No more assessments or accidents. Now I can and will teach you what you need to know to stay alive, or at least as close as you're going to get."

We laughed and made a toast to everyone's long life as I downed the rest of my red. Carlos knew I was still hungry and was kind enough to risk overexposure among the thronging hoards in search of refills.

Since we'd had our mea culpa moment, I wasn't interested in wasting any more time. Considering Alaric's age and my track record, who knew how long either of us had? I got right to the point. "Alaric, I need to ask you something. Beau Pre has been catching me up on history. He's great at reciting the textbook versions of everything…"

He shook his head in understanding. "He should be, he wrote half of them. What *blanks* would you like me to fill in? I can hear the word racing through your mind."

"What can you tell me about Dorius and Aryan? I don't care if it's something you know, you choose to believe, or it's something you heard eons ago. What can you tell me?"

He took a long time to think about the question. I wondered in amazement at what it must be like to think back literally thousands of years. Before he'd said anything Carlos came back carrying a full tray of drinks.

Alaric thanked him, took a sip of whiskey, and eased back in the chair. "My young Prince, your three distinctions—knowledge, belief, and rumor—have very little, if any, import regarding the question. No one in my living memory was present while either of them lived. The fact of their existence is not in question. They were as real as you or I. What was written about them, some of which I read personally, was destroyed by Caesar in Alexandria. I spent three years, on and off, at the Library and Museum before the fire, which was as much our fault as Julius'. If I'd drained Mark Antony when I had the chance, things might be different. The world will never know what was lost when I foolishly spared his life.

"As for Dorius and Aryan, the tales of their battles and triumphs were as renowned as the stories of their suffering and loss. Achilles and Patroclus in Homer's writings are inspired by their legend. Perhaps in another time and place we can talk about those aspects of their life.

"What you want to know about is their deaths, and I can only tell you what was written. Dorius, even though he was born here, was not human. He was Anunnaki."

"Yes, Beau Pre told me about this. He was from the royal bloodline of Marduk."

"That's right. None of the other clans, even the Nephilim, had such a leader. None of their Houses today are descended from that line. The others fed freely on whomever, whenever, they chose. Dorius would only draw blood from Aryan. After his conversion, Aryan fed upon and transformed only those who were needed to keep Dorius alive and safe while the others grew fat with armies and formed treasonous alliances out of fear and jealousy. Dorius and Aryan had no children, for obvious reasons. Some of the others from Marduk did bear offspring with humans. Some were more prolific than others.

"That's where the Nephilim draw the basis for their claims. Only the unions that produced *naturally conceived* offspring were considered legitimate lines of heredity. No Dorian has any vampire blood, other than

Dorius. The royal blood of the Anunnaki was only ever shared with one human, Aryan. You, me, Charles, even Carlos, we're all directly descended from Dorius and Aryan. Each of us is half human, half Anunnaki.

"With only Aryan's blood to nourish him, Dorius began aging and slowly grew old. He and Aryan finally settled in a valley on the Albanian coast when Dorius was too old to run any longer. They lived away from the others and took only what they needed to survive. Over time they were found out. After a few centuries, word had spread about the wondrous kingdom at the edge of the sea, its marvels of rich green fields on the sides of mountains, plazas and gardens hanging in the air, indoor plumbing… and a library."

We both stopped, blinked, and reached for our drinks at the same time. I could hear and see the rumblings of a brewing storm in the darkened distance. His glass of whiskey lit up like molten amber every time lightning struck nearby.

"The other tribes gathered around them in the northern countries waiting for word of Dorius' death." Alaric was all wound up by then. Hanging on his every word, I didn't dare interrupt when Carlos threw in the towel, brought more drinks, then quietly went to bed. I feared no matter how long I lived, I would never get to hear the same story again.

"After several more centuries, those younger, and their instigators, began sharing tales of clandestine excursions into the land of milk and honey. It only took a few more years before they became emboldened enough to attack and overrun the kingdom. Too old and weak to fight, Dorius was captured."

Lightning was going off all around us. The water wasn't troubled at all by the giant flames being tossed about in the sky, but, when it began pouring rain, I was personally bothered by the monsoon and, more especially, the prospect of watered-down drinks. We sought shelter under a canvas canopy where Alaric finished his Olympian story.

"Aryan fled into the forest but was eventually captured and prepared for execution. The others had no qualms about separating him from his head because of his human origins. In the final act of his life, he cursed his captors, calling them mongrel dogs, and vowing they would never rule man or vampire. Believing Dorius was already dead, Aryan said he would return to exact revenge and they would all die at his hand in a single day. As the axe swung toward his neck, those present claimed they'd read his final thoughts. He swore he would rise again during a time of peace, young and powerful, fearless in the face of the western sun, to end the Great Conflict and unite the remaining tribes, both great and small for all time.

"Dorius, on the other hand, was not so easily dispatched in spite of what Aryan believed. The other tribes were mortally afraid of spilling the ancient one's sacred Anunnaki blood. The eldest among them believed they'd be cursed for all time by taking the life of a royal. Arguing with the younger tribesmen, they pointed toward the heavens, reminding them of the fate that befell Marduk when the rebels raised hand and sword against the emperor."

The storm was directly overhead at that point. I had to lean in close to hear Alaric.

"So what happened to Dorius? Did they kill him?" I asked.

"No, fear won out and they bound the *being of light and great stature* in silver chains, placing him in a sarcophagus with an enormous, solid-stone lid, larger and heavier than could be lifted by ten of their strongest men.

"Poor Aryan should have kept his mind closed in those final minutes. Taking his threats seriously, they hacked him to pieces, and across great time and distance scattered his remains in the farthest corners of the Earth."

"Now I think I see. All these crazy people today still believe those old legends and think I'm Aryan reborn or some such horseshit. Wow, that's incredible. What a fucking story! Any idea what they did with Dorius' body?"

"The scrolls I read in Alexandria said they stood guard over his tomb night and day until only Aryan's heart remained to be dispatched. When the last of their kingdom had been dismantled and no trace remained, its inhabitants long since driven from their lands, they carried Dorius' body out of Albania along with Aryan's heart, burying them both in a faraway place at the edge of the sea. One of the scrolls said, when the lid was removed to place Aryan's heart inside, Dorius was still alive."

CHAPTER NINETEEN

Professor Beau Pre came around the next evening and nearly every evening thereafter. Once I'd devoured and digested all the books in the safe, he brought more. After eight weeks I felt I might be passing his courses, which I'd stopped referring to as Musty Mythology. Of course, as you might imagine, I asked for everything ever written on Dorius and Aryan.

In human history, I could only trace them back to ancient Illyria. The Dardanians were the last vestiges of their lost kingdom. Alaric told me the word was originally a derivative of both their names combined. *My great-great-great-whatever Grandvamps were two gay dudes. How cool is that?* As ridiculous as it sounds, I was so excited for a time, thinking I'd discovered the gay-vampire gene. No one except me seemed to care or have much interest in fabled love stories about the last Anunnaki prince and his human-vampire husband. Real or not, it was one hell of a legacy, and it was mine.

The degree to which vampires had shaped the world was mind numbing. *Revisionist history* couldn't begin to describe what I discovered in my crash courses on the truth, or at least our version of the truth. We were seemingly behind, or in the shadows of, numerous events that would forever define life on the blue planet, Earth.

Confuse, confound, distort as needed. Repeat often. Even The Havens itself was built upon the mantra, "what's up is down." Remote, detached from the rest of the world, Down Under was, and is, the perfect moniker. Sydney has the world's highest per capita income and the world's deepest basement of vampires. The true story of how that came to be is one of pure genius. I've often wished I'd thought of it.

BLOOD: THE SANGUINE PRINCE

Aboriginal indigenous tribes occupied the continent, relatively undisturbed until late in the 1500s. Two centuries later, we persuaded the British Parliament to help these tribes start cleaning up their acts. For our purposes, it was a perfectly arranged marriage, and formed the foundations under which The Havens were built.

Transportation was a new and growing industry. Prisoners were more easily accounted for offshore. Abundant native food and highly-skilled imported labor built two great cities in New Holland—one up, one down. We controlled both. New South Wales quickly became the place to leave your troubles behind. The first prisoner ships arrived in the world's largest natural bay in 1788. Two hundred years later, our plans were fait accompli. Sydney was a world-class city, about to host the Olympics. A few of its elders were extraordinarily excited by the honor. They'd been instrumental in organizing the first one 2,500 years before...

The Nadir was, and is, its own raison d'être. The Havens primes Sydney's pump and robust economy with excellent universal healthcare and a more than adequate social-safety net. Because of plentiful jobs that pay living wages, everyone always knows where their next meal was coming from. That particular lesson would not be lost on me. I was on my way to Gravesend, a whole new life, and I was determined to make it the best one I'd ever had.

You can't out-give God. My mother said it so often, it was permanently seared into my mind. If I could manage to stay alive long enough, I intended to test the theory. The God of the Old Testament had never struck me as particularly benevolent or philanthropic. My own Grandvamps, Charles, seemed like a much better model, excepting, of course, the forsaking your own son part...

They were all in on it, the mind games. Stillman, Carlos, Beau Pre, the always-evil Alaric, even the security guys took great delight in my mental torture. The physical part of my Nadir training wasn't nearly as taxing. It's one thing to be worked like a dog, regardless of breed, but exercising the mind can be much more painful and exhausting. I wasn't allowed to answer the door without knowing who was there. Ditto for the phone.

Telepathic texting isn't as easy as it sounds. My nails could shave the neck off a wine bottle in a millisecond with a diamond-polished finish. They were great for craft projects or severing a jugular, but hitting those tiny cellular keys in response to a question asked only by ethereal carrier pigeons proved much more challenging. Smells, sights, sounds, feelings, thoughts, and all other sorts of sensory exercises seemed to be the real thrust of the Nadir. *Control the mind. The body will follow.* In six weeks' time, the training had managed to turn me into a blood-sucking Kung-Sufi mystic, though I never have been able to harness the powers of Android technology.

Luckily, I suppose, depending on your point of view and the wind's direction, I did manage to get a whiff of a really old Nephilim when we docked in Dubai. Fresh from an undoubtedly first-prize finish in the Stinkiest Vampire contest at the Hotel Burj Al Arab across the water, he'd come on-board and I was supposed to locate his room. Sugar and spice, not so much. The sickeningly sweet smell was more like rancid raisins. I felt surprised they hadn't evacuated the floor, when I stepped off the elevator, and right back on again.

The days and nights flew by as the tainted memory of his rotting corpse eventually faded from my nostrils, though it would always be with me and, I suspected, the ninth floor's carpeting in some way.

Never having the luxury of boredom, unlike some, I sensed a sentry daydreaming one afternoon. I'd seen him several times before. Young, muscular, and, if my opti-mystic intuitions were correct, he had one hell of an overbite.

Listening to his mind meandering was like watching a porn video starring myself. It was the one and only time I had a theatrical release involving one of the guards. Crouching at the door, I waited eagerly until the moment he was adjusting himself, then flung the door open and snatched him inside by the neck. After demonstrating that a workplace erection lasting longer than four hours is not always a bad thing, I fed him some well-deserved dinner and tried sending him on his way. His hesitancy to leave convinced me he was still hungry. Putting our heads together, we gave each other a hand and whipped up a quick dessert that he must've enjoyed tremendously. In no time, he was gushing more appreciatively than anyone I'd ever met.

Later that evening, fully refreshed from a heightened sense of security, I walked into the gym. Alaric was waiting for me and he wasn't alone. He'd persuaded the guard I'd plucked from the hallway to join us for the evening's exercise. *Well now, isn't this awkward,* I thought.

"Rip his heart out!" Alaric thundered. To my shock, I realized he wasn't making a decidedly unfunny joke. I sure as hell wasn't laughing—neither was the sentry.

Dumbfounded, I recoiled at the idea and tried, unconvincingly, to defuse the situation. "Doesn't fucking his brains out count for anything?" When it became apparent we weren't starring in an episode of *Candid Camera,* the bile began building in my throat for obvious enough reasons, many of which I could count in the poor man's terror-filled eyes.

Alaric screamed again, "Do it now, or you both die!"

The invective charge of his voice was only surpassed by my own overwhelming need to vomit. Blood, it seems, is indeed thicker than water. I offered proof all over the gymnasium floor and into the hallway. Hearts thundered and blood boiled in my overcrowded ears as I stabbed at the elevator button repeatedly.

I feared my face and reputation were both in ruins as Carlos waited for the doors to open. I couldn't stop crying. All the way up, I'd been repeating the same words, "I'm not a killer. I'm not a killer. I'm not a killer."

"Of course you're not, *mon ami.* Let's get you inside." Memories came flooding down the hallway, engulfing my mind. I was drowning in the lead-smelted, toxic sludge of my own past. Sinking deeper and deeper as the bloody body count rose, I watched bloated corpses of long-dead cowboys come bobbing by, one after the other, as I fought my way back to the surface.

Slamming the door behind me, I choked on the memories of their clotted remains all the way to the bathroom. I tried in vain to wash the crimson stains from my hands and face. They just kept coming and I didn't need to be a Sufi mystic to know why. Each of their voices was coming through loud and clear.

By the time I finished crying a river into the bathroom sink, I'd lost a lot of blood and turned to Blue Boy for some semblance of comfort and a refill. Seldom lacking for solutions, he held not only a bottle of southern Greek comfort, but a message as well. They both bore familiar seals, only one of which was embossed with gold. Taking a brimming glass of Selene and the blood-soaked towel out on the terrace, I did the Christlike thing and performed an act of contrition by turning the ruined towel into food for hundreds of hungry sharks.

Flinging the confessional bits of red and white confetti overboard, I felt something akin to relief as they fluttered downward, spiraling into the sea. Sipping at the wine, my body began to feel replenished. It made me wonder whether or not forgiveness was possible for the soul. Since having met Sebastian, I'd always assumed I no longer had one.

After the frenzied sharks finished feasting away at my sins, I sat for the longest time staring at the envelope before tearing away its golden seal. Prescient, short, and to the point as always, the note inside was packed with meaning although it contained only a single sentence: *Nicholas, may you never forget how true greatness is born not always from strength or adversity, but sometimes from the smallest acts of kindness. Welcome to Gravesend.—CHB.*

CHAPTER TWENTY

Other than hearing the blaring of horns, I hardly noticed when my ship came in. Alaric and Camuel had already said their goodbyes. Carlos… what can I say? I pleaded with Charles to let me keep him. Grandvamps, unpersuaded by my pubescent pleas, suggested I get a puppy, but I refused to give up my one and only Etruscan god without a fairly fantastic fight. On and off again, we waged a bloody, three-day grudge match in which Carlos proved more formidable than I'd been led to imagine. Surrendering in the end wasn't easy and I didn't do it out of weakness. It was the only thing I had left to give. After two mind-clearing months at sea, I felt like my head might finally be on straight for a change, figuratively speaking of course.

The mob of reporters, cameras, and microphones waiting on the pier was a decidedly unwelcome sight. Without so much as a pitchfork or flaming torch among them, they still drove my Zen-like ass back on board, much to Captain Stillman's delight. Between great peals of laughter, he and Peter, the smartly assed Purser, managed to stuff me inside a seaman's trunk and wheel me, free from assault, to safety. It was the one and only time I've ever wished my fag license included a drag endorsement.

Blind faith is all good and fine unless you're locked in a seaman's trunk, with no seamen to help pass the time, and feel yourself being hoisted into the air and summarily dropped inside yet another trunk, then, with a giant *thunk*, that trunk gets slammed on your head. I wondered, other than the ones kidnapped for ransom, was I the only millionaire playboy who had to endure such humiliation?

Several stops, starts, and turns later, on hearing the car's engine being put into park, I hoped I was being let out to pasture. I was a tad dizzy, my legs were beginning to cramp, and I hadn't the faintest fucking clue how far we were from Gravesend.

In aspiring toward the back seat, I noticed how spacious the Rolls' trunk was compared with my Caddie's, all the while admonishing myself for doing so. The driver was trying to introduce himself as he hoisted me out of dry storage onto wet pavement. "Welcome to England, Sir. We've been anticipating your arrival for some time now. I can't say how sorry I am it had to be by parcel post."

"Let's not dwell in the past. It's just good to be home. Where is that by the way?"

"I'm sorry, Sir Nicholas. Let's try this again. My name is Edward. I'll be driving you to Thornecrown," he said slightly more soberly while opening the back door.

"Thornecrown? I thought we were supposed to be going to Gravesend."

"Yes, Sir. Thornecrown is the name of the estate. We're about an hour and a half outside London by car. Maybe forty minutes by High Speed One."

"High Speed One?"

"Yes, Sir. It's the bullet train from County Kent into central London. At our end it connects with the Chunnel. You can take the train to Calais, or, if you prefer, I can drive you across. It's really quite convenient."

"Thank you, Edward. I may take you up on that offer once I get settled in." Leaning back against the seat, I relaxed until we'd left the city. Watching the soft hills as they endlessly rose and fell was almost hypnotic, like rhythmic breathing. Even at night it was a lovely drive with the moon's light casting a milky pallor across the darkened fields.

When the car, its rear window down, turned off the main road, I realized I'd been dozing. Its tires were clamoring in noisy protest as they claimed the cobblestones of an ancient bridge. Intent on the sound, I almost missed the darkened figure dashing through a thicket alongside the car. At first I thought it was an animal until it stopped and stood on two legs.

"Edward, there's someone out there."

"Yes, Sir," he replied in a rather nonchalant way. "I imagine that's Cornelius. He's been excited about your arrival all week. He thought you were coming in last night. We had a hard time getting him to bed this morning. He probably hasn't slept much."

"I'm not sure I understand."

"He's really quite harmless. Your grandfather brought him back to the estate many years ago from Paris. He was in the process of conversion when Sir Charles discovered him wandering in an alleyway in the 1960s after being bitten and left for dead. He's mute as far as anyone can tell and rather slow or feebleminded, but he's really very sweet. He's just very excitable. I suspect he'll grow on you. Except for Hilda, we're all very fond of him."

Pulling through the last of a wooded glen into an open expanse of green lawn, I was amazed at the sight of a quite large man galloping beside the car on all fucking fours! Once we came to a stop, I could barely see the house through the smudged window.

"Edward, will you please make him get down? He's licking the goddamned window!"

"I assure you, Sir, he's completely tame."

"Tame, lame, whatever. He's still baring some pretty damned-serious-looking fangs."

"I know, Sir. It's a sign of affection with Cornelius. I imagine he likes the way you smell. If you'll pat him on the head and say hello when you get out of the car, he'll be fine. I promise you he's well fed and as far as I'm aware, he's never bitten anyone."

Edward came around and opened my door, followed by an extremely excited, overexuberant Cornelius. Much to my relief, within seconds he was nuzzling against my leg instead of chewing it off. In and of itself, that wasn't so bad, but trying to extract his head from my crotch as I attempted to exit the car was completely disconcerting in ways I'd never hoped to imagine.

"No, Cornelius, get out of the car!" Edward yelled, as my overeager companion bounded from between my legs into the empty seat beside me, panting and staring happily in my direction. I was surprised the Rolls could contain his hulking, quivering frame, even with him on his knees. With his slightly gamey breath shooting down the collar of my shirt in short, fitful gasps, I didn't suppose there was much point in trying to make a run for the front door.

Matching him breath for breath, I stared squarely into his animated eyes, attempting to implant an old Sufi proverb in his boisterous brain. *I like you, dude, but not enough to sleep with you. Capiche? And besides, you've got some serious possum breath there, buddy.*

Once I'd tamed the bewildering beast, I was able to get a look at the house, if you can actually call something with four stories a house. Even though the Elizabethan architecture wasn't particularly to my taste, it was still spectacular. With my haplessly devoted, overspirited companion attached to my hip, as the front door opened, we were greeted by a very tall, completely bald vampire in a black suit and rail-thin black tie. I couldn't help but think of Lurch from *The Addams Family*. Undoubtedly, my karma was kicking in from having called Carlos "Uncle Fester" one too many times.

"Welcome to Thornecrown Manor, Sir Nicholas. My name is Thadius."

I tried looking up to, around, and through his shoulders, but my mind couldn't change the channel broadcasting his face. I even tried for a commercial interruption. "It's nice to meet you Thadius, but please call me Adrian."

"Very well…Sir Adrian. May I show you to your room?" *Dry and gravelly. Probably made to eat dirt as a child,* I surmised, without the aid of a crack pipe or British accent.

Cornelius led the pack up the massive double staircase before my eyes could begin to absorb the majesty of the entry hall or Lurch's light-eclipsing shoulders. The place definitely looked like Charles. It smelled like him, too.

At the top of the stairs hung an enormous tapestry. It was so large, in fact, I could make out entire scenes on either side of Thadius' shoulders. While contemplating the possibility of an extra tour of duty inside another seaman's chest, I heard Edward depositing my bags on the landing behind us. *This place is the fucking museum of unnatural history,* I thought. Everything in it was a relic. Frozen fixtures, pasted faces from the past, everything ensconced in gilded gold—I'd obviously been framed. Only

Cornelius seemed alive…*No wonder Charles gave me millions. I'm being paid to be the fucking crypt keeper.*

"In case you were wondering…Sir Adrian," Thadius interrupted, "the house was built in the 1880s by a wealthy shipping magnate, Lord Atterly. Sir Charles acquired the estate from his heirs in 1927. I've been managing the property for…about forty years. I hope you'll find it to your liking. It's very tranquil here."

The ornately cast bronze knob turning in his hand could have only been fashioned for the Less-Than-Jolly Green Giant, I speculated as he opened what I presumed to be the master bedroom doors. If not, Lord Atterly sure as hell had intended to intimidate his guests.

Standing commandingly aside to let me enter, Thadius slowly said, "I couldn't agree with you more…Sir Adrian. The place could sorely use some updating. If I can be of any assistance…"

Isn't that great? Lurch is not only a butler and decorator, he's also a mind reader.

Smiling in a way that can only be understood by the eternally damned, he said, "No offense taken, Sir. I don't care much for television…especially American television."

Cornelius waited outside, even when Edward brought in the luggage. Somewhat puzzled, motioning toward the door, I asked Thadius, "Why isn't he jumping on the bed or something?"

Dry as the Sahara he replied, "I'm not sure, Sir. Maybe it was something you said about him having possum breath." Edward and I both died laughing, sending Cornelius racing up and down the hall. Thadius' stoic expression never changed. I was considering calling off any further search for life on his barren face when I spotted the corners of his mouth turning up in the faintest of smiles. It was painful watching the lump of coal slide down his throat.

The verve in his voice, when he next spoke, was quite a juxtaposition from his earlier undertaker tone. "Cornelius sleeps in the carriage house over the garage. If he ever becomes a pest, you can tell him to go to bed. For the most part, he minds very well. Please make yourself comfortable, Adrian. If there's anything you need, please let me know. I'll have Berta unpack you tomorrow and introduce you to the rest of the staff. May I get you something to drink, Sir?"

"Yes actually, now that you mention it, I think I've unearthed an appetite."

"Red or gin?"

"Let's start with gin. It's been a very long trip."

"Very well. I'll have it brought to the salon. We'll see you downstairs in a few minutes." He walked out the door, saying, "Come, Cornelius."

Not exactly quaint (by any of those standards to which I was accustomed), the salon was the size of a hotel lobby and crowded with overstuffed furniture, way too many portraits, and an Oriental carpet large enough to blanket the better part of Manhattan. From across the room, the fireplace's interior seemed so massive, I imagined it could easily accommodate a toasted s'more the size of a Buick. But, even with its colossal, gargantuan scale, given enough time I thought I might grow used to Thornecrown Manor as long as the place didn't keep trying to grow on me.

Cornelius leapt off one of the divans and cowered behind it when a plump, older woman wearing an apron came in carrying a tray of drinks. I couldn't say I blamed him. She had an all-weathered, no-nonsense air about her, which was supplemented by a rather lethal-looking fly swatter tucked handily at the ready in her apron's holster pocket. *This must be Brunhilda,* I thought.

Peering from behind the sofa, Cornelius warily watched Thadius make the introductions. "This is Hilda. Hilda, this is Sir Nicholas. He's asked that we use his middle name, Adrian."

"Pleased to make your acquaintance, Sir Adrian. My sincerest condolences on the loss of your uncle. May he rest in peace."

"Thank you, Hilda," I said, as she made the sign of the cross and left the room.

I asked Thadius, "How many people are on staff here?"

"Fourteen year round, including myself and Edward. Most are local townspeople who work the grounds or tend the fields. We have stables if you'd like to ride. Sir Charles said you're fond of horses. Eric, the groomer, can fit you with some tack and gear. He's a very pleasant lad. The family's been with us for generations. His father, Eldon, was the farm's general manager for the longest time before retiring a few years back.

"We have about two hundred acres under agricultural production. Most of the food is donated to area food banks. The rest feeds the workers and their families. We keep several hundred head of cattle for the pantries as well. The other eight hundred acres comprise a dedicated wildlife sanctuary. Oh, and lest I forgot, the emus."

"Emus?" I asked.

"It's a long, sad story, I'm afraid. We must have at least a hundred, maybe a hundred and fifty of the nasty things by now. I'm uncertain whether they're multiplying or immigrating. Either way, one of the local farmers invested heavily in them some years back, thinking he'd strike it rich. Obviously his dreams of wealth were nothing more than a birdbrained scheme, otherwise we'd have never inherited the nasty, noisy creatures. Your grandfather, in all his benevolent wisdom, bought the entire herd to save the man's reputation and we've been saddled with them ever since.

"I have heard the steaks can be quite tasty. Should you have a hankering for barbeque, by all means, please speak up. The flocks are called *mobs*, I suspect for very good reasons. The only practical use I've found for them thus far comes from the oil from their skin. Not that you'd care or need it, but, since we're on the subject, it has the unusual ability to dissolve wrinkles as well as age spots. It's part of my daily beauty regimen." Patting his cheeks, he said, "It's how I maintain my healthy, vibrant glow. Aldridge, our ranch foreman, complains every six months about having to rebrand them because the tattoos in their ears keep disappearing."

"I'll be damned. I've never heard of such a thing. I guess I should've eaten an emu steak when I had an appetite." From the corner of my eye, I was watching Cornelius, cautiously, carefully reclaiming his divan while I asked Thadius, "How many rooms are there here at Thornecrown Manor?"

"Honestly, I haven't the foggiest. I've been here forty years and I doubt I've been in half of them. If you have a few weeks, I suppose we could count them. Shall I give you the tour?"

"Lead the way."

After an hour we'd toured maybe half the downstairs, ending up in the kitchen. It was a romantically warm, comfortable place in need of children, laughter, and gossip. *I could provide two out of three, I suppose. My mother would love this room.* Sadly, I hadn't thought of her in what seemed like ages.

"After all the walking, my appetite may have improved somewhat," I said, still thinking about my mother as Thadius unlocked the warmer and poured us both a glass of red.

"There's another one in your bedchamber's study as well. I'll get you keys and show you the phones and security systems tomorrow after we get you settled in."

"That sounds great. Thanks for the tour, Thadius. I think I'll say goodnight and get some rest for now."

Walking up the stairs, I heard Thadius telling Cornelius it was time for bed. The kitchen door slammed loudly shut behind him.

Closing myself in, I wandered through the three rooms that had been Charles' private refuge. The artwork and furnishings were gifts fit for a king, though they only managed to give me fits as I surveyed the lackluster faces and two-dimensional landscapes. Downing the uninspired red in my hand, I set the glass on a table and fell backward onto the massive four-poster bed. Down, down, and downier I sank into the white cocoon of sheathed feathers until only my extremities remained exposed. I'd survived nearly drowning at sea and I'd be damned if I was going to go the same way in bed. Finding a much less effusive sofa in the next room, I tried getting some sleep.

Visions of my mother and an acute longing for chrome and glass kept me awake. The house was morbidly quiet as I paced the floor followed by the eyes of what I assumed to be mostly dead and assuredly overdressed ancestors watching my every move from mahogany-paneled perches. Opening the veranda doors to the more comfortably familiar, haunting sounds of the night, I spotted the huge wingspan of a giant owl blotting out the stars in a lazy spiral until it came to rest on a far ledge of the roof, its song full of queries to which I had no answers. Finding my own cups empty, it flew away in search of a livelier, more informative companion. I laughed, thinking, *Fine, be that way. See if I give a rat's ass next time you need a friend.*

Back inside I sat at the desk scribbling a note to call a decorator while staring at the myriad buttons on the phone, wondering if a call downstairs would be long distance. A bottle of gin was calling my name and I intended to answer whether toll charges applied or not.

With nothing but mixed signals and a frustrated finger to show for my efforts, I finally gave up and sought relief on foot. Hilda must have heard me rattling around in the kitchen. She came in, asking, "May I help you, Sir?"

"Yes, thank you. Would you be a lamb and find me a bottle of gin, some tonic, a bucket of ice, some limes, and a great big glass? I can't seem to sleep. Another cocktail or six might be just what the doctor ordered."

"Would you like me to bring it up to your room, Sir?"

"That's very sweet of you to offer, Hilda, but I think I need to learn my way around."

"As you wish, Sir. Let me show you the pantry. We keep most everything in here."

"No fucking shit!" I exclaimed, hoping I'd said it silently. The pantry was enormous. I'd only thought I was rich before. Now I knew I was truly loaded. The walls were lined with boxes, bags, sacks, and bins of almost everything imaginable. The far end was filled with the contents of a well-stocked liquor store. I was in heaven. On the way out, clutching bottles in either hand, I noticed an entire section of assorted foils and Ziploc bags. We were prepared to withstand a long, hard, nuclear winter. And as long as the ice wasn't yellow, I thought I might have actually found a home at last.

"This is the ice fridge. Let me get you a bucket and a tumbler," she said. *Please, dear God, don't tell me the staff reads minds as well...* While she was getting the glassware, she nodded toward the Sub-Zero and said, "Limes are in the left keeper, Sir."

I handed her a couple that she expertly wielded into wedges with enough gusto and precision to embarrass Benihana's best. "Thanks for your help, Hilda. I think I'll fix myself a toddy and wander around a bit. Good night."

"Good night, Sir. If there's anything else you'll be requiring, my number on the telly is star twenty-nine. I'll be here 'til seven when Berta comes."

I wandered the second floor until nearly daybreak. It was easily as depressing as the lower floor, only the carpets were smaller. I wasn't sure whether I needed a decorator or an exorcist. The place had to be more haunted than my own moribund dreams.

Berta came in the back door as I was contemplating another tour of beauty on the third floor. The smell of pleasant perfume and hellaciously strong, black coffee drew me away from the affronting lines of overcarved furniture and spying eyes.

Once we had dispensed with introductions and she'd poured me a cup of Joe, Berta politely showed me the back door. Since the prognosis for sleep was growing dimmer as the morning dawned and I was still on Australian time with a handsome seaman on my mind, I took the hint and went for a walkabout. Passing through the portico underneath Cornelius' room, I was almost certain I could hear him snoring. *Thank god he sleeps all day. At least the possums can get some rest, even if I can't.* Obviously I'd awakened on the wrong side of the featherbed and was missing Carlos' bubbly-butted personality when I caught an unmistakable whiff of horseshit.

The coffee had begun working its magic by the time I reached the stables. The structure itself was much too elegant to be called a barn. Briefly, I flashed back to the polo matches in Dallas, but quickly let that train of thought roll down the tracks as I ducked inside, out of the morning's glare. It took a couple of seconds for my eyes to adjust to the softer light of the stables. Once I'd regained my focus, I saw, standing before me brushing a beautiful Arabian, an even more beautiful Brit. Eric looked up as I walked in with the coffee cup to my lips. In about ten seconds, from what I'd seen so far, I was going to need a much larger mug if there was any hope of masking my unexpected and rapidly growing delight.

Ironically he stopped what he was doing about the same time my heart failed. I was considering asking if he knew how to perform CPR when he patted the pony's ass and came at me armed with a smile warm enough to melt the sun and everything in its orbit, including my knees.

"Hello. My name is Eric, Eric Forsythe. You must be Sir Nicholas." *No, I'm butter and you're toast if you keep smiling like that big fella.* "We heard you were coming in from Down Under. It was such a shock when we heard the news about Sir Charles. I still can't quite believe he's gone. He was something of a legend in these parts."

He wiped his hand against his overalls and thrust it in my direction. "It's nice to make your acquaintance, Sir." I took his hand as both our smiles and eyes locked together in some like-minded, kindred terminus of understanding. I think he may have even been blushing a bit. I know his heart was racing. I could hear it thumping like a wild stallion's inside his chest.

"Eric, it's lovely to meet you. But would you please do us a secret favor and call me Adrian? I actually hate it when people call me *Sir* anything, and especially, Sir Nicholas."

He grinned like the Cheshire cat, or Donny Osmond. (They both have so many teeth—I'm always confusing the two.) "I think I can do that, Adrian. Would you like to meet some ponies?"

Why not? I've already met one stud. Two cups…I was definitely going to need two cups of coffee, I muttered silently, trailing awkwardly, stiff-leggedly along behind him to meet his mare.

"This is Sadie. Isn't she a beauty?"

"Incredible," I replied, only I wasn't referring to the horse. My comment may have been a bit too transparent because I was certain he was flushing again and I could visibly see the rhythmic blue bulge of the artery pulsing, teasing along the side of his neck.

I was taking a sip of coffee when he asked, "Do you like to ride? I'd be glad to saddle up the boys and take you out sometime."

I was trying desperately not to choke or laugh while sporting that much wood and a hot mouthful of coffee at the same time. Somehow, I strongly suspected I was going to like mornings much, much more than the ghostly, owl-eyed evenings at Thornecrown Manor.

"That sounds perfectly splendid, Mr. Forsythe. Maybe tomorrow morning, say around seven? I confess, I'm not much for the afternoon heat."

We smiled and clasped each other's hand. There was no need to invade each other's inner diaries. We seemed clearly to be on the same page.

"Damn! Somebody shoot me!" I exclaimed while walking away shaking my head. I hadn't realized I'd said it out loud until a wrinkly-faced gardener stopped midprune, casting a suspicious, squinty-eyed glance in my direction.

It felt good to be out of my mind for a change. Two months at sea still hadn't completely cleared my senses of the undertow from Down Below. That place certainly had a knack for sucking the life out of a person, one way or another. That's probably why Carlos chose the oceans. Even in their sorry state, they still had more life in them than The Havens.

To say a place is teeming with half-life is one thing, but Thornecrown had chosen the nuclear option in terms of those secret compartments and hidden passageways that are standard fare for creaky old mansions. "Extra-whitening if they have it," I'd yelled over my shoulder at Berta in the kitchen while making the corner into the hallway. Three seconds later I would have missed the fresh flowers and framed photos on the table sliding back into place as Thadius disappeared down the staircase.

Perfectly deceptive, the table's legs seemed to touch the ground, but there were no scuffmarks of any kind. I'd been trained to look down first. The table was attached to the wall, not the floor as it appeared to the eye. It had a very solid feel when I knocked on it.

"Yes, Quaker Oats and molasses, I'm making treats for the horses," I yelled toward the kitchen while waiting for someone to answer the wall. Five seconds later I heard a clicking sound and the entire panel, table and all, starting sliding stage left to reveal a very startled, but relieved, Thadius.

"Oh good, it's you, Sir. For a moment I thought we had rats, and I absolutely despise the miserable things. Since you're here, if you'll follow me, I'll introduce you to the rest of the staff. They're anxious to meet you. I thought you were still upstairs resting."

"I wish that were true, but I'm afraid not. I've been milling around all morning. What is this place?"

"Originally, it was a root cellar and basement storage when Lord Atterly constructed the house. It's been expanded any number of times since

Sir Charles purchased the property. If you like technology, I'm sure you'll find it fascinating."

Next to the word "Prince," "technology" has to be my least favorite term. If I hadn't been so curious, I'd have turned around and gone back to the stables.

Descending a long staircase, we came to a landing that was indeed a dimly-lit root cellar and storage space for the overstuffed overflow from upstairs. As we crossed the room, the wall in front of us opened automatically on our approach. Inside, gleaming light revealed a starkly white, modern interior. Down another short flight of stairs and we were standing in a futuristic looking command-and-control center with banks of computers and monitors lining the walls.

A strikingly handsome vampire sat behind a desk containing a large console and four or five small television screens in front of him. I wondered why I hadn't noticed the launching pads in the garden earlier…

When we approached, he stood and firmly grasped my hand. "Ah, Sir Nicholas. It's a pleasure to finally meet you. My name is Ambrose. I'm head of Dorian security. Glad to see you made it in one piece. It was looking a little touch-and-go there for a while. Please, if you would, let me show you around."

"Thank you, Ambrose. I wasn't too sure about it myself, but I'm here now and no worse for the wear, although I am a much stronger swimmer. But if you'd don't mind, I'd prefer you call me Adrian."

"Certainly, Sir. If you'll follow me."

Anyone would have been impressed. Personally, I was astounded. It was an entire complex, easily larger than the house above it. *What's up is down,* I reminded myself as we walked down the windowless hall past a full-size gymnasium, tennis and racquetball courts, Olympic half-pool, and a large, comfortable lounge with billiard tables and a bar at one end where several people sat talking over drinks. Off to one side was a substantial library that looked like it belonged upstairs with its wood paneling, soft lighting, and plump upholstery.

Ambrose was kind enough to show me his own quarters. *Even though he had no dragon, I'd certainly lived in worse places.* Everything was black leather, steel or chrome, and glass or acrylic. I couldn't help myself. "Ambrose, can I move in with you? I'll gladly pay half the rent!"

Once they both quit laughing, Thadius said, "I don't think that will be necessary, Sir. When we get back upstairs, we'll call Penelope, the decorator. Besides, there's a *no pets* policy downstairs and somehow I think they'd notice if you tried sneaking in a dragon."

Thadius, you fucker, quit reading my mind. "Alright, you two, Ambrose said, "let's save the fisticuffs for the gym. Sir, there's one other thing I'd like to show you if you have time."

"Certainly, lead the way." I could sense Thadius smirking behind my back as we made our way down the hall toward a very heavy-looking steel door. Sliding open, its sound reminded me of the old *Star Trek* television series. But the armory inside was anything other than a movie set. The weapons lining the walls sure as hell didn't appear to be stage props either, although some of the more advanced munitions looked as if they had been conceived of by George Lucas and company for another *Star Wars* production.

Passing through the door at the far end of the room, I couldn't have been less prepared. Swimming pools and libraries in a basement may be unusual, but not unheard of. This was something of an entirely different nature altogether. Dozens of people hovering about stopped whatever they were doing when we joined them in the twenty-second century.

Ambrose looked at the now-frozen room and said, "As you were." I'd never been on a military base and didn't even own a pair of combat boots, but I'd seen enough films to know a military command center when I saw one. The only difference was this one appeared to be very much real and several decades ahead of my comprehension.

"We call this the War Room," Ambrose said to my gaping mouth and unbelieving eyes. *I'm sure you do. I should have bought a season pass to The Havens when I had the chance. Jesus fucking Christ!* I saw no need to say it out loud since everyone was so fond of reading my mind.

"From here, we monitor events around the globe, keep tabs on the other Houses, and do a little old-fashioned spying on governments and multi-nationals on an as-needed basis, which is most of the time. It's also how we communicate with The Havens. Almost everything that happens here is directly communicated to them in real time via a band of satellites ringing the planet."

I had to ask, "I assume there's a mute and a pause button somewhere?"

He laughed lightly, along with several others. "Of course, we even have the capacity to transmit false data and images to any network in the world. Obviously, we try to keep that sort of thing to a minimum, otherwise…"

I added, "everything would start to look and sound like FOX News." They all thought that was funny until Ambrose glared at some fellow, who quickly bent his head, turned, and walked briskly out of the room.

"Sorry, Sir," Ambrose said. "That was Garrett. When he actually works, he's one of the world's best cryptologists. On his nights off you can catch his lounge act in the bar at seven."

In my peripheral vision, I noticed a herd of holographic deer running through a holographic forest. I was about to ask when Ambrose offered an explanation. "This is where we monitor all movement on the estate. If it moves or gives off a heat signal, we pick it up here. The reason you saw the deer is because of the multiple large signals moving quickly together. The computer would filter out a swarm of insects. Anything much larger, and we get a live feed. Lack of preparedness is not something we're fond of here at Thornecrown."

"Is the house upstairs monitored?"

"No, Sir. There's no point. We're surrounded by a thousand acres and nothing would stand a chance of getting anywhere near the house without us knowing it. All entrances and exits are closely monitored on the grounds and here in the tunnels as well."

"Tunnels?"

"Yes, Sir. We have an extensive system of tunnels below the entire estate. If we were to be assaulted, we could come at the threat from any point underneath. I understand you've been through Nadir training. I know I'm not a prince, but maybe you could show me some moves in the gym someday. I've always been curious…"

Once I'd sufficiently cringed, I shrugged in agreement. No one had bothered to tell me Nadir training was a state secret reserved for princes.

"Some of the tunnels serve transport needs for men and material. We can come and go without being seen by humans on the estate. I'll have someone give you a tour later." He stepped over to another table and swiped his hand in the air. Images began jumping and swirling in a cloudy haze. "This is where we monitor vampiric movement. The Havens has a database of every vampire known to exist. It's not infallible, but the computer would instantly recognize anyone not belonging here. We'd assess the threat level and take appropriate action if some sort of treaty violation were to occur."

"If there's a treaty, then why…? *Never mind, forget I asked. An ounce of deterrence is worth more than a pounding from bloodsuckers.*

Later, back upstairs, as I sat with my head pounding in Thadius' spartan office, he tried to hand me a large ring of keys. Uncertain if the seismic activity was being picked up downstairs, I banged my head on his desk in protest nevertheless.

"Sir Charles didn't like keys either, but you may actually want this one. It's for the Bayswater flat in London. James is usually there most of…"

"I didn't know we had a flat in London?"

"Three floors, actually. We constructed the building, of course. It's across the street from Hyde Park. Really lovely views of Kensington Gardens. I'm almost certain you'll like it."

"That reminds me, Thadius, you said we'd call the decorator. I'm drowning in goose feathers upstairs, and, while we're at it, is there a room downstairs I might use for a study?"

He was already scribbling a number when suddenly his face lit up like Christmas. "Sir, I think I have the perfect room for you." He wasn't asking, or waiting for, me to follow. He knew exactly where he was going. From the darkened hallway he inquired, "So what do you think? I know it gets the morning sun, but you're an early riser…"

"That I am, Thadius. That I am. These windows are to die for! Can we have the furniture and drapes removed before the decorator comes?"

"Certainly, Sir, and I couldn't agree with you more regarding the windows. Speaking of death, don't forget the solicitor will be coming around this evening at seven.

"I took the liberty of putting a list of numbers on your desk upstairs with instructions on how to use the phones. There's also a cell phone and charger, but you must never call The Havens from anywhere except downstairs on a secure line."

I thanked him and slothed my way upstairs to change. After freshening up, I went to the desk and found the items he'd mentioned were all laid out. There was also something he hadn't mentioned, a luxury-car catalogue. I picked it up and took it downstairs.

Thadius came in with two glasses of red and saw the catalogue in my hand. Offering me one of the glasses, he smiled. "I see you found my little surprise. Ambrose and I were talking after your swimming lesson and agreed it might be better if you had a new car for security reasons. Nearly anyone in town would instantly recognize one of ours. I'm sure the media frenzy will die down soon enough, but until then, we can't be too careful."

The two of us were still talking when the ancient, decrepit solicitor came round, wheeling in stacks of papers and an oxygen tank. Time stood still until his nearly wooden carcass was seated. Whereby…he slowly, painstakingly proceeded, ad nauseam, to explain the will, assets, and other minutia of the estate until I was virtually coma-toasted after the fifth or sixth drink. Remarkably, possibly miraculously, two-plus hours later, he left wheezing, but breathing.

Having obeyed Charles' first commandment, it was truly a testament to my own internal fortitude, which from the smell of things, the poor man himself had abandoned long ago. If the Grim Reaper ever went blind and became the Grim Groper, I had little doubt he'd be able to find the elderly anyway.

Closing the door on the dear, nearly departed attorney, I heard Grandvamp's clock chiming in the salon. It was time for my Great Tunnels of England tour and down the rabbit hole I slipped. This time Ambrose wasn't there. It was Superman, sans the cape. I swear to God, the guy looked identical to Christopher Reeve. When he introduced himself as Clark, it hit me squarely in the funny bone. With an embarrassing degree of difficulty, I finally managed to stop laughing and apologized.

"I get that reaction a lot, Sir. When I'm in public, I usually make up a name."

"I would too, if I were you."

"You're here for the tour, right? Let me get Chad up here to show you around."

In a few minutes a smallish young boy walked into the room. His innocent face didn't appear to be a day over seventeen. After introductions, while walking down the hall, I asked, "Chad, are you sure you're old enough to drive?"

He smiled and said, "It should be okay, Sir. I've had my learner's permit for over twenty years. As long as you've got a real license we should be fine." I suspected Chad and I were going to get on famously.

The garage was full of vehicles, everything from sedans to large commercial trucks. The walls were also lined with another arsenal of weapons. Chad was heading toward a Land Rover, which didn't exactly float my boat. Pointing to an open Jeep, I asked if we could take it instead. Rovers, at least in my experience, were nothing more than four-wheel-drive hearses.

The overhead door rumbled open and we drove into a well-lit tunnel encased in concrete.

He drove very fast, the same way he walked. I was considering asking to see the actual learner's permit when he handed me his wallet, laughing. "I was converted at eighteen, Sir. I'll be forty-four next week. I look kind of young, don't I, Sir? My husband, Thomas, calls me Claudia—you know, from *Interview with the Vampire*."

We kept speeding through intersections, crisscrossing other tunnels in a near blur. I was contemplating whether it could legally be called vehicular manslaughter if Chad mowed down a vampire in one of the crosswalks when, mercifully, we slowed and pulled onto a ramp. I could smell unconditioned air for the first time since we'd left as the armed guard waved us through. My neck nearly snapped backward as I realized how drop-dead gorgeous the guy was when we pulled past.

I was in the process of opening my mouth to make a complete fool of myself when Chad saved me the trouble. "Thank you, Sir. He's still as handsome as the night we met in London twenty-five years ago when Thadius introduced us. Thomas and I have been together ever since."

Driving out of a large metal warehouse, we pulled onto the main road. After touring the perimeter of the grounds for almost an hour, we stopped in front of another warehouse with a large, cheerful painted sign over the door. *Thornecrown Farms* sounded much nicer than *Death Merchants Wholesale* I thought as we drove inside.

CHAPTER TWENTY-ONE

Seven o'clock the next morning found me heading out the kitchen door toward the stables. I hadn't worn boots in ages and they felt like old friends on my feet as I tromped through the dewy grass on the way to make new ones. I'd gathered my balls and courage, the blue ones for Eric, the sticky ones for the horses, as I walked through the barn door. Thus far, first or second dates had always made me slightly nervous and nearly everyone else dead. I was hoping to turn over a new leaf rather than shovelfuls of the same old fresh earth for a change...

Eric was waiting with a heart-melting super-nova smile plastered all over his face. He was wearing tight jeans and a sleeveless red-checkered shirt; he must, I imagined, drive the locals wild in that outfit. He was certainly driving me to distraction and I hadn't even started my engine. "Good morning, Adrian," he blushed in that *aw shucks* kind of way. I didn't know if there was such a thing as choking to death on a beefcake sandwich, but I was sure as hell willing to give it the old college try.

"How are you this morning, Eric? I brought treats for everyone."

He eyed my big sticky balls and laughed. "They'll love you for that, especially Alexander here. He'll eat anything and everything. Napoleon is kind of finicky." Within seconds all the horses were eating out of my gooey hands and that settled that. *Now if it could only be that easy with their groomer, I thought.*

After I hosed the molasses off my hands, we mounted and rode out to the fields. Eric took Napoleon into a full run. Easily enough, Alexander and I were able to keep up with them. He was an exquisitely beautiful and powerful animal. After a teeth-rattling ride, we slowed to survey the crops and cattle. I even got a gander at the emus. When I commented about what ugly, noisy creatures they were and how with their giant inquisitive eyes, I could see the familial resemblance to roaming bands of reporters desperately trying to scratch out a story, Eric laughed and explained how the herd was called a *mob*. He could tell me things I already knew anytime he liked. I just loved hearing the sound of his voice speaking to my newly discovered soul.

The less-harried ride through the woods on our way back was a shady breath of fresh air until my thoughts turned to Dallas, polo ponies, and tears. We were perfectly timed and I'd just fallen in single file behind Eric's strong shoulders when he said, "Come on, I want to show you something." Luckily he didn't turn around as he goaded Napoleon into a slow trot. We cut across a shallow stream and took a well-worn path along the creek's bank until we encountered a stepped waterfall cascading into a natural pool. It was every boy's wet, dreamy place of wonders untold, blood oaths, and spit-bound secrets. I tried washing as many of them from my face as I could while Alexander drank from the spring-fed creek.

"I've been coming here since I was a boy. This is one of my favorite places," Eric whispered. "Sometimes I come here to think, or go swimming, or just forget about the world. I keep a bottle stashed over there," he said, pointing to an outcropping of rocks, "in case you're ever thirsty."

"If that's an invitation, I accept. I think I could fall in love here, Eric, with this place."

When I turned in his direction, several shades of crimson were breaking out all over his brightly flushing face. Avoiding my gaze, his head bent low studying the tip of his boot drawing wavering lines in the sand.

Once we'd both recovered, he looked at me again. "My rock is your rock, and it makes one hell of a diving board too, mate. I'd warn you to be careful in the deep end, but the TV says you're a really good swimmer."

Alexander turned toward me, as if asking, "You're not really going to let him get away with that are you?" I couldn't. I just couldn't. I wanted to kiss him desperately, but I couldn't bring myself to do it. I wasn't even certain why. I knew he wanted me too. I could see the hungry anticipation in his eyes and smell the nervous desire clinging like perspiration to his skin.

While putting my foot in the stirrup and mounting the horse, I tried communicating how much I wanted him with my eyes, but he seemed to be the only one at Thornecrown who wasn't psychic. Mystified, he looked hurt and disappointed. I was, too. "Thanks for showing me around, Eric. This place is magical and incredibly beautiful, but I'm afraid I have business to attend to this morning. I've got to get back to the house."

Riding toward the stables in silence, I knew I'd blown it. I would regret not kissing him then and there while I'd had the chance for the rest of our lives. I already did.

Handing him Alexander's reins and stroking the horse's head, I said, "Thank you both for a lovely morning. I hope we can do it again soon." His smile was not nearly as broad when he turned and walked away with the horse. Neither was mine, but for the most part, we were both still alive. It was at least a start.

Two chairs and a small writing desk were the only pieces of furniture remaining in my new study. Fortunately, Thadius' allergy to sunlight had prevented him from removing the drapes over the two-story, mullioned, bay window. It was just as well. I'd had more than enough vitamin D for one day. Even with the curtains closed I could still see Pretty Boy's face in the darkened room. Randolph Howard Theis III, consummate asshole, arrogant prick—I'd killed him simply for treating me like a once-prized toy that had lost its luster. I couldn't, I wouldn't let that happen to Eric.

My decorative mood had completely soured by the time I poured a glass of red and sank into bed with the car catalogue. Spitting nails and feathers both, I couldn't make a decision about either the car or Eric. In my struggles with my conscience and molted geese remnants I did manage to nod off for a few hours until my new cell phone rang for the first time.

It was Vanessa and she sounded chipper enough for someone calling from the bowels of hell. "How are you, handsome?"

"In every way imaginable, of course." I didn't have any tonic left and the limes were gone, so I was forced to take everything literally.

She laughed at my stupid joke while I gargled with gin. "Why don't you call down tonight when rates are cheaper? We can talk then. Ziegfried is saying hello."

"Tell him hi. Is everything okay in Sydney?"

"Everything's fine. We'll talk tonight. Bye."

I thought it was weird, but maybe it was easier than sending encrypted messages from satellites. I was in the bathroom washing my face when the landline started ringing. My recent surge in the polls was refreshing and annoying at the same time as I groped for a towel, the receiver, and another swig of Bombay Sapphire. It was blue, it matched my mood, and it was 100-percent proof that Listerine isn't the only way to fight germs or bad breath. I'd never touched the stuff, yet I hadn't been sick in years and couldn't even pronounce gingivitis.

I could however pronounce salvation, and it was mine. The decorator was on the line; she had an appointment in Kent the next day and was wondering if I'd be available. "God yes! I'm a desperate man. Please come. I don't care if it's midnight." I told her to bring, "samples, lots of samples, and a firm mattress if you happen to have one." She was still laughing as she hung up the phone. Obviously, the bitch had no idea how gravely dire my circumstances were. I wasn't completely certain when molting season was in England, but winter was coming and I could hardly imagine trying to survive another one.

Feeling nostalgic and hopeful after talking to Vanessa and the decorator, I decided to call Theo in Dallas. We hadn't spoken in two months and he was probably thinking I was dead. Half a ring later, he answered. Astounded, I said, "Hey, big daddy. That was fast. I don't think you've ever picked up on the first ring. Are you out of weed or did your buzz saw break?"

"Hey, fuck wad! How are you, man? I thought you were Caroline. We're supposed to hang out tonight and watch some chick flick. I voted for *Transformers,* but she's being a bitch. It's all your fault. You haven't been around to keep her and Ad'ragon company. Any idea when you're coming home? He's eaten like two or three puppies and we're starting to get fleas and shit."

"I miss you too, asshole. I should be back in the next week or two. I'll let you know. Can you pick me up at DFW?"

"You know my piece of shit car would be lucky to make it to Love Field."

"You can take my Caddie."

"I have been," he laughed nervously. "It was just sitting there anyway. That reminds me, it's almost out of gas. Can you send some money?"

"No, but, Theo, there is something I want to talk to you about." The lie I was about to tell had actually just dawned on me. "I've met a girl, and I think I might propose."

"You've got to be shitting me!"

"No, I'm not shitting you. I'm deadly serious and she's seriously hot. The only problem is she doesn't like the States. We've talked about it and she won't even think about leaving Sydney. So, if I do pop the question do you think you might want to buy the loft?"

"Dude, I probably couldn't come up with enough scratch to buy the teepee. Maybe Caroline will buy it for me. She's a trust-fund babe."

"Excellent idea. I like a man who thinks with his dick. Alright, my brother, I have to go now. I'll see you soon. Give Caroline a big kiss for me."

He was saying something about tongues when I clicked off the line.

I'd been thumbing through the car catalogue while we were on the phone. Page forty-six, there it was right in front of me. It looked pricey, I'd probably have to spend a whole month's allowance to pay for it, but it was British, an Aston Martin DB9 Coupe, Limited Edition Carbon Black. I'd never fallen in love twice in one day.

Flying around the corner with the magazine in hand, I nearly ran into Thadius.

"Whoa there, young Sir. Where's the fire?"

"I found the car I want. Look, this one," I said, pointing at the page as if he were about to go blind and I needed to hurry before his eyesight failed completely.

He whistled and raised his eyebrows. "Excellent choice. Why not get two?" From the look on his face, for a second or two I thought he might be serious. "I'll call London tomorrow and see if we can get one sent out. You do want the black, correct?"

I nodded vigorously in the affirmative. Cornelius had been quietly giving me lessons.

Thadius walked away thinking it was good to have some life in the old place for a change. It had been way too quiet for decades...He wasn't the only one who could read minds.

Full of manic energy, I made a trip down to the Bat Cave, which is what I'd decided to call it. The place looked like Wayne Manor anyway. It seemed only fitting.

Ambrose was back at the front desk. I asked him if he'd call Chad for me. We were going to finish the underground portion of our tunnel tour on foot. He smiled and dialed. Chad was there in a flash, looking forever young.

In the garage walking toward an exit, he asked, "Fast or slow?"

"Fast."

He opened the door and said, "Follow me, Sir."

I had no choice. He'd already vanished. I could only follow in the wake of his scent. Finally he stopped about midway to let me catch up.

"My God, how can you move that fast, Chad?"

"I ran track in high school," he smirked. "I wanted to show you one of the substations. There's another one like it on the other side of the property. We keep personnel at these posts 24/7 in case of emergencies."

Inside, we met the sentries. The place looked like an ordinary apartment, except for the grenade launchers and particle accelerators hanging on the walls in place of art. I assumed they did most of their shopping at Battlestore Galactica, but considering I was losing the war with duckless feathers, I refrained from commenting.

After introductions and a brief tour, we excused ourselves and went back into the tunnel. Before Chad could ask, I said, "Don't even think about it fucker, we're walking."

On the way back to the Bat Cave he explained why we're faster than humans, which was one story I hadn't heard. I was fascinated to learn that once conversion begins, our bones and muscles strengthen, but slowly become lighter. Our organs are less taxed by not consuming food. The blood we drink is full of compounded minerals and pure elements that act like super vitamins loaded with antioxidants. I thought, *Turbo charged V-8. I can see the TV commercial.* "How red is your red, neighbor? Well, that's not red enough!"

"The Havens' scientists figured out years ago," he continued, "how and why we're anatomically different than humans. Over time we lose a great deal of density, but very little mass. Our bodies become less solid and more gas which is why mirrors are such a pain in the ass." *Now you're preaching to the choir, buddy.* "When I was human, I weighed about one hundred and thirty. Today I'm the same size but I only weigh ninety pounds. I bet you dropped a lot of weight in the first couple of years, too?"

"I never understood why, but you're absolutely right. I weighed one seventy then. Now I weigh one thirty and my body, if anything, is better than ever." I read his dirty, flattering mind and blew it at the same time by quipping, "Thanks. You're not so bad yourself, Claudia."

Photon beams may be hazardous to one's health, but the look Chad shot me was infinitely more lethal. I only hoped it wouldn't be everlasting. "The reason I'm faster than you, *Sir,* is because I'm lighter and smaller and I converted at an earlier age. Since I wasn't a *child...*"

Mentally I pleaded forgiveness. *Okay, I'm sorry Chad! Enough with the emphasis already.*

"...my bones and muscles were dense and developed enough, but not as dense or developed as yours. I was also converted twenty years before you, so my atomic structure is composed of more gasses than yours. Those gasses have less wind resistance than the solids that still comprise more of your body at this point."

"So I'll keep changing," I asked, "but I'll probably never be as light or fast as you? Pardon the pun, but if we get more gaseous as we age, could the legends be true? Do you think some of the oldest vampires really could turn into vapor and rematerialize in solid form?"

"I've read the legends, too. I don't know anyone who's ever seen it happen, but, theoretically, I don't see why it wouldn't be possible."

We were back at the Bat Cave and I thanked him for another round of show and tell while fervently vowing to never call him Claudia again. It seemed I'd piqued his indignation only slightly less than he'd stoked my own curiosity about our physiology. In the dual spirits of forgiveness and scientific discovery, I asked if he and Thomas would care to come upstairs for dinner one evening soon.

"We'd be delighted to, Sir," he responded without a hint of emphasis. "We'll have to come through the front door though. No one from the basement is allowed to use the stairs. We wouldn't want the staff seeing people walking through walls." Although it sounded a bit racist, he did have a point. With all the dead ancestors hanging around upstairs, I wasn't completely convinced anyone would've noticed in the first place, but if he wanted to use the front door, it was fine by me.

Lying to most of my friends back in the States about my upcoming nuptials to Vanessa, I'd finished the handwritten notes that needed to be postmarked from Sydney. Dialing the phone to break the news and heart of my nearly betrothed, I realized I'd forgotten to call The Havens earlier. Neither the spirit nor the flesh was willing to trudge back down to the Bat Cave. Ambrose ran interference while I tackled a sack of some poor goose's life's work and fell asleep dreaming of misty vampires and boys who like horses.

Upon waking, I thought I'd been dreaming of Eric, which was understandable since there was more blood in my dick than in my brain. Sometimes our dreams have a funny way of duping us into believing what we want instead of seeing what's actually there. Even fully awake, it can be difficult knowing the difference.

Trying to fall back asleep with less and less success, I finally succumbed to consciousness and a bath, shedding the fuzzy build-up of dark dreams and duck lint before the decorator arrived at five.

She was right on time, of course. The English tend be annoyingly punctual, a decidedly non-American habit. Penelope Atkins was literally bubbling with timely British enthusiasm so, considering I hadn't had a cocktail yet, Berta's double gin may have inadvertently saved the woman's life. Even after removing dozens upon dozens of fabric samples from her trunk, there still wasn't enough room to fit Chatty Cathy inside.

I was contemplating asking Edward to bring the Rolls around front when she exclaimed, "Oh my heavens! What a wonderful room! Look at these ceilings. And that window! I've been out to the estate several times, but I've never seen this room. The proportions are absolutely perfect."

"Thank you. That's why I chose it. I like the scale. If you don't mind, Penelope, I'm going to look at furniture catalogues while you measure and sketch." Flipping through the pages I happened upon a kidney-shaped desk with a lacquered top of highly glossed bird's-eye maple. The legs were chromed elephant heads with sharply pointed tusks and long trunks tapering gracefully to the floor before curving back up for good luck.

"That was easier than I expected. I found a desk I like, which gives me another idea. Come look at this. Since the legs are chrome, can you get someone to silver leaf the picture frame moldings and veneer the inset panels in the same maple as the desk?"

"God, Adrian, that's an exquisite idea!" *And to think I was having trouble being referred to as a Prince...* "The walls would look striking as a backdrop. I would've never thought of it. I don't suppose you need a job, do you?"

"Thanks, but I'm pretty well set for the time being. Now if we can find some fabric for the draperies...Honestly, I've never cared much for curtains, but these windows are screaming for some sort of treatment."

"So is my husband," she replied without a hint of sarcasm. "Why don't you come to London when you get back from your trip? With your gorgeous good looks and my biggest purse, we could nick some really nice art." We were on our third cocktail and I was beginning to like her much better in spite of her questionable ethics or ability to accessorize.

"Thanks, Penelope, it sounds like a completely captivating adventure. Unfortunately, I've recently met our antiquarian solicitor and we'd be long dead before making bail, assuming he could somehow find the jail."

Thadius was in his office when I popped in to tell him, thanks to Penelope, we'd never pay retail again. I also wanted to know about the car. For someone who'd been so nonplussed a few days ago, now I could hardly wait. He motioned me to a chair.

"You must have stayed up all night picking that particular model in Cobalt Black. The biggest dealer in the country can't get his hands on one for three months."

I would've cried, but, since I hadn't had dinner yet, I didn't feel I could spare the tears. Instead I slumped my shoulders and tried looking as dejected as possible.

"Sir, please stop doing that. You look like someone's just run over your puppy. I've phoned a friend and he persuaded them to bump some poor, soon-to-be-disappointed soul down the list. The car will be here tomorrow afternoon. Are we happy now?"

I jumped out of the chair and bounded around the desk intent on giving him a big hug. He stopped me cold. "I know you haven't fed tonight, young Sir. My obligations to the House of Dorius may be plentiful, but most certainly do not include breastfeeding its heirs."

"That's fine, Thadius, but don't even think about asking to borrow my car if you're ever lucky enough to have a date again. And remember when you're really, really old a few short years from now, I'll be the one picking your room in The Havens. I'm sure they'll have something left with a nice ocean view.

"Speaking of hot dates, I ran into Thomas and Chad downstairs. I invited them up for dinner one evening soon. I hope you'll join us. Chad told me you're the one who introduced them. Among your many other talents, I had no idea you were a matchmaker, too."

"I'm not, and, yes, I'd love to join you for dinner. If you swear to keep your fangs sheathed, I'll tell you how that *situation* transpired."

"Consider them corked. Am I going to need a cocktail for this?"

He buzzed Hilda for drinks and launched into his story. "It must have been twenty-five, thirty years ago. Several of us, including Thomas, were in London letting off a little steam for the night. We'd gone to one of our favorite haunts and the place was packed. It must've been the seventies because all I remember was disco music and bell-bottoms. There was this young boy there, too young to be there, and he kept looking at me from across the room. I was ignoring him because, as you've probably surmised by now, I don't play for your team."

Obviously Hilda must have been as psychic as everyone else at Thornecrown. She brought the whole bottle and a bucket of ice. I poured while Thadius talked. "Anyway, most of the guys had already picked up their first date or two and I was enjoying watching them plying their wares. Once they'd exhausted the A's, B's, and most of the type O's, we decided to move on before someone reported us to the Red Cross.

"I forget the name, but we'd only been at the next watering hole for minutes when I spotted the boy again. His nostrils were slightly flared and he kept staring. There were a couple of younger good-looking B negatives there, which are relatively rare, and Thomas didn't seem to notice them at all. He only had eyes for the famished little waif, although none of us knew it at the time.

"There was a lovely young lass bartending and we needed another round anyway. I offered to fetch the drinks and while I was busy persuading her that Yul Brynner really was her type, the young boy approached me at the bar. He'd been wanting to meet Thomas all evening, but was too shy to approach him of his own accord.

"Back at the table, we teased and taunted Thomas until he and the boy left together. I genuinely thought he'd have a snack and send the little Keebler Elf merrily on his way. No one at the estate heard from Thomas for over a week. We'd begun to think he'd died of graham-cracker poisoning by the time he returned. Three months later, Charles gave his permission for Thomas to convert Chad and they've been together, for better or worse, ever since."

As Thadius was finishing his story, I remembered I hadn't called The Havens. It still struck me as odd to go down to the Bat Cave and find Superman sitting at the reception desk. When he saw me on the stairs his lips were saying, "Good evening, Sir." His mind had an entirely different greeting. *Please don't start laughing again, Sir.*

I shook his hand and asked if he could get me a line to Ziegfried.

"Of course, Sir. Give me just a moment. There's an office two doors down on the right. I'll ring you in there when I have him on the line."

Looking around the sparsely decorated, windowless office I was wishing Penelope could nick something colorful for the drab walls and put in a window or two when the phone rang.

"Adrian, it's so good to hear your voice. I've missed you terribly. How are things in bloody old England?"

"Other than dying of bucolic boredom, things are going swimmingly. I've taken the Great Tunnels tour and auctioned off most the dead relatives' portraits to pay for my new car which should be here tomorrow."

"What did you get?"

"Aston Martin DB9 in Cobalt Black."

"You bastard! Can I lick your leather?"

"No, but I do have something else…"

"Don't start. My hand is already calloused from thinking of you."

We both know that's a lie. Your hands and heart were both calloused long before you met me. "Is Vanessa where I could speak with her?"

"No, she's out tonight, but you can try her cell. She was here last night, but you stood us up. We waited by the phone for hours."

"I know, I'm sorry."

"I'm only joshing you, Adrian. Ambrose called and said you were with Chad touring the tunnels. He's a fast little fucker isn't he? And have you seen that über hot husband of his? It makes me weak, I tell you."

"I'm having them for dinner in a few days."

"You'll have to let me know if he tastes as good as he looks."

"Ziegfried, do you ever pull your fangs out of your dick for even a minute?"

"Only if I can sink them into someone else's. The art of self-fellatio is completely underappreciated by moderns. You should try it sometime. Very relaxing and much more stimulating than yoga."

"Thanks, I'll try to remember that. I hate to tear away from this riveting conversation, but I need to speak with Charles. Can you put him on?"

"Please hold. I'll see if he's in."

"Very funny, dick lick."

Charles came on the line saying, "Nicholas, I'm glad you arrived safely. How are you getting on? Is Thadius taking good care of you?"

"Yes, Sir. He's a diamond in the gruff and everyone else is an absolute jewel. They've all helped me get settled in and I'm pretty well situated by now. I've toured downstairs with Ambrose and Chad. I've even covered most of the grounds with Eric. Talk about beautiful."

"Whom, the grounds or Eric?"

"Both, Sir."

"Yes, he is a lovely lad, isn't he?"

"I don't know if you've heard, but I'm getting a new car. I'd been thinking of putting a spoiler and some racing stripes on the Rolls…"

It felt good to hear him having a big belly laugh. After he'd recovered he said, "I think the new car may be a better option, all things considered. I trust you found something fun?"

"An Aston Martin Coupe."

"Excellent choice, Nicholas. I had one many years ago. I'm glad they've made such a comeback. The company was about to go under in the seventies and when I heard the government wasn't going to help them, I arranged some assistance. I have fond memories of that little car."

That explains a lot presumably…Phone a friend, my ass. "Charles, last night when I was with Chad, he was telling me about our physiology. I found the conversation fascinating. How can I find out more? None of the books I've read have mentioned it."

"If we'd had more time while you were here, I'd have taken you on a tour of our research facilities. Much of what Chad was talking about is relatively new science. I'll have someone put you together some reading material, but you'll have to leave it downstairs."

"That would be great, thank you. Oh, there's one last thing. I'm not sure when I'll be leaving, but I'm going back to Dallas in a few days to put my affairs in order. I don't think it should take very long."

"Poor word choices aside, I'd rather you didn't, but I understand if you feel you must. I know we'd all like to see that whole unfortunate *affair* as you so aptly describe it, as far behind you as possible. Please be careful, Nicholas. There's a great deal at stake here."

"I know there is, Sir. I promise I'll be careful."

Vanessa sounded miffed when I reached her. "Hello, stranger. I thought you didn't care about me anymore after last night."

"Nothing could be farther from the truth. You know that, my darling." I was trying to channel my inner Cary Grant or James Mason, and probably failing miserably. "Vanessa, my love, nothing would make me happier than if you'd consent to be my wife. Do say yes, you know how poorly I handle rejection."

"I wasn't aware of anyone ever rejecting you in the first place."

"True, that's why I handle it so poorly. I have so little experience with it."

She laughed and asked if I was on drugs or being serious.

"No...and almost. I need to FedEx you some letters and have you post them from Sydney. They're notes to people in the States telling them I've fallen madly in love with the girl of my dreams and moving to Sydney. Tell me the truth, do you feel terribly used?

"Sullied maybe, but never used. Not even you could afford that, Mr. Wellstone. Speaking of heartbreakers, I talked with Carlos yesterday. He said to give you his best. How was that by the way? I've always thought he was food for the gods."

"He does just ooze ambrosia, doesn't he?" I teased conspiratorially.

"I wouldn't know. I'm hanging up now to go buy your fucking stamps, and if you know what's good for you, there'd better be an engagement ring in that FedEx."

It seemed like things were finally settling down and possibly, just possibly, I could see the beginnings of a new life taking hold. Randomly I pulled a book off the shelf after pouring a glass of red. It was about the history of Gravesend. Its storied past was quite surprising.

Mary Shelley had written about it in *Frankenstein*. Joseph Conrad used it in *Heart of Darkness*. Even Pocahontas was laid to rest in the town's church graveyard. I didn't even know she'd been a real person. For some reason there was not a single mention of Thornecrown or what was buried in its basement...

The historical record kept running from the pages as my mind and heart wrestled and raced with each other regarding Eric. *Never in the nest. Give love a chance. Free pony rides forever. You can't do this to him. His life is just beginning. But imagine how sweet...*And I did, at least in my dreams.

The next day came right at the crack of dawn. I'd heard that can happen in the country. Eric was still on my mind and I couldn't seem to buck him. "Fuck it!" I said aloud and slipped on my boots. I knew I was going to have to face him sooner or later and I supposed the longer I waited the more awkward it would become.

"Good morning, Berta. May I please have two cups of coffee?"

She poured the coffee and off I went. His face was hard to read when he saw me coming.

"Top of the morning to you, Eric. How are you today?" *Well that sounded completely fucking lame.* He probably thought I'd swallowed a leprechaun.

He took one of the mugs and said, "Thanks. I'm fine, Sir."

"I was wondering how busy you're going to be today? I'd like it if we could ride out to the waterfall again this morning. I regretted not being able to stay longer yesterday. I hope you won't think I'm being a pest, but I do have one other favor to ask."

He was definitely curious and trying not to show it. "Yes, Sir?" he asked calmly.

"I'm having a new car delivered to the house this afternoon. I was hoping maybe you'd take me into town and show me around a bit."

Gravesend's most beautiful grin was wanting to break out all over his face. He was trying so hard not to smile, but the sparkle in his eyes betrayed him.

"Well, Sir, I'd like to, but I tend to smell like a barn by the end of the day. I'm afraid that new car smell would turn to day-old horseshit before we could make it to the highway."

It was official, we were both laughing. I could see and feel all the hurt feelings and confusion melting away in both of us. I was beyond happy and hoped he was, too.

"Then go home and change sometime after lunch, silly, and come back this afternoon. I'll even take you to supper wherever you like. Please don't make me beg."

He was hesitating just to mess with me. Casually he asked, "So what'd you get?"

"Aston Martin DB9 Coupe. Limited Edition, Cobalt Black."

"Sweet. Count me in. Can I drive?" he teased.

"Of course. I never learned to drive a stick. I was hoping you'd show me." We were both cracking up again. He was absolutely the most beautiful thing I'd ever seen when he laughed. My heart was about to beat right out of my chest. I had to do something before it made a mess everywhere. "So how about that ride? If you'd be kind enough to saddle up the boys, I'll be right back."

Opening the kitchen door, I yelled, "Berta!"

She came running out of the pantry looking completely panicked. "Yes, Sir. Is everything alright, Sir?"

"I'm sorry, dear. I didn't know you were in there. Do you happen to have a thermos?"

"Yes, Sir, of course we do. Let me get you one."

I followed her into the pantry. Of course there were at least a dozen shapes and sizes of the damned things. After picking one out, I walked across to the liquor store and nabbed a bottle of Irish Cream. "Oh my God, a carton of Dunhills!" I hadn't smoked a cigarette since I'd fallen off the boat. It felt like shoplifting, but I took a pack anyway. After filling the thermos with coffee and Irish Cream, I was hauling my elated ass back to the stables when I realized I'd forgotten the horses' molasses balls. Turning around, I saw Berta on her way out the door with them in her hand. *God I love these people!*

The boys were all rearing to go and two of them knew I'd brought treats. We rode hard out to the falls. I fed and watered the winded horses while Eric spread a blanket on the damp grass next to the bank. Filling the thermos lid full of spiked coffee, I offered it to Eric and fished in my pocket for the pack of smokes, only to realize I hadn't brought a lighter. He handed me the cup and went to his saddlebags for matches.

Tossing them to me, he said, "Always be prepared for everything."

"So I've heard. That seems to be the motto around here." We drank and smoked in silence while I summoned my courage. It took longer than expected. By the time I found it, I was glad I'd brought a whole pack and the large thermos.

Finally I drew a deep breath, exhaled, and blurted out, "Eric, I like you."

"I like you too, Adrian."

"No, I mean I *really* like you, Eric."

"I understand. I really like you too, Adrian."

I felt like I was speaking Leprechaun again. He was grinning slightly in what I assumed to be amusement as he turned his body toward me, resting his chin on his pulled-up knees. Just sitting there staring at me, smiling, rocking back and forth until it seemed as if he might be dozing off, he was really a bit disconcerting.

I bumped his shoulder with my own to make sure he hadn't fallen asleep with his eyes open. He hadn't. He bumped me back. Smiling uneasily, I said, "Eric, I'm going away for a few days…"

That seemed to wake him up. "Not right now, you're not." Grabbing my shoulders, he pushed me back on the blanket and kissed me like he really meant it. No one before or since has ever kissed me again or tasted the way he did. Lying there beside the creek next to him that morning I can truthfully say I fell in love for the first time. My heart and jeans both felt as if they would burst under the weight of his beautiful lips and soul. Every minute his body was pressed against mine, I kept dying from emotional electrocution and was reborn again each time we came up gasping for air and sanity.

When I felt the tears welling behind my eyes, I knew I had to stop him. Wrapping my arms tightly around his neck and back, I pulled him as close as possible without breaking him and rolled us over with me sitting upright straddling his waist. He seemed remarkably, exquisitely composed for a man who'd just finished wrestling a vampire in the throes of ecstasy.

Folding his hands behind his head, he flashed me that million-dollar smile. "I wanted to give you something to remember me. I hope you're coming back soon. I've got needs too, you know." Rubbing my crotch and laughing, he tried locking his legs around my waist in a scissor hold. I knew if I let him, the blanket and my britches weren't going to be nearly large enough. Forcing his knees and ankles apart, I used them to stand up. His bottom lip wasn't the only thing protruding as I turned away, pretending to stretch.

Alexander's bored expression indicated he thought we should get a stall or something. I started laughing. Rearing his head and whinnying, he apparently thought it was funny too until I leapt on his startled back, gigged him hard, and yelled, "Fly, Alexander, fly!"

We were racing toward the house when I heard eight hooves on the ground instead of four. Twisting in the saddle, I saw Napoleon hot on our heels.

When we found Eric wandering through the woods, he was wearing the proudest, widest grin I'd ever seen. My heart begged my tongue to remain silent and not spoil the perfect shade of blushful bliss on his face as I handed him Napoleon's reins. We rode back in near silence, with the exception of the construction project screaming away in my pants. By the time we'd arrived I was sporting enough wood for a sizable addition to the house. After carefully, painfully dismounting the horse, I waved from behind, saying, "See you at four," and limped off stiffly toward the kitchen deliriously happy, with one leg only slightly shorter than the other two.

CHAPTER TWENTY-TWO

Thadius was trying to reach me through the dense, feathery fog. Barely audible, he was saying something about not being certified for sunlight. Even with superhuman strength, it was nearly impossible wrestling my way out of that fucking bed while grappling with the receiver. Sleeping like an angel is all good and fine, but to then wake up spitting feathers and venom sort of defeats the whole purpose.

Needing to meet the driver and sign for the car, I was padding bleary-eyed and barefoot around the bedroom trying to find pants and a CD when I tripped and spilled the entire rack, along with my ass, all over the floor. Sitting there naked rifling through the cases, I could almost smell the obsidian leather and hear Harry Connick Jr. belting out show tunes through the Bang & Olufsen speakers. I could hardly wait. By the time I'd lumbered down the stairs and opened the door, the truck was pulling into the driveway.

The porcine driver rolled out of the cab sideways and jiggled onto the cobbled pavement saying, "I have a delivery for a Nicholas Wellstone."

"That would be me," I replied, picking away at the last of the feathers lodged in my teeth.

"I kinda' thought so from the look on your face," the driver wheezed. "This is one hell of an early Christmas present. Santa must really like you."

"Something like that. I suppose that's why they named me after the fat bastard."

The driver was sneering, slobbering, and thinking, *what a lucky little cocksucker. Wonder how many knobs he's polished to get a car like this?* I was thinking about revoking the sweaty asshole's membership in the land of the living when I realized I'd probably never get the car off the damned truck by myself. Although I'd lied earlier when I said I didn't know how to drive a stick, I doubted I'd be able to drive, much less hide, a semi loaded with sports cars and a dead fat dude in the cab.

As he backed the Aston slowly off the truck and peeled away the protective paper, I thought the car should have been unveiled. But his arms were entirely too stubby for any sort of sweeping flourishes. In spite of the driver's shortcomings, exquisite was the only descriptor that came to mind as I stared at the layers of pearlescent paint shimmering in the afternoon sun. After signing his paperwork, I gave the driver a generous cash donation toward the dick he and his wife had always longed for, and gladly watched him drive off grinding away at what was left of his teeth and the truck's gears.

Getting high off the leather, I was sitting in the driver's seat when Eric came coughing, spewing, and sputtering up beside me in his pickup. Several minutes after he'd turned off the ignition, the truck finally, fitfully died of what I could only assume to be old age and natural causes. Once the billowing cloud of smoke cleared, I was checking the ground for fallen sparrows when he rolled down the passenger-side window. And yes, it was the kind with the cranky-knob sort of thing on a handle. I wasn't certain whether I'd ever seen one in operation.

"Don't laugh. This was my first car and I can't stand the thought of trading it in. Where should I park the old bucket of bolts?"

I smiled, trying with modest, intermittent success not to cough through the clouded outbursts still inexplicably shooting out the tailpipe, exhausting his dilapidated muffler which had long ago failed to live up to its name or original intent. "Right here. Come sit on my lap. We'll have one of the groundskeepers bring a backhoe for the truck."

Laughing, he asked, "Do the seats recline?" I sincerely hoped it wasn't a rhetorical question.

"There's only one way to find out, big boy. Let's go, and, like I said, you can drive." I stepped out and tossed him the keys through the open window.

"Are you serious? I thought you were just playing this morning."

"As I recall, we both were, but I still want you to drive, unless you're afraid of a little horsepower between your legs."

As we were heading out to the main road I thought about people in town seeing him driving the car and said, "Eric, if you don't mind, when we get into town, if we see people you know, I'd prefer if you'd introduce me as Adrian, a friend from London."

"What's the matter? You don't want to be seen as the lord of the manor cavorting with the peasantry?" I knew he wasn't being serious. The mile-wide grin was a dead giveaway.

"No, you beautiful asshole, but lots of people would be willing to sell pictures of our love child. And from what I saw this morning, you're already showing." I rubbed my hand teasingly along his leg to emphasize the point.

"Adrian, if you don't stop that, I can guarantee at least one baby will be coming sooner than you think."

Crossing the cobblestone bridge, I spotted Cornelius tracking us from the darkening woods. He was up way too early for anyone's good, including mine. I'd have to call Thadius and have him put away before we came home. I couldn't imagine seeing the look on Eric's face otherwise. Everyone knew we had some strange birds on the estate, but there are limits and Cornelius more than happily defied most of them.

Out on the main road, Eric gunned it and started shifting through the gears. The sound alone was a thing of amazement. When he hit ninety and it felt like we were still in a school zone, I put my hand back on his leg.

"Okay, Speed Racer. Let's not kill ourselves or get arrested on our first date."

"First date?" His head tilted like he'd heard the phrase uttered for the first time in human history. "First date." His smile went supernova again. "I like the sound of it. I've never been on a date with a guy before. I've been on one or two with a girl. I even tried having sex once. Her name was Charlotte. Oh God, it was such a disaster, I never tried again. Honestly, I've never wanted to…until now."

Turning the stereo down, I thought I'd heard him incorrectly. "You've got to be kidding me, right? You, of all people, sitting there looking like you look, and you're telling me you're…a virgin?" I could barely get the words out of my mouth I was so stunned. "Eric, come on, you can't be serious."

He shrugged, so matter of factly it was as if we were discussing the weather. "I thought I told you this morning at the waterfall. When *I* kissed you…" he reminded me, "…what can I say? I knew I might lose my job over it, but, for the first time in my life, it felt right. All I can say is, Adrian, you're a much better kisser than any horse I've ever cared for."

We were both still laughing when I felt his nails running along my leg. He was right. That one simple touch felt more natural than anything I'd ever experienced in either life or death. Nora Jones was winding through some sultry tune when I realized I didn't know the song, the day of the week, nor possibly the year and didn't care in the least. I was hopelessly lost in the moment as we exited into downtown.

My mind's eye had conceived of Gravesend as a quaint little village out of a Dickens' novel. It was nothing but an ordinary city full of commerce, stinking industry, and lots of people littering the streets. Even the small, older shops had no charm with the supertankers towering behind them in the distance. Giant cranes shot metallic fingers into the evening sky at sadly regular intervals. If I wanted a romantic hamlet, I supposed we'd have to look elsewhere.

Eric could sense my disappointment. "Let's go see one of my favorite places."

"By all means. We've got a full tank of gas. How far to the next village?"

He drove and twisted through the narrow streets until we came to a park of rolling hills dotted with beautiful trees on the bank of the Thames. There were no supertankers in sight. I was liking it before we even got out of the car. Walking down by the water, we sat on a bench without anything to offer the hungry, noisy ducks. Thankfully, they soon waddled away seeking more fertile lands and bread-filled hands.

We were alone at last when I felt his arm slip over my shoulder. Smiling sweetly, he asked, "Do you mind?"

"Not very well, I'm afraid. I was difficult, even as a child. It's no wonder my parents sold me to the gypsies."

We both chuckled softly as I laid my head on his shoulder. It felt oh so good and ever so right, but after a few minutes I thought our heavy breathing might sound better with gin.

I sat up and was about to say so when he turned my face toward his and kissed me until the stars I saw were outshining the setting sun. His lips and tongue were a powerful enough tonic I almost forgot about the gin. If not for the *adults only* festivities taking place in my pants, I could've easily imagined being a child again making out for the very first time.

We were still tongue-grooming each other's faces when the ducks came back with an axe to grind. Apparently Moses, the misdirected Mallard, had taken them on a wild goose chase instead of leading them to the Promised Land and they were pissed. We had no loaves or fish to offer, so they drove us from our bench and out of the park. We were a blighted people without cocktails, condiments, or sustenance of any other kind.

Not being very religious, I was as surprised as anyone when I gazed up and saw a sign beckoning to us from the heavens. It said "Now Open." Next to it in glowing blue neon was the universal symbol of hope, the outline of a martini glass.

Forty stair-steps later we'd arrived at the Pearly Gates, which were somewhat disappointing in tarnished brass, although I suppose in the greater scheme of things they did complement the tacky walnut paneling and red-flocked wallpaper. St. Peter seemed pleasant enough, dressed in his maître d' uniform. Not a single question regarding our religious affiliations or sincerity of beliefs—he seemed to have only one concern. Did we want to be seated inside, or outside in the garden? We opted for a candlelit corner table near the window.

La Trattoria del Mar's menu was primarily seafood. The last time I'd eaten, I'd had seafood, only this time I didn't expect to be choking anyone afterward. Gagging, however, was almost a given. Glancing at my watch as the waiter set the plate of crab tortellini in front of me, I asked him to bring me another double in fifteen minutes and a separate glass of ice. The food smelled deliciously nauseating as I sprinkled on the parmesan and crushed pepper.

Eric kept eyeing the window nervously until I asked if something was the matter.

"Do you think someone will mess with the car if we leave it there?"

"Not if they want to live," I replied matter-of-factly. Thinking it sounded a bit harsh, I set my fork down and tried using a nicer tone when saying, "So tell me about your family, Eric."

"Well, my mom died of cancer when I was ten. My dad is still alive, but he's not doing so well. He started aging pretty quickly after she died. They'd always wanted children, but couldn't have any. They adopted me when I was two. This is where I grew up and that's pretty much it."

"Do you live with him?"

"Yeah, he can't live alone at this point. He worked for your uncle at the estate most of his life. He and Sir Charles were very close, even after dad retired. Pops took it really hard when he heard the news. We all did. Your uncle was just one of those people I guess we all thought would live forever."

"I understand. It's been rough on all of us. I'm sorry, but will you excuse me for a moment? I need to find the little boy's room. Order some dessert if there's something you'd like. I'm stuffed."

I went to the bathroom, called Thadius about putting up Cornelius, and barely made it to the toilet before my crabs grew wings and began flying around the room. I washed my face and went back to the table lamenting the fact that coke wasn't on the menu. For some reason I've never understood, vomiting always makes me crave a big fat line to settle my stomach.

Eric ordered molten chocolate something or other that he seemed to enjoy with an almost religious zeal while I tried turning as few shades of green as possible and ordered another cocktail after downing the one in my hand.

He looked concerned. I rattled the ice in the empty glass and said, "I don't get to have a designated driver very often, especially not such a cute one who likes kissing boys and horses."

"Are you feeling okay, Adrian? You've looked a little pale since you came out of the loo."

"I didn't eat anything earlier today. I think the food was too rich for my empty stomach."

"Why don't you let me drive you home? Maybe you'll feel better if you lie down."

"I think you may be right. I've had a wonderful evening, though, in spite of the hateful protestors in the park. Isn't it a shame what religion can do to otherwise perfectly nice ducks?"

Eric seemed to think all my lame-ass jokes were funny. If they made him laugh then I'd be deliriously happy to keep telling them forever. We drove home to the soothing underwater sounds of Vivaldi. Carlos had given me waterproof earbuds and a snorkel while I was on board the *Empress*. I'd become addicted to *The Four Seasons* submerged in three hundred gallons of water.

It did nothing to dispel the feeling of floating when Eric kissed me goodnight leaning against his pickup truck. After I opened the creaking door for him, he grabbed my crotch as he was sliding into the seat, winked at me, and said something about sitting there and jerking off.

Fuck, I'll never get to sleep now with that autoerotic image in my mind. I really wanted to go driving anyway, I just didn't want to go alone or with Eric. I knew we'd probably be at third or fourth base before I could ever hope to make it out of second gear and I wanted to wait a few days before getting slobber all over the seats.

I had no Bat Signal, but I did have two perfectly good legs and a third that was in danger of petrification. Taking a carefully orchestrated walk downstairs, as luck would have it, I found Superman on duty. Thanks to Eric's overly vivid imagery I was reduced to thinking of Clark sitting there naked pleasuring himself wearing only a red cape while he phoned Chad, who must have been nearby. He was there in a blinding flash. *No, Adrian, you can't call him Flash and you sure as hell can't call him Claudia. And stop perving on Clark before he smacks you in the face. With all those muscles I doubt he hits like a girl.*

"Good evening, Sir. How's that new car working out? It sure is a looker."

"Damn it, Chad. I was going to surprise you. Wanna go for a ride?"

"I'd be glad to, Sir," he smiled omnisciently. "If you would, Sir, could you drive around to the warehouse and come through the tunnel? I need to have a monitor placed on the vehicle. It'll only take a minute."

"Sure, but the car already has LoJack on it."

"No Sir, it's not for antitheft. It tells security the car is one of ours. Without it, every time the car moves, we have to manually override the system. All the cars on the estate have one. I'll open the warehouse doors and meet you in the garage."

Fifteen minutes later we were at a dead stop in the middle of the road. I smiled and said, "Are you ready? Let's see what she can do." Working through the gears as fast as I could shift, nine seconds later we'd hit a hundred and ten with no complaints from the car. One twenty around the first curve, and I could barely feel myself leaning into it. I didn't want to imagine what it might take to get two wheels off the ground. Chad was laughing as we slowed down.

"What's so funny, Speedy Gonzales? Think you can do better?"

He grinned shyly. "No, Sir. I'd blow you away in a quarter-mile drag race, but this baby would make my heart explode in an endurance test."

I'd conjured up images of the Monty Python players in ball gowns and high heels running track and field against the Queen Mother while he explained how our blood is like oil in a car. "If you run it dry, you explode. It's the same thing as throwing a rod."

Throwing a rod? Blowing me away? Exploding? I wondered how many sexual metaphors Chad might be able to fit into a sentence and whether Eric was parked on the side of the road somewhere pounding out new ones? Either way I was unfit to drive and desperate to shift mental gears. Letting Chad take the wheel, I tried getting a grip on something other than my overactive gonads. On the drive back to the estate I asked if he and Thomas would like to come for dinner the following evening before my trip to Dallas.

When I casually commented that Thadius would be joining us, I also made some flippant remark about Ziegfried and how I hoped he wouldn't drop by drooling all over dinner and Thomas' leg. I probably shouldn't have, in retrospect, because Chad visibly bristled at the mention of his name. "What a complete waste of immortality and good German bones. As much as I'd like to scrape the meat from them and make a big bowl of hearty soup, I've discovered you can't reduce the irreducible."

CHAPTER TWENTY-THREE

The next evening's dinner, or, rather, the thought of what to serve, left me feeling wholly unprepared. Ziegfried's Wiener schnitzel on a platter would have been a big hit, but I had no idea what to use for sides, even with a pantry the size of a smallish Walmart. "How about nine o'clock?" is fine for pot roast or stir-fry, but in the Estate That Never Sleeps, something else seemed in order.

Out of desperation I called Charles. Jealous he couldn't attend, he told me to go to hell, straight down the stairs, take a left, and within those nethermost regions I would find two bottles of Selene he'd stashed in an old sofa some years back. Beyond the cobwebs under a long-forgotten Countess' watchful, suspicious eyes, I found the buried treasure between two formerly over-plumped crimson velvet cushions.

Making my way back up the stairs, my cell started ringing. It was Chad. "Sorry to bother you, Sir. I tried you on the house phone and no one answered. Thomas wanted me to ask what time tomorrow night?"

"How about nine o'clock? And while you're upstairs, there will be no *Sir* anything. My name is Adrian. Do we understand each other, soldier?"

"Loud and clear. Sir is not allowed in the house of Adrian."

"Good. Then we'll see you tomorrow night." Hanging up the phone, chills ran down my spine. I'd never heard anyone utter the words *House of Adrian*.

I took the wine to the pantry and redialed Chad's number. Even if curiosity does kill the cat, I was already dead anyway and I couldn't let it pass. "Chad are you off duty now?"

"Yes, Sir, I'm at home. Thomas doesn't get off for a couple of hours."

"Good, then I'd like to ask you…"

"But, Sir, I'm a married man!" I could hear him trying not to laugh.

"That's not…Never mind, I know you're joking. Can we please be serious for a moment?"

"I'm sorry, Sir. Ask me anything."

"What do the people downstairs in the Bat Cave say about me?" The dead silence on the other end told me I'd hit a nerve.

"With all due respect, Sir, I think you should talk to Ambrose about this. It's not my place, Sir."

"It's your place if I ask. If I wanted Ambrose's opinion, I'd ask him. I'm asking you, but if you'd prefer, we can call it an order."

"That won't be necessary, Sir, but this could take a few minutes."

"I've got all night."

"People's opinions vary as much as the people themselves." I could hear the nervous hesitation in his voice. "Some believe our Prince has gone round the bend by self-imposing his own exile in The Havens. They see it as arbitrary and I imagine some of them blame you for his decision. Others, including myself, know he's kept us safe, prosperous, and at peace for many years now. We believe he knows what he's doing. And the rest, I would guess they're still sitting on the fence waiting to see what happens."

"Thank you for the candor, Chad. Obviously this is not a dinner topic for tomorrow night or else we wouldn't be discussing it now. If you'll answer one other question, I promise I'll let you off the hook. I'm curious as to what's being said among the other Houses."

"I understand your question, Sir, but anything I might say would be nothing more than rumor or conjecture. You must know by now that gossip…"

"Yes, Chad. It's the blood sport of immortals. I've heard."

"Good, because I don't have any direct access to the other Princes, or their counselors, for that matter. The rumor mill, and that's all it is, says some of the leaders, mostly among the Great Houses, are laughing at us behind our backs. They see this as an attempt on Sir Charles' part to strengthen the Dorian's dynastic prospects or else the ramblings of a messianic lunatic peddling prophecy for profit by trying to frighten everyone with his grand theatrics.

"Others aren't so cynical from what I hear. Especially among the Lesser Houses, some of the Princes believe the legend is true. Like Sir Charles, they see you as the fulfillment of the prophecy. Honestly, that's about all I can tell you."

"I see. Thank you, Chad. Again, I apologize for putting you on the spot. I'll try not to make a habit of it. I know I've asked a great deal of you, but I'd really appreciate it if this could remain between us. I'd rather neither Thomas nor anyone else know we've had this conversation."

Hanging up the phone, I knew how completely, utterly screwed, fucked, boxed, and painted in I was—and none of the coloring was with my own crayons. In another world, I would have been graduating from college, but, in less than five years, I'd died, been reborn into solitary eternal damnation, reborn again as the grandson of a Dorian Prince disguised as a now-dead English nobleman who no longer existed to 99.999 percent of the world, and finally, without my permission or consent, I was being reborn yet again as Aryan.

In no way did I relish the thought of becoming my own great, great, great grandpa, or ma, whichever it was. For some reason I'd always assumed that Dorius was the top…Either way I couldn't sit there brooding while everyone else busied themselves cooking my goose in their own legendary juices preparing to offer me up for the next dysfunctional family feast. I was more than tired of being shaped, molded, and reconstituted to serve over and over again as some sort of immortal mystery meat. I thought if the Buddhists, Hindus, or Christians felt for a second they had some sort of monopoly on being reborn, they should try walking a mile in my fangs.

The same dread of certainty washed over me as on the night I'd been swept out to sea, only this time I had a feeling there would be no cute sailors in lifeboats. The only floating white orbs would be the pasty faces of dead relatives dutifully watching the clock on the kitchen stove. *Is he done yet? Should we turn him over again? No, he's much too pretty a bird. Turn the temperature down and baste him some more. We don't want to burn him. Not yet anyway…*I could hear them cackling. Chad had said they were laughing at me behind my back, but fuck them and their twisted sense of humor. I wasn't finding anything remotely funny about being the recipe for disaster or the plastic baby Jesus in the King cake Charles was apparently trying to bake.

"Be the spider, not the fly," I said under my breath. Alaric had drilled it into my head a thousand times. I'd been both, and I suspected I'd rather be a Texas-sized spiderman than a flaming British flyboy. Crashing and burning in someone else's tangled web of myth-spun mischief was sounding less and less appealing by the minute. If I wanted out of the silky white, plushly overstuffed coffin, I'd have to use the Nadir and crawl between, beneath the nearly invisible threads which were itching, twitching to play me for a siren's song.

John-Paul Sartre once famously stated, "Everything has been figured out, except how to live." That's fine for most folks, but when you're already dead, it can be a more daunting aspiration than one might imagine. Sitting in the teepee just being me was about as far as my imagination could roam. Dallas and a very firm mattress were calling me home.

If I stayed in England, no priest or amulet, prayer or potion could save me from becoming who and what they wanted, either a boy king or a boy toy. I was certainly no one's king and one person had died already for treating me like a toy. How many more would have to die before I was remade to their liking?

All I really wanted was to fall in love with the stable boy and live happily ever after, but, with things as they were, I didn't see how that was possible. How could I ask him to become what I was if I couldn't be sure myself what that was? *Either I'm a goddamned unicorn with fangs or a pawn on an invisible chessboard. Fuck it, I'm going to bed. They can all kiss my mythological ass.*

No one was kissing anything in my dreams. It was all cops and cowboys, meth-addled Mexicans, and masked raccoons. I kept running and running only to fall flat on my face in the same place with wild stallions stampeding toward me in a frothing, furious cloud of dust.

Thinking I'd awakened from the nightmare, I tried sitting up in bed but my body was paralyzed. I screamed but no one could hear my muffled cries through the feathered wings of the angel holding me in its supernatural grasp. I struggled and screamed again and again. *Let me go! You can't make me!* I was shouting so loudly the ceiling began cracking and falling apart. *I'm not your prisoner! Let me go you motherfuc...* Before I could finish cursing angels, the entire roof collapsed, filling my gaping mouth with debris.

I woke up gasping for air, choking, and sobbing. I'd come completely undone and so had the bed. The weight of four stories, a basement full of vampires, and the toxic sludge of my own putrid past had pressed me so far into the depths of downy hell, I'd been trying to claw my way out in my sleep. When my eyes fluttered open, there were feathers floating in the air, littering the carpet, and plastered all over my bloody body. From the look of things it had been one hell of a cockfight I'd had with either Gabriel or Michael. I never could keep my archangels straight, but since the roof had caved in and collapsed the house, I was guessing it was Gabriel I'd wrestled in my dreams. If he'd chosen to blow me instead of that stupid fucking horn, the room probably wouldn't have been such a wreck and all those geese wouldn't have died for nothing.

Stepping my tarred and feathered ass into the shower, it was one of those rare occasions I was grateful I couldn't see myself in the mirror. I must've looked like a Santeria ritual gone terribly wrong. The drain kept clogging with feathers and coagulated blood. Somehow, I had to get out of there. In reality, I knew I should've never come in the first place. I wouldn't have fallen in love with Eric nor fallen victim to the histrionic visions of overzealous, forked-tongued evangelists bent on reshaping the world using my image. I'd been willing to be Adrian, but seemingly even that wasn't enough to satisfy the demands of so many princes and their principalities.

Kings and Queens be damned. Dallas was looking and sounding better by the minute, and that was no small task in and of itself. Once I'd plucked and patted myself dry, I started rehearsing my speech knowing it would have to be the perfect lie or they might not let me leave without somebody getting hurt. In Nadir training I'd been taught the best lies are the ones that most closely approximate the truth. The story I fabricated was woven so tightly to reality all I had left to do was go downstairs bubbling with enthusiasm about how I couldn't wait to get back.

Thadius was in his office bent over a ledger. "Knock, knock. Sorry to interrupt, but if you're not too busy I wanted to talk to you about my flight to the States. Do you have a minute?"

"For you, Sir, I have centuries." Nothing in his face or demeanor indicated he was aware of my intentions or the bloodbath I'd taken upstairs earlier. "Regarding your flight, I'm not sure what happened with that near meltdown in Sydney, but Belmont Industries has its own jet. Although I've asked, I've yet to get a straight answer as to why you were ever allowed on a commercial flight at that distance in the first place. Any idea of when you'd like to leave?"

"How about tomorrow night? Oh, and if they can just drop me off at LaGuardia, I'll catch a commercial flight to Dallas. It's a direct route and a friend's picking me up at DFW."

"Are you sure, Sir? It's really no…"

"Nonsense. Stop worrying. It's only three hours." I stood up to leave before he could insist and remembered we had company coming as I was turning around. "Oh fuck, I'm sorry. I can be such an airhead sometimes. I almost forgot Chad and Thomas are coming up for dinner tonight. You will join us, won't you?"

"Of course. I'll look forward to it. Why don't we have Edward drive you to Heathrow tomorrow? We wouldn't want anything happening to that new car of yours, would we?"

"Absolutely not. Then, if it's settled, I'm going to go upstairs and pack. I'll see you tonight at nine. Oh, by the way, come with an appetite. I'm planning something special."

"Please, Sir, tell me it's not pork chops again? That would be the third time this month."

Flipping him the bird, I laughed and said, "Emu steaks," while walking away with thoughts of Calgon floating on the bubbly, effervescent surface of my mind.

Shortly after dark, I found Hilda humming away in the kitchen to the tunes of what I could only assume to be the greatest hits of the Third

Reich. I asked if she'd seen Cornelius and explained I was having guests later. She hadn't, but made the generous offer to find him and put him away.

I wasn't trying to mask my thoughts or expression when I said, "No, but if you'd be kind enough to find him and bring him in the house, you can have the rest of the night off."

Watching her hand reflexively creeping toward the fly swatter, I shook my head back and forth. *Don't even think about it Frau Goering, unless you want that thing flying up your own ass in a blitzkrieg.* She didn't have to be the least bit psychic to read my mind. Nervously her eyes dropped, scanning the counter for a dishrag. Opening the kitchen door, she let loose a blood-curdling whistle loud enough to awaken Pocahontas in the town cemetery if the wind had been blowing in the right direction.

She was long gone by the time Cornelius came flying in the door with an expression fit for Heath Ledger relishing an afterlife reprisal of his role as the Joker. Tiny tufts of fur and ample smatterings of blood swathed his insanely happy face, reminding me of a demented taxidermist returning from a wildly debauched, drunken weekend of partying on Noah's Ark.

"Good boy, Cornelius, let's get you cleaned up. Did you get a deer?"

He smiled agreeably, nodding with enough enthusiasm to put a chiropractor's kids through college. I could smell the possum on his breath... regardless he was still adorable. After washing his face, I asked, "Now can you go to your room and put on some clothes like these?" I was pointing at my jacket when he started shaking his own head back and forth, which wasn't something I'd taught him.

"Why not?" I asked.

He grabbed the edge of my coat and tried pulling me toward the back door. Once he understood I was coming with him, he let go of my sleeve and tore off in the direction of the carriage house. I found him waiting upstairs by the open door.

I'm not sure what I expected exactly, but his quarters were not something from an Industrial Age novel. Plain, clean, nothing fussy—he'd obviously been using Thadius' decorator—nevertheless they were more than livable. He even had a television, video games, and a VCR with several racks of tapes, most of which appeared to be Bugs Bunny cartoons.

Embarrassed by my own prejudicial notions, I went through his wardrobe and chest of drawers while he rifled through his collection of *Looney Tunes,* seemingly searching for some particular title. I'd found some corduroy pants and was still looking for a presentable shirt when I heard Daffy Duck lisping childworthy obscenities at thirsty mice.

We went back to the house after he'd changed his pants to finish dressing. My largest, loosest shirt and belt were a stretch, and he thought it terribly funny when I tried helping him tuck in the tails. He kept undoing and redoing the process with enough gusto to almost rub the back of his hand raw. Finally, I removed the belt, although the shirttails themselves proved to be an endless source of delight for the rest of the evening. His brief encounter with one of my neckties deserves a story all its own. Between his fascination with stuffing and jerking the shirttails in and out of his pants and the dangling noose around his neck, Marcel Marceau would have been hard pressed to equal his quietly comical performance of autoerotic asphyxiation.

I'd almost given up trying to prevent him from choking when we were saved by the bell. I had one end of the tie in my hand attempting to loosen the knot. It nearly cost me an arm when he went tearing down the stairs like a crazed cosmetics saleswoman who'd won a coveted pink Cadillac at the annual Mary Kay convention. I was yelling for him to come back at the same moment Thadius stuck out his foot, thwarting Cornelius' poorly timed assault on the front door.

Tables can be repaired, but I thought my guts would never heal as I sat laughing on the landing while our guests picked their way across the scattered remnants of a once-fine foyer.

"Where's Hilda?" Thadius asked as Cornelius bounded up the stairs seeking refuge behind my still heavily heaving shoulders.

"I sent her home early," I cried, choking back tears of laughter.

"How very thoughtful of you, Sir," he snarled while working a rose from the shattered vase into the buttonhole of his jacket's lapel.

"Welcome to our home!" I exclaimed gleefully while firmly crushing Cornelius by the hand as we made our way slowly down the stairs. "Please pardon the mess. Today is the maid's day off." After casting a glancing blow in Thadius' direction, I shrugged and said, "I'm sure we'll manage somehow. Won't you come in?" The look on everyone's face was worth far more than my Aston Martin out in the driveway.

Herding us into the salon, I parked Cornelius beyond Thadius' reach and shook Thomas' hand. "We've waved, but I don't think we've had the pleasure, Thomas. I'm Adrian, and I hope Chad's told you the house rules for tonight. Please make yourself at home."

Thadius appeared to have pulled the last leg of the entry table from his ass when I offered everyone a drink. "Chad, as usual, you look like you're rapidly approaching seventeen, so I'll need to see some ID."

I couldn't be completely certain, but I thought I heard a bone snapping in Thomas' upper arm when Claudia smacked him for laughing. I took drink orders and played bartender while Chad served. I fixed Cornelius a "What's Up, Doc?" improvised of sparkling water and grenadine. He loved the name, the red bubbles, and the miraculous straw for blowing more of them.

While handing him his cocktail, Chad stroked Cornelius' hair. "You look very handsome tonight."

It probably pained Thadius, but he added, "Yes, Cornelius, you do look very handsome this evening. That's a very nice shirt," he said, shooting me a look, "even if it does seem a little snug on you."

I was telling Chad about my conversation with Charles and how he'd offered to have the latest white papers sent from The Havens on vampire physiology. Naturally, he wanted to be in the loop. Only partially joking, I told him he could be my science advisor at Thornecrown.

After consuming a real glass of red through a straw, I sent Cornelius to change and go play outside. Amazingly, he did exactly as I asked, waving frantically goodnight before slamming the kitchen door. Thadius looked at me and sighed. "I don't know why anything you'd do at this point might surprise me, but that one, Sir, nearly put me in an early coffin. I don't think I've ever seen him quite so calm, especially in front of guests."

"We watched cartoons in his room before everyone arrived." Standing up I added, "I don't know about the rest of you, but I'm ready for dinner, and tonight we have something special on the menu I think you'll like."

Thadius motioned for me to sit back down. "Please, allow me. You've been doing all the work. Enjoy your guests."

"Thank you, Thadius." I asked the boys, "Now if either of you can tell me the name of this particular vintage, I'll be most impressed. I only discovered it recently myself. Let's see if you can identify the secret ingredient."

When he'd uncorked one of the bottles and realized what it was, Thadius turned to me in surprise. "If you don't mind my asking, Sir, where on earth did you find this? I haven't seen a bottle in years."

I smiled and said, "I picked it up at the duty-free shop when I got off the boat."

Everyone sat sipping in silence until Thomas, who was still nursing his arm, foolishly quipped, "It's very fruity, more so than even Claudia here." There was no mistaking the cracking sound of his ribs when Chad retracted his elbow from his lover's side. I couldn't help but notice how Thomas seemed to favor his left arm afterward. Silently I vowed to never use the word Claudia again. I hadn't been at Thornecrown ninety days yet and my insurance probably hadn't kicked in.

Thadius refilled everyone's glass. "I know the vintner and the vintage, but I'm sworn to secrecy. Her sweet name shall never cross my lips," he taunted.

It was good to see him relaxing and getting into the game. When it was my turn to do the teasing I made sure I was well beyond the reach of Chad's right hook. "Now come on you two, show some fang and venture a guess."

Clueless, Thomas shrugged, winced, and waded in with, "Strawberries?"

"Sorry mate, it's back of the trolley for you." I really was starting to sound sort of British; too bad I wouldn't be around to perfect the accent. "Next up, please, pay your money, take your chances. Everyone's a loser in our little shop of horrors."

"Kiwi!" Chad jumped up exclaiming like a crazed jackrabbit-in-the-box. Thomas pulled him back down by the seat of his pants. "Shut up, you ninny. It's not kiwi, and if you hit me again I'll report you for elder abuse."

"That's right, Pee Wee, it's not kiwi," I laughed as I leapt behind the sofa for safety and comedic effect. Peering above the back, I made sure everyone was still seated before saying, "Okay, you tasteless fuckers, time's up. The game is over, and as expected, neither of your lovely wieners is a winner."

Chad winked at me and chuckled. "I don't know about that, Adrian. You haven't seen Thomas' yet. Show it to him, honey. I'm sure he'd love to see it. Isn't that right, Adrian?"

Score one for Pee Wee.

Thadius interrupted the presumptive outflowing of manhood. "Alright, boys. Before you shed any more of your…decency and start making pale comparisons," he said while hitching up his trousers, "if you'll excuse me, I think I'll leave you lightweights to it. When you're done, if you'd be so kind as to return the furniture to its upright position it would be greatly appreciated. And if you must draw funny faces on the portraits, please don't use permanent markers."

We were all snickering as he walked out of the room, waving goodbye like a drag queen exiting the stage after her grand finale. If only his air boa had been real…

When he'd rounded the corner, Thomas said, "Wow, Adrian! I'd have to hand it to you if my arm weren't broken. I can see what a positive impact you're having on him. I don't think I've ever seen him so lively. It's a tad freaky, to be honest with you. After Cornelius earlier and now him, what exactly is it you're putting in these people's red?"

We were still laughing when I confessed, "By the way, it's pomegranates you're tasting. Her name is Selene. She's one of our donors in Greece. She stomps them with the grapes using her bare feet and drinks nothing other than pomegranate juice for a week beforehand."

Chad nearly barfed. "Eewww, gross! You could have told us before the second glass." After Thomas and I polished off the bottle, I felt like a bloated tick. "Okay, you two lovely deviants, sadly, I must take my leave because I have a plane to catch tomorrow." I gave them both a heartfelt embrace and wished them goodnight. It was difficult not being sad because I doubted I'd ever see either of them again.

Sitting upstairs at the desk, I made a long shopping list with instructions for Berta. Guessing at Cornelius' sizes, I intended, although I'd never see it, to dress him like an adult rather than the son of a sharecropper. In bestowing parting gifts it occurred to me that planning a party was the perfect cover for my escape. I added evening gowns to the list for Berta and Hilda without an explanation as to why. Ambiguity, I'd learned in Nadir training, can be more powerful than a torrential river of lies. *Never let them see you coming or going.*

Ten boxes of Quaker Oats and a jug of molasses later, I'd finished the list, signed my life away, and was headed for the hottest bath I could stand. Washing away the rumors, lies, and half-truths of war and unwanted destinies wasn't easy, but I scrubbed so long and hard, I turned beet red enough to convince even myself that I hadn't passed my expiration date.

Bright, glowing orange licked and lapped at my skin after dawn, waking me from an otherwise restful sleep. Berta was making coffee in the kitchen. I said good morning and gave her the list while I gathered my thermos and the Irish Cream. After swiping another pack of Dunhills, I asked her, "Do you have any matches or a lighter, by chance?"

She found me a box of stick matches and said, "Thank you for the dress, Sir. I'll put the other things in your closet."

"Oh, I forgot one thing. Can I see that note again, please?"

I scribbled "two pairs of ladies heels" and handed it back to her. "What's a new dress without new shoes?" I kissed her cheek, grabbed my goodies, and headed for the stables.

Eric was brushing Sadie. He looked up when I walked in. "Where are my boys?" I asked.

"We're all right here, Sir." I liked the sound of the words almost as much as the way his mouth formed them. Sadie ate from my hand while he finished brushing her.

"Eric, I have to leave for the States this evening. I thought maybe we could take a ride this morning before I go?" I dangled the thermos temptingly, as if he needed encouragement. While he smiled approvingly, his less than sparkling eyes revealed the unspoken sadness we both shared.

"I'd like that. If you'll put Sadie in her stall and bring you-know-who, I'll saddle Napoleon." Alexander looked at me questioningly with one raised eyebrow. He knew something other than a ride was up. Napoleon could have cared less; he was more than placated by his treat and saddle. We took a longer, less-hurried path to the waterfall. Eric was untying the blanket when I walked around Napoleon and kissed him with as much sincerity as I could afford.

"I'm going to miss you very much. You know that, don't you?" I asked, stroking his cheek and hair.

He responded by picking me up like a sack of fingerling potatoes. After a thorough lip-smashing tongue-lashing, he set me down and asked, "Adrian, how much do you weigh? You're almost as big as me, but it's like you're made of air."

Attempting to pick me up again, I pushed him away. "Watch it there, cowboy. Blue bloods are built to last, but we carry ourselves lightly. It's part of our royal charm. And I'll have you know, my great, great grandmother something or another was an Albanian Queen."

He was about to make an off-color joke when I shook my head and put a finger to his lips. "I really wouldn't if I were you. She was also known as the Butcher of Bulgaria." Without waiting for a response, I grabbed him by the front of his shirt and threw him against the side of the startled horse who tried to bolt, but I had them both in a vise-like grip. By the time I finished mauling Eric's face and neck, he'd completely lost any interest in the topic of my weight.

Gasping for air and sanity, he said more with the gleam in his eyes than all the world's languages could ever convey. His eyes and heaving chest spoke of love and longing, hope and desire. He dared dream with his beautiful blue eyes while mine, nearly the same color, were forced to lie.

Sharing the spiked coffee and pilfered cigarettes, we sat watching the horses grazing on tender shoots of wet young grass. Between caffeinated kisses and puffs of ephemeral smoke he talked of the future, our future. I was able to contain myself until he spoke of riding off into the sunset together. Knowing I was about to cry, I handed him the cup and nuzzled my head in his lap, obscuring my face. My tears may have been red, but their source was clearly the same as anyone else's.

"Adrian, don't be so sad," he said, weaving his fingers through my dark strands of hair. "You won't be gone forever. I'll still be here when you get back. I'm not going anywhere."

He bent down to kiss my temple. I knew he'd see the bloody tears welling in the corners of my eyes. I'd never wanted anything as much as I wanted to be human again at that moment. Without thinking, instinctively, I jumped and stood upright faster than should have been possible. Before he could remark that my eyes were bleeding, I had no choice but to make him forget what his own had seen.

Once I'd washed away the blood from my eyes and his memory, I reached out my hand to help him up. Understandably, he was slightly confused. "Wow, Daddy-O! I'm not sure what you're putting in that witches' brew you call coffee, but it's making me dizzy as shit. I hope I don't get in trouble with the boss for drinking on the job."

I kissed him one last time and reluctantly let go of his shoulders while trying to memorize his face. "Eric, you have no idea how much I'd like to fire you right now and tell you to pack your things. I'd give the world if you could get on that plane with me tonight."

He was still a little punch drunk. He had me by the ass cheeks grinding his crotch into mine, slurring something about, "I dare you to, you handsome fucking Albanian Prince."

Albanian Prince? Now he's doing it, too. Why did I have to go and open my big fucking mouth? "I'd love to, you uncommonly perfect peasant, but we have to consider the children. Alexander would probably never speak to either of us again."

I must have overdone it a bit on the mind-bending. Eric was definitely high on persuasion. He threw his head back laughing uproariously. "Seriously? If that horse is talking to you, you're way drunker than I am. Do we have any of that shit left? I should get the recipe and slip a little in my old man's Ensure. He'd sleep like a baby 'til next week."

When he turned around and bent over to get the blanket, I whacked him hard on the ass.

Jumping, he yelled, "Ouch! Save that shit for your talking horse, rich boy!"

I picked up the thermos and snatched Alexander by the reins. "We'll race you and that mute mare of yours to the barn!"

Heads down, riding hard, they beat us by several outstretched lengths. In his condition, I was worried Eric would fall off and kill himself. Other than maybe by insulting his horse, it honestly wasn't my fault they won. I could only surmise that Alexander let Napoleon win. They obviously had a thing for each other. It seemed only natural. There was a lot of love at Thornecrown and I was going to miss every last bit of it.

Roaming the mansion's gloomy halls well past sunset (not that anyone, once inside, could actually tell whether it was night or day), I tried recording its details, the myriad faces and smells, until they were all indelibly seared into my senses. I wanted to leave with something, even if it were only the small hope that somehow Thornecrown might never become just another long-distant, fog-filled dream, as had so much of my past. I needed it to go on living inside me; I just didn't think I could go on living inside it.

CHAPTER TWENTY-FOUR

Tromping down the stairs, bags in hand, I ran into Thadius. He asked, "Do you need help, Sir?"

"No, I'm fine. Thank you. I'm not taking much. I have everything I need in Dallas or else I can live without it. I don't want to have to bring it back."

"Yes, Sir. Take only what you need, as our Prince would say."

"The Dorian creed. I think we really should have pamphlets printed. Oh, Thadius, I sent Berta into town earlier to buy some clothes for Cornelius. I told her to leave them in my closet. Except for the unfitted suit, can you make sure he gets the rest of them and see that they fit properly? I was just guessing at his sizes. I'll help him with the suit when I come back. Make sure he gets socks and shoes, too."

"By the way, Sir, that was very nice what you did last night. He was quite dashing and I don't believe I've ever seen him as calm or happy, certainly not both at the same time. You seem to have a remarkable way…"

"He's a very special person, Thadius. He has his own unique and lovely magic."

"That's funny, Sir. Only recently I was thinking the same thing about you."

Several minutes later, still stinging from his compliment, I absentmindedly walked into the kitchen to ask Hilda if she could find Cornelius for me. Innocently enough, she went to the door without a word, opened it, and let out the most blood-curdling whistle in human history, causing several of the emus to miscarry on the spot, and, if my Sufi-magination was correct, one to conceive a calf scheduled to be born several months later with two heads. Right or wrong, Cornelius came barreling in like a whirling dervish on crack cocaine with a look of absolute wonder writ large across his face, which, from the appearance of things, had recently suffered a head-on collision with a rabbit. The snowy white tufts of bloodied fur protruding from his grill were a dead giveaway.

"Hey Cornelius, you're a good boy for coming when I call you. Yes, you are, you're a very good boy." Taking him by the hand, I led him into the salon, perched him on the same divan he'd been on the previous evening, pulled up a chair, and sat down beside him.

"Cornelius, I have to go away for a few days, but I'll be back very soon. I'm going to miss you. Are you going to miss me?"

He nodded vigorously enough to make the perfect martini if you like them shaken rather than stirred. With the proper attachments and motivation he could've probably made one hell of a margarita as well. I reached out and put my hand around his neck, kissed him on the top of his head, and soaked in the scent of his wildly disheveled, dirty-blonde hair.

"I'm going to miss you so much, Cornelius. Promise me you'll be a good boy while I'm gone? I'll be home soon. Now why don't you to go out and see if you can catch a possum, this big!" I held my hands far apart for illustrative purposes. His head flew back in great gales of pantomimed laughter as he mimicked the measurement and clapped madly. It made me think of a late-night reality show I'd seen with drunken rednecks noodling for catfish using only their bare hands in a muddy river bottom. Remembering how funny it had been to watch, I regretted there hadn't been time enough to take Cornelius fishing at least once. I know he could and would have given new meaning to the phrase, *carpe diem*.

Skulking around the corner, I could smell Hilda's talcum powder scurrying away as I slid the chair back into place and sent Cornelius outside to play. She was busily cleaning an already spotless counter when I walked into the kitchen. "Hilda, I want you to go out and buy a lovely dress and shoes comfortable enough to dance the night away. We're going to have a party when I get back. Berta went shopping today. I want everyone and everything to be beautiful, including that lovely face of yours. Of course there's probably not much we can do for Thadius, other than teach him to smile. But before I leave, there is one favor I'd like to ask of you."

"What's that, Sir?"

"Please try and be kind to Cornelius. He may be strange and simple, but we're the only family he has and this is his home, too."

She had her head down busily fussing with the front of her apron when I kissed her on the cheek. "Take care of yourself, Hilda. I'll be home soon."

"Yes, Sir. Thank you, Sir. Have a safe journey."

I walked out of the kitchen and found Edward standing in the recently renovated foyer where someone had removed and replaced the broken table from the previous evening's melee.

"Your bags are in the car, Sir."

"Thank you. It's good to see you, Edward. Where've you been hiding lately?"

"Likewise, Sir. I've been spending more time downstairs getting reacquainted with a lady friend who's just returned from overseas. I heard you talking to Hilda about the party. It sounds like fun. It's been a long time since…"

"In that case, consider you and your lady friend invited."

"Thank you, Sir. Shall we be off? Your taxi slot at Heathrow is in two hours and if we miss it I'm not certain how long it would take to get another one."

Driving away, I'd been holding my hand out the window trying to capture Thornecrown's breeze between my fingers when I saw Cornelius running alongside the car in the woods. I pretended not to notice. I'd already wept enough tears over lost loves at Thornecrown. Getting away from Gravesend was the only way I could see to keep from shedding even more blood.

The clattering noise of the tires on the cobblestone bridge sounded like rubber bullets ricocheting in my ears as we crossed over. Even with my heart impossibly heavy and my head bent, I knew I had to press forward. I had to, for everyone's sake. Soon enough I would be far removed from the echo chamber of salivating prophets spreading lethal lies along with the prying eyes of their minions following my each and every move on the estate.

Ironically, Thornecrown wasn't the problem, it never had been. What lay buried underneath was the source of my bereavement. On the surface it was such a beautifully bucolic place, a peaceful home, a life I'd live happily over and over again. But the underbelly, the Nadir, was what I wanted more than anything to escape. I'd learned to live without killing, and, in spite of my preeminent qualifications, I refused to be listed as the leading cause of death, regardless of species.

If running forever would keep my name out of the record books, I'd have to keep on running. They couldn't very well drag me back, tie me to the throne, and force the crown on my head. *Kingdom of one?* Hell yeah! *Your order is ready. Please drive through.* I intended to because destruction wasn't my calling. It never had been. If I were to be any sort of god at all, I wanted to be a creator, not a god of destruction like my maker. Dominion meant mastery of myself, not others. Unlike the Nephilim, I didn't see power as an end. It was a tool for building a better world, not subjugating a species to eternal damnation in the name of bloodthirsty empire.

While the Rolls was barreling toward London, my deceptive departure was creating an uproar at Thornecrown. Thadius stomped down the stairs barking decidedly unhappy orders at Clark. "Get The Havens on the phone now!" Without waiting for a response, he marched down the hall and nearly splintered the office door slamming it shut behind him. Snarling into the receiver, he snapped, "This is Thadius. Find Sir Charles and tell him it's urgent!"

Soon a calmer voice came on the line saying, "Yes, Thadius, is there a problem?"

"Yes, Sir. They just left for the airport. He's not planning on coming back."

"I see...and what makes you say that?"

"It was in his mind, Sir. I know this must sound silly, but he was using the Nadir to project bubbles for some reason. I saw it underneath the surface when some of them popped."

"You saw what exactly?" Charles asked.

"He was bringing his bags down. I asked if he needed help with his luggage. He said no, that he had everything he needed in Dallas. For an instant, I could see the intent behind his words. He has no plan of ever returning to Gravesend."

"Forever's a long time as we both know, but I can't say that I blame him, Thadius."

"I'm sorry, my Prince, but I don't understand. This doesn't bother you?"

"Of course I'm bothered, Thadius, but I think you're underestimating Adrian. He has a great deal on his plate right now, as do we all. I can only imagine how much of the world's weight he feels on his shoulders. Pray tell, who would want that burden?"

"Adrian thinks he's doing the noble thing and trying to save himself at the same time. He'll figure it out. Give him time. You can't very well drag him kicking and screaming to his own destiny. He'll come home when he's ready, and, I suspect, that will be sooner than you think. I know who he is, Thadius. I've always known. He'll make the right choice, but it has to be his choice."

"Yes, Sir. I understand. I hope you're right, Sir."

"Is there anything else, Thadius?"

"No, Sir."

"Then I'll say good night."

While they debated my intentions, I was busy beating back tears, fending off demons, and denying myself the men of my dreams to keep them safe. I'd fallen in love with Eric and wanted more than anything to believe he'd fallen in love with me. Cornelius was a gift, a magical being living in a world of wonder that he'd have more than gladly shared if we'd only had the chance. Cruel beyond imagination, the pain I felt made me want to tear the tormented heart from my chest and hurl it out the window. Death seemed my only birthright, and I would've rather been damned than let them pay the price for my sins.

Far too many guns were pointed at and away from me for anyone's safety. There was too much hanging in the balance, including the ever-tightening noose around my own neck. Political rivalries, deadly games of bat and mouse, millennial intrigues over alliances made only to be broken—none of these were the makings of a happy home. I could see it playing out. I'd come home at the end of a long, hard day in the killing fields. He'd ask, *"Hi, honey! How was your day?"* I'd respond by tossing a severed arm on the entry table and growling, *"Not tonight, Eric. The Great Conflict completely kicked my ass this afternoon. Can you just fix me a drink and get your sewing kit? I'm wiped out."*

The Great Conflict, coming to a theatre of war near you soon… Somehow, Beau Pre had forgotten to mention that one tiny detail and how it perpetually seemed to swirl around me like a category-five tornado. Alaric, whether intendedly or not, had been kind enough to catch me up to speed on the inclement, looming apocalypse soon to be waged against and sponsored by *yours truly*. In all his innocence, Chad had nicely finished filling the nail holes in my custom-fitted coffin, blotting out any last remaining rays of hope.

I'd been dressed to kill and schooled in the fine art of stakesmanship, fashioned into a reluctant force of one harboring an immortal army buried beneath my storied feathered bed—an army who were waiting, watching for me to defy or succumb to yet another death. What everyone failed to recognize was that I had no fight left in me because it had never been there in the first place.

Wars are, and always have been, the provinces of politicians and generals. I was neither. I hadn't even played with plastic soldiers as a child. Who were we supposed to be kidding? I sure as fuck had no intention of toying with real people's lives, on or off the battlefield. During the entirety of the cowboy and Indian wars in Dallas there'd been only one casualty, a chipped tooth when some kid fell off his bike. Even back on Chestnut Street in Atlanta, how many times had my parents been about to kill each other when I walked in and shut down the latest production of *Hellraiser, the Prequel* with one of my lame-ass jokes?

Life, and the lack of it, taught me that people are not toys. They're not pieces to be moved around like pawns on a chessboard. I'd always tried to be a peacemaker, not a game player, with the possible exception of miniature golf, and look how well that turned out…Conflict wasn't my style. It never had been. In my experience someone was always left clutching at the short, sharp end of the stick while getting royally fucked up the ass by some guy named Victor.

Breaking up fights between my parents or my buddies Glen and Brad was the closest I'd ever come to great conflict. More often than not, the reason was the same, ironically. If some girl happened to glance in my Dad or Brad's direction, then, according to my Mom or Glen, there was sufficient justification to stop the world from spinning long enough to toss the libidinous Lotharios off, deserved or not. Without ever sacrificing life or limb, I'd always been able to keep them from ending up bloodied, dead, or in jail. Once or twice it was close, but somehow I was always in the right place at the right time to prevent all hell from breaking loose.

Wait. What did I just say? Somehow I've always been in the right place at the right time to keep all hell from breaking loose. The Great Conflict? Why does that have to mean all-out war. I've prevented it before. Maybe I'm wrong. Maybe we're all wrong. The thought was staggering enough, I felt as if someone had cold-cocked me with a cheap shot to my head and stomach at the same time. Laying my head back against the seat, I tried catching my breath but I was getting more and more nauseous as the city lights whirred by at ninety kilometers an hour while my mind and emotions spun, crashed, and convulsed headlong into each other in a juggernaut of hope and fear.

The prophecy hadn't said anything about a Great War, only that after the Great Conflict He would unite the Houses, both Greater and Lesser. *Fuck! How could I be so stupid?* I'd assumed from the beginning all the manpower and hardware in the Bat Cave was meant to wage war. Why couldn't it be used to prevent one?

The One from the West will be born in a time of peace, before the Great Conflict. I'd read it myself and that's all it said. My stomach was retching in protest to the bare-knuckled brawl between the wildly competing thoughts slugging it out in my mind. *Don't do this, Adrian. Don't be a fool. If you go back everyone could die.* Holding my hands over my ears and stomach at the same time wasn't an option. My brain and belly were both hemorrhaging and I couldn't quite seem to settle the argument. *What if you're supposed to bring peace instead of war? Think about it, Adrian.*

"Shut up! Just shut the fuck up!" I screamed.

Edward turned and looked at me. "Are you alright, Sir? Who are you...?"

"Pull the car over. I think I'm going to be sick."

It was too late. I couldn't wait for him to stop. Throwing open the door, my stomach seized so violently, my body lurched forward and I hit the ground, not running, but rolling over and over again until my leg exploded against the guardrail. I'd barely made it to my hands and one good knee in the gravel-strewn ditch when I felt the convulsive sobs and dry heaves turn to bitter mouthfuls of acrid blood. Each of the spasms erupted with such volcanic velocity, I was quickly covered in rivulets of red bile ricocheting back into my face, clothing, and hair. It was as if Jackson Pollock had risen from the dead and taken up portrait painting with a psychotic fervor previously unknown to humankind, art critics, or the auctioneers at Sotheby's.

With my masterpiece finished, I prayed it was Edward's hand I felt underneath my arm pulling me up out of the pool of crimson-colored filth. Otherwise I was being arrested or carted off to the hospital. Either way, there was enough blood on the ground to guarantee that someone from Scotland Yard would be investigating a double homicide come morning. Limping out of the ditch in dire need of a roadside knee-replacement, I tore off the stained shirt and asked Edward to open the trunk.

"Are you alright, Sir?' he yelled over the din of traffic while unzipping the suitcase as I rubbed what was left of the tattered white rag across my face and neck. Half naked and covered in matted blood, I barely noticed the cars whizzing by at breakneck speed as I tried fumbling with the fresh shirt.

"Here, Sir, let me help you." I didn't have the power to resist as I slumped against the rim of the trunk while he wrestled my arms into the sleeves. After one button, I swatted his hands away. He asked again, "Are you sure you're alright, Sir?"

"Not exactly, but I think I'll live."

"Excellent choice, Sir," he shouted as he opened the car's door and helped me inside.

"Take me home, Edward," I sighed, collapsing into the seat.

"Another excellent choice, Sir."

The drive back to Gravesend required only one brief emergency stop. Considering I looked like death, and not exactly the warmed-over sort, Edward was kind enough to run in the liquor store and spare everyone the panic. At that point I hadn't mustered the motivation to finish buttoning the goddamned shirt, nor did I particularly care. Sometimes homicidal hobo is the best you can do and since I was about to be drinking from the bottle anyway…Don't get me wrong, room-temperature martinis are fine for the most part, unless you happen to somehow rub the shit in your eye, and then like an idiot, in the other one, too.

I'd finished my cocktail and regained partial vision in my left eye, so things were looking up by the time we recrossed the cobblestone bridge. Feeling a wee bit tipsy, but infinitely better, I asked Edward if he knew how to whistle. I'm reasonably certain, from the way he looked at me, his opinion regarding my level of intoxication may have differed from my own, but nevertheless he said, "Yes, Sir, I believe I do."

"Then, if you would, please stop the car, get out, and whistle."

He acted as if I'd asked him to strip naked and dance on the hood, but he did open the door, step out and whistle, timidly at first, until I laughed and said he sounded like a boy lost in the graveyard after dark. Weaving and tottering my way out of the backseat, I said, "No, Edward, pucker and blow like this." I was trying to pinch his lips together with my fingers but the pavement kept moving each time I made a grab for them. After several passes he stepped back and used his own fingers with much more satisfying results.

While thanking him profusely and slurring something about the possumbility of lessons, I heard the familiar sound of snapping twigs and trampled leaves under Cornelius' rapidly approaching feet. I'd staggered back to a seated position when his hulking frame flew across my lap and banged head first into the glass with a resounding thud.

"Edward, would you be a lamb and roll down the back windows?" Once Cornelius had regained some variety or another of consciousness he stuck the upper half of his torso out to catch the breeze on his face. Watching his jowls flapping happily in the wind, I thought *why the hell not?*

Pulling into the drive, we were hanging out of our anything-but-respective windows when the Rolls came to a stop. Lumbering Jack saw no need of remaining seated or standing on formality. He simply jumped out the window while I tried to insinuate myself back into the seat and wait for Edward to open the door.

Thadius was standing stoically on the porch shaking his head while Cornelius ran laps around the car. First one scuffed shoe dropped, then the other, as my shaky feet sought solid ground. Slowly, painfully I braced myself against the car as best I could and tried standing.

Partially upright, I could relate to a broken, dispirited Neanderthal returning to the cave without a damned thing to show for a hard day's hunting and gathering. Sheepishly taking one tentative step after another, I joked, "Hi honey. I'm home," to an unappreciative audience.

The look on Thadius' face wasn't much prettier than my own. It indicated he was taking measurements of the man I'd once been, wondering which size straightjacket might fit me properly as I hobbled toward the door. Of course my broken knee had to buckle as I attempted to traverse the first step onto the porch. Reaching out, he grabbed my elbow as I fell. "Sir, should the occasion ever present itself, please remind me to never go on holiday with you under any circumstances, no matter how brief the excursion."

Looking down, I didn't need a mirror to see what a complete mess I was. One misaligned button held my bloody, untucked shirt together. The lacerations on my arms and torso as they'd bled through the white cotton fabric had adhered to it, creating a festive new spin on the tie-die, why, yes-I-did, thanks-for-noticing look. Both knees of my blood-soaked pants were obliterated, and I felt confident my face and hair were perfectly paired for that freshly train-wrecked look I'd worked so hard to achieve.

In spite of my haphazard makeover, I could see the early warning signs of a smile wanting to break out on the sides of Thadius' mouth as he helped me limp through the door.

Hilda was waiting in the entry hall. "Oh my heavens! What on earth…?"

I shrugged and laughed. "What can I say? I got homesick."

She was quickly losing her color and about to pass out when I yelled for Edward. "Can you please do us all a favor and persuade Hilda to be a dear and take the rest of the night off? She looks like she's coming down with something and I'm in no position to catch anything. Oh, and I guess we should probably cancel the plane."

Pointing toward the salon, I told Thadius, "Park me near the bar and find some ice. I think this calls for a drink, maybe two. Edward, after you've seen Hilda out, why don't you join us? I'm afraid we're too late for happy hour, but I just so happen to have a tab and a trust fund."

Cornelius didn't need an invitation or directions. He claimed his usual seat, on all fours as soon as Hilda walked out the door. I didn't have the energy to scold him considering I was on the verge of clawing myself to death while my itching wounds tried to heal. The knee was by far the worst. There was no way of getting at the bone underneath the scabbing skin and it was driving me completely fucking crazy. Edward came back with an ice pack and a change of clothes. Two cocktails and a glass of red later, I was marginally limping again.

Thinking it might be easier going down than trying to get up the stairs, I gingerly made my way to the Bat Cave, knowing I'd have to talk to Charles sooner or later. In the office waiting for him to come on the line, I prayed I'd made the right choice. Five years and a couple of lifetimes ago, my mother yelling at me when I screwed up or made poor choices was about as severe as the consequences would get. She could be a real bitch, but no matter how mad she got, I couldn't remember a single occasion when she'd tried driving a stake through my heart.

"Nicholas, that must've been the shortest intercontinental flight on record. Please tell me you didn't trade the Rolls for a Concorde?"

Neither of us was laughing. "You knew I wouldn't leave, didn't you?"

"Let's just say I had my suspicions."

"Why didn't you tell me about the Great Conflict? For some reason Beau Pre never bothered to mention it either."

"Truth be told, it was to avoid exactly what happened tonight. Knowledge has to be chewed and digested slowly, otherwise we fall into gluttony or choke to death from trying to swallow it wholesale. You weren't capable of hearing the whole truth. We have to learn to walk before we can run. How's that knee coming along, by the way?"

"Very funny, Grandvamps, but let's not change the subject. Alaric mentioned it in passing and Chad pretty much told me everything else."

"Nicholas, Chad is a very sweet lad and I'm glad the two of you are getting on so famously, but I can assure you, he doesn't know everything. People either believe according to their greatest hopes or what they fear the most, often both. None of us, however, are immune from our own perspectives, much less the manipulative minds and tongues of others.

"I promise we'll talk about this and anything else you like tomorrow, but, in the meantime, you've got a party to plan and bones that need healing. And as we all know, sunrise comes early at Thornecrown."

"That it does, Sir. There is one other thing."

"Yes?"

"I really prefer the name Adrian. Nicholas just doesn't suit me. Every time someone refers to me by that name, it reminds me of Santa Claus."

Laughter wasn't the reaction I'd expected. "I was wondering how long you'd let me get away with it. As you yourself said, I'm not that fat or jolly. Trust me, my boy, you'll grow into it eventually, but until then, good night, Adrian. Pleasant dreams, my dear boy. And stop worrying so much. A little jolly never hurt anyone. We'll do everything we can to keep the rascals at bay."

Surprisingly, I slept well enough, although the pleasant dreams Charles had promised woke me up long before sunrise. I'd been making big plans while I slept and needed to get an early start if I wanted to live the dream. Stepping into the shower for a quick rinse, I couldn't find a trace of shrapnel from the previous night's roadside bombing other than a stiff knee and an even stiffer Jolly Roger.

I'd made a pot of coffee and was sitting at the counter clipping words and letters from old newspapers and magazines when Berta came in. Rolling the horses' oat balls, she intently eyed my activities with silent suspicion. When I asked where I might locate a bottle of glue, she could no longer contain the curiosity of her tongue or the need to laugh.

"Forgive me for saying so, Sir, but, from the looks of things, I'd say you've already been in the glue. And that may be the last bottle we had. If I can ask, what is it you're doing there?"

"Oh, this is a ransom note. I'm kidnapping Alexander this morning."

She laughed again, saying, "I wasn't aware we were having money troubles? If it would help, I can hold off cashing my check."

Looking up soberly, I said, "Berta, we're not having money troubles. By all means, dear, please go cash your check, but first could you find me that glue? I'm afraid I'm in a bit of a hurry this morning."

Napoleon was snoring away until he heard me affixing the note to his stall door. Alexander was already awake and watching my every move as I took his tack and saddle from the wall. Moving at lightning speed with the horizon beginning to glow yellow orange, we'd narrowly made it across the open field into the woods when I heard the death rattle of Eric's old truck coughing, sputtering, and finally giving up the ghost with a loud booming bang before collapsing in an exhausted cloud of smoke alongside the barn.

Dodging trees and low-hanging branches, I kept my head down as we raced through the woods in a beeline for the creek while Eric read the note: *Bring your heart and twenty-seven million dollars to the waterfall at sunrise, or you'll never see Alexander again. And don't try anything ducky.— The Army of God.*

The horse and I were both huffing and puffing, but we'd made it. I'd already stripped out of my clothes when I saw the empty vase on the blanket next to the thermos and Dunhills. In my haste, I'd skizzed out on the forget-me-nots, so set off buckass naked and barefoot in search of wildflowers. For supposedly being the "Garden of England," County Kent wasn't exactly afire with color. I was making a mad dash for a clump of daffodils when I heard Napoleon's hooves blazing a trail in our direction.

As I bent over to place the spartan arrangement in the vase, Alexander decided to be a comedian and stick his cold, wet nose in the crack of my ass, sending me face first into the pot of strawberry preserves, thoroughly squashing my dignity and the still-warm biscuits. Although I thought gooseberry jam would've seemed more appropriate, I let him lick the preserves off my nose anyway before diving into the seizure-inducing, icy cold water. So much for planting Jolly Roger in Eric atop the rocks…My formerly proud, smoking-hot sausage was reduced to a frozen, shriveled cocktail wiener by the time I'd reached the waterfall.

My teeth were still chattering as I heard Eric unbuttoning the snaps of his overalls. Continuing the harried search for my missing scrotum, from behind the rocks, I yelled, "Did you bring the ransom?"

"Yes, Sir, at least what I could raise on such short notice."

"How much do you have?"

"Six quid and change."

"Did you bring the heart?"

"That I did, Sir. That I did."

THE END.